# Praise for

# *THE ENCORE*

"*The Encore* is a debut whose voice soars like a rock star from the first note and never lets go. Read this book now so you can be the person in your book club who gets to say you discovered Juliet Izon 'first.' Her writing will stop you in your tracks."

—Ali Rosen, bestselling author of *Unlikely Story* and James Beard– and Emmy-nominated journalist

"A gorgeously layered exploration of artistic ambition and abiding love, as cutting in its portrayal of the glories and pitfalls of career obsession as it is romantic about love's possibilities for redemption. I devoured Izon's debut with reckless abandon."

—Ashley Winstead, *USA Today*–bestselling author of *This Book Will Bury Me*

"*The Encore* is a big-hearted novel that depicts how love and loss, tragedy and joy, are not only necessary dualities in life, but also intrinsically connected. Izon writes with a playful exuberance; fans of Taylor Jenkins Reid will find a lot to love in this charming, utterly readable debut."

—Gabriella Burnham, author of *Wait*

"With witty dialogue, a quickly unfolding plot, and a simmering will they/won't they romance, *The Encore* offers readers a backstage pass to the rewards of chasing a long-held dream, the perils of fame, and the intertwining influences of art and destiny."

—Sarah Landenwich, author of *The Fire Concerto*

"Part *Daisy Jones & the Six* and part *Tomorrow, and Tomorrow, and Tomorrow,* Izon's stunning debut is a backstage pass to the music industry, the perils of stardom, and the complexities of sacrificing love and life in service of art. Propulsive, sweeping, and populated with characters as nuanced as the songs they write, *The Encore* deserves a standing ovation."

—Daria Lavelle, author of *Aftertaste*

"Juliet Izon's debut is a layered exploration of ambition, sacrifice, family, and love, all set to one truly iconic soundtrack. But most of all, *The Encore* is a celebration of art—the pleasures and perils of making it, and the enduring power it has to heal us, even when we fear we're broken beyond repair. Read this book—I promise it will leave you feeling starry-eyed with arms stretched high, dancing at your favorite concert."

—Grant Ginder, author of *So Old, So Young*

# THE ENCORE

# THE ENCORE

## JULIET IZON

UNION
SQUARE
& CO.
NEW YORK

Cover design by Patrick Sullivan
Cover images by Alamy: DedMityay (man);
Shutterstock.com: focuslight (woman), Lemon Twig (picks)


Union Square & Co.
Hachette Book Group
1290 Avenue of the Americas, New York, NY 10104
unionsquareandco.com
@unionsqandco

First Edition: March 2026

Union Square & Co. is an imprint of Grand Central Publishing, a division of Hachette Book Group, Inc. The Union Square & Co. name and logo are registered trademarks of Hachette Book Group, Inc.



Print book interior design by Jeff Stiefel

Library of Congress Cataloging-in-Publication Data has been applied for.

ISBNs: 978-1-4549-6122-2 (paperback), 978-1-4549-6123-9 (ebook)

Printed in Canada

MRQ-L

10 9 8 7 6 5 4 3 2 1

*For my parents,*
*who taught me the beauty of words and music*

# PROLOGUE

Right before the show starts, they cut the lights.

The audience bubbles itself into a frenzy when this happens, the noise cresting like a fast-moving wave that crashes at the front of the stage.

The bass drum kicks in first, pushed so high in the sound mix it feels like it emanates from deep inside your sternum. Then, a single spotlight flashes onto the drummer, who slowly starts beating out a half-time shuffle. Soon the guitarist and bassist are illuminated too, all three communicating with nearly imperceptible signals: a strum of a power chord here, a quick twirl of the drumsticks there. They jam for a few minutes, picking up the tempo only to ease it back. The crowd is getting itchy, impatient, restless. This is what the band is aiming for.

Those on the far side of the stage see her first as she readies for her entrance, igniting another round of cheers. She does her best to focus inward: takes a quick swig of water, adjusts her inears, and exhales slowly. Sometimes, she crosses herself, a vestige of a life she's long left behind. When she finally strides onto the stage, in a simple black leotard and a pair of high-waisted jeans, a deafening, febrile wall of sound rises up from the seats, striking her with a nearly physical force. She smiles. She's home.

Her fingers skim the hands of those lucky enough to be in the front row of the pit, gold bracelets clanging up and down both slender arms. They throw flowers, throw letters, throw their bodies toward her. Eventually, she takes her place in front of the mic, closing her eyes and swaying her body languidly to the beat of music she knows so well it might as well be her own heartbeat. After a minute or two, she raises her left hand: the cue to the band that she's ready. The drummer smashes the hi-hat and she begins to sing.

She sings in a voice as clear and strong as a mountain stream. She sings about him, about her. About what did happen, and what should have, and what didn't, and what might. She sings to them even though they're not there. She sings to them even though they don't know she's there. She sings because music and love became entangled so long ago, she doesn't even remember when they were separate.

She sips Irish whiskey with a splash of water between songs, says it's there to help her remember, but they all know it's there to help her to forget. Sometimes, she's bleeding by the end of the night: on her shin, or her elbow, or her forehead. She can never tell you how it happens. It doesn't really matter, anyway. Her mascara runs down her flushed cheeks, her long hair hangs limp and sticky from sweat, her jeans are ripped. And it feels so fucking good.

The next day, they do it all over again.

# ONE

## Lottie

*New York*

May 3, 2024

Charlotte Thomas woke up alone on the morning of her sixteenth birthday.

This wasn't unusual. But Charlotte—or Lottie as she'd been called since birth—had somewhat foolishly hoped her uncle Aidan might stick around long enough to wish her happy returns in person. The silence blanketing the town house like down, however, assured her he'd either left for an early meeting, or never returned home at all.

She allowed herself the small luxury of a few more minutes in bed, basking in the spring sunlight that was just beginning to tickle her bedroom's large bay window. Her cat, a fluffy Persian named Cajun, leapt up onto her chest, purring delightedly to see someone else in the house finally awake.

Eventually, she gathered her wavy brown hair into a messy topknot and padded downstairs. Their home, a six-story prewar on an immaculate block between Fifth and Madison, was laughably roomy for the two of them: there were entire floors that went unused for months. But when Aidan's considerable talent for design had catapulted him into the heady territory of running his own fashion label, it was his first major purchase. "I needed something fit for this princess," he'd say, twirling one of her curls around his finger.

Cajun chirped and weaved in and out of her legs once Lottie got to the kitchen, equally ready for her own breakfast. Displayed on the white marble island was a bottle of Dom with a red bow, a comically large bunch of gold balloons, and a Breads Bakery Nutella babka (her favorite) with numeral one and six candles stuck haphazardly in the middle. Resting next to it was a small envelope with the word *Lottie* scrawled in loopy cursive. You could fault Aidan for many things—promoting underage drinking among them—but penmanship was not one. She pulled out the card.

> *My love!*
>
> *Have the most fabulous day. So sorry I couldn't be there to give you a morning birthday kiss, but will catch you tonight.* DON'T *drink that before school.*
>
> *x,*
> *A*

She shook her head and smiled to herself. Aidan was her legal guardian, but at thirty-eight, he operated more in that ambiguous realm between brother and confidant. When he was actually around—the vagaries of the industry often had him jetting between Paris, Milan, and London, sometimes in a single week. She'd grown used to spending most mornings and many nights by herself; her de facto custodian was really Beatriz (nickname Bee), her erstwhile nanny and now Aidan's fastidious housekeeper. Lottie heard her key in the garden door lock now.

"Where is the birthday girl?" Bee trilled from outside before bursting into the kitchen, arms occupied with a large gift bag. "There she is!" she exclaimed, quickly unloading everything onto the counter, then wrapping Lottie in a tight embrace. "*Feliz cumpleaños*," she said, sprinkling her cheeks with kisses. Lottie scrunched up her face, but she was grinning.

"Where's Mr. Aidan? Did he leave already?"

Lottie shrugged as she ripped off a piece of babka.

Bee clucked her tongue, then noticed the champagne on the counter. "Ah! No. No, no." She narrowed her eyes at the bottle, then quickly snatched it. Lottie began to protest and Bee silenced her with a finger. "*¡Eres demasiado joven!*"

"I'm not too young! Sasha had a champagne *fountain* at her sixteenth birthday party."

"Sasha's parents can pay for her therapy later, eh? No." She tucked the bottle under her arm. "I'm bringing this back to the cellar."

"Not even a mimosa?" Lottie looked at her pleadingly.

"*Mi amor*, do not push it!"

At 8:00 a.m., when Lottie arrived at Pembroke, her all-girls school a few blocks away, a gaggle of her friends was already waiting at the ornate blue front door, bearing Billy's Bakery cupcakes and even more balloons. All of them were sporting identical gray skirts rolled up just long enough to pass dress code, with some variation on a tiny, fitted T-shirt on top. (Aidan insisted on tailoring her skirt: "If they're gonna force you into that miserable poly blend, the least I can do is make sure it's flattering," he'd grumbled, hunched over the sewing machine. "These box pleats look like they were made by a five-year-old." He paused. "They probably were.")

"Happy birthday!" the girls squealed in unison, pouncing on Lottie and snapping selfies at the same time.

"This bitch is finally sixteen!" Sasha—of the champagne fountain—yelled as she started filming her.

A figure cut in brusquely just then between Sasha's phone and

Lottie. "Ladies, first bell's in three minutes." Pembroke's head of Upper School, Ms. Santos, tapped her watch. "Finish all this inside, please? And happy birthday, Lottie," she said with a smile, giving her shoulder a squeeze. "I know today might be tough," she added quietly. "Let me know if there's anything I can do."

Lottie carefully extracted her arm and offered Ms. Santos what she hoped was a convincing-enough smile. "I'm fine."

Ms. Santos gave her another pat anyway. "Wonderful."

Pembroke's moratorium on in-school birthday celebrations meant Lottie's day unspooled rather normally, which was her preference anyway. There wasn't much she felt like commemorating; every year only carried her further away from when things had made sense.

Her friends, however, knew the best present they could give was to keep her occupied. After school, they dragged her to Butterfield for soft serve, Sasha presenting her with a sprinkled swirl cone nearly as large as her head. The girls walked desultorily home through the park, frantically licking the cones before ice cream dripped down between their knuckles. For Lottie, their excited chatter was calming—the same way white noise could be—but just as meaningless.

Once outside the house, she could spy Aidan through a parlor-floor window, scurrying around the dining room table to plop a big bunch of white peonies into a vase. His ear was glued to his phone, as was customary.

"My love!" he mouthed when she walked in, and rushed over to plant a big kiss on each of her cheeks. "Yes, Ernesto, like I said, I want it in the poplin for summer, not the silk. No . . . *poplin*. Okay? Okay. Great, I gotta go." He blew a lock of blond hair out of his eyes with an irritated puff. "Phew! Happy birthday! School good?"

She nodded, then frowned. "I think my friends get a bigger kick out of my birthday than I do, though."

"I think your friends will use any excuse for a party. Maybe that's why I like them so much." He grinned at her and then narrowed his eyes at the peonies before rearranging them minutely.

"Hi, Lots!" Aidan's boyfriend Gregory was in the kitchen, topping off cocktails with the purloined Dom. He raised an eyebrow in her direction. "I won't tell Bee if you won't?"

She mimed a zipper on her lips.

"Go get changed; I left you something upstairs," her uncle said with a wink.

Lying across her duvet was a red silk bias-cut dress, complete with a custom tag on the inside: "For Lottie, on her 16th birthday." She smiled: her friends' heads would explode when they saw it. Aidan hadn't taken measurements—his eye was good enough that he never needed to when he made something custom for her—but it fit, naturally, like she was born to wear it. And even she could appreciate the artistry: Lottie, much to her friends' (and Aidan's) chagrin, was rather lukewarm on fashion.

She bounded back downstairs, twirling for them both on the landing. "It's gorgeous, thank you."

"Just like you." Aidan smiled, eyeing his handiwork, and reached out to adjust a strap. "Hope you're hungry." He nodded toward the dining room.

Neither Aidan nor Gregory, an interior designer, was exactly a proficient cook, but they were both masters of ordering in. And while the duo gladly would have taken her out to whatever downtown spot she fancied, she greedily wanted them both to herself. It was rare to get through a meal out with Aidan where someone didn't approach the table to gush over his new collection or want to chat business.

For tonight, the men had convinced their favorite West Village sushi chef to take up a one-night residency in their home. He was still in the kitchen expertly fileting fish, but the dining table was already set with jewel-toned displays of maki and sashimi, along with towering piles of edamame, dumplings, and seaweed salad.

"You guys ordered enough food for a hundred people," Lottie murmured, taking in the spread.

"You only turn sixteen once, right?" Gregory walked in with the cocktails and handed one to her. "Cheers, doll." The three clinked glasses; Lottie took a small sip and relished the tiny bubbles buzzing up the inside of her nose.

"Shall we?" Aidan gestured to the table with an exaggerated flourish.

Between prepping for the end of the school year and getting ready for all the various fashion weeks, respectively, Lottie and her uncle had been ships in the night. She filled him in on the latest injustice from her taciturn algebra teacher Mrs. Reiner; whether she wanted to go to the end-of-the-year mixer at Pembroke's brother school Hoxton; the latest piece she'd been noodling around with on the piano. Aidan told her some delicious gossip about two *Vogue* cover models who were in a secret relationship and—less sexy—his and Gregory's new plan to go keto.

Toward the end of the meal, Aidan cleared his throat rather dramatically. "I do have a couple more gifts for you. Some things you weren't supposed to have just yet, but, well, you know how I feel about rules." He flashed her an apologetic smile and slid a blank envelope across the table.

Lottie eyed it curiously, then slit it open with an index finger. Inside were New York State minor emancipation papers, already signed by Aidan. She looked up at him, confused.

"A judge owed me a big favor, let's just leave it at that," he said enigmatically. "And to be clear, you're never getting rid of me, but I can't give you the other thing until you sign these and are technically an adult in the eyes of the law. You understand?"

She nodded. She did.

Lottie didn't remember being told she was adopted; it was always understood. Maya Thomas, Aidan's sister, was a single mother by choice and never hid the fact that she wasn't Lottie's birth mom ("It was fate, not biology, that brought us together," Maya would tell Lottie proudly). Maya was, however, less than forthcoming on what she knew about her daughter's origins.

As Maya had gently reminded her whenever she'd asked, Lottie's birth mother had requested no contact with her until she was an adult. She'd also refused to share any information with Maya on the identity of Lottie's father—whether that was because she didn't know who it was or didn't want to share was anyone's guess. All that Maya would divulge was that Lottie was born in Ireland and came back to LA with her just a few days after she was born.

"It's not because she doesn't love you," Maya would be quick to note when Lottie asked, repeatedly, about the no-contact clause. "She wanted you to make your own way in the world. And it could be confusing to have her in your life, right?"

It was a rhetorical question, of course: Lottie didn't have any say in the decision. But when you're that young, the world your parents present to you seems whole and complete. Her birth mother wasn't her mom, and who Lottie was, genetically, was a blank on any form. It was an unassailable truth, like the freckles on her nose, or her dark blue eyes. And by the time that world view had cracked, Maya was dead and Aidan proved to be just as tight-lipped as his sister.

"I just want to know where I come from," she'd beg him, when yet another school project had them tracing their family tree, or asking what cultural holidays were traditional in the household.

"I know, sweets. I'm sorry," he'd say, shaking his head. "I'd help if I could." That the refusals pained him was evident; she rarely insisted on anything.

Aidan and Bee had done the best they could to provide Lottie with some form of surrogacy, but neither saw themselves as a parent, nor did she expect them to. And it wasn't that she was looking for another mother: far from it. By her estimation, she'd lost three parents already; it seemed foolhardy to be vulnerable enough to let someone in again. She just wanted to feel a little less untethered, to find that rope that lashed her to whatever came before.

But her uncle remained impenetrable. So she focused instead on turning eighteen, when, according to whatever agreement Maya had signed, she'd be granted access to her records. And with them she could fill this lacuna, bridge the gap to this other mother, the one whose face appeared blanker the harder she tried to imagine it. That absence, in its own way, was sometimes as devastating as Maya's.

Aidan was considerably proud of himself for finding a clever workaround. "The youngest age for legal emancipation in New York State is sixteen, or I would've done this sooner," he continued. "I wasn't there when all those papers were signed, but"—he exhaled—"I'm who's here now. And I think you have a right to know where you come from. Or, at least, decide for yourself when you're ready."

Lottie was silent as she stared at the forms. What difference would two years make? Maybe nothing: her birth mother could be dead already. But still, there was that faint, hopeful flicker: What if? What if. The thought was a skittish, wild thing: if she got too close, it darted away like a hummingbird.

"I'll sign," she said finally, quietly. Aidan proffered a pen and Lottie quickly initialed next to all the red arrows, signed where it was requested. She pushed the papers back toward him.

"Congratulations, you are officially emancipated." He pulled another envelope from inside his blazer's pocket. "Do you want this now?"

She hesitated. "I'm gonna . . . I'm gonna need some time on that."

He nodded once and tucked it away. "Whatever the birthday girl wants."

The next morning, she awoke to her uncle uncharacteristically crashing about in the kitchen. He was set to leave that day for Paris, but Lottie was delighted to not wake up alone again. By the time she made her way downstairs, Aidan was busy concocting some sort of sludge-colored smoothie in the Vitamix, the carnage of the effort evident by the many open containers and bottles on the counter.

"You want? It's adaptogenic." He raised up the blender.

She wrinkled her nose. "I'll pass, thanks."

He slid onto a bar stool next to her and made a face as he took his first sip. "Not my finest."

She chuckled. "When is it ever?"

"Fair point." He put the glass down and placed his hand on hers. "Sorry I'm dashing so soon. Everything at the atelier is a mess and I—"

"It's fine, I get it. We had last night."

She wanted him to stay. She always wanted him to stay. But she'd never tell him. Her guiding principle since moving in was to fit her life into his, never the reverse. She was aware what a colossal imposition she must have been: he'd been barely thirty and single when he inherited a motherless eight-year-old.

Over the next eight years—half her life—they'd fought hard to will this new family unit into existence, and then to keep it alive. Both were shoved into roles they were never expecting to play, the bright stage lights of this reality, somehow, still jarring. But considering how fraught some of her friends' relationships were with their own parents, sometimes Lottie felt lucky to never have to fight those battles. Sometimes, she thought about what she didn't know she was missing.

"I'll call every day," he said, then slurped the last of his smoothie and made another face.

She tilted her head doubtfully. “You hate the phone.”

“True. I’ll text?”

“Deal.”

“Oh, before I forget.” He reached into his vest pocket and pulled out the envelope from the night before. “You don’t need to do anything with it, but I wanted you to have it while I’m gone.” He slid it across the table. Lottie stared at it as if it might start leaking noxious fumes at any moment.

“Whatever it says, doesn’t change who you are.” He leaned over and kissed her cheek. “Okay?”

She forced a smile. “Okay.”

After Aidan’s town car left for the airport, Lottie grabbed the envelope and trudged back to her room. Bee didn’t work weekends, so she’d have the house to herself unless she invited people over. (Aidan, trusting perhaps too fully in Lottie’s maturity, hadn’t bothered to arrange any supervision during his absences since she started high school.) Once upstairs, she flopped onto her bed and held the envelope up to the light to see if she could discern any writing without opening it. No luck. Tossing it onto her bedside table, she picked up her phone to text Sasha.

“r u up?”

“kinda. FT?”

Lottie FaceTimed her. Sasha was still in bed, her hair a haloed mess of tangled curls.

“Why do you look so awake already?” Sasha said with a tinge of disgust, rubbing her eyes with her free hand.

“Aidan left this morning for Paris. We had breakfast early.”

“Ugh, the life. But that means empty house? Wanna do something?”

“Dunno. Maybe. Can you walk over, though? . . . I need to show you something.”

Sasha sat up, suddenly alert. “Are you okay? Do I need to, like, look at a mole on your butt or something?”

"Ew, no! But easier to explain in person."

"'K, gimme, like, fifteen? Maybe twenty?"

Lottie smiled. "I'll see you in an hour."

"You know me too well." Sasha blew her a kiss.

Out of the fizzy gaggle of Lottie's posse, Sasha was her best friend. She was bubbly and extroverted to Lottie's more reserved and measured disposition, but loyal to a fault. Punctuality was never a strong suit, though: she arrived over an hour later, balancing iced matchas and a bag of croissants in her arms.

"Okay, so what's going on?" she said, plopping onto the giant, modernist couch, sunglasses still on.

Lottie grabbed a croissant and chewed thoughtfully for a second. "Aidan gave me legal emancipation papers."

"What?" Sasha leaned forward and pushed her sunglasses up on her forehead. "Why?"

"So he could give me this." She picked up the envelope from the coffee table. "My birth certificate. With my birth mom's info."

Sasha's eyes grew large. "Fuck. Did you open it?"

Lottie shook her head. "I didn't know if I wanted to, and then I didn't want to do it alone." She sat down heavily next to Sasha and handed it to her. "I've begged Aidan for this for, like, ever. But now? All of the sudden, I kind of like not knowing. 'Cause once I open that—once I know—I can't . . . *un*know it." She leaned back on the couch, exhausted just from the contemplation. "But I can't not know forever, either."

"Well . . ." Sasha examined the envelope and took a sip of her matcha. "You're technically an adult now. I think adults can do hard things."

"Are you listening to Glennon Doyle again?"

"I'm sorry, her podcast is actually amazing."

"You open it, if you're so wise." Lottie flicked it with her thumb and forefinger.

"No! It's your birth certificate." Sasha tried to pass it back to her.

"Just read me her name," Lottie said quietly. "Please?"

"You sure?"

Lottie nodded and closed her eyes briefly. She heard Sasha rip it open.

"There's a few sheets in here," she murmured. "There's your birth certificate, and then there's . . ." She unfolded more sheets of paper and spread them flat with her palm. "Some music?"

Lottie sat up abruptly. "What?"

On the table were four sheets of staff paper, covered with handwritten notation. "For Charlotte," it read at the top in careful cursive. "A Lullaby."

# TWO

## Anna

*Boston*

September 2003

It was an accident that Anna and Will met at all.

She was getting settled in one of the piano practice rooms, arranging her papers on the music rack. He tripped in a few minutes later, sporting a well-worn navy polo shirt and beat-up khakis, brown hair flying out at all angles. Anna was familiar with the type: he looked like every New England boy she'd gone to boarding school with. And, compared to the almost comically serious guys she'd met at Brookfield so far, his tatterdemalion state was a welcome change.

Half of his papers had fluttered to the ground when he'd stumbled in. He held the door open with his foot as he collected them, not noticing her until he'd gathered everything haphazardly in his arms and stood up. "Oh! Hi, sorry . . ." He walked back outside the door to check the room number. "Did you reserve 346E?"

"I did." He was cute. Also a welcome change.

"Ah, crap. I think the booking system must've screwed up. Lemme see if there's another room. Sorry again." He waved, a little awkwardly, and closed the door behind him.

Anna resumed laying out her music, pulled her auburn hair into a ponytail, and had just started playing when there was a knock on the door. He poked his head in.

"So, there's no other free rooms . . . And I wouldn't normally ask, but would you be okay if we shared? I just have to get the first draft of this piece done by tomorrow and I, uh, haven't really started," he finished with a mumble.

Normally, this would be a fast no for her; it wasn't her fault that he (presumably) forgot to book a space. But his rumpled attire and the fact that it was still the first month of freshman year were making her feel a little more charitable than usual. "Um, sure. Let me run through this a few times, and then she's all yours." She patted the Steinway. "I'm Anna, by the way."

"Oh, right. Will. Pendleton." He walked over to shake her hand. "Nice to meet you."

"Likewise. So, are you gonna stay or . . . ?"

"Oh, can I?" His eyes lit up at what she certainly didn't intend to be an invitation. "I love hearing what everyone else is working on." He'd already dropped his backpack in the corner and now sat down on the floor. His enthusiasm was rather endearing, she would admit. "Are you a music comp major?"

"No, vocal arts and piano."

"Double major? Damn, I didn't even know they let you do that."

"They don't, normally." She tried to contain a proud smile. "I'd love to write more, too, though. You're comp?"

Will nodded avidly. "With a minor in conducting." He smiled, bashful. "Sorry, I'm a dork with this. I'm just pumped to be finally doing it for real."

"I know the feeling," she said with a quick grin. "Anyway, I'll get going." She wiggled her fingers over the keys.

"Right, sorry. Do your thing. You won't even know I'm here."

She took one more look at the music and then began Ravel's

*Gaspard de la nuit*: not a favorite by any stretch, but a necessary slog. She'd barely gotten through the first few bars when she heard Will clear his throat behind her. "What?" She lifted her hands from the keys without turning around.

"Nothing, you sound great. Amazing, even. But the piano's out of concert pitch."

"Doubt it. Sounds fine to me."

He smiled placidly. "Wanna bet?"

She thought about it for a second, then finally rotated to face him. "What're we playing for?"

Will was already rummaging in his bag for his tuner. "Um . . . if I'm right? You have to play in my midterm recital. And if *you're* right—which, you're not, I'm sorry to tell you"—he looked up from his backpack and grinned—"then . . . I'll do your laundry for the whole semester."

Later, when Anna discovered how impeccable his ear was, she would never bet against him when it came to anything related to pitch. But at this first meeting, all she saw was another kid trying to flex his musical muscle, and she had no doubt she could best him.

"Fine, deal."

Will scrambled to the piano and struck middle C. "It's sharp." he said, tilting his head as he listened intently. He stuck the tuner next to the soundboard and played the note again. He stared at it, and then waved it at Anna triumphantly. "Boom."

Her jaw dropped. "For real? How the hell'd you do that?"

He shrugged. "Born with it."

She shook her head, blue eyes wide. "That's just unfair, dude."

He grinned again. She liked his smile; it made his eyes crinkle.

"Promise there won't be *too* many polyrhythms in your solo," he said, nodding toward the piano.

"Ha, thanks."

"Well, go 'head. Sorry for the interruption." He motioned for her to continue and retreated back to the corner to start working on his piece. She ran through the Scarbo movement a handful of times, gritting her teeth through a few of the trickier passages, and then they swapped places at the bench. He'd written a surprising amount of music in an hour.

"You do that in your head?" Anna said, attempting to sight-read the sheet over his shoulder.

He nodded, jotting down a few more notes before clicking his pen shut. "You wanna stay and listen?" He swiveled to face her. "I could use an extra set of ears. Even if yours aren't perfect," he added with a crooked smile.

"I'll ignore that. But sure, why not?" It was hard not to be curious about what he'd come up with.

Will flexed his fingers, arranged his music, and started to play. He wasn't at her level of proficiency—few were—but it didn't matter. The inchoate piece was already striking: she could hear elements of minimalists like Reich or Glass, but this was younger, more playful. Anna found it beautiful from the first time she heard it.

She spent the next hour ostensibly working on her music theory homework, but mostly just listening in awe. Anna didn't doubt her own talent—no one got into Brookfield if they didn't have it in spades—but his seemed nearly effortless. Watching him almost unthinkingly spin out gold from the page to his fingers, she could admit she was a touch envious. But mostly she felt, in a surprising way, complete. In Will, even at eighteen, she saw a kindred spirit, someone whose North Star was the same as hers.

"I think that's all I can wring out tonight," he said as he finished. "Whaddya think?"

"It's good." She saw no reason to inflate his ego any more than necessary.

They walked back to the freshman dorm block together, discovering they actually lived in the same building, just on different floors. From that day forward, they were hardly apart, except during their respective classes. Mornings would start with Anna carefully picking her way through his shambolic room and nudging him awake with her foot. At breakfast, over half-eaten bowls of cereal and sharing one set of earbuds, they'd trade playlists on their iPods, debating the merits of Sufjan Stevens's arrangements on *Michigan*; or challenging each other to name ever more obscure Eastern European composers.

And, per their bet, every Sunday Anna dutifully attended Will's rehearsals for his midterm recital, along with a few other first-years he'd roped into playing. He was an electric conductor, she'd discovered, which was unexpected. In his everyday life, Will was laughably disorganized: hair never brushed, barely remembered to eat if Anna didn't remind him. But to put him on top of the podium was to witness a person transformed. Even with a group of teenagers, he was able to coax out nuanced performances, pushing each to their technical limit without it resulting in tears or a thrown bow. She never tired of watching him work: of the burst of elation on his face when he finally teased out a difficult passage, or his kinetic glee of hearing a quartet perform his piece for the first time.

And while, undoubtedly, there had been an undercurrent of flirtation the night they met, they'd never acted on it. Anna had, instead, started casually dating a junior, a jazz comp major named Marcus. Will found him insufferable and made no secret about it, so they mostly avoided the subject. And for his part, Will stayed mum on his dating life. She'd occasionally spotted him sloppily making out with a few random girls at parties, but none of them seemed to stick, which was fine by her. The thought of sharing him made her feel strangely territorial, even if she knew she was already doing the same to him.

A week or so before Thanksgiving, they were walking back from rehearsal to the dorm, looping arms to stay warm.

"When do you head out?" Will wrapped a big wool checked scarf tighter around his neck. The glory of Boston fall had given way to the gray bite of early winter.

"I'm gonna stick around here, actually."

"You're not going home?" He looked at her with surprise.

"Nah. It's such a pain to get down there and back." Anna was on a full ride to Brookfield (as she had been at Oak Grove, her boarding school), and money was tight. But her reasons for not going to Tennessee didn't have much to do with finances. Will was probably nominally aware that things were strained with her parents, but she quickly changed the subject whenever he brought them up. At some point, he stopped asking.

"So, what are you gonna do for Thanksgiving dinner?" He was concerned, in the way that only someone with a functional family could be.

She shrugged. "Hadn't really thought about it. I'm sure they're doing something for the international kids in the dining hall."

They'd reached the door of the dorm and were standing outside. "But that's depressing. And the international kids don't even care about Thanksgiving." He scuffed his shoe nervously on the pavement. "Do you, maybe, wanna come to mine?"

She honestly hadn't planned on doing anything, but it was tempting to be with an actual family and not alone with cafeteria turkey. "Oh. Well, that could be nice. But you'd need to ask your parents, yeah?"

"I did." Will's cheeks blushed crimson. "I mean, I was talking to my mom and she said that, hypothetically, if I had friends who didn't have a place to go, she'd love to have everyone over. So, the offer is open. If you want."

"I'll think on it." She rubbed her hands together to stay warm. "Thanks."

He scuffed his shoe again. "She makes a really good pumpkin pie . . ."

"Whipped cream?"

"Duh."

She smiled. "Fine, I'm sold."

So it was that the next Thursday morning, Will's dad Charles picked them up at the dorm in a shiny Mercedes M-Class.

"Anna, it's a pleasure. Will's told me so much about you," Charles reached around from the front seat to give her a sturdy, WASP-dad handshake.

"Not that much," Will mumbled grumpily from the front seat.

Having already spent four years of school in New England, Anna had had a pretty good read on Will's background before she met his family. The wrecked Barbour jacket; his mentions of summers in Kennebunkport; a family of Trinity College grads, minus him. But even she was surprised when they pulled up to the house—a stately, white-shuttered brick colonial that towered three stories high, surrounded by deftly manicured boxwoods and leafy, mature white oaks.

Will stepped out of the car and immediately started sneezing. He shrugged apologetically. "I'm a sun sneezer."

Anna raised an eyebrow. "That's not a thing."

"It is a thing! Look it up."

Will's mother Betsy—blond, pearls—was already waiting at the front door, beaming. "I'm *so* happy to finally meet you," she said, drawing her into a tight hug. Anna could detect a slight twang. "It'll be nice to have another Southern girl here for the holiday, too," she said conspiratorially, and wrapped her arm around her, leading her inside.

Will was the youngest of four boys, all of whom possessed the same mop of brown hair and the same infectious grin. He and his three older brothers, Charlie, Ben, and Matt, were all about two years apart, which lent a bit of an obstreperous frat party energy to any Pendleton family gathering. Anna, as an only child, loved the chaos: the brothers were like a litter of puppies always tumbling over one another, but were genuinely excited to be reunited.

Unlike Will, however, the rest of the family wasn't much musically inclined. His father and brothers regarded his prodigious skills curiously, the way one might a professional juggler or an expert whistler. Interesting dinner party trick, sure, but what was the real utility in it?

Betsy, on the other hand, was clearly smitten with her youngest, and understandably proud of his talent. She managed to weave Brookfield into a surprising number of conversations, even when they didn't involve him. And Will's own ability to put others at ease was clearly a skill he had inherited from her. Regardless of what anodyne anecdote Anna was relating to her, Betsy made her feel like she was the only person in the room, even when her rambunctious brood was in the middle of tackling each other on the living room floor. Anna, who considered herself an exacting judge of character, liked Betsy immediately.

After a round of introductions (she was positive she wouldn't keep any of the brothers or their last-name-for-first-name girlfriends straight), they all sat for dinner at a massive, Federal-style table beneath an understated gold chandelier. A giant shellacked turkey held court in the center, surrounded by overflowing bowls of glossy cranberry sauce, yellow squares of cornbread, and oval baking dishes of green bean casserole. The brothers traded embarrassing childhood stories the whole meal, sending everyone into alternating gasps or hysterics. All that was missing was Norman Rockwell to paint the scene. It was everything she'd always imagined Thanksgiving could be; it was nothing like her own.

Like all good New Englanders, Betsy and Charles paid no attention if anyone under legal age was drinking. The red wine and vodka bottles formed a teetering pile in the kitchen sink; the port came out swiftly with multiple pies. Will wasn't lying about his mother's baking skills: the pumpkin was superb. By the end of the meal, Anna was stuffed, happy, and a little drunk.

"Would you two consider playing something for us?" Betsy turned to them, eyes bright.

"Mom, I don't know . . ." Will groaned and raked his fingers through his hair. His nervous tell. "I don't wanna put her on the spot."

"Anna? Sing for your supper?" Betsy pleaded.

"I don't mind if he doesn't." She elbowed him gently.

His brothers started pounding the table like a snare drum. "William, William! WILLIAM!"

"Ugh, fine. *Fine*." Will sighed, pushed himself up from the table with exaggerated effort and walked toward the living room piano—a Steinway, naturally—with the rest of the crew trailing close behind. He slid onto the bench and pointed at Anna. "But she's singing."

"Then scooch," she said, and sat down next to him.

They'd spent so much time messing around together in the practice rooms that Will didn't even tell her what he was going to play. Hearing the first few notes, Anna launched into a stripped-down rendition of "Lilac Wine." The two moved through the song almost like figure skaters: flinging each other across the melody, but always in tandem.

By the time Will took his fingers off the keys, Betsy was wiping away tears and even Charles looked misty. Will's family sat in stunned silence for a moment before Betsy rushed to embrace Anna and Will at the piano, kissing the tops of their heads.

"That was beautiful. It's like you two have the same brain. Will, honey, I might have to let you go to adopt this one," she said, giving Anna another squeeze. "Sweetheart, your voice is like something from the *angels*. How does all that sound come out of such a tiny thing? You're gonna be a star one day, I can feel it right here." She put an outstretched hand to her chest.

Anna blushed. Her own family had never been big on compliments.

She'd planned on taking the train back to the dorms after dinner, but the Pendletons were aghast at that, and insisted she spend the night. It wasn't as if they didn't have the space: Betsy led her to one of multiple guest rooms, where a new pair of pajamas and a mini toothbrush and toothpaste were already displayed on the blue chintz, canopied bed. "Of course I wasn't gonna let you leave," she said with a wink before she closed the door. Anna quickly changed, brushed her teeth, and sunk gratefully into the down pillowtop.

There was a knock. "Annie?"

"I'm in bed already."

"Are you decent?"

"Ha, yes. You may enter." She propped herself up on the pillows.

Will stuck his head through the door. "Nice jammies."

"Your mother has exquisite taste."

"So I've been told." He yanked at his collar nervously before continuing. "I'm glad you came. That was really fun. Even if you may have replaced me as my mother's favorite."

She grinned. "What can I say? I'm good."

"Night, loser." He rolled his eyes and closed the door.

Anna settled back down into the warm flannel sheets, replaying the night. It had been months since she'd been at home with her own family, years since she'd lived there full-time. She'd never doubted she'd made the right decision to leave, but it was hard, sometimes, to not feel unmoored on her own. Seeing Will's happy clan was a gut punch: How often had her Thanksgiving dinners not devolved into a screaming match? A rhetorical question, of course. The answer was never.

The next morning, Anna awoke to the fuzzy, sweet smell of cinnamon rolls baking. When she arrived downstairs, Betsy had already put the boys to work: juicing oranges, whisking eggs, setting the table. There were magnums of Dom chilling in an ice bucket, too.

"Oh, morning! Here, sit." Betsy ushered her to the breakfast bar in the sunny, oversized kitchen, where one of the brothers' girlfriends (Hadley? Halston?) was perched. "Coffee?"

"Sure, thanks. How can I help?" Anna was happy to forget much about life in Tennessee, but proper Southern manners were ingrained.

"Just by being your pretty little self. I always make the boys set up the morning after a holiday. It's the one benefit of having so many of them," Betsy said in a mock whisper before whipping around to scold her son at the counter. "Charlie, that's enough oranges!"

The rest of the day passed in a blur of mimosas, family board games, and a few encore performances at the piano for Will and Anna, with Charles even making a guest appearance to belt out some Beatles tunes. And, after some light begging from Betsy and a quick swing back to the dorms to pick up more clothes, she ended up spending the entire holiday weekend Chez Pendleton.

It was the start of a years-long tradition: Anna became a mainstay at their family gatherings, whether Christmas break, Easter, or Fourth of July. Betsy and Charles grew to consider her the daughter they'd never had, even as Will's siblings settled down with serious girlfriends (which would prove to be a point of contention more than once).

Whether they ever asked him if there were anything romantic between them, Anna never knew. But if she could guess from the way Betsy looked at them when they were playing a four-hand piece, or Monopoly, or just helping with dinner prep, it was what she hoped.

Later, when Will's family was long gone from her own life, Anna would allow herself to open this glowing box of memories only on the rarest of occasions. Mostly, it remained stowed away on a high shelf, growing dusty and forgotten.

# THREE

## Lottie

*New York*

May 4, 2024

Lottie quickly sight-read the music before gathering up the papers and marching them over to the grand piano in the living room. Aidan had purchased it for her the week she'd arrived in a well-meaning attempt to keep some semblance of continuity in her life. She had clung to it the way other children might a stuffed animal; its curves and corners were now as familiar to her as her own fingers. She laid the sheets out on the music rack and scanned them one more time before placing her hands on the keys.

She knew this piece.

Her mother had put this on the stereo all the time when she was little. Lottie had never asked her where it came from, and by now it had been probably a decade since she'd thought about it. It was surprising how easily the melody returned to her, almost like it had been imprinted on her subconscious. The song unlocked a torrent of memories: of the old house in Malibu, of languid summer naps in a hammock, of her mom.

But who had been playing on that recording? Maya didn't play herself. Did she ask one of Lottie's piano teachers? Maybe Aidan would know.

Lottie finished the piece and sat quietly for a moment, staring at the music. That was her handwriting. Those were her music notes. She was a musician. Lottie felt something click into place inside, like a key slowly moving through tumblers in a lock.

"That was beautiful," Sasha said. Lottie had almost forgotten she was there. "I still can't believe you can play like that."

Lottie's musicality was apparent from the time she could talk. As a toddler, she sang more than she spoke, and could carry a tune a cappella practically from birth. During baby ballet or music classes, she was fascinated by the piano, often so mesmerized that she would drift over to watch the keys rather than participate in class. At home, she would drag coffee table books to the bench seat one by one, piling them up until she was high enough to play, and then spent hours plinking out songs of her own making.

Maya finally found a piano teacher willing to take on a preschool student, and Lottie started lessons when she was around three. She looked forward to the sessions the way other kids did to the playground or the zoo; nothing delighted her more than creating new sound from the keys. And she was a quick study: her teacher had had her reading music and playing two-handed pieces within weeks.

A few months after she'd started lessons, Lottie was sitting on the back porch with Maya, listening to the ceiling fan whir. "Mama, this fan makes an A noise, but the one in front is a C."

"What do you mean, honey? It's shaped like an *A*?"

"No, its sound is an A. Like ayyy." She sang the note.

Maya stared at her. "How do you know it makes an A?"

Lottie looked at her like she was an idiot. "Everything makes a note."

"Does the car engine make a note?"

She nodded solemnly. "F."

"And the fridge?"

She hummed it. "A C-sharp." It came out more like *shawp*.

Maya nodded slowly. "Okay. Come with me to the piano, baby?" Lottie slid off the couch after her mother.

Maya played a single note on the baby grand. "What's that one?"

"B-flat."

She struck another key. "And this?"

"F-sharp."

"And these?"

"A, B, and G. They don't sound very good together."

"You're right, they don't." Maya came to kneel in front of her, putting her hands on Lottie's shoulders. "There aren't many people in the world who can do what you do. Do you know that?"

Lottie shook her head, brown curls bouncing.

"I knew you were one of a kind from the moment I saw you." Maya drew her into a tight hug. "But I didn't know I'd get this lucky."

Lottie stood up from the piano in a daze and sat back down next to Sasha.

"You all right?" She leaned her head on Lottie's shoulder.

"My mom used to play a recording of that for me. I just never knew it was from . . . her."

"You wanna know her name?" Sasha asked softly.

Lottie exhaled. She would have said no ten minutes ago, but the music had cracked something open inside her and she needed to fill the void. She nodded.

Sasha unfolded the certificate and squinted. "I forgot you were born in Ireland."

"Sash."

"Sorry! It's Anna. Buckley."

"Anna Buckley, like the singer Anna Buckley?"

"I dunno how she spells it, but yeah."

Oddly, Lottie had never really thought about what her name might be—something Irish?—but Anna seemed fine. A palindrome. The same forward and backward. Past and future.

"You wanna know more?"

"What else is on there?"

Sasha scanned the paper. "Her birth date, where she's from . . ."

"Fine, hit me."

"Okay. She's American. Born in August '85."

Lottie's curiosity finally got the better of her and she snatched the paper from Sasha. "She's American? I always thought she'd be Irish." She quickly read the rest of the document. No father listed. That secret would remain a secret for now. But 1985. That would have made her twenty-two when Lottie was born. Not a teen mom, but certainly not old.

"Wanna Google her? If we've got her full name and birthday, shouldn't be too hard to track her down. She's probably on Facebook if she's in her thirties."

Lottie paused, then grabbed a pillow from the couch and smushed it over her face. "I don't think I'm ready," she said, muffled. "Let me sit with this for a little."

"Want me to sit with you?"

She nodded.

Sasha grabbed her own pillow and leaned against her. "Okay. We can do that."

Eventually, though, Sasha had to head home, and Lottie wandered back to the piano to play the lullaby a few more times through. Now that she knew how to read music herself, it was easy to see that the piece was written by someone who was classically trained. Anna hadn't just jotted down a simple melody, but included the three-quarter time signature, beamed the notes, and added dynamics. Lottie bent down to inhale the paper, as if the old ink might, somehow, reveal answers she couldn't see.

But being alone in the empty house, with only the sheet music and Anna's name for company, would probably send her spiraling into a place she'd rather not visit. Lottie quickly shot off a text to the group chat to see if anyone wanted to swing by for an impromptu sleepover. But Sasha, of course, had already put out the APB that Aidan had left for Paris. By 10:00 p.m., the house was crawling with kids from nearly every private school on the Upper East Side.

Lottie tried weakly to protest as people started arriving, but they all knew she always relented. And the truth was that, tonight, the buzzing hum of so many voices and music so loud it made her ears ache was maybe the only solution to drowning out what was already blaring in her head.

As far as personalities went, Lottie wasn't a natural fit for her rather boisterous crew. But—bluntly—she had a glamorous, famous uncle and a huge town house that was often empty. That was enough to offer her entry into whatever social stratum she desired, not that she paid much attention to the hierarchy. And her friends were fun, as well as adept at keeping her from retreating too far into herself. She was aware that many at school were curious—if not outright envious—of her unorthodox living situation. She doubted any of them would trade places. There was such a thing as too much freedom.

But with Aidan gone so frequently, she mostly didn't mind kids descending upon the house nearly every weekend. It was noisy and exciting, and the beer lubricated everyone to their most uninhibited selves. It wasn't a family, but it did offer a cheapened sense of belonging. She'd settle for that.

Around eleven, a rowdy group of Hoxton boys arrived, lugging a case of vodka and enough White Claws to quench the thirst of a small nation.

"Let's get litty!" one of them yelled as they walked inside, to hoots of approval from almost everyone. Lottie rolled her eyes.

The boys made themselves at home in the kitchen, pulling open the giant Sub-Zero in a hunt for limes and ice. Bee was going to have her ass if this wasn't cleaned up by Monday morning, but she'd deal with that tomorrow.

A few minutes later, her friend Tyler sidled up to her and placed a vodka soda with a flourish in her hand. "A gift for our most charming hostess."

"So very kind, sir." She raised the glass in a mock toast.

Tyler and Lottie had known each other since fifth grade, when they were paired together during summertime STEM camp (clearly Aidan's idea, not hers). Tyler's friends and hers often made their way to each other's parties during weekends. She'd always found him cute, but he was normally too preoccupied with the exploits of his crew to pay her much attention.

"Heard you had a birthday yesterday," he said, taking a sip of his beer.

Lottie nodded, took a swig, and made a face. "Jesus, did you actually put any soda in this?"

"A splash. So, are we celebrating tonight?"

She shrugged. "Trying to get in the spirit. I had a . . . day."

"Yeah? Anything you want to share?"

Why not? She took another big gulp and winced. "Found my birth mom. Well, kind of. Found her name."

"Whoa. So now what?"

"Dunno. Doubt I'll make any decisions tonight." She gestured with her drink to the pandemonium around them.

"Well, as you may recall from my absolute domination over everyone at camp"—Tyler grinned—"I'm pretty good with a computer. If you need help with any light stalking, lemme know."

Lottie chuckled. "Noted."

The night tumbled further and further into entropy from that point thanks, in part, to Tyler's subpar bartending skills. There was beer pong on the dining room table, a Chappell Roan singalong, and multiple late-night pizza orders. Lottie managed to corral everybody out by about 2:00 a.m., which felt unimaginably mature.

But she woke up the next morning still in her clothes from the night before, accompanied by a hammering headache and Cajun the cat rumbling loudly on top of her head. When her eyes finally adjusted to the light outside and she could check her phone, there was already a text waiting from Tyler.

"wasn't kidding. lmk if u need help on the hunt."

Her hangover had also doused her with more than a little self-pity. This seemed like a cure, at least, for that. "i think I do," she texted back. "eli's at 1?"

Tyler was already sitting with his laptop and lunch when she walked into the shop. "I know this is the most expensive sandwich in America, but damn, they know their way around a ham and cheese. Want some?" He waggled a half in her direction.

Lottie laughed and slid in across from him. "Honestly? The thought of eating anything right now makes me wanna puke."

"You have fun, at least?"

"Yeah, I did." The truth, surprisingly.

"My job's done, then. Now, whatcha got for me?" He opened his computer.

She reached into her bag and handed him the birth certificate. He read it quickly and then pulled up a set of commands on his screen.

Lottie eyed them curiously. "What is that?"

"It's not the dark web, but it's, like, not *not* the dark web. It's the easiest way to get people's contact info. We type all this in here . . ." His fingers flew across the keys like hers on the piano. "And then it should pull up a list of anyone with those parameters . . . here." He turned the screen toward her. "Voilà. There is only one American Anna Buckley born August 14, 1985." He clicked on her name. "And she's in New York."

Lottie leaned in closer, brow furrowed. "She's not in Ireland?"

"Nope, looks like . . . Soho, Crosby Street." Tyler typed the address in Google and then whistled. "Damn, sweet digs." He paused, squinting at the search results and was quiet for a moment before turning the laptop back to himself. "Uh, Lottie? Do you know there's a singer named Anna Buckley?"

"Yeah—guess it's kind of a common name?"

Tyler's face, softly illuminated from the glow of the screen, grew serious. His fingers clicked out a staccato beat on the keyboard as he looked something up.

She frowned. "What?"

"So, *that* Anna's birthday is August 14—" He paused. "1985."

"No, she's gotta be younger than that." She dismissed what he was trying to tell her with a quick wave of her hand.

Tyler swiveled the screen to face her, with Anna's Wikipedia page pulled up. The resemblance, even in the thumbnail photo, was uncanny. Anna's hair was lighter, more of an auburn to Lottie's dark brown, but they shared the same dark blue eyes, the same smile, even the same ears.

"Oh," Lottie finally said when she realized she had to say something. She had the distinct sense she was breathing in helium instead of air; her head felt precariously close to detaching. She grabbed onto the table to steady herself.

"You didn't know?" he asked. "Like, at all?"

"No," she said, gripping the edge even more tightly. "No, my mom never told me anything."

Tyler nodded, Googled more images of her, and slowly scrolled through. "This is wild. You look just like her." He clicked on a performance shot: Anna straddling a piano bench, head arched back and hair flying behind her like flames. "You know her stuff?"

"Yeah, some," she mumbled, still staring at the photo.

"Is it good? She's, like, won Grammys."

"I guess so." In that moment, it was difficult to decide whether she'd prefer Anna's career to be a staggering success or an abject failure. Because, if the former, whatever she'd achieved had only been possible because of what—of whom—she'd given up. And if the latter, then had it been worth it at all?

Tyler turned to her, a mischievous glint in his eye. "Wanna go to her apartment?"

"Right now?"

"Hell yes, right now."

"And do what? Ring the doorbell and be like, 'Surprise! Remember me?'" She shook her head. "No way."

Tyler acknowledged that with a considered nod and kept typing. "Fair. But I'm sending you her address. Just in case." He shut his laptop softly. "Can I ask you something? You don't have to answer."

That was never a promising start. "I guess?"

"I know you live with your uncle, but he's not related to your birth mom, right?"

She nodded.

"So . . . what happened to your parents?" He looked apologetic to even be asking.

"Ah." She exhaled. "Well, I never had a dad: my mom adopted me on her own. She died in a car crash in LA when I was eight. And her parents were dead already, so Aidan drew the short straw and got me."

"Shit, Lottie." Tyler leaned back in his seat. "I'm sorry, I didn't know."

She shrugged. "I mean, it's not really something I lead with. As much as everyone loves an orphan," she added, throwing him a sardonic smile.

"Well, Aidan's lucky to have you," he said, and held out a fist for a bump. "Lemme know when you need more snooping done."

Lottie made her way home as if blinkered by the news: she tripped over a stroller and nearly walked into oncoming traffic on Madison. The questions were pouring out of her like water from a smashed hydrant. Had Anna been in New York this whole time? Did she know Lottie was here? Had they ever ended up in the same subway car, or the same restaurant, or the same elevator?

Had she written songs about her?

Lottie let herself into the empty house and found herself in front of the piano again. The lullaby seemed to be taunting her: this melody that had been with her for a lifetime was suddenly not so sweet. It was terrifying to think of what else might get distorted. She slammed down the piano's fallboard with a bang and walked away.

# FOUR

## Anna

*Boston*

April 2007

"Ah, fuck, I'm too nervous. I can't open it." Will stood up abruptly from his desk and started pacing his living room, hands behind his head.

"Oh my god, Will. The anticipation is killing *me* at this point. Just click the link!" Anna was perched on his ratty couch, legs curled under her and snacking on Teddy Grahams.

"You do it. Those things are disgusting, by the way." He waved distractedly at the box.

"You really trust me not to fuck with you if I open it?"

He stopped walking and considered this. "No, actually."

"Smart man."

He resumed pacing. "Okay. Okay. If I don't get in, then—"

"You're gonna get in."

"If I don't get in," he said again, shooting her a look of irritation. "I can still move to New York. I can still be a working composer." He was saying it like a mantra.

"Of course you can. But you're gonna to get in." She threw a teddy at him.

He swatted it away. "Why are you even here?"

"Because I'm excellent moral support." She popped another one into her mouth.

He snorted. "I fear for whoever you end up with."

She made a face at him. "Pot, kettle, black."

Will collapsed next to her on the couch and groaned. "I want this so bad, Annie."

"I know you do." She leaned her head on his shoulder. "Just *open* it."

He was still for a second, then finally nodded and popped back up. "Okay, here goes." He took a swig of root beer, leaned over his desk, and clicked the link. They both waited for the page slowly to load. "Come on!" he moaned.

And then, in big fat letters on the screen: "Congratulations!"

"Holy shit. I'm going to fucking Juilliard!"

Anna hooted and raised her arms over her head. Will ran toward her, picked her up off the couch, and spun her around.

"Told you," she said. He set her back down, arms still around her. They stared at each other for a second, then bounced apart like magnets turned the wrong way.

"Dr. Will Pendleton has a nice ring to it," she said, plopping back down on the couch.

"Yeah, but then when people ask what kind, I have to say doctor of musical arts. That sounds like something out of, like, Roald Dahl."

"If they ask for a doctor on the plane, what're you gonna do? Compose someone out of a heart attack?"

"Decompose, more likely."

"The dad jokes are only gonna get worse for you in grad school, aren't they?"

He grinned. "You have no idea."

Senior year had crept up on both of them like an unexpectedly high tide. It was as if they blinked and then were standing knee-deep at the start of their adult lives. Second semester, in particular, was an interstitial period that Anna found hard to parse. She was trying to enjoy the last few months of school, but, uncharacteristically, still didn't have her post-grad plans in place. And the amorphous nature of what came next was making her more than a little anxious.

She'd loved the structure and rhythm of Brookfield, but unlike Will, grad school didn't appeal. Over the last four years, she'd veered away from thoughts of a career in classical music—finding it too stifling—and instead had come into her own as a songwriter, accompanying herself on piano or guitar.

And, after a disastrous first summer teaching piano lessons to sticky-fingered, entitled kids in Newton, she'd found a steady gig during school breaks working as a piano player at the Ritz. By no means did it excite her creatively and she had to contend with far too many gin-soaked finance types making passes at her, but the money was surprisingly good. And while covering Tony Bennett in a hotel lobby wasn't exactly Carnegie Hall, discovering that small, symbiotic spark with an audience was intoxicating. Performing was better sustenance to her than any meal; it heightened her senses and left her fulfilled in a way she hadn't known was possible. Which was what she was trying to explain, unsuccessfully, to her advisor the next morning in her office.

"If you really don't want to go the orchestra route, you'd be a fantastic session pianist or vocalist. You're a fast learner," Dr. Sharma told her. "Play one of the Chopin études, some Copland, and sing whatever art song you want for the showcase, and I promise you'll be booked up for the next five years."

Anna leaned back in her chair and sighed. "I mean, thank you for the vote of confidence, but . . . I don't want that. I've been working on my own stuff all year. That's what I want to perform. That's what I want to do, after graduation."

"It's risky, I don't need to remind you of that. But ultimately, it is your decision." Dr. Sharma paused. "I don't want you to have unrealistic expectations, here. And part of my job *is* trying to make sure all of you graduate with some sort of a plan in place."

"I'm going in with eyes wide open, promise. But if I don't do this now, when else am I getting the chance?" Anna said, the urgency in her words pushing her forward on the seat.

Brookfield invited a slew of industry professionals to attend the senior showcase: label heads, agents, managers. More than a few students had landed record deals on the strength of their performances alone, which was the brass ring that Anna (and everyone else not pursuing classical) was intent on grabbing.

"Never, which is why whatever you do needs to be flawless." Dr. Sharma put her hands up in surrender. "I've said my bit. You have to make this call yourself."

"Promise to thank you in my Grammy speech," Anna said, grinning.

She smiled back. "Nothing would make me happier than to be proven wrong."

Anna spent the next month hardly sleeping and virtually living in the practice rooms. Will was also required to present an original composition for graduation, but his acceptance into Juilliard meant that the showcase was more of an afterthought for him. Instead, he was in the rooms nearly as much as she was, offering up (mostly) helpful tweaks for her melodies or pointers on her stage performance.

The night before the showcase, he cajoled her into taking a break and smoking a joint with him on the main quad. Anna wasn't a huge stoner, but acquiesced. She'd need something to blanket her frantic thoughts if she had any hope of sleeping.

He was lying on his back, staring up at the cloudless sky. "Would you ever get a tattoo?"

"Um, dunno? Doubt it. Only if something, like, really monumental happened. You?"

He shook his head. "Those needles make me nervous. And

my mother would disown me." He took a hit and passed it to her. "What's your dream scenario for tomorrow?"

She took a long drag and pondered that while she held the smoke in her mouth. "An agent? A record deal? Multiple labels fighting over me?"

"What's your worst case?"

"Thanks for the vote of confidence." She lay down next to him. "Mm, that nothing happens, I guess? That, at some point, I'd have to stop."

"So what's your plan? If you don't get any of that after the showcase?"

"You're a real ray of sunshine over there."

He glanced at her quickly, then studiously went back to looking at the sky. "I just—I just wanna know where you'll be, I guess," he said quietly.

Anna hadn't wanted to tell him until later, but she had made one Hail Mary backup plan. She'd applied for a songwriting residency in Ireland, in a small town called Doolin on the west coast. It was a hub of traditional music, and some of her family had emigrated from there, albeit many generations ago. And what better place to focus on writing an album than a misty, windswept Irish village?

She took another hit and blew out slowly. "I got into that residency, in Ireland."

Will, surprised, rolled over onto his side. "For real? When'd you find out?"

"Couple days ago."

"And you didn't tell me? Are you gonna go?"

She shrugged. "Kind of depends on what happens over the next few weeks." She turned to face him. "Sorry I didn't say anything sooner. But talking about it makes it real and I'm not ready for it to be real." She passed the joint back to him. "I just wish I knew how it all worked out already."

He took a puff. "I'm really high, so, you know, take this with a grain of salt. But you're really fucking talented, Annie. Those songs . . ." He mimed his head exploding. "I don't know. They make me feel really good inside."

It was a level of earnestness they didn't often reach; most of their compliments were couched in gentle ribbing.

"That one bridge would've been terrible without my help, though."

She punched him in the arm.

"Ow! What? It's the truth," he laughed.

Even after the joint, Anna found it near impossible to sleep. She was caught in restless half-dreams of attempting to play the piano, only for the keys to turn into soft clay, her fingers mashing and no sound emitting. When she tried to sing, it was as if her throat was stuffed with cotton balls: she nearly choked from the effort.

Arriving at the concert hall the next morning, it was clear she wasn't the only one battling a bubbling mix of nerves, insomnia, and a touch of hubris. After all, this was the first crucible of their fledgling music careers: they knew not all of them would emerge intact. Everyone milling around backstage could barely make eye contact with one another. It was eerily quiet as people pored over their music one final time, or sat with their earbuds in, trying to chase an elusive moment of zen.

Will and the other comp majors had their showcase the next day, but he'd snuck backstage for moral support. Anna appreciated this more than she let on.

"Anna Buckley?" one of the techs called out before spotting her. "You're up next."

"You okay?" Will asked, holding her lightly by the shoulders.

She nodded.

He put his forehead to hers with a grin. "Good. Fuck 'em up, Annie."

Afterward, she would find it difficult to recall what exactly transpired once she got onstage. It was as if her fingers, her voice belonged to a different, wilder creature that unzipped itself from her when she began to play. There was a video—it popped up on YouTube after her first album came out—but she'd never had a desire to watch it. That Anna did not know how it all worked out. She'd let her have her peace.

But she did remember what happened when she finished playing, slowly taking her foot off the sustain pedal at the end of her last piece. A brief silence hung in the air like a balloon, and then burst into a booming wave of applause. It took her by surprise. She looked to the wings first, where Will was goofily pumping his fist, and then out to the audience, where a few students had risen to give her a standing ovation. She blushed, gave a little wave, and nearly ran off the stage.

"Jesus, that was fantastic!" Will threw his arms around her as other students high-fived as they walked by. "You feel good?"

She shook her head in disbelief. "I have no idea."

While the performance students were understandably itching to go out and celebrate, nearly all of them were pulling double duty by playing in the comp showcase the next day. Unsurprisingly, Will had recruited Anna for his piece, and he'd organized a final rehearsal that evening. Though *rehearsal* was probably too ambitious a term: he'd rolled up with plenty of six-packs and a tray of brownies that looked far too suspect for Anna's taste. Before long, the night had devolved into live piano karaoke and half-finished games of Never Have I Ever.

Anna was sitting on the floor with Jess, a bassoon player, both sipping vodka-cranberries out of red Solo cups. Will was playing OutKast on the piano, which was both terrible and kind of good at the same time.

"Can I ask you something?" Jess was sweet, but Anna found her a little dull. She assumed that was a bassoon thing.

"Shoot."

"You and Will. Are you, like . . . you know?"

"Like . . . together?" Anna laughed. "No, definitely not."

"Really? Like ever?"

Anna shook her head no. "Like ever."

"Huh. So, it would be okay if I . . ."

"If you—Oh, no, go for it." Anna gestured toward him with her cup. "That 'Hey Ya!'–playing maestro is all yours."

Jess grinned. "Cool, thanks."

Anna didn't think he'd go for her, but she wasn't exactly sure why the whole conversation made her uneasy, either. She didn't have much time to contemplate it, though; soon everyone roused themselves for a wobbly walk back to the senior apartments. Will was far drunker than she'd realized—typical that he'd still be able to play that well—and Anna was shouldering about half his lanky body as he stumbled down the path.

"Do you need help?" Jess asked eagerly.

"No, I've got it," Anna said quickly. "Go get some sleep."

"Oh. Okay." Jess looked crestfallen, but she reluctantly turned back toward her building.

Anna managed to maneuver him to his front door and punched in his code. "Easy, buddy, let's get you some sleep. Big day tomorrow." She led him to his bed, slowly lowered him onto his mattress, then set about taking off his sneakers.

"Annie?" He raised his head.

"What?"

"Nothin'." His head flopped back down.

"I'm gonna grab you some water. Don't move." As if he could have gotten up if he wanted to. She filled a glass in the bathroom sink and brought it over to him, coaxing him up into a seated position.

"This is good water. You're so nice," he hiccupped. "If you leave, I won't have anyone to bring me water." He shook his head sadly. "Please don't go." He slumped over onto her shoulder. "I'll miss you too much."

She patted his head. "It'll work out, promise. But right now, you gotta rest. I'm setting your alarm for you, okay?"

He nodded like an agreeable four-year-old and allowed her to put a comforter over him. "You know what I was thinking?" His eyes were closed; he was already half asleep. She'd never noticed how long his eyelashes were.

"What were you thinking?"

"If we had babies, they'd be, like, really good at music. So good."

Anna laughed. "You really are wasted."

"But I'm right, right?"

She sighed. "Yes, hypothetically, little baby Mozarts."

"Or Gershwins."

She indulged him. "Sure, or Gershwins."

He smiled and rolled over. "Okay."

She smiled back and turned off his bedside light. "Okay."

Composing majors at Brookfield had to perform an original work for graduation, but the parameters were loose. Will had put together his own chamber orchestra, many of whom had been playing for him since their freshman year. It was bittersweet: most likely the last time they'd all be onstage together for the rest of their careers, but also probably the biggest audience they'd ever played to.

There was little doubt that Will was the most talented composer of the senior class: he was probably the best Brookfield had graduated in a decade. So it was no surprise that the auditorium was standing room only: not only did younger comp majors want to see what he'd been working on, but many of the record execs and agents as well, even if they knew he was committed to grad school in the fall.

And while Will himself was unperturbed by not only the showcase, but the star power in the room, Anna and everyone else was fairly giddy to perform his work. It was a contrapuntal piece in a presto tempo that reminded Anna of galloping horses weaving in and out of each other's way. Her piano part was one of the more challenging she'd ever attempted, but knowing he wrote it for her made her especially wary of striking a wrong note.

All of them may have been suffering from various degrees of hangovers, but you'd never have known once Will raised his baton. (Anna *had* allowed herself to watch this performance, which had also shown up on YouTube when Will started gaining notice for his film scores. She couldn't resist reading the comments, either: "is that anna buckley on piano? mother was mothering even then?!" She almost liked it, then thought better of it.)

Four years of conservatory training had made Will even more confident and graceful on the podium; watching him was like sound in physical form. And because all of them knew each other's playing styles so intimately, there was an unspoken shorthand on stage, an intuition of when to speed up or slow down. They moved as one. It was one of the most effortless and joyful performances of Anna's career, and a memory that became a touchstone in later years, when it was sometimes hard to remember why she was still doing it at all.

The coda finished with a bang: the brass roaring, the strings playing legato, and Will with his arms in the air and hair in his face, triumphant like a prize fighter. She was—they all were—proud to know him in that moment.

With the showcases finally over, it felt like the campus heaved a giant, collective sigh.

And now, the waiting began.

As was tradition, any of the industry types who had been in attendance were asked not to contact specific students directly, but their advisors instead. Every senior had a meeting the Monday after the shows, where they were informed who was (or wasn't) interested in working with them. Colloquially, it was known as D-Day, in which the *D*, ostensibly, just stood for *decision*, but the more cynical ones would tell you it stood for *dirge*: the song of mourning.

Anna's meeting was late in the day, which made for an excruciating wait. When she finally arrived at Dr. Sharma's office, she'd played out virtually every possible scenario, vacillating between joy and terror all day. At this point, though, she just wanted to get it over with. She stood outside for a moment before knocking, her hopes both alive and dead like Schrödinger's cat.

"Come in, Anna," Dr. Sharma called out.

She tried to parse her voice for any giveaways: no luck. With a deep exhale, she tentatively pushed open the door. Dr. Sharma had a folder on her desk for every one of her advisees; she pulled out Anna's as she walked in.

"Your performance was lovely. I enjoyed it very much. And that was wonderful work on Will's as well."

"Thanks, Dr. S." Was there a but coming?

"But I know you don't really care what I think, at least not today," she said with a knowing smile. "And, luckily for you, I did hear from quite a few people whose opinions I do think you care about."

Anna could barely contain herself from lunging across the table and ripping the folder from her hands. "And?" she managed to squeak out.

"You've got interest from half a dozen agents and three labels. But—and this is a big but—they need to see more of your work before anyone wants to move forward. If I were you, I'd spend the next six months to a year writing and then recording demos, and then reach back out when you've got close to a full album's worth of material."

She was nonplussed. It was hard to decide if this was good news or just disappointing.

"I know you wanted to walk out of here with a contract, but that so rarely happens." Dr. Sharma reached out to touch her hand. "This is a fantastic outcome, Anna, truly. I want you to be really proud of yourself. Push through this next year and then I have no doubt you'll get signed somewhere."

Anna nodded. The upside was that now she had a plan. And she thrived on a plan.

"Are you going to say yes to that residency?"

No friends, no family, no distractions. "Yeah," she said. "I think so."

The next few months felt like she pressed fast forward on an old VHS tape. Certain frames stuck, but mostly everything passed by quickly in a Technicolor blur. Graduation came and went without much fanfare; she told her parents not to bother coming up and they offered no resistance. Anna and Will both received awards for their majors, a feather in their caps certainly, but didn't mean much in the real world.

Will, however, had been offered a commission from the New York Philharmonic on the basis of his showcase performance. The irony was not lost on her that out of their entire graduating class, the person least hungry for approbation was the one who landed arguably the biggest coup. But she was mostly excited for him; he deserved it.

Now it was already August and she was leaving for Doolin the next day. Will had moved into his new apartment in New York, but had come back up to Boston to help her pack and say goodbye. Neither knew exactly when they'd see each other again. She assumed she'd come back to the States briefly for his NY Phil show, but her residency was technically a year long.

Anna's room was almost empty: all that remained were a few posters affixed to the wall behind her bed. The Jeff Buckley (no relation, but she didn't offer that up unless asked) *Live at Sin-é* pulled off easily, but the corner of her Tori Amos *Little Earthquakes* was stuck. "Shit," she said as she tried unsuccessfully to launch herself higher off the bed to reach it.

Will was watching amusedly from the floor, taking slow sips from a now-lukewarm Sam Adams. Kings of Leon's *Because of the Times* was playing softly from a portable speaker.

"Anna. Anna! Stop, I'll get it." He stood up and took a few shaky steps toward her on the mattress.

"No, I've almost"—another failed jump—"got it."

He chuckled. "You almost definitely don't." He put a balancing hand on her, stretched his arm up and grabbed the corner, stumbling into her as he peeled the poster off, his mouth grazing the side of her cheek. "Sorry," he mumbled, but he didn't move away. His hand remained lightly on her shoulder, his palm warm.

Anna was still. This touch—this proximity—felt, somehow, inevitable. But she was afraid to shift and break the spell. The poster dropped with a clatter onto the floor. Behind her, Will's breath deepened, tickling the top of her spine. After a moment, he reached out and slowly slid his index finger along her collarbone, pushing her tank top strap off her shoulder. Then he bent down to kiss it, barely touching her skin with his lips. When she didn't pull away, he got a little bolder: left arm encircling her waist to draw her closer. Anna could feel her heart pounding in her throat, but still, she tilted her head to the side. He kissed her earlobe, her neck, her shoulder blade. She closed her eyes. Now that it was happening, she couldn't believe they'd had the self-control to wait this long.

"Do you want me to stop?" he whispered into the back of her

neck. His hand drifted toward the waistband of her sweats as he said it, and then dipped below. She inhaled sharply, but shook her head no.

Finally, she turned around, her eyes darting over his face almost as if she'd never seen him before. In a sense, she hadn't. They were both breathing a little heavily now. Anna stood on her tiptoes and, without stopping to think, kissed him fully, her hand reaching back to cradle his head. Will reciprocated quickly, pinning her against the wall before his hands reached up under her tank top, pulling it off in one fluid motion. She did the same with his T-shirt, running her fingers up his abdomen before lowering herself onto her mattress, pulling him down with her by his neck. He landed on top of her; she could already feel him through his shorts.

Will had told her once that one of the most difficult parts of conducting was not letting your heartbeat dictate the pace of your movements. It was so easy, he said, to go faster and faster because that's what your pulse was telling you.

He reached back to unhook her bra while he kissed her neck. "Annie, are you sure?" He stopped for a moment to search her face. "I don't wanna do this if—"

"Stop talking," she whispered. She pulled him back closer to her and plunged her hand inside the front of his shorts.

"Oh, fuck," he murmured.

The rest of their clothes practically evaporated off: a fury of hands and legs and lips. But then he hesitated, propped up on his arms looking down at her. They were both aware they were tumbling straight into the Rubicon. "Okay?" he asked softly, one more time.

At this point, she'd rather drown in there than stop.

"Okay."

After, they lay on her bed, the right words slipping through their fingers like sand, so they were silent. On one hand, Anna could chalk up what happened to too much beer and nostalgia for a time in their lives that wasn't even over yet. They were drunk and they were young and they were sad. On the other, there was no one who understood her better (there was almost no one who understood her at all, if she were being honest).

Even so, she was surprised at how well their bodies had fit; how wordlessly they could move together. She would have thought that familiarity might breed awkwardness, but it turned out to be the opposite. They could anticipate the other's move; he could make her every part hum. That night, they fell asleep in a tangle of the other's limbs, chests rising and falling like a harmony.

But the next morning, with antiseptic daylight washing over them, the possibilities from the day before were scrubbed away. They both woke up naked, nursing hangovers, and unsure how to address what exactly had happened. Anna wrapped the sheet around her with a nervous smile.

"I've seen it all now." Will poked her shoulder and grinned mischievously. "You don't really have to cover up."

It broke the tension like a finger on a bubble. Anna burst out laughing. "I guess you have." She buried her face under the sheet. "Fuck, Will! What did we do?"

He wrapped his arms around her, kissing her shrouded cheek. "I don't know. But it was fun."

Eventually, they could delay the inevitable no longer. They peeled themselves from the bed, got dressed, and Anna sat on the last of her suitcases while Will zipped them closed. He lugged them easily down three flights of stairs and she was reminded that conducting was a far more athletic pursuit than anyone gave it credit for.

Will offered to drive her to Logan, blasting Feist's new album *The Reminder* on the way. "I Feel It All" started playing just as they pulled up to the drop-off. He cranked the volume, flicked his hazards on, and hopped out of the car to open her door.

Anna squinted up at him. "What are you doing?"

"Dance with me." He held out a hand.

"Here?" she said dubiously.

"Yes, here. I'm not gonna see you for a very long time. So, I want you to dance with me." He thrust his hand out again.

She sighed, but she let him take hers. He pulled her up out of the car and they started to slowly sway, smack in the middle of the lane. Cars started honking almost immediately. This was Logan, after all.

He kissed the top of her head. "I love you, okay? You do whatever you want with that. But I needed you to know before you got on that plane."

She wrapped her arms around him tighter, her cheek against his chest. They stayed like that until they couldn't.

This was the moment that both would return to, late at night, when it felt safe to slip into it. This was the moment that they'd each capture, again and again, in song or in symphony. This was the moment that everything changed. And this was the moment that they said goodbye.

# FIVE

## Lottie

*New York*

May 5, 2024

How strange, that she'd been there all along—in magazines, on the radio, in New York—but that Lottie never knew to look.

It was Sunday night. She was alone, again, in the echoes of the house. Briefly, she considered calling Aidan to tell him she opened the letter, but then remembered it was the middle of the night in Paris. There was a chance he was still awake, but if so, he was either burning the candle at both ends at the studio or blowing off steam at a private club somewhere. Neither scenario was exactly ideal for a heart-to-heart.

Lottie eyed her closed laptop on the kitchen counter, which she'd resisted opening since getting back from Eli's. If—well, really, once— she started Googling Anna, she knew it would be nearly impossible to claw her way out of that rabbit hole. There must be thousands of videos of her on YouTube, hundreds of photo shoots and interviews.

Her friends' parents were lawyers or doctors or worked at hedge funds; they didn't have dedicated websites, or magazine cover stories, or supercuts from concerts. Or fans—there were already a dizzying number of people who followed Anna's every move: what she wore, where she ate . . . who she slept with. And all of them knew more—a lot more—than Lottie did. It was silly to feel territorial, but still, it didn't seem fair.

So, after grabbing a slice of cold pizza from the fridge, Lottie decided she'd start learning about her in the only way that made sense: through the music. She pulled up Spotify, loaded the This Is Anna Buckley playlist, and songs from her first record, *Cliffwalks*, began playing softly on the living room sound system. There were threads of Anna's eccentric, singer-songwriter predecessors like Kate Bush, or even Björk—she didn't shy away from harmonic dissonance or unusual time signatures—but her work wasn't derivative. It was complex, and vibrant, and a little haunting with its mix of virtuosic piano sections and electronic flourishes. Irrespective of how Lottie or anyone else might feel about her songs, objectively, Anna was extraordinarily talented.

Lottie checked the release date of the album: the year after she was born. If any record mentioned her, even obliquely, she'd have to imagine it would be this one. She pulled up the lyrics and read them for any mention of Charlottes or Lotties (unlikely, she knew), or even babies, but found nothing. Anna's writing, in general, was fairly esoteric: there was little chance she would have spelled out the situation straightforwardly in song. There was, however, a link at the bottom of the web page to the liner notes: she clicked it and a photo from the CD booklet popped up.

She scanned it quickly: it was mostly thank-yous to Anna's crew and recording team. But then, there it was. The very end of Anna's acknowledgments: "And to Charlotte, who inspired these songs more than she'll ever know. I hope, one day, you'll let me tell you all about it." Lottie's phone jumped out of her hand and clattered to the floor. She felt like she'd been kneed in the stomach.

It was one thing to know, intellectually, that this person was related to her. But it was another to see a message that Anna had written *to* her. (Lottie wondered if she had ever been the discussion on an Anna Buckley subreddit: Who *is* Charlotte?) It was incontrovertible, tangible proof; and that was much harder to ignore.

And it was almost a dare, wasn't it? Anna had said she hoped one day she could tell her all about it. Well, maybe Lottie was ready now.

But how, exactly, she wanted to orchestrate this meeting, she wasn't sure. Contrary to what Tyler suggested, she had zero desire to roll up to Anna's doorstep and knock (plus, doormen: she'd never get past the lobby). It would be better, she thought, if there were a way to make it happen more organically. And, maybe, if Anna weren't Anna, she could. But fame, as she knew far too well from Aidan's own experience, erected roadblocks that could be impossible to circumnavigate. She would be hard to find for a reason.

And so, Lottie needed reinforcements, of the sort who were adept at curating chance encounters by obsessively collecting crumbs through social media. Luckily, Lottie was sixteen: this description applied seamlessly to all her friends. She quickly texted Sasha: "found her. she's in nyc! help."

Sasha texted back a bunch of exclamation points, then FaceTimed her. "How'd you do that so fast?"

"Tyler."

"Ah, that makes sense. So who is she?"

"Sash, it's *that* Anna Buckley. The singer Anna Buckley. Not a random one."

Sasha, uncharacteristically, opened her mouth without a sound. "Shut up. *Shut up*," she finally said, once she'd recovered.

"Swear to god. This is so weird."

"I mean, yeah, but . . . kinda cool? Like, isn't this what everybody always dreams about? Finding out your parents are actually famous?"

Lottie made a face. "I think it just makes it more complicated. It's not like she works in, I dunno, a grocery store somewhere. There's a lot more red tape. Like, what am I supposed to do? Email her . . . manager? They're gonna think it's some creepy parasocial thing."

Sasha considered this while tapping her chin. "Okay, true. But did you check her IG yet? See where she goes?"

She shook her head. "I haven't wanted to look yet. Feels like I'm spying."

Sasha nodded. "I got you. Lemme see what I can find."

"Thanks, Sash. Love you."

"You're, like, an actual nepo baby now. You know that, right?" Sasha grinned.

Lottie rolled her eyes. "You have to be famous to be a nepo baby. But if you tell anyone, I *will* murder you."

Within the hour, Sasha had sent her an email with a comprehensive list of places Anna had either geotagged herself or been spotted. The commitment to detail was impressive (and color-coded): Sasha's mother would have probably lamented that her daughter never spent that long researching her American history papers.

The list was a lot of the usual suspects for someone like Anna: Electric Lady Studios, Zero Bond, the Bowery Hotel. They were tricky spots to engineer a run-in for anyone, let alone a teenager. And while she knew Aidan, with his considerable connections, would probably be helpful, Lottie felt, for whatever reason, that she needed to do this without his help.

Sasha had also left a note at the bottom of the email: "She takes a lot of photos at a studio somewhere, but I can't figure out where. Looks like one of those old factory spaces in Soho that they converted into little offices. Remember that one where we used to get our brows done by that Russian lady? What was her name? Like that.

"And I know you didn't ask specifically, but don't think she's married or has kids . . . Well, other kids."

Helpful-ish? But she didn't feel much closer to finding her and more snooping would have to wait. Tomorrow was the start of the school week, and finals were approaching.

Lottie's weekends certainly involved their fair share of hard seltzers and afternoon naps, but no one made the mistake that Pembroke wasn't rigorous. She had untold hours of homework, private tutoring, and after-school activities every week. Aidan felt that his own education at an arts-focused high school had left him with major gaps in his cocktail party knowledge, and he would tolerate no such deficiency for his only niece. In her more cynical moments, she wondered if he sent her there just for the bragging rights, but as a voracious reader and a naturally curious person, it was a good fit, regardless.

Understandably, however, her mind was elsewhere by the time she arrived at school. When the core of your identity has been sucked out like so much water from a straw, it can be difficult to concentrate on, say, algebra. Or Shakespeare. Or anything, really, except how you're going to get down to Soho and find the woman who gave you up and look her straight in the eye and ask her why. And ask her and ask her until you have an answer that makes sense.

"Lottie. *Lottie!*"

She plummeted back down into her body when she heard her name. Mrs. Reiner, her moody, awful algebra teacher, was standing in front of her desk with her arms folded primly. "I said, if your value of $x$ is seventeen, then how did you get fifty-four for $y$?"

Lottie stared up at her, unblinkingly. "You know? . . . I really don't give a shit." As Mrs. Reiner sputtered, Lottie pushed herself back from her desk, stood up, and walked out. The stunned tittering of her classmates grew louder as she closed the door behind her.

But once in the hallway, she realized she had no idea where to go. Eventually, she made her way to the bathroom, splashed some water on her face, and gave herself a minute to cool down. She'd never done anything like that before: more often than not, she felt like she was already taking up too much space. Her default was to make room for others, whether at the cafeteria table or in conversations. It didn't take a world-class therapist to unpack the reasons why, but she'd never given much thought to *not* doing it. It was a little unnerving how good it felt.

"Lottie? There you are." Eugenie from her algebra class was holding the bathroom door open. "Ms. Santos is looking for you."

Pembroke was all about expressing your individuality and finding that unique light within each girl, to a point. Lottie knew she was going to be in deep shit for snapping at Mrs. Reiner, who, to be fair, didn't really do anything wrong.

She walked down to the lobby and knocked on Ms. Santos's open door. She was at her desk, face stern, hands clasped in front of her. She gestured for Lottie to sit across from her.

"You wanna tell me your side of the story?"

Lottie shrugged. "She probably got it right. I just . . . snapped. Sorry. I'll apologize to her, too, of course."

"This isn't like you. At all. Something going on you wanna talk about?"

She picked at a hangnail until it started to bleed. "I dunno. Maybe."

"Lottie, work with me, here. It'll be easier to get her off the ledge if you do."

Lottie looked up and smiled slightly. At least she wasn't the only one who thought Reiner was miserable. She exhaled, her ribs still tight. "There's some . . . stuff happening at home."

"Yeah?" Ms. Santos cocked her head. "I'm gonna need more than that."

"Family stuff?"

"Lottie."

"Fine." She swallowed. "I found my birth mom."

Ms. Santos leaned back in her chair, her mouth a perfect O. "I see. You met her?"

Lottie shook her head. "But I know who she is. And she's here, in New York . . . somewhere. So, I'm a little bit—a lot—distracted."

"Do you want to schedule a time to see Dr. P.?" Like every private school worth its $60,000-plus tuition, Pembroke had an army of specialists to help with every problem, real or imagined. Dr. P. was the school psychiatrist, who was always a touch too keen on how little orphan Lottie was coping with life's woes. She loathed being treated like a pity case and avoided him whenever possible.

"Not right now."

Ms. Santos nodded. "I'll talk to Mrs. Reiner. But you know I'll need to call Aidan. And you're definitely LOP'd for the rest of the week."

That stood for Loss of Privilege: it meant no eating lunch off campus and extra community service hours, among other indignities.

"Yeah, figured. First time for everything, I guess?" She smiled, just a little.

"Don't make it a habit." Ms. Santos raised an admonishing eyebrow. "But my door's always open if you need to talk; what you're dealing with is a lot. Still, no more cursing at Mrs. Reiner. I literally thought I saw steam come out of her ears." Her eyes were wide. "She scares me, too, sometimes," she added in a stage whisper.

Aidan FaceTimed her a few minutes after she walked into the house.

"I know I'm really terrible at this disciplinarian stuff, but you wanna tell me what happened? I had a missed call from school and I need to know what I'm getting into."

They hadn't spoken since he'd left for Paris. Even texting proved to be a little too heavy of a lift when work got intense.

"You want the long version or short?"

He looked at his watch. "Short." Of course.

"I told Mrs. Reiner I didn't give a shit about algebra."

He let out a stunned chuckle. "No, you did not. Charlotte Anne Thomas!"

"I'm sorry! I don't know what happened."

"You don't know?" His tone was dubious. "Or you don't wanna say?"

She shrugged sullenly.

He groaned. "Okay, I don't have time to pull this out of you. Are you in trouble? Is this a make-a-donation type of thing?"

"Yes. And no. Just some extra hours helping out Mr. Shean."

"Remind me who that is again?"

"One of the music teachers."

Someone was speaking in frantic French behind Aidan, trying to get his attention. He turned away from the phone to address him: "*Attends. Attends!*" He sighed heavily and looked back at her. "I have to go. We can't find our lacemaker. Everything is always a fucking disaster with these people." He pointed a finger at her. "Be good."

Lottie smiled indulgently. "I will."

"We'll talk more about this later."

They wouldn't, but she nodded anyway. "*Bonne chance, mon oncle.*"

Lottie's LOP punishment wasn't really much of a punishment, but she certainly wasn't going to let Ms. Santos know that. Mr. Shean was head of the music program at Pembroke's Upper

School and one of Lottie's favorite teachers. Her job that Tuesday morning was to arrive at school early and help him set up for first period orchestra, which she was a part of, anyway.

He gave her a quizzical look as she entered the auditorium. "*You're* my LOP?"

"At your service," she said with a bashful smile.

"Never thought I'd see the day," he said with an exaggerated shake of his head. "Well, get down here and start pulling chairs. I'll throw some music on." He walked offstage and soon, a chill, indie rock mix was piping through the speakers. "What'd you do?" he asked when he reemerged.

She waved off the question. "Doesn't matter."

He put his hands up. "Fine by me. I'm happy for the company, especially someone I can chat recital with. How d'you think we're sounding?"

"Good, I think. And I like the Gershwin better than I thought I would. How do *you* think we're sounding?"

He wavered his hand: *così così*. "Getting there. Strings section could use some work, but we're not exactly playing with Sarah Changs, are we?" He raised his eyebrows conspiratorially.

"Are you implying the Pembroke orchestra isn't Juilliard-level?" Lottie said, faux-aghast. "Don't let the parents hear you, they'll have you canceled in a day." She grinned at him and moved a music stand into place.

He laughed. "I mean some of you are very talented. You think more about doing that solo?"

"No," she said quickly. "I mean, it's not my thing. Playing with everyone is more my speed." Lottie's stage fright had gotten progressively worse over the last few years. She'd play for Aidan, or for friends occasionally, but the thought of being the only one onstage filled her limbs with an icy dread.

"Well, the offer stands, if you change your mind."

A familiar song started playing: it took Lottie a few seconds to realize it was Anna's. Mr. Shean looked up and shook a finger toward the speaker. "Speaking of piano: You know her? People don't realize how good of a musician she is. Her skill level is insane. Conservatory-trained and everything."

"Who is this again?" Lottie's voice came out squeaky. Acting was probably not her forte.

"Ah, Anna Buckley. You should listen. You kinda look like her, actually," he said, pausing to squint at her. "Anyway, she's great. *Incredible* live. I think has a lot of demons, judging from her lyrics, but, y'know, that always makes for good music."

"Huh. Well, cool. I will check her out," she said with as much enthusiasm as she could muster.

The bell rang for first period. "I need to grab something from my locker," Lottie mumbled, and bolted for the door. Anna's voice was nothing but invasive and dissonant in this space.

Wednesday after school, Lottie found herself with a rare, free afternoon. Her piano teacher had come down with the flu and her homework load was surprisingly light.

She popped in her AirPods for the walk home, shuffling through some of Anna's later albums. After listening to her exclusively for the past few days, there was a familiarity now to her intakes of breath or her tremolos, but it was difficult to be objective on how she felt about the music. It seemed important, all the same, to learn her full body of work. Almost as if hearing it would, somehow, provide the answers that she actually wanted from Anna herself.

Soon, Lottie realized that she was headed toward the subway station, not back home. The 6 train went direct to Soho. She relented, let whatever it was propelling her take charge, Anna and her piano still threading their way through her eardrums.

She hopped off the train at Spring Street and checked Tyler's email with Anna's address; the building was just about a block over from the stop. It was what she'd envisioned: a slick loft conversion with huge floor-to-ceiling windows and an arsenal of doormen. And not that Lottie had expected her to be standing outside on her phone or emerging from an Uber, but the street was empty, minus a few tourists lugging giant Prada shopping bags.

Her attention turned to the windows, as she tried to discern which ones might be Anna's. (Tyler would have reminded her she could just pull up the floor plans, but that seemed a step too far.) An overhead light blazed to life in one living room, but it was impossible to see who turned it on. Lottie suddenly pulled out her earbuds and stuffed them back in the case. It felt a little too on the nose to be listening to Anna's music while standing outside her apartment like a stalker.

After another minute, she decided to call it. One of her favorite record shops, Schoolhouse, was around the corner, at least. The door jingled as she opened it: inside it smelled of old cardboard, dusty rugs, and just a hint of patchouli. Everyone who worked there was an insufferable music snob who was always lamenting about how much better New York was thirty years ago. Lottie adored every inch of the space.

She pretended to be interested in the latest Maggie Rogers LP in the new releases, but could feel her attention getting pulled to the B section like a zipper being snapped into place. She finally gave in. There was lots (and lots) of Jeff Buckley, of course: this was downtown Manhattan. But the shop carried a decent selection of Anna's as well. She pulled out *Eleusinian Mysteries*, her second album. The cover shot had her in a vaguely Greek ensemble, her auburn hair piled on top of her head with crisscrossed gold bands.

"That's an okay one," said the dude behind the register, sipping a yerba maté out of one of those gourd cups. High praise, coming from him.

She turned toward him. "Yeah?"

He shrugged. "Maybe I'm biased, though. She lives around here. Nice gal."

Lottie knew the best way to keep these guys talking was to say nothing at all. She smiled brightly and nodded.

"She likes Joplin a lot, Zeppelin." He took a slurp through his metal straw. "But she got St. Vincent and San Fermin the last time she came in."

Lottie busied herself with examining the track listing on the back of the record.

"She works real hard, that one. I think she comes down here when she needs a break."

"Oh?"

"Yeah, well, it's convenient." He pointed a finger up. "Her studio's right there."

# SIX

## Anna

*Doolin*

Fall 2007

**From: anna.buckley@gmail.com**
**To: maestro.will@gmail.com**
**September 16, 4:29 PM**

WP!

Sorry the phone tag has been so intense. I'm keeping odd hours and the time zone difference doesn't help.

Here is everything you need to know so far: Doolin is teeny, adorable (thatched roof cottages!), and crawling with musicians.

The residency provided housing, but what I didn't know was that I'd be living *with* someone. I'm staying in her cute little house, actually. Her name is Maeve Kilian. I think she's probably in her fifties, and she takes in a new boarder, like yours truly, every year. They pay her for her trouble (although, as you know, I'm excellent company), and I get a full Irish breakfast with a view of the sea every morning. Also, she takes bullshit from absolutely no one and I can only hope to be as cool as she is when I grow up.

Speaking of grown up: I've got my very own studio down the road with a piano, acoustic and electric guitars, amps, etc. So mostly spending days there, and then messing around on the keyboard back in my room at night. Not exactly action-packed over here, but honestly? It's kind of amazing. Maybe I'm more of a hermit than I realized.

Tell me things from NYC. Making friends? Are the Juilliard practice rooms everything I would dream them to be? Are you remembering to, like, eat and do your laundry?

Miss you,
A

**From: maestro.will@gmail.com**
**To: anna.buckley@gmail.com**
**September 18, 6:58 PM**

Banana—

I seriously thought you'd fallen into the bogs. You absolutely are a hermit—are you just realizing this?

Here's my update: New York fall is really inferior to New England fall. I didn't realize how much I'd miss the leaves. Or just that crisp smell in the air. It smells like garbage here, everywhere. I'm turning into my father much earlier than I thought.

Doesn't really matter, though, because I'm never outside. Basically living in the studio like you: we have our first full orchestra comp due in Nov. Really wishing you were here for the piano, but Juilliard students . . . don't suck? So, I guess it's an OK compromise. They are *very* serious though, so haven't really made inroads with anyone. And yes, the practice rooms here are ridiculous. I'll show you when you come.

Speaking of: it's looking like the Phil gig will be May, if you want to pencil in? You think you might come back for the holidays, too, or nah?

I'm remembering to eat every couple of days. Are you sick of potatoes yet? Have you seen the sun? How are the songs coming? Send more clips! Loved what I heard so far. Of course.

Miss you too,
WP

**From: anna.buckley@gmail.com**
**To: maestro.will@gmail.com**
**October 3, 12:19 PM**

Billy boy:

Love what you sent me last week. That second movement . . . fuck. Can't wait to hear it for real. Did you get your date for May yet? As excited as I am to see you, I think I'm mostly excited to see the sun and eat a goddamn real piece of pizza.

Although to be honest: the rain here does make it delightfully moody. I'm writing/composing some kind of dark shit, but it feels fitting. As for food: obviously I continue to be sick of potatoes, but I'm kind of sick of . . . everything. Took a (rare!) day off to see Inishmore in the Aran Islands (you would be so into the sweaters they make there) and the boat ride was awful. Been feeling nauseous since then. Had no idea seasickness could last this long?! Ireland, man.

Attaching some new stuff here, let me know what you think. Still feels so strange to not be able to play it for you live.

xo,
A

* * *

Anna had been fairly incapacitated since returning from Inishmore, which, like she mentioned to Will, she assumed was some sort of odd, prolonged seasickness. The smell of most food sent bile racing up her throat, and she was sleeping for at least ten hours a night, which was probably double what she normally managed. An exhaustion seemed to emanate from deep inside her marrow, radiating outward into all her limbs.

On the third morning of this, when Anna had to hold back a gag as Maeve scrambled eggs, Maeve decided she'd had enough. "I'm not sure if you have the flu, or food poisoning, or what, love, but this is not seasickness. I bought you whatever I could find at the pharmacy. It's all in a bag up in your bathroom, go have a look." She shooed her off with a mug of tea. "Do it now. Your face is greener than the hills."

Anna felt too nauseated to protest and trundled up the creaky stairs. There was a white paper bag sitting on the bathroom counter, along with a warm bottle of 7 Up. She sat down on the toilet seat and peered inside it. A box of paracetamol, anti-nausea hard candies, and . . . two pregnancy tests. *Quite presumptuous*, she thought. Plus, she'd gotten her period. It'd been much lighter than normal, but she'd chalked that up to the stress of moving across the Atlantic.

When was that, though? She did the math in her head, frowning. Well over a month ago and she hadn't gotten another. But she figured it was coming soon: her boobs had been so tender she could barely wear a bra.

The penny dropped.

There was no way, was there? They hadn't used a condom, but she was on the pill (though it was possible in the frenzy of the move that she'd skipped one or two). She shook her head quickly to herself. Her cycle was probably just messed up from all the changes. Taking the test would ease her mind, vanquish any niggling doubt.

She ripped it open, scanned the directions, peed on the stick, and set it down on the Formica counter. It said it could take up to two minutes for results, but far faster than that, one, then two bright, angry red lines appeared in the window. She stared at it for a second, uncomprehendingly, before fumbling open the directions and reading them again. Two lines: positive.

Fuck, fuck, fuck.

She leaned forward and put her head in her hands. Her heart was pounding so furiously it felt like it might explode through her temples. She inhaled and held her breath, allowing it to sneak into every crevice of her rib cage before she slowly let it go.

Maybe it was a dud test. That's what was happening. She'd take the second one and that would be negative and she'd just . . . ignore the first result. With a nod to herself, she pulled the other out of the bag and repeated the steps. She managed, this time, to avoid looking at the window until the full two minutes had elapsed.

Two red lines. Bars on a cage.

"You have to be fucking kidding me," she muttered.

She had to get this taken care of. Fast.

Maeve was peering up from the bottom of the landing when she walked out; Anna watched her attempt to scurry back to the kitchen without being noticed. She slowly descended the stairs, then sat down at the table, staring blankly ahead.

"How far along are you, then?" Maeve asked quietly, pretending to be busy cleaning the stove.

Anna looked up. How did she know? Did it even matter? "About two months, I think," she finally said. "There was only one time it could've . . . happened."

Maeve nodded, scrubbing the burners. Eventually, she turned around and leaned back against the stove. "I can help. Whatever you decide."

“I mean, I already know,” Anna said quickly. “I don’t want to—I can’t be . . .”

Maeve put a hand up to save her from spelling it out. “It’s not legal here, you know that, right?”

Christ, maybe she did at one point, but getting an abortion wasn’t exactly on her Irish bucket list. She slumped back in her chair. “So what do people do?”

“Fly to England. Manchester, mostly, it’s cheaper than London. Or you can take the ferry to Liverpool.” Maeve walked to the table and sat down next to her, placed her hand on top of Anna’s. “Just let me know. We’ll get you where you need to be.”

**From: anna.buckley@gmail.com**
**To: maestro.will@gmail.com**
**October 7, 11:09 AM**

Call me.

Will buzzed her around noon. He must have seen her email as soon as he woke up in New York.

“Hey.” He sounded sleepy. “Are you okay?”

She hesitated. “I’m pregnant, Will.”

It took him a moment to respond. “What?”

“I’m pregnant.” She paused. “It’s yours, obviously.”

She heard him exhale loudly. “You sure?”

“You want me to mail you the fucking test? I took two. I’ve got an extra.”

“Sorry, just asking,” he mumbled. “Did we not, um . . . use protection?”

“I’m on the pill.”

“But it didn’t work?”

“No, it didn’t work.”

"Okay." He exhaled again. "Fuck. What do you need me to do?"

"I'm taking care of it," she said evenly. "You don't need to, like, fly over or anything. But I thought you should know."

"Well, yeah. Are you sure? On, you know."

"Don't be ridiculous. Of course."

"I can fly over."

"I don't want you to," she said abruptly. "Sorry, I mean it's fine. I can handle it."

"Okay, whatever you want to do," he said carefully. "It's just—I'd hate for you to have to be alone for . . . that."

She knew he was trying to help—Will was generally always trying to be helpful—but the fact that he was (partially) responsible for this in the first place was making it hard to be equanimous. "Like I said, I can handle it," she said tightly. "I don't need you to do anything. Well, anything else. You've done enough."

"That's not fair, Anna," he said quietly.

"None of this is. I gotta go." She hung up before he had a chance to protest and she to change her mind.

Maeve helped her find the most reputable clinic in Manchester, and Anna bought a plane ticket leaving from Shannon in three days' time. In the interim, she found it best to stay busy. She was clocking ten hours at the studio—even with this relentless exhaustion—simultaneously penning lyrics, composing new melodies, and honing songs she'd already completed.

But this was a rhythm with which she was familiar. Working tirelessly on her music had been her reliable escape since she was barely out of middle school. To stop meant inviting the more spiky and sticky thoughts to rise up, like water in a clogged drain. Staying in motion kept everything flowing.

Will had called every day, of course, but she sent him straight to voicemail. She couldn't countenance speaking to him about any of this, but didn't know how they could possibly avoid it. So she ignored him.

But by the day of her flight, Anna hadn't been able to keep much food down for forty-eight hours. She dry heaved into the toilet as soon as she woke up, and vomited the water she drank after. The only thing she seemed to be able to stomach were those crumbly digestive biscuits that she, for the life of her, couldn't understand why anyone in Ireland enjoyed. (Later, when she was in a position to request a rider for shows, her only nod to rock star excess was to require these banished from the premises. The smell of them still made her gag.)

"You cannot get on a plane," Maeve said that morning. She was standing at the door of the bathroom looking down at Anna curled around the toilet bowl. "I don't even think you can stand up."

Anna's head was pounding from dehydration, and she was dizzy with hunger. She shook her head into the bowl. "It's fine. I'll be fine." She retched again.

"We can reschedule—"

"No." Anna tried to stand and felt all the blood rush from her head. It felt like her bones were made of water; she had to hold onto the counter to keep herself upright.

"Anna . . ." Maeve's voice had an edge of warning.

"Please, don't. I've gotta get on that plane," she said, still leaning unsteadily over the sink.

Ultimately, though, Maeve got her way. Anna had tried to take a few tentative steps toward the door, but her vision quickly went black. When she came to, she was lying on the bathroom floor, head in Maeve's lap.

"We're going to the clinic, love," she said softly, patting her head.

Anna was too tired to fight her.

Maeve insisted on walking in with her: a relief because she didn't want to ask, but she also wasn't sure she could stand on her own. Soon, she was in a small exam room, hooked up to IV fluids and finally feeling as close to normal as she had in weeks. She was lying propped up on the exam table when Dr. Callahan came in, looking over her chart.

"So what have we, here? Dehydration and emesis?" He had some of the most magnificent eyebrows she'd ever seen. They were like two furry caterpillars traversing his forehead. "Feeling better with the fluids?"

Anna nodded, transfixed by his face.

He continued scanning her chart. "Ah, you're pregnant. Well, that'll do you. How far along?"

She swallowed. "Couple months?"

He looked up. "Have you not had your first appointment?"

She shook her head.

He set the chart down and smiled. "Well, we can take care of that now, while you're here."

"Oh, no, that's all right. I don't need it . . . right now."

He waved her off. "We're jacks of all trades here." He gestured to the ultrasound machine behind him. "Don't even need to switch rooms." He was already walking over to turn it on. "Just pull up your shirt, m'dear."

Her brain was screaming at her to run before this went any further, but her body wasn't cooperating. She watched with no small amount of horror as he squeezed freezing cold gel onto her abdomen and used the probe to move it around. An image materialized on the screen: a small, white oval with tiny appendages inside a much larger black one. She knew, intellectually, what she was looking at, but it was incomprehensible that it could be inside of her.

"But I got my period," she mumbled, staring at the screen.

"Well, that's what we call implantation bleeding," he chuckled. "I'd say you're spot-on eight weeks, and everything looks right as rain. And give me a minute . . ." He reached up to click a knob. The fast whoosh-whoosh of the heartbeat flooded the room. *Allegretto tempo*, she thought. *Three-quarter time.*

She and Maeve drove home in silence, Anna both trying to process and desperate to forget what she just saw. Outside, blurry green meadows flashed by under a gunmetal sky. She wanted to fling open the car door and run and run until her legs gave out, scream until her throat was raw.

"I'll make us a cuppa?" Maeve said when they got back home. Anna nodded and slid into a chair in the kitchen. Dozens of hypothetical scenarios paraded across her mind. Every outcome seemed worse than the one before.

Maeve deposited a cup in front of her before sitting down herself. "It's ginger. Should help with the nausea."

Anna held the warm mug in her hands, let the steam tickle her face as she inhaled. "I don't think I can do it," she whispered into the cup. "I can't keep it, but I don't think I can do it."

Maeve nodded. "Okay," she said softly. "We'll figure it out."

She finally called Will that night.

"Jesus Christ, where the fuck have you been? I've been trying you every day."

"Sorry. I needed a minute."

"What's going on? Are you all right?" He was frantic.

"Yeah." She paused. "It's done."

He was silent for a few seconds. "Okay," he said quietly. "How are you? When can I come see you?"

Anna had to hold the phone away from her and cover her mouth with her hand to let the cry escape unnoticed. Her chest felt like it was going to crack in two. "You know, I don't think that's a good idea."

"What?"

"I think, maybe, I need some time alone."

"What do you mean? What does that mean?"

"I think it would probably be better if we didn't talk for a while."

"Anna, no, come on. Don't be ridiculous. Just let me—"

"Will, please, *please*. I can't." She was starting to hyperventilate. "I'm sorry, but I can't." She hung up the phone just before she doubled over in sobs, the grief rolling over her like a thunderstorm in June.

# SEVEN

**Lottie**
*New York*
May 10, 2024

Mr. Martinez wrote *nature vs. nurture* in large red letters on the whiteboard. "You're all familiar with this term?"

It was Friday, third period psych class. The girls nodded.

"It was popularized by Sir Francis Galton, who, pardon my French, was a racist asshole. But it refers, as you know, to the relative effects of genes and environment on one's personality. Who can give me an example?"

Lottie's classmate Christina raised her hand. "It's like in those twin studies, where they're separated at birth, but then they both become, like, the same type of neurosurgeon. So that would be nature over nurture. And then nurture over nature . . . Let's say somebody adopts a baby, and that baby grows up to be way more like their adoptive parent than what was in their genetics. So maybe they're both artists, or something."

"Basically," Mr. Martinez said. "And you're right that much of the research has come from twin or adoption studies."

Lottie felt a few eyes dart toward her and quickly look away.

"Different traits have been shown to have low, medium, or high heritability," he continued. "Religious preferences, for example, are quite low. And then something like eye color, obviously, is much higher. Creative skills, like painting or musicality, are somewhere in the middle. And who can tell me how epigenetics relates to all of this?"

A girl to Lottie's left raised her hand.

"Liz?"

"Epigenetics is how your environment can actually affect how your genes express themselves."

"Correct, but give me more?"

"So it means it's not nature *or* nurture: it's always both. Things that happen to you, or when your mom is pregnant with you, can actually change how your genes work. Like, a really stressful childhood can change your epigenome, and that can get passed down to future generations."

Lottie raised her hand.

"Lottie?"

"That's not the whole story, though," she said, with a touch of irritation. "There can be positive changes, too. And it said in the reading the latest research shows there are ways to reverse the negative ones."

"Of course," Mr. Martinez said. "A lot of this area of study is uncharted territory. Take microchimerism—fetal cells crossing the placenta into the mother's tissues and vice versa. Those cells stay in that new body for a *lifetime*. We all—literally—carry our family tree inside of us. But we're still very much learning how who we were born as relates to who we might become." He paused. "I bring this up not just because it'll be on the final." Mr. Martinez took a seat on his desk and scanned the class. "I know how high expectations are for all of you: from your parents, from school, from wherever. And sometimes, it probably feels like your whole path is already predetermined." He pointed a finger at them. "Remember: that's not true. Nothing is set in stone, and you have agency. I want all of you to be captains of your own ship."

* * *

"Wait, do you like this one?" It was Saturday night. Sasha was holding up a neon green tube dress to herself. "Or this one?" Hot pink, one shoulder.

"The pink," Lottie said, putting the finishing touches on one of her space buns in the mirror.

She and a handful of her friends were getting ready to head to the Brooklyn Island for the Summit Sunrise show, a DJ duo from Australia. Lottie's friend Poppy's father owned the record label to which they were signed, which meant the twenty-one-or-older rule for admission was really more of a light suggestion—Poppy's dad would get them all in.

But they were pregaming anyway, just in case: Poppy was brandishing a bottle of Grey Goose and making everyone take swigs straight from the bottle. Lottie hazarded a sip and shook her head to help choke it down.

"Guys, we can find drinks there. This feels really unncces-sary," she said, wiping her eyes.

"It's just the appetizer, anyway. I've got the good stuff for when we get there." Sasha grinned and pulled out a plastic baggie from her clutch. "Happy pills!"

Poppy put the bottle down and came over to inspect, squinting. "What is that? Molly? From who?"

"My sister, it's legit. But it's not for now." She stuffed it back into her purse. "The last thing I want is to be rolling while we're stuck on the FDR with Poppy's dad." She collapsed into giggles.

Half an hour later, the girls piled into a waiting Escalade: Poppy's dad, Carlos, up front with the driver and the rest of them in the back, a mess of glitter-flecked limbs and vodka breath. They blasted house music the whole ride from the Upper East Side to East Williamsburg, rolling down the windows on the highway to let the wind tickle their cheeks.

Carlos had arranged for VIP seating so he could keep an eye

on them, but once the girls realized there was a crew of Hoxton boys in general admission, there was little chance of them staying put. Poppy told her father they were going in search of snacks and the bathroom, and they made a quick escape soon after arriving.

By New York standards, the outdoor venue was gargantuan, and tonight's crowd was the largest Lottie had seen. She was doubtful they'd find their friends, but didn't mind being in the scrum. It was a sticky, sweaty, thumping mess—even now, before the DJs took the stage—the perfect escape after the incomprehensible week she'd had.

Shockingly, though, Sasha managed to get enough cell reception to connect with the boys. The girls hooked arms and plowed through the crowd, finally spotting them in a back corner near one of the bars.

"Ladies! You look lovely tonight. When does your spaceship leave for Mars?" Tyler said, flicking one of Lottie's buns.

"Don't be jealous of our sparkles," Sasha retorted. "You all look so boring in your T-shirts. I hope you're not planning on having a boring night." She pulled out her baggie and waved it at them.

"Sasha! Discretion!" Lottie exclaimed, pulling the bag down from eye level.

"Lottie, I promise everyone else is already too fucked up to notice. Now: open up." Sasha removed one pastel pill at a time and stuck them under everyone's tongue. Lottie demurred.

"Lots, stop. You really want to be here all night without a little boost?" She was waggling the pill tantalizingly in front of her face.

Tyler put his hands on Lottie's shoulders from behind. "She's right for once. Gonna be way more fun if you do."

"I'd really rather not," Lottie said, trying, unsuccessfully, to back away from Sasha.

"Come on," Tyler implored, right into her ear. "Don't be like that. I promise it'll be worth it." He squeezed her shoulders gently. "You've gotta loosen up every once in a while."

There was nothing, Lottie thought, like peer pressure. Especially when you were already a people pleaser. She sighed and opened her mouth. Tyler grabbed the pill from Sasha and popped it in for her.

"Attagirl," he said, giving her a pat on the arm. "You won't regret it."

Soon the hot, squirming mass of people started pushing all of them toward the stage, driven by that ineffable feeling that something was about to happen.

"Don't let me get trampled!" Lottie yelled to Tyler.

He placed his hands on her waist, steering her through the crowd until they were almost at the barricade. The lights finally dimmed for the show around 1:00 a.m.: it felt like all of Brooklyn let out a collective roar of pleasure. But maybe that was just the molly kicking in.

Halfway through the set, it began to pour: big, fat, warm raindrops that splashed off their foreheads and formed puddles that sent them skidding on the slick dirt. Lottie felt purified. She felt weightless. And, for the first time in weeks, she felt happy. She turned toward Tyler, hands lifted over her head as she danced; the thrum of the bass so loud, it felt like it supplanted her own heartbeat. He smiled, drew her in closer, and kissed her.

The memory of how, exactly, they got home had vanished along with her wallet, but Lottie woke up on Sunday in her own bed. The house was still except for Cajun, who was meowing dramatically to be let out of the room.

Her phone buzzed soon after she woke up: Aidan, FaceTiming.

"Is that . . . glitter?" He was squinting into the screen.

"Probably. We went to a show at the Island last night."

"So I hear."

She looked at him quizzically.

"There was a pretty frantic text chain last night when you guys wandered off."

Lottie grabbed a bottle of water, took a large gulp, and shrugged. "We were fine, though . . ."

"I mean, glad to hear it, but can you guys be a little more careful next time?"

She rolled her eyes.

"What?"

"Nothing. Just . . . you're not even in the same country right now."

"So?"

"So why do you care?"

He furrowed his brow. "Hey. Of course I care."

She sat herself up with irritation, cranky to be having this conversation so early in the morning. "You don't have to pretend like you're worried. I mean, now you *really* don't have to, right?"

Aidan looked confused and a little hurt. "That's not why I did that and you know it. And I *was* worried." He sighed. "I'm putting on the uncle hat for a minute: Carlos thought you guys were on something last night—molly?"

Lottie bit her lower lip and finally shrugged.

"Fuck, Lottie, really? I don't want you near that shit. You do anything else?"

"No."

"You swear?"

"Yes, *god*."

He stared at her through the phone. "This isn't like you. Neither is this attitude. What's going on?"

"Nothing. I'm just hungover."

He sighed again. "You know I'm pretty lax about a lot. But not this, okay? It is so easy for it to spin out of control." He paused. "You wouldn't believe how fast it can happen. And you wouldn't believe to who," he added quietly.

"Message received. But I can handle a night out by myself." She lay back down on her bed, holding the phone up over her face. "I can handle a night alone, too. There're a lot of them."

"Do you want me to come home? Is that what you're trying to say? I will get on a plane."

The first ticklings of a headache were forming. She grimaced. "No. That's the point. I don't need you to. I'm fine. Everything is fine."

She could see him groping for the right words. But what he landed on was "Want me to send over that sushi chef?" Aidan's guilt over traveling so extensively often manifested in any number of extravagant gestures.

"Jeez, no."

"I get it. You're a big kid. Doesn't mean I don't want to make sure you're safe." He hesitated. "I was mostly calling to see how you're doing today."

Lottie frowned. "Why? What's today?"

"It's, uh . . . Mother's Day."

"Oh. Hadn't realized." She exhaled and sunk back into her pillow. "Great."

"I miss her, too, Lots," he said softly.

They were both silent for a moment. "There's a lot I'm starting to forget. About her," she finally said. "I couldn't remember the sound of her voice the other day. How is that allowed to happen?"

"I don't know. It's not fair." He shook his head; this ice was too thin for either of them to cross over the phone. "I'm sorry, I've gotta run."

"Oh . . . okay."

"Did you look, though? At the papers?"

She shook her head no.

"All right, well, love you."

She forced a half smile. "Love you, too."

# EIGHT

**Anna**
*Doolin*
November 2007

She couldn't tell him. She knew this with a conviction so absolute it was almost calming. To tell him what she wanted to do would be the same as destroying him. And if she told him, and he told her what he wanted, it would, she was sure, destroy her. The only solution—the only way forward—was her silence.

Anna may have been unwavering in this decision, but it brought her little peace. Will had been as elemental to her as her sense of hearing. And without him, she had no choice but to learn a new way to communicate. It was exhausting, and alienating, but necessary.

He was still calling every day and writing an email every few, but she archived them all without opening. Every change in her body—seemingly overnight she couldn't button her jeans any longer—was a prickly reminder of him and that night. And to not be able to share something so monumental with him left her with the uncanny feeling that he was dead.

She did her best to return to the comfort of rhythm she'd established: days at the studio, nights on the keyboard. Maeve mostly left her to her own devices, while tacitly keeping watch. Her bedroom light was always glowing when Anna returned home, even if it were after midnight. Other days she'd find prenatal vitamins on her bathroom counter, or a slim volume on childbirth left on the bedside table. Anna appreciated the discretion: discussing any of this out loud felt like summoning a specter she wasn't ready to see.

A couple of weeks after her trip to the clinic, the overpowering nausea, thankfully, started to wane. Anna came down to the kitchen hungry for what felt like the first time in months. Maeve, as usual, had intuited this: she was stirring a golden pat of butter into a big bubbling pot of oats.

"That actually smells amazing," Anna marveled.

"Sit. You need to eat," Maeve barked.

She complied and Maeve placed a steaming portion in front of her, sprinkled with brown sugar and sliced strawberries. The Irish, Anna would readily admit, certainly knew their way around a bowl of oatmeal.

"Proper meals from here on out," Maeve commanded, pointing an accusing finger. "If you're doing this, then you're doing it right."

She nodded and hungrily scooped another spoonful into her mouth. It was like she'd never eaten before.

"We're going out tonight, too."

Anna looked up, bemused.

"You've been in Doolin for weeks now and haven't even been out for trad music yet. What's the point of being here at all?" Maeve didn't wait for an answer. "So McDermotts it is. Be home by six."

Doolin was a speck of a town, but its deep musical roots made it as much of a pilgrimage for a certain type of traveler as Mecca. Every night, the handful of pubs filled with locals (and a hearty dose of tourists) looking for a way to escape via the transporting sounds of tin whistles, fiddles, and bodhrans.

Anna hadn't realized how much she'd missed the company of other musicians until she walked in and felt the staccato thump of the drum square in the center of her chest. It was like she'd been asleep for weeks and was finally jolted back into the sonic world of the living. The minute she arrived, she never wanted to leave.

It was standing room only inside the red-and-white-painted pub; Irish flags festooned the ceiling. Maeve, unsurprisingly, knew almost everyone and made introductions all around.

"Can I get you a pint, girls?" said Donal, one of the accordion players.

"Sure, for me. This one will have a water," Maeve answered for both of them. She turned to Anna and nodded toward the musicians in the corner. "You know any trad songs?"

"Actually, yeah," Anna said with a small smile. "I had to learn a decent chunk when I was playing a hotel in Boston."

Maeve's eyes sparkled. "Then we've got to get you over there." She turned toward the bar. "Donal! Bring her with you when you go, aye? Don't take no for an answer!"

Anna shook her head furiously. "No way! Not with those guys."

Donal strode over with the two glasses and gave one to Maeve. "Sláinte," he said, clinking her mug before grabbing Anna's hand. "Come on, then. You can't argue with her, you haven't learned that by now?" He grinned, sat down on the bench, and patted the seat next to him. "What do you want to sing?"

Anna froze, eyes wide, as she looked out at the crowd. "Oh my god. I don't know. 'Spancil Hill'?"

He clapped his hands once. "You heard her, lads!" He pulled his accordion across his lap and gestured for her to take the mic. Anna tentatively grabbed it as he signaled with a twirl of his finger for everyone to start playing.

*Last night as I lay dreaming*
*Of pleasant days gone by,*
*My mind being bent on rambling*
*To Erin's isle I did fly . . .*

Soon, much of the band joined in singing, which made the endeavor a little less risky. She finished the song to hoots and cheers, Maeve's voice the loudest among them.

"Well done!" she exclaimed as Anna maneuvered out from the corner bench. "But they'll never leave you alone now."

"That's true," said an unfamiliar voice behind her. "Once they know you can sing, you're sunk." Anna turned around; he'd already stuck out a hand for a shake. "I'm Rory."

She stared at him, perplexed. "I know who you are," she blurted out. "Sorry! I mean—what are you doing here?"

He laughed. "I'm from here. Grew up singing with that whole lot." He nodded toward the bench.

Maeve elbowed him with a smile. "And then wee Rory O'Shea went and became a big rock star. Now he graces us with his presence every so often just like the sweet baby Jesus."

He smiled sheepishly. "Something like that. But really, you were class up there. I hope it wasn't a one-time thing."

Anna was still having trouble finding her words. Rory was about a decade her senior and the lead singer of the Vagabonds, one of the hotter rock bands of the moment. She was surprised Maeve had never mentioned him, but then again, there were musicians pouring out of every crevice of this town. "Thanks," she finally managed to squeak out. "It was fun."

"Do you play, too?"

"She's more classically trained than your faffing-about arse," Maeve butted in. "Anna's a real musician: she's here working on her album."

"Well, not exactly," Anna interjected. "I mean, on the album part. Hopefully one day it's an album. But I am a real musician." Oh my god, she needed to shut up.

Rory nodded, blond hair falling into his face. "Well, if you need pointers or anything . . ."

"She's fine. You should hire her to look after yours." Maeve poked him in the chest. "That last one was a right mess," she added with a cackle.

Rory turned toward Anna with a sardonic smile. "You can see why I love coming home. Always great craic."

Later, the breathless articles about the start of their relationship would all get it wrong. This is where they really met: that night at McDermotts, both of them hiding their fair share of secrets, and hoping the music could help them forget.

The pub didn't end up being a one-time thing, as Anna had assumed it would. Singing with that crew had felt like her first taste of freedom since the bars had gone up around her, and she was loath to give it up. Especially since she wasn't sure how social she'd be once she really started showing: there'd be so many questions, and answers no one wanted to hear.

But she also felt a surprisingly deep connection to the music, especially the improvisational nature of it all. They could sing "The Wild Rover" night after night, but every version carried a different flavor, depending on the crowd, or the musicians' moods, or how many pints deep they were. It was as different a training from the conservatory as treble from bass, and just as valuable.

Every few nights, on days she left the studio at a healthy hour, Anna would pop by on her way home. She'd sing a few songs with the band, learn some new ones while she watched, and, increasingly, chat with Rory about everything from tour life, to their favorite bass guitarists, to where they wanted to be in ten years. Apart from Maeve, Anna hadn't met many people in town because she was nearly always working. She'd forgotten how pleasant it could be to engage in the simple act of casual conversation.

"So I take it you're not a drinker?" Rory asked one night a couple weeks later, while he was walking her home. Her place was on the way out of town to his parents'.

"Oh, yeah. Trying something new with that."

He nodded. "That's cool."

They'd arrived at her doorstep. Rory rocked backward on his heels nervously, hands behind his back. "So this is my last night in town for a while." He hesitated. "I think you've probably guessed by now that I like you. I don't generally escort every American home from the bar," he added with a grin. He had dimples, which Anna hated that she'd noticed.

"Really?" she replied. "I thought that was just part of the famed Doolin hospitality." She liked spending time with him, too. And he helped keep her mind off Will, which was perhaps his best quality. But present circumstances dictated that he—and anyone else—was certainly off the table.

"No, door-to-door service is reserved for our VIPs." Rory smiled and curled a finger into one of her belt loops, pulling her to him. Then he leaned forward and kissed her. Anna thought she'd resist, but found she couldn't quite force herself to do it. It felt nice to be wanted. It felt nice to pretend to be somebody else. But when his hand started sliding down toward her stomach, she pushed him off quickly.

"Sorry! Sorry. It's just . . . late."

He put his hands up. "My mistake."

"No, it's not that." She paused. "I do like you. It's—now's not a good time."

He nodded. "Understood. See you when I get back from this leg?"

Who knows who she'd be by then? "Sure. Good luck."

He tugged on her jacket sleeve. "Learn some new songs while I'm gone?"

She smiled. "I can do that."

After Rory left, the weeks slogged by more or less identically, apart from her swelling midsection. She could still hide it under a sweater (and it was always sweater weather here), but she wasn't sure how much longer that would suffice. Maeve had gently inquired about what she planned to do a handful of times, to which Anna would only respond that she had it under control.

One day in December, the two of them were driving into town to grab groceries. Anna had a craving for lasagna and told Maeve she'd cook them dinner. The chances of them finding all the ingredients she needed were approximately zero, but it gave her something to do.

"I found someone," she said, apropos of nothing. "For the baby."

Maeve kept her eyes on the road and her tone noncommittal. "Oh?"

"Yeah. Her name's Maya. She's been trying to have a baby on her own for a while. Lives in LA. She seems great."

"That's grand, then," Maeve said with a smile. "How do you feel?"

"Relief?" They drove in silence for a minute. "I don't want you to think I'm a bad person," Anna eventually said, staring down at the floor mat because she couldn't risk looking at Maeve. "'Cause I'm not keeping her."

Maeve slowed and then pulled the car over. She put it in park and turned to face her. "If you're not ready, then it would be awful for both of you if you did." She put her hand on Anna's leg. "You're doing what's best for you and that baby. Don't let anyone tell you otherwise." She pulled back onto the road. "So, it's a girl?"

Anna nodded, a protective hand flying to her stomach before she even realized it. She'd just started to feel her move that week, which had catapulted the situation unnervingly from the hypothetical. "Yeah. It's a girl."

"Do your parents know, love?"

Outside, it was starting to spit rain, leaving fat splatters on the windshield. She'd miss this weather whenever she did leave. There was a newfound kinship with its unpredictability. She shook her head no.

"Why not?"

Even after these last few months, Anna could still be surprised by Maeve's bluntness.

"You think they wouldn't understand?" she prompted.

Anna thought that over while she looked out the window. "No, I think they would. That's the problem."

Maeve nodded, eyes still on the road. "And will you tell him?"

She was quiet and finally shook her head again. "What's best for him is not knowing."

**From: betsy.pendleton@aol.com**
**To: anna.buckley@gmail.com**
**December 25, 7:06 AM**

Hi honey,

I woke up early today and thought maybe, just maybe, you'd be my surprise present under the tree. I know that's silly: it's a long way to come from where you are. But it won't be the same without you two at the piano bench on Christmas morning.

I won't pretend to know what's going on between you and Will, and I'm not asking you to tell me. And he certainly doesn't know I'm emailing you. But I wanted to make sure you knew how much we all love you and miss you. You're a part of this family now, whether you like it or not. And regardless of anything—*anything*—this home, and our hearts, are always open to you. So please don't be a stranger, OK? Merry Christmas, Anna.

Love,
Bets

# NINE

## Lottie

*New York*
May 12, 2024

With all of her friends presumably out to brunch with their intact families for Mother's Day, Lottie found herself with an open Sunday. And while she told herself she'd stay in, watch some old episodes of *Gilmore Girls* before she started her homework, she knew she'd be downtown within the hour.

The building where Anna purportedly had her not-so-secret studio was fairly iconic Soho: a pre-war, twelve-story cast-iron, whose floors had been subdivided into a warren of tiny offices for people like therapists, facialists, and, really, any other -ists who might not need a ton of space but wanted the fancy downtown address.

The directory was helpfully outside the building, which meant she could study it without immediately alerting the security guy within. There was, obviously, not a listing for Anna Buckley, nor was there anything else on the alphabetized chart that seemed promising. With upward of probably eighty businesses within the building, trying to find hers might mean walking it floor by floor. And, depending on the level of dispassion of the guard, that could be either quite easy or nearly impossible.

But she had to start somewhere: Lottie scanned the list until she found an orthodontist, which seemed plausible enough. She flounced into the lobby, big grin on her face. "Hi! I'm here to see Dr. Zuckerman?"

The guard stared at her. "On a Sunday?"

"I have an emergency with . . . my retainer."

"I haven't seen him come in. You sure he's there?"

She nodded.

"Whatever. Fourth floor." He jerked a thumb toward the elevators.

"Thanks *so* much!"

As it turned out, each floor was built around a central atrium and staircase. It would be easier than she anticipated to snoop since she wouldn't have to double back onto the elevator. The building was quiet, of course: no one was working on Mother's Day. She walked a cursory loop of the fourth level, but there was no door that looked likely to be Anna's.

Lottie spent the next half hour or so climbing the stairs, circumnavigating each floor, and then moving on to the next. She did find a pretty sweet-looking tarot card reader, but no sign of any studios or pianos. Or birth parents.

She was about to call it a day and assume the record store guy had been mistaken when she noticed a doorway marked STAIRWELL off the main hall of the eleventh floor. She pushed it open and found a small staircase leading up to the twelfth. A dusty skylight overhead illuminated all the particles in the air; it was silent except for her footsteps.

A squeaky door at the top of the stairs led to a small hallway with three offices on the left and a large window at the end that looked out over Broadway. Lottie stood on tiptoe to peer inside the first room: from the Persian rug and the book-lined shelves, she guessed a psychiatrist. The second was basically bare: just an empty desk and an unlocked door. Her pulse started racing as she approached the third; she nearly turned around before she got to the doorframe.

The lights were off, but she could see a piano and a couple of guitars in the corner, a stack of sheet music piled on a small table. The nameplate on the door read DOOLIN PRODUCTIONS. She tried the handle: locked, of course.

So: that was that. Maybe hers, but she wasn't even there. Lottie was starting to get frustrated at these near misses, that, really, felt much more like far misses. Anna could be literally anywhere on the planet right now. Or, she realized with a touch of irony, having Mother's Day brunch with her own family somewhere.

This whole expedition had not only been fruitless, but foolish. So she told herself she wasn't coming back. She told herself she didn't need her. She told herself this was insane. But she came again the next day, and the next, and the one after that.

Lottie canceled all her tutoring and piano for the week, and every afternoon convinced the building guards she had intensive orthodontic appointments (even though, thanks to Aidan, her teeth were perfect). From the lobby, she made her way up to the twelfth floor, then did her homework in the unlocked spare office.

And on the fourth day, just like the sun, moon, and stars, Anna appeared.

Lottie heard her, first. She was on the phone, she assumed, with one of her producers.

"Yeah, we sent the stems over already . . . Am I satisfied? What do you think?" Anna laughed, a raspy sound, then closed the door behind her. Lottie realized then she'd never actually heard her speak, only sing.

Sound carried well through the thin walls between the rooms and Anna hadn't soundproofed her studio; it seemed more like a place for her to experiment than ever record. When she started noodling on the piano and singing along, Lottie might as well have been beside her on the bench. In a way, it wasn't so different from listening to her on a speaker: she still couldn't see her. But in person, Anna's voice was as rich and clear as on any of her albums, which was surprising. So many of Lottie's favorite pop stars were dripping in autotune, she'd forgotten some could sing without it.

As she studied (or attempted to), Lottie heard threads of songs get woven into full cloth, others ripped apart and stitched together anew. It was a master class in the creative process, even if Anna didn't know she was teaching.

Learning about her in such an oblique way felt more than a little invasive. But Lottie also savored this chance to drink her in without pretense, to solidify a sense of who Anna was when she thought no one was looking. She was intensely focused, that much was obvious from behind the wall, but focused in a way that made Lottie wonder what she might be neglecting in order to be so.

And she knew this observation period was finite: she couldn't stay in that empty little office forever. Surprisingly though, the end of this split coexistence turned out to be Aidan's fault. Lottie would have sworn her phone was on vibrate, but when he called one afternoon, it was, somehow, cranked to full volume. The Talking Heads' "Once in a Lifetime" started blaring obnoxiously.

"Shit," she muttered, and fumbled to silence it. Next door, Anna stopped playing. Lottie heard her piano bench scrape against the floor as she stood up. In a panic, Lottie scrambled from behind the desk and ran out the door, sprinting down the hallway.

"Hey!" Anna called after her. "Wait!"

Lottie slammed the door behind her and half tripped down the stairs. She didn't stop until she was back on the eleventh floor, squatting against the wall and safely out of sight of the staircase.

“Hello?” Anna said hesitantly from the top of the stairs.

Lottie held her breath, but Anna didn’t walk down. Eventually, she heard the door close, and soon after piano notes began to drift again through the stairwell.

She couldn’t even begin to discern the thoughts ricocheting through her head. But one kept repeating, like a needle catching on a record.

She’s real. She’s real. She’s real.

# TEN

**Anna**
*Doolin*
May 3, 2008

She should have known it was coming. A few days earlier, Maeve had taken no more than a cursory glance at Anna's belly as she carefully made her way down the stairs and declared the baby dropped.

"You uncomfortable?" Maeve had asked, setting a bowl of yogurt in front of her. "Calcium," she added, though Anna hadn't asked.

*Uncomfortable* barely touched the outer reaches of what she was feeling. It was as if she were straddling a bowling ball every time she took a step. Her ribs ached constantly. She hadn't slept more than a few hours at a stretch in weeks. Anna nodded, after a moment.

"She's getting ready," Maeve said, cleaning a plate at the sink. "I won't ask you if you are because no one ever is."

Over the months, theirs was a relationship that had been molded by actions, rather than shared intimacies. Much of Maeve's life remained a mystery to her: Anna was preoccupied with her own collapsing, and Maeve was reticent to share details of hers, anyway. But her presence—the fact that Anna hadn't been forced to navigate this pregnancy fully alone—was likely the only reason Anna could still be sitting at that dining room table.

"You won't be the same," Maeve said quietly. She had stopped washing dishes and was looking out the window at the sea now. "I guess that's a silly thing to say. Of course you won't. But you'll still be you." She turned around to face her. "Even if it takes some time to find yourself again."

The deep velvet hush that fell over the town after the pubs closed made it easier for Anna to write. Her most productive hours lately had been these, when it felt like she was the only one awake in all of Doolin. Maybe she was. At the moment, it was coming on 1:00 a.m. and she'd been trying to finish the bridge of a song that had been eluding her for days. The melody had been buzzing around like a pesky fly, but whenever she tried to catch it, it flitted away. Sleep seemed elusive until she could find it.

She was working from her bedroom: the walk to the studio had started to get rather exhausting in her current state, and Maeve was quite vocal with her displeasure about Anna being out there alone deep into her third trimester. Anna didn't mind being home: it was less opportunity for the inevitable stares. For someone as private as she was, to have this secret so obviously, so heavingly exposed whenever she stepped outside was nearly intolerable. There was comfort in the solitude of the house, where she could control the narrative better.

The baby kicked her hard in the ribs. Anna jumped and rubbed her stomach absentmindedly. "I can't tell if I'm keeping you up or the other way around," she murmured. The two of them had fallen into a (mostly) comfortable coexistence. She liked testing out chord progressions on her acoustic right up against her belly; when the baby grooved, Anna figured it was a song worth pursuing. Likening her to a collaborator was the only way Anna could make sense of their relationship, anyway. She was not this baby's mother now; she would not be this baby's mother later. And just like at the end of producing a record, they'd part ways when it was over. What would be left was the music.

The contractions, at first, were little more than a nuisance that kept her from focusing fully. When one hit, she'd slowly maneuver herself up to standing, walk around for a stretch, and then dive back in where she left off.

A couple hours in, however, she felt bile race fast and hot up her throat, and barely made it to the toilet before vomiting. She allowed herself to rest her head on the side of the cool seat for a minute, then splashed water on her face and slowly padded back to her room. *Braxton Hicks and dehydration*, she thought. *That's all.*

It was also two weeks before her due date, and while Dr. Callahan had been very clear about those dates being nothing more than a suggestion, Anna had still taken it as gospel. With so much in flux, she was clutching at whatever semblance of order she could find.

But by the time she was back in her room, the next one struck with such a force it made her audibly gasp. She put a hand on her swollen belly, which had gone rock hard. It felt like giant claws were trying to pull both sides of her apart from the inside. She was leaning over her desk, arms splayed, slowly rocking side to side when Maeve knocked.

"Anna? I heard you in the bathroom. You all right?"

"Mm-hmm." She couldn't muster much more.

Maeve opened the door without waiting for a response and looked her up and down. "Ah. How are you doing?" she asked carefully.

Anna nodded, holding her breath until the pain relented. "Fine. It's nothing. I'm just uncomfortable, can't sleep. Sorry I woke you."

"You don't look fine," Maeve said slowly. "You look like you're having a baby." She approached her tentatively and put a hand on her shoulder.

Anna shook her head. "It's not time yet. It's just—" Another wave hit her. She let out a tiny moan in spite of herself.

"How long have you been having these . . . not-contractions?"

"I don't know, a bit." Anna waved it off, as if downplaying it would make them stop. "I haven't really been paying attention." She gestured to the keyboard. "I've been busy." She was still swaying in an effort to alleviate the discomfort.

"You know"—Maeve moved her hand to Anna's lower back and started rubbing softly—"babies have their own minds when it comes to their birth days. And I think this one has decided."

Anna shook her head again: petulantly, like a child. "I need until at least next week. I'm not even done with—" Just then, she felt an almost imperceptible snap inside her, and a warm trickle started running down her leg. She looked at the floor where it began to puddle. "I think my water just broke," she whispered. Her eyes were big like a wild animal's, one who couldn't believe it had finally been caught in a trap.

Maeve gently steered her to the bed. "Okay. It's time. Do you have a bag ready?"

Anna shook her head no.

"We'll pack one together, then." Maeve was doing her best to keep her from toppling into panic. "Do you want to call Maya?"

Anna nodded. "But she wasn't planning on coming until next week."

"I'm sure she'll figure out a way to get here faster." She hesitated. "Is there anyone else you want to call?"

Yes. Yes, of course. "No."

"It's not too late," Maeve said softly.

Anna forced herself to swallow the hard lump in her throat, and shook her head. "It's too late."

By the time they finished packing, Anna's contractions were coming nearly on top of one another. She'd never fathomed her body was capable of producing this much pain. It seemed impossible that she could contain it inside herself, that it wouldn't radiate out and strike anyone nearby.

Maeve, blessedly calm in the face of crises, hustled her into the car and prayed out loud that she wouldn't give birth on the way.

"Keep those legs crossed, love!" she yelled from the front, looking at her in the rearview mirror. "Guess someone should have mentioned that to you nine months ago," she added with a chuckle.

"That is really not helpful," Anna moaned from the back seat.

Thankfully, there was no one else on the road at this hour: Maeve floored her tiny Volkswagen Golf and Anna did her best not to howl every time they hit a bump.

The hospital center was small enough that Maeve had called ahead to let them know they were on the way. There was an orderly waiting outside with a wheelchair, which Anna found ridiculous until she tried to stand up from the car. She doubled over from the pain; he and Maeve exchanged a knowing look and helped her into the chair.

"You don't have to stay," Anna managed to gasp out.

"Don't be daft, I'm not going to leave you here."

Anna's protests were feeble. As much as she prided herself on her independence, facing the next few hours alone seemed insurmountable. She looked up at her. "I'm not sure I can do this."

Maeve reached down and cupped her cheek. "You're stronger than you know, love."

Dr. Callahan had urged Anna to sign up for a class or to come up with some sort of a birth plan, but to do so meant acknowledging that she was actually giving birth. It was a lot easier to pretend you weren't having a baby if you avoided contemplating the whole labor bit. So she never did. By the time she arrived at the hospital, she was deep in active labor, with no more knowledge than her few cursory glances at the pregnancy books Maeve had quietly deposited in her room.

He arrived soon after she got situated in her hospital bed, caterpillar eyebrows as lively as ever. "Got here just in time, looks like." He smiled kindly, pulled on a glove, and gestured toward her. "May I?"

Anna nodded, then grimaced as another contraction came roiling down her abdomen. She gripped the bedside handlebars until her knuckles went bone white. The phrase *urge to push* had struck her as nonsense when she read it in one of Maeve's books. But in this moment, it was suddenly all her body was capable of.

Dr. Callahan emerged from under her legs, eyes wide with surprise. "You're crowning."

She sat up with alarm. "What?"

He chuckled. "Be glad you didn't wait another hour to come."

Maeve walked in then, took one look at Anna's panicked expression and addressed the doctor directly. "Everything all right?"

"Everything is fine. Textbook, really. But baby's coming now. Right now."

She was born on May 3 at 4:22 a.m., just about fifteen minutes after they arrived at the hospital. The baby squawked loudly just once, and then was silent as she took in her new surroundings with, what felt like to Anna, resignation. She stared, transfixed, as they rubbed the baby's limbs with a towel, weighed her, and checked her vitals. It all seemed so surreal, it was difficult to parse her emotions. There wasn't much joy, if she were being honest. More a churning mix of disbelief and fear.

Dr. Callahan placed her gently on Anna's chest with a pleased smile. "Here she is."

"She's okay?" The baby's own warm, tiny chest was rising and falling under her hand. She'd loomed so large in Anna's mind (and felt so, while inside), but now, in the flesh, was nearly impossibly small.

"She's little, but perfectly healthy."

Anna looked down at the quiet newborn, who already had a full head of dark brown hair. Will's hair. How utterly strange to see someone half her and half him. In a way, it almost felt like the logical end: they'd created so much together already, why not this, too? But to be holding her, and not holding his hand as well, was a reality that was difficult to reconcile. She wondered if in some odd, cosmic way, Will had intuited that his own life had just changed as well.

Maeve bent down to get a closer look. "Well done, Anna. She's beautiful. And I promise you can't say that about most of them when they first come out," she added with a wicked grin.

Anna gingerly touched the baby's finger, marveling at the size of the miniature nail. "She doesn't feel like she's mine," she said quietly.

"Maybe it's better that way." Maeve softly stroked the top of the baby's head. "When you're ready, you'll make your way back to each other." She stood up and stretched her arms overhead. "You two should get some rest. I'll be back first thing."

Anna nodded, uneasily cradling the baby.

"You'll both know what to do," she responded to Anna's unasked question. She kissed her fingers and placed them first on top of the baby's, then Anna's head. "Promise."

Both of them slept for hours after Maeve left. As Dr. Callahan had commented, it was hard work being born, too. By the time Anna finally woke, it was noon and there was no bassinet next to the bed.

"She's in the nursery," said the nurse taking her vitals. "Figured it was best while you were sleeping. You want me to bring her back?" Her name tag read ORLA.

“No,” Anna said, perhaps a little too quickly. “I mean, maybe. In a bit.” She wasn’t sure if all the nurses knew the situation. Probably: everyone knew everyone’s business here.

Orla smiled kindly and touched Anna’s arm. “I wasn’t sure if you’d want to try to feed her? We can do it in the nursery, if you’d prefer.” She knew.

Anna had never planned on it, because she’d assumed Maya would be here when the baby was born. Now she was facing, at least, a day alone with her. This prospect mostly paralyzed her with terror, but was also somewhat of an unexpected comfort. A few hours where they could make believe things were different.

“I guess you can bring her in when she’s ready.”

Orla beamed. “She’s the cutest one in there. That head of hair! My goodness.”

The baby, now awake and fussy, got rolled in about half an hour later. Her cries pierced a primal part inside that Anna had never known existed. Orla deftly unswaddled her and placed her in Anna’s arms, while she unsnapped the top of her gown. “Quiet down, miss. Your mam’s gonna feed you in a minute—” She stopped, realizing what she’d said. “I’m sorry. I didn’t mean . . .”

“It’s okay,” Anna said, softly rubbing the baby’s back. “It’s confusing for me, too.”

“Well, anyway,” Orla recovered. “Skin-to-skin contact is really good for her, helps to regulate her breathing and her heart rate now that she’s on the outside.”

On the outside. Anna still couldn’t comprehend she’d made a human. In her arms, the baby rooted, then latched nearly instantly and fell silent. Anna gasped quietly.

Orla laughed. “Smart girl, this one. I’ll be back when she needs burping.”

It was quiet in the room, except for the baby’s gentle sucking. Anna used this time to get a proper look at her: she had her same large blue eyes, but her coloring, with that shock of dark hair, was closer to his. Anna wondered if she'd get a spray of freckles across her nose like Will did when he spent too much time in the sun. She gently lifted up the baby's arm: there was a small birthmark on the inside of her right forearm, like someone had left a light thumbprint.

How strange, and how beautiful, she thought, to sync her heartbeat and her breath to another's, even for just a few minutes. Eventually, they both drifted back to sleep, Anna cradling the baby protectively: her warm body and soft murmurs the balm she didn't know she needed.

Maya arrived from LA that night, all flushed cheeks and red eyes and unkempt, short dark hair. The two of them had Skyped frequently over the past few months, but this was Maya's first visit.

The baby was sleeping, swaddled, in the bassinet, a hospital hat with a comically large bow atop her head. Maya covered her mouth and tried to keep from crying as she gently touched her cheek. "She's perfect, Anna." She sat down on the bed next to her and reached out to squeeze her hand. "I'm so sorry I couldn't get here in time. How are you?"

"Better than twenty-four hours ago," she said with a tired smile. "I'm okay. Sore, but okay. You can pick her up." Anna gestured to the bassinet. "She's yours."

Maya carefully reached in and scooped her up; the baby cooed softly in her sleep. "I was gonna name her Charlotte, if that's all right with you? Call her Lottie." She started rocking her and bent down to kiss her on the forehead. It all came so naturally to her.

"It's perfect. Suits her."

"Good. I wanted you to like it, too." Maya turned to her, eyes suddenly clouded with concern. "I know I've asked you this, but are you sure? I need you to be one hundred—one thousand percent—sure on this, Anna."

"I've never been more sure of anything." Maya was going to be an incredible mother: kind, compassionate, present. It was what she wished she could have had herself.

They signed the formal papers the next morning, including a provision that Anna had requested on no contact until Lottie became an adult.

"If you change your mind, you know that door is always open," Maya said. "But I understand."

"It'll be easier, healthier, this way. But"—Anna grabbed an envelope from the side table and handed it to her—"I do have one thing for her. It's nothing much, but I wrote her something."

Maya bent down to envelop her in a tight hug. "Thank you," she whispered. "You'll never know what this means to me. I'll take good care of her." She nodded toward the baby. "I'll let you have some time before we go." She walked out, closing the door quietly behind her.

Lottie was unswaddled and dressed, ready to be popped into a car seat for the ride to the airport. Anna gingerly picked her up and laid her on the bed, their faces almost touching. She tried to drink in every one of her exhalations, every tiny eyelash, that sweet, intoxicating, milky baby smell.

"Hey. You're here," she said quietly as she brushed Lottie's cheek with her finger. "I'm sorry this is how it has to start for us. I'm sorry your dad's not here. I'm sorry I won't see you for"—she exhaled in a short burst—"a long time. But you're going somewhere better, with someone who loves you so much." She smoothed back some of the baby's soft curls and suddenly realized she was humming a lullaby aloud, one her own mother had sung on the rarest of occasions. She stopped.

Lottie's eyelids—framed with Will's long lashes—were fluttering closed. "This is where we say goodbye," she whispered, as much to herself as the baby. "But this is how it's meant to be."

* * *

She returned home the next morning, although by the time she walked in the door, she couldn't even remember leaving the hospital. Maeve hurried her straight to bed; and Anna, even in this fogged-out stupor, could see how worried she was. For days after she'd returned, Anna heard her door creak open in the middle of the night, Maeve tiptoeing over and putting a hand under her nose to make sure she was still breathing.

Mostly, Anna felt like she was disintegrating. She was bleeding. She was leaking milk from sore, swollen breasts. She was waking up in the middle of the night drenched in sweat, hair plastered to the back of her neck. And she was crying in her sleep. Or so it seemed. There was no other explanation for eyes so red and dry she could barely pry them open in the mornings.

But it felt deserved. It felt like penance. Not necessarily for the baby, for she was undoubtedly in a safer place. But for what she'd done to him. And the physical pain, in those early days, was overwhelming enough to crowd out all the other kinds. So, she succumbed to it all: letting the salty wave of guilt bury her until she was nearly drowned. Then she'd emerge—briefly, gasping for air—until pulled back again by the undertow.

Maeve left her cabbage to put inside her bra to stop the milk from flowing, and a steady supply of industrial pads to help with the blood. She quietly removed the pregnancy books she'd bought her, the vitamins and tea. It wasn't until much later that Anna would wonder how she knew to do any of this. They never spoke of it.

But it all helped. A few weeks after Lottie's birth, Anna began to put herself back together, bone by bone. It was almost as if she'd drained herself of everything that came before: what remained now was harder, sharper. Impenetrable.

She needed to get back to work.

One foggy morning, she forced herself into real clothes for the first time since the hospital and made her way downstairs.

"I'm gonna go for a walk, maybe swing by the studio?" she told Maeve. Not that she needed her permission, but she wanted her blessing.

"Go on. Bring a jacket, it's chilly." She smiled kindly at her.

Anna was halfway into town when she heard someone call her name. Rory came bounding up next to her, bright-cheeked and wearing a leather jacket that was hilariously incongruous with the verdant countryside around him.

"Hiya." He grinned. "Haven't seen you for a minute. Did you go somewhere?"

"Hey. No, just been busy." She instinctively wrapped her coat tighter around her abdomen.

"Ah, okay. Listen, I was hoping to run into you. We're leaving soon for the new leg and our opener just dropped out."

"Oh, that sucks."

"Ah sure, look it. They were some dryshites. But I was hoping you might give it a lash?"

"What?" She still hadn't mastered a lick of Irish slang.

He laughed. "I mean consider it."

Anna tilted her head to the side. "Consider what?"

"You know, opening. Coming with me and the boys."

"Opening?" Now she had to laugh. "For you? With what songs?"

"Don't be daft, I know you've got loads. And you can test stuff out on the road. It'll be grand." He threw his arms out in front of him like a circus showman.

"Rory, I appreciate the offer, but I'm not ready for something like—"

"Stop that, you're fuckin' brilliant. But you don't have to give me an answer now." He winked. "I gotta grab some eggs for my ma. Just think on it." He jogged off in the other direction before she could respond.

It turned out it was all she could think about. Anna spent the next few days at the studio ostensibly writing, but mostly just fantasizing about what a relief it would be to let someone else take the lead. Show up, perform, sleep, and do it all over again. There'd be no time to think. She needed that even more than she craved being back on a stage.

When she got home from the studio one night that week, Maeve was still up, sipping tea in the kitchen and reading the sort of saucy romance novel she favored.

"Productive day?"

Anna nodded confidently.

"That O'Shea lad was looking for you here."

Anna had to laugh that Maeve would still refer to him like that; he'd never be anything else to everyone in town.

"Yeah? We ran into each other a few days ago."

Maeve raised an eyebrow.

"He, uh, invited me on tour," Anna said, fiddling nervously with her jacket zipper.

"Did he now? Huh." Her disapproval was hard to miss. "What'd you say?"

"Nothing, yet."

"You want to go." A statement, not a question.

Anna nodded again, after a moment.

"You think it's a good idea?"

"No." She let out a hollow laugh. "No, it's probably a terrible one."

"Then why do it?"

It was the same question she'd asked herself all week. "Because I'm scared of what might happen if I don't."

# ELEVEN

**Anna**
*New York*
May 16, 2024

Transcript from the *New Yorker*'s "An Evening with Anna Buckley"

> ***The New Yorker***: Hi, everyone! I'm Sophie Miller, a music critic at the *New Yorker*. Thanks for joining us here at the Crosby Street Hotel for a very special chat with singer-songwriter and Grammy winner Anna Buckley. As you probably know, Anna exploded onto the indie rock scene fifteen years ago, with the release of her debut LP *Cliffwalks*. The album was one of the best-reviewed releases of 2009, earning a coveted 9.3 rating from *Pitchfork*, platinum status from the RIAA, nominations for Best Alternative Album and Best Songwriter of the Year, and a win for Best New Artist from the Grammy Awards. Since then, she's won three more Grammys, completed multiple world tours, released four more albums that have also gone platinum—and she's about to release a sixth. Anna, when do you *sleep*?

> ***Anna Buckley***: [*laughs*] I'm happiest when I'm busy, I guess.

*TNY*: Has that always been the case? I'd love to hear more about what you were like growing up. Was music a big part of your household?

***AB***: I guess I've always been pretty driven, even as a kid. I grew up in a small town in Tennessee; my first exposure to music was at church. I started singing in the choir when I was little, and I loved performing right away. There was also this big, old organ there that I was fascinated by, so I actually learned how to play that first. And then gradually made my way over to piano and guitar.

*TNY*: Wow, that's a lot of instruments. Who taught you to play?

***AB***: A lot of little old ladies at church, at first. And then when I was fourteen, I went to Oak Grove, a boarding school for the arts, so that's where I started my more intensive training. And from there to Brookfield for college.

*TNY*: Your parents must have been so proud.

***AB***: Well, I think they would have preferred if I'd kept to church songs and maybe didn't leave home quite so early. But I knew from a really young age I wanted to make music and share that with the world. And it's pretty difficult to do that from where I was.

*TNY*: How do they feel now?

***AB***: You know, we have quite different ways of . . . seeing the world. I think what I do and what I choose to sing about isn't exactly their cup of tea, to put it gently.

***TNY***: Do they come to your shows?

***AB***: No. But it's better that way.

***TNY***: Do you get back home often?

***AB***: Also no. If I'm being candid, I don't think it ever really felt like home.

***TNY***: Hence the leaving early?

***AB***: Hence the leaving early.

***TNY***: How did it feel to be on your own at fourteen?

***AB***: Incredible? My high school was for all types of artists, so there weren't just musicians, but painters, sculptors, fashion designers, you name it. The interdisciplinary collaborations were electric. It's also not hyperbole to say that I wouldn't be here without the support of some of my classmates.

***TNY***: I'd love to hear more about your time at Brookfield, too. There were quite a few major talents there when you were.

***AB***: Yes, definitely. It was transformative to be surrounded by so many other people who valued music as much as I did. And solfège. [*laughs*]

***TNY***: I was looking up your graduating class and I didn't realize that the composer Will Pendleton was your year.

***AB***: Uh . . . yes. Yes, he was.

***TNY***: Did you two ever overlap in classes or work together?

***AB***: [*pauses to take a sip of water*] We did collaborate on a few things. Will is, as I'm sure you know, brilliant. He could hear a piece of music once and play it from memory, and keep a whole symphony's worth of instruments in his head when he was composing. I've never known anyone with a brain like his.

***TNY***: That's amazing. Are you still in touch?

***AB***: No.

***TNY***: Let's switch gears. You had quite the interesting path to releasing your first album.

***AB***: I was very lucky. I spent the year or so after graduation in Doolin, Ireland, working on my music. And while I was there, I met Rory O'Shea from the Vagabonds. He saw something in me that I couldn't see in myself and asked me to open for them even before I had a record deal. It was a trial by fire, for sure, but such a formative experience to learn how to live on the road, play that many dates, read a crowd, all of it. And I met a lot of people in the industry through that, which allowed me to get signed and, eventually, release my first album.

***TNY***: Let's talk about that album. For me—and probably many of us here—*Cliffwalks*' themes of loss, grief, and regret really resonated. Can you walk us through what was happening in your own life when you were writing it?

***AB***: I've said this before, but I've kept the specifics of that creative process pretty private. I guess that probably applies to most of my work, actually. But I think albums can connect with listeners based on their own experiences: you don't need to know my life story to have a song connect with you.

***TNY***: True. But I've noticed you don't perform songs off that album as much as others. Is it fair to say you'd prefer not to revisit that headspace?

***AB***: So, that's a loaded question. [*pauses*] I wouldn't be where I am now if it weren't for that period of my life and those songs coming out of it. But you're right that it was a pretty dark place. So it's not particularly . . . comfortable to jump back in and inhabit who I was then.

***TNY***: Would you say you're in a better place now?

***AB***: Sure.

***TNY***: What brings you joy?

***AB***: The same as always: making music, touring, connecting with fans.

***TNY***: You actually topped our readers' poll of best live performers. You're known for your improvs. Tell me a little about that?

***AB***: When I'm offstage, I can be . . . exacting. On myself, on a lot of things. But up there, I think I give myself license to loosen the ropes. To imagine all the possibilities of what could have been, what could be.

***TNY***: What is it about playing to an audience that you love?

***AB***: Not to sound too dramatic—and this will, sorry [*laughs*]—but being onstage is like . . . breathing. Performing to a crowd makes me feel complete and alive in a way that nothing—or no one—else can. When I'm up there, I can be naked—well, not literally, most of the time—and raw without ever feeling self-conscious or any kind of shame. It's as if I'm there as a conduit for the music; without any other labels attached to me. If any of that makes sense?

***TNY***: Yeah, and I wish I had a place like that. Your fans are also known for being some of the most passionate in the industry. I'm sure that contributes to your love of performing.

***AB***: Of course. I couldn't do what I do if I didn't have people who wanted to come to my shows. I'm very fortunate to have such a wonderful community. It's like a big extended family, and a *chosen* one, so even better.

***TNY***: Hopefully this isn't getting too personal, but you don't have a partner or children.

***AB***: [*sips water again*] That's not a question.

***TNY***: Sorry. Do you feel like your fans kind of fill that role instead? I know some of them consider you to be a mother figure.

***AB***: I love my fans, but I do find it irritating that there seems to be this endless need to always identify female performers as mothers. It's not a role that's right for everyone. And you never see this question asked to men, truly.

***TNY***: Apologies, I shouldn't have—

***AB***: I'll say this: I made a decision at the beginning of my career to put my craft—to put music—before everything else. It wasn't an easy choice, and it wasn't a choice that didn't have . . . repercussions.

***TNY***: It was also a choice that's brought you an incredible amount of success.

***AB***: Yes, which, if I'm being honest, happened more quickly and at a level that I never anticipated and wasn't prepared for. It didn't leave a lot of time to dwell on the what-ifs. But—and this isn't an exaggeration—I wouldn't be alive if I couldn't compose and sing and perform. So for me, it was—it remains—the right choice.

***TNY***: And we're so happy to have your music in the world. Unfortunately, that's all the time we have. Thank you, Anna, for sharing a little bit of your life with us. And make sure to check out her new album, *Constellation Story*, dropping next Friday.

Anna emerged from the stage, ripping the lav mic with irritation from her dress. "What the hell was that?" she said, storming toward her publicist, Kendall. "Did you not vet these questions?"

"I'm sorry," he said, flummoxed, as he flipped through papers on a clipboard. "She went off script. I can show you what they sent me?"

She waved it off. "Too late now. Jesus. For the future, though?

And I've told you this before: no questions on my family." She paused. "And nothing about Will, either."

"I mean, *I* didn't even know you guys knew each other."

"It was a long time ago," she said tersely. "But I'd rather not have our names together in the press."

"Noted and noted." Kendall widened his eyes in exasperation as he scribbled some notes down.

She narrowed hers at him. "What?"

"Nothing, I'm just writing."

"I can see your face. What?"

"It's just—" He sighed, putting his pen down. "Will's kind of a big deal right now. You're kind of a big deal. It's gonna set off red flags if I have to say something before interviews. So if there's some shit between you that's gonna come out, even if it's from twenty years ago, I would really like to know. As your publicist. As the person that you literally hired to put out fires."

Anna considered this for a moment. "You think Will's a big deal?"

"*That's* your answer? Christ." He pinched the bridge of his nose. "Let's see. He got nominated—twice—this year for an Oscar. Two different film scores. Won, by the way. Youngest composer ever, blah, blah, blah. I think he got a Grammy this year, too."

"He did—I mean, I think he did," she added quickly.

Kendall raised a dubious eyebrow. "Great for Will, I guess? Are you gonna tell me anything else I need to know?"

"I am not." She smiled benignly. "And I'm getting out of here. The piano awaits."

"Remember this conversation!" Kendall called after her as she walked away. "I'm doing my job!"

# TWELVE

**Lottie**
*New York*
May 16, 2024

All of her notebooks were still sitting on that desk in the empty office.

Lottie didn't even realize she'd left them until she was getting off the train uptown. At that point, she was too flustered to contemplate returning, and it was getting late, anyway. She figured she could swing by the next day after school to grab them, and hopefully time it so that Anna would be elsewhere.

Aidan was finally back from Paris, although they hadn't seen much of each other since she'd been holed up in Soho most evenings. He didn't keep a close enough eye on her weekly schedule to ask where she'd been; he probably assumed some extracurricular or other that was running late.

And conversation between them had been a little strained since their call after the Island night. Lottie wasn't exactly sure what was making her so frustrated: Aidan himself wasn't behaving any differently. It seemed more that she was noticing everyone's absences more profoundly.

Surprisingly however, he and Gregory were home when she

walked in. Although, from the looks of it, not for long: both were kitted out in tuxedos.

"What's the occasion, gentlemen?"

"Bianca's film premiere. I can't even remember what it's called," Aidan said distractedly, fixing Gregory's bow tie. Bianca was an actress whom he dressed with some regularity. "Where are you coming from?"

"Piano." It was kind of the truth.

He caught her eye briefly in the mirror. There was a look of surprise on his face that he quickly tried to bury.

"What?"

"Nothing." He shook his head as if to erase the thought. "You just reminded me of someone." He walked over and put his hands firmly on her shoulders. "You good at home? Did you eat? I'd say there's food in the fridge, but I'd be lying."

She sighed, but smiled. "I'll order something."

"Sorry. Have Bee get groceries tomorrow?"

She nodded.

"Okay, we're off!" Aidan gave her a quick kiss on the forehead. "Let's hope Bianca behaves herself."

"I looked. At the thing . . . at her name." They were halfway out the door already; she had no idea why she chose then to blurt it out.

Aidan turned around, opened then closed his mouth.

"I don't want to talk about it," she said, heading off the question at the pass. "But I know who she is." She gave them a tight smile. "Go, we'll catch up later."

"We don't have to?" Gregory said haltingly, looking at Aidan.

"Yeah, it's not a big deal," Aidan added, walking back toward her. "We can stay home."

"No, I shouldn't have said that right as you guys were leaving. That was dumb. Go, seriously. I'm tired, anyway."

The two exchanged concerned glances, but she made a

shooing motion toward the door. "Don't let the tuxes go to waste."

Lottie made a beeline for the train as soon as school ended the next day: she wanted to stop by the office as early as possible to avoid any potential run-ins. Thinking about how narrowly she'd avoided direct contact with Anna had felt like stepping off a curb only to have a car whiz by. She didn't get hit, but it was close enough to make her far more circumspect: she'd already decided to avoid returning to the building, at least until she figured out what she wanted to accomplish from an actual meeting.

The security guard, inured to her by now, waved her by when she walked into the lobby. Lottie stuck in her AirPods for the climb up: she was still taking the elevator to the fourth floor and then the stairs, just in case the guard was watching the security cameras. It was good exercise, anyway. Pearl Jam's "Alive" was blasting in her ears: she'd been on a big '90s kick this week.

What this meant, though, was that Lottie couldn't hear anything as she clambered up to the top floor. She didn't think to check if Anna was next door because she'd never seen her arrive this early. So she didn't hear her playing the piano. She didn't hear her footsteps in the hall. And she certainly didn't hear Anna open the office door as she was gathering her notebooks.

Anna was casually leaning in the doorway with an iced coffee when Lottie turned around from the desk.

"Fuck!" Lottie jumped, nearly dropping her books, and yanked an earbud out. Eddie Vedder stopped wailing.

"Talking Heads," Anna said unperturbed, and gestured to her with her coffee. She was slighter than Lottie would have thought. In a pair of joggers and a ratty blue T-shirt, she looked barely older than her, too. Her eyes were unmistakably, almost uncomfortably, identical to her own.

"What?" Lottie's pulse was already deafening in her ears.

"You're the Talking Heads." She motioned to Lottie's phone. "From yesterday."

"I . . . I don't know what you mean," Lottie stumbled.

Anna rolled her eyes in impatient irritation. "If I called your phone right now, you're telling me it wouldn't be 'Once in a Lifetime'? Great track, though," she added.

"My phone's on vibrate," Lottie mumbled.

Anna shot her a deeply skeptical look and took a sip of her coffee. "That's a non-answer. But doesn't really matter: you're not supposed to be up here. It's private."

"Sorry, I was just leaving." Lottie shifted the notebooks in her arms and started to walk toward the door.

Anna didn't move from her perch in the doorway. Instead, she looked around the empty room, puzzled. "What are you doing in here, anyway?"

Lottie cast her eyes about, willing something—anything—to appear that would make it plausible for her to legitimately be there. "Um, homework? It's nice listening to you play," she offered.

"Thanks, I think?" Anna wrinkled her nose. "I mean, I generally don't think of my songs as good homework accompaniment, but I'll take it." She looked at Lottie directly for the first time. "Do you play?"

Lottie couldn't decide if she should try to make a break for it or answer honestly. Ultimately, she was too rooted to the floor with fear and fascination to move. She nodded. Anna tilted her head toward her studio.

"Play me something."

"Oh, I don't think—"

"It's only fair. You already heard me, now you have to go. C'mon." She motioned to her with a wave behind her back and walked away without waiting for an answer. Lottie hesitated, then followed behind; her legs were pushing her forward while her mind frantically hunted for a way to redirect them.

Anna was already standing next to the upright and gestured to the bench. "Or guitar, if you want?"

Lottie shook her head. "No, just piano."

"She's all yours."

In the last few weeks, it felt to Lottie like her brain and her body had been operating independently of one another. She was blurting out things she didn't mean to, finding herself in places she didn't intend to be. It happened again now as she sat down at the piano. Of the hundreds of songs she knew, the only one that surfaced in that moment was the one that Anna had written for her.

Lottie sat down and played her lullaby.

When she was finished, she left her foot on the sustain pedal, the last note hanging in the air like an unanswered question. She could feel the prickly sensation of Anna watching her, but she resisted the urge to turn around. Eventually, Anna quietly approached the bench and sat down to Lottie's right. Looking down at Lottie's arm, Anna carefully and slowly pushed up Lottie's sleeve. There, on the inside of her forearm, was a birthmark. Like someone had left a light thumbprint.

Anna stared at it silently for what seemed like a full minute, then exhaled slowly. "Okay," she finally said. "You're here."

"I know I'm not eighteen—"

"I know how old you are," Anna said softly. She was looking ahead at the piano. "How'd you find me?"

"It's kind of a long story. I'm legally emancipated, so, an adult. I got access to my records."

Anna nodded slowly as she took that in. "Fuck. Sorry, I just wasn't expecting . . . this today. Or, for a while, I guess." She finally swiveled to face her, her eyes darting from the top of Lottie's head down to her fingertips. "Jesus, you're so grown up," she whispered, then shook her head quickly. "I mean, of course you are. It's been a long time."

"Sorry I didn't reach out in, like, a more formal way. I wasn't really sure how. And I really didn't think you'd be here. I just came by to grab my stuff."

"How long have you been coming by?"

"A few days."

Anna nodded again, as if calculating what Lottie may have heard. "You don't owe me an explanation." She paused. "I, on the other hand . . ." She trailed off.

Lottie was finally in the moment that she'd fantasized about since she learned how to daydream. And it was entirely destabilizing to be in the reality and no longer the hypothetical. The infinite possibilities of who Anna was had been a towering house of cards, one that Lottie had painstakingly designed and balanced over the course of years. But today, she'd pulled one card out, and all the others—all those endless, branching hopes and terrors—collapsed in a pile on the floor. Now she was left with just this one flesh-and-blood version: her own flesh and blood. This Anna couldn't be manipulated in Lottie's mind to say and do what she wanted her to because this Anna was no longer a figment of her imagination, but a real fucking person. She needed to get the hell out of here.

"I don't think I can do this right now. I'm sorry." Lottie pushed herself up from the bench.

Anna looked almost as fractured as she did. "Okay . . . But wait, hold on." She stood up and walked over to the desk, where she scribbled a number on a piece of paper, ripped it off, and handed it to her. "If you want it."

Tyler texted her as she was walking home from the train. They hadn't seen each other since the Island, and she wasn't even sure he remembered what had happened. But, to be fair, she hadn't given it a ton of thought: she'd been understandably preoccupied.

"u see this? from today." He had sent her a link to an interview with Anna that had just been posted to YouTube.

"whoa, no. tx." She left it at that. She wasn't about to attempt an explanation over text. She couldn't even explain it to herself.

Lottie arrived home to an empty house, but thankfully, a full fridge. This was her preferred outcome: she needed the quiet to begin processing what the fuck had just happened, and sustenance to keep from passing out. Maybe she'd watch that video first: she wasn't quite ready to replay her own encounter with Anna just yet. After dumping turkey meatballs into a bowl, she beamed the interview from her phone to the TV.

The video materialized on the screen: Anna, with her hair in a braid, looked the same as when Lottie had seen her at the studio. She must have walked over soon after, which explained why she was there earlier than usual.

She doubted Anna was revealing anything she hadn't said before, but since Lottie had studiously avoided Googling her, it would all be new to her, anyway. She certainly didn't know Anna was from the South: she'd scrubbed any trace of an accent from her speech.

*"And then when I was fourteen, I went to Oak Grove, a boarding school for the arts . . ."*

Lottie stared at the screen, fork frozen in midair. She must have misheard her. Stuffing the last bite of meatball into her mouth, she rewound the interview back a few seconds.

*"I went to Oak Grove . . ."*

Oak Grove was where Aidan went to school.

She'd heard dozens of stories from his time there, mostly about sneaking vodka and pot into the dorms, or making out with supposedly straight boys in the dark room. But nothing, obviously, about her. She paused the video. A sludgy, black feeling was coalescing in the pit of her stomach. Aidan and Anna were the same age.

Lottie stood up abruptly from the couch; she was almost positive all his yearbooks were on a shelf in his office upstairs. When she was much younger, she had loved to look at the pictures of his student fashion shows in their pages, to marvel at all the marabou and chiffon he favored back then.

She nearly sprinted up to the third floor, where Aidan kept a small home workshop. Behind rolls of muslin and batting and a dressmaker's dummy was a large floor-to-ceiling bookcase, mostly filled with oversized coffee-table books that he used for inspiration.

She quickly scanned the shelves, looking for the titles. "Come on, come on, where are you?" she murmured to herself. Finally, she spotted them up top: four shiny volumes of the Oak Grove *Quercetum* standing at attention. She pulled the sliding step ladder over and scrambled up, grabbing all four in her arms, then throwing them down onto his drafting table.

2003 was his senior year: she'd start there on his personal page. As a little kid, she used to pore over it because there were pictures of a much-younger Maya. The book's spine cracked open easily to the page: plenty of photos of the family, of course, but also many with friends, which she'd never really bothered to examine closely.

She found Anna in the bottom right corner.

Aidan had his arms around her and was giving her a kiss on the cheek. "With my Queen B.," the caption read.

Lottie pushed the book away from her in disgust. Hot, bristly tears of anger were forming in the corners of her eyes. She knocked over the dummy and slammed the door on her way out.

# THIRTEEN

**Anna**
*New York*
May 16, 2024

"This is Aidan."

"She's not eighteen yet. We had an agreement."

"Anna." She heard him exhale deeply through the phone. "I was wondering when I'd get this call."

Anna was pacing her living room like a tiger at the zoo: furious and trapped. She was, obviously, blindsided by Lottie's showing up, but what had her truly incandescent was her lack of agency. Having the reins wrested from her had slingshot her back to a time and place she'd never wanted to revisit.

"Well, here I am." She was gripping the phone so tightly she was surprised it hadn't shattered. "How the hell did she just show up at my studio?"

"She came to your studio? Today?" He sounded alarmed.

"You didn't know?"

"No, I didn't. Fuck. What'd you say to her?" She couldn't quite tell if his tone was accusatory. It had been so long since they'd spoken.

"Not much; I think she got spooked pretty fast. Nothing about you, if that's what you're asking. You didn't answer my question."

He paused. "You know, when all of this went down with you and Maya, I was never comfortable with what you made her agree to. I felt like I'd always be lying." He considered this for a moment. "I *have* always been lying."

"Well, wonderful moral high ground you have there, but it wasn't any of your fucking business."

"Maybe at the time it wasn't," he said calmly. "Sure as shit is now."

She was quiet, chastened.

"I have hated keeping your secrets for you," he continued. "And I've hated keeping them from Lottie even more. So I gave her emancipation papers and her birth certificate on her birthday. Which was earlier this month."

"I know when her birthday is," Anna snapped.

"Respectfully? I have no idea what you know or not anymore."

"Well, would've been nice to get the heads-up."

"To be honest, I didn't even know she'd looked at it until last night. And she didn't tell me she'd found you. But"—he laughed, a bit ruefully—"I also don't owe you anything. She's not yours."

"Fuck you."

"That was your choice, Anna! And to be very clear, I don't blame you for making it; it was the right call for everyone. But you were also very clear that you didn't want to see either of us after everything happened with Maya." He stopped to think. "I'm only hearing from you now because she found you. So there are consequences to your actions: you cannot have it both ways. And forgive me if I don't take your feelings into account when it comes to Lottie."

"I get it. I'm a piece of shit." Anna suddenly realized getting through this conversation without a drink would be impossible. She wandered over to her bar and poured herself two fingers of whiskey. "Why bother telling her at all?"

"That's not what I said." He was exasperated. "Look, she's been dying to know where she comes from; I think she deserves the truth. None of this mess is her fault."

"Trust me, I'm aware whose fault you think it is." She sat down on her couch, swirling the drink in her hand. "I didn't even recognize her, Aidan," she said quietly. "What kind of person doesn't recognize their own fucking kid?"

They were both silent. Below on the street, a commotion was erupting: Anna could hear a cab leaning on its horn and a gaggle of voices yelling.

"I know it wasn't easy for you. After." His voice had softened a little. "And I know you weren't expecting this. But she was always gonna find you, eventually."

She chuckled lightly. "You think a day goes by where I could forget that?" She took a long, bitter sip of her drink. "I guess I thought I'd be different by then. Have my shit together."

"Yeah, well, welcome to the club," Aidan said dryly. "She's an incredible kid, Anna. So goddamn smart, so talented." He paused. "There's a lot of you in there. I don't want you to miss out on more than you already have."

Anna bit her lip. She didn't want to know what she'd missed. That was kind of the whole point of staying away.

"If you're ready, that is," he added. "If you're not, then you can stay the fuck away."

"Jesus, Aidan, you didn't really give me much of a choice."

"Neither did you," he shot back. "Doesn't mean I didn't do the right thing. Doesn't mean you can't, either."

Anna felt as if she had been dropped into a foreign country where no one spoke her tongue: every emotion was new and unintelligible. She was desperate to see Lottie again, to touch her face, grasp her fingers, confirm she really existed. But to do so meant having to hold herself accountable. And how do you look your child in the eye and tell her the reasons why you left?

"Does Will know?" Aidan asked cautiously.

Her voice was frayed, a string pulled too taut. "No."

"At all?"

She took another deep swig. "No."

"Jesus. It's time, Anna. He needs to know."

Before there was Will, there had been Aidan. In a platonic sense, of course: no one would ever have confused him for straight. They were two of the only Southern kids their year at Oak Grove, and while both worked assiduously to dissolve their accents by the end of the first semester, they bonded over their otherness in those early months (and their mutual distaste of New England–style cornbread).

But their continued friendship was based on more than just geographical proximity. Aidan was one of the few able to tap into Anna's playful side, which she often buried in favor of a laser-beam focus on her music. He made her feel like a kid again (for the first time, really), and Aidan, in turn, found Anna's white-hot ambition bolstered his own. By the time he left for Parsons and she for Brookfield, they were each other's shadow: two souls who saw the world through different but equally kaleidoscopic creative lenses.

Anna's punishing double major at Brookfield didn't leave her too many free weekends, but she always managed to escape down to New York a few times a year. Aidan would take her dancing at dark, sticky-floored bars on the Lower East Side until the sun came up, then to early-morning breakfasts at a diner. And he adored visiting Boston, finding New England's Americana so on the nose as to be charming. (Anna thought the real reason he came was to flirt with all the geeky orchestra boys, but regardless, she appreciated the company.)

Will was suspicious, at first: Anna chalked it up to misplaced jealousy. Eventually though, he came to appreciate Aidan's ability to dig out Anna's elusive goofiness. And by senior year, he looked forward to the visits almost as much as she did.

All throughout high school and college, Aidan had kept her breathlessly updated on the exploits of his much older sister, Maya. She was a successful film agent in LA, but always seemed to be drifting from one ill-fitting boyfriend to the next. By the time Anna was at Brookfield, Maya had decided she wanted to have a baby on her own, but multiple rounds of IVF had failed so far, and she was unsure how many more times she wanted to put her body through the grueling process.

So it was Aidan who Anna called from Ireland, when she finally forced herself to reckon with the fact that she wouldn't be pregnant forever. That there came an after, and with it, an actual baby.

"I'm going to tell you something, and you have to swear on your fucking life you will not tell a soul," she said when he picked up.

"Um, okay? Good morning to you, too?"

"Aidan, I mean it."

"Okay, fine. Promise. This feels very serious."

"Yeah, well. I'm pregnant."

He coughed. "What? With whose baby? You told me you've barely left the studio."

She exhaled. "It's Will's."

"*Will* Will?" He guffawed. "You were sleeping with Will?"

"Slept. One night. But I guess that's all it takes," she added dryly. "That's not exactly why I'm calling, though . . ."

Anna, present condition aside, was nothing if not a meticulous planner. She laid out her many reasons for giving the baby to Maya: financial security, less red tape than going through an adoption agency, and of course, Maya's deep desire for a child. Aidan was, understandably, gobsmacked at first, but Anna argued a convincing-enough case that he promised he'd talk to his sister.

"And Will's all right with all of this?"

She was silent for a long time. "He doesn't know."

"What?"

"He can't know, okay?"

"You're joking." She could feel how wide his eyes were through the phone. "You're not telling him? Anything?"

"It's not up for debate, Aidan. This is how it's gonna happen."

"Fuck, Anna!" he exclaimed. "Then why are you telling me?"

"I don't have anyone else I can tell," she said quietly. "And I felt like someone needed to know. And I know I can trust you."

With regards to Will, Anna swore Aidan to such secrecy that not even Maya knew who Lottie's father was. And while it was never explicitly discussed, Anna's blanket refusal to have any contact with her daughter meant her friendship with Aidan had no choice but to become a de facto casualty. Lottie became an ocean between them: deep, and wide, and impossible to cross without getting sucked under.

And so, in the course of a year, Anna lost not just Will, but Aidan, too.

She told herself that it was necessary: that, eventually, she'd be fine without them. And, for a while, the ruse worked. But lying to yourself is an athletic pursuit: at some point, you get tired. At some point, your feet are blistered, and your lungs are burning, and there's sweat in your eyes, and you stumble.

# FOURTEEN

## Lottie

*New York*
May 16, 2024

Lottie had thought she might be calmer by the time Aidan came home, but it turned out stewing in her fury had only brought it closer to a rolling boil. By the time he walked in, she was dangerously close to spilling over.

"Hey, sweets, how was—" He stopped dead when he saw the yearbooks fanned out in front of her on the kitchen counter.

"You knew this whole time," she said, staring down at the books and trying to keep her voice level. "You knew *her* this whole time."

"Lottie, let me explain." He had his arms out, as if bracing for a right hook. "What did she tell you?"

She looked up. "What do you mean, what did she tell me? How do you know I saw her?"

He grimaced. "Shit. I mean—"

"Did she call you? Did you call *her*?" She wiped her nose on her sleeve. "This is so fucked."

"No. No, no. Hold on." He sat down heavily on the stool next to her and took a deep breath. "Okay. Obviously"—he gestured to the pile of books—"we knew each other. We were friends.

And that is how she found Maya." Lottie started to interrupt and Aidan held up a finger. "But we have barely spoken since you were born. She called today to tell me you'd shown up at her studio. Which, clearly, I didn't know you were planning on doing."

Lottie was silent while she thought this over. "But if she called you," she started slowly, "then she knew not to call Mom, didn't she?"

"Yeah. She knew," he said quietly.

They were both still for a minute, Maya's presence as palpable as their own heartbeats.

"How could you keep this from me? How many times have I asked you?" She was trying very hard not to cry, to seem like the adult that she now technically was. "How many times have you *lied* to me?"

"I was just trying to do right by what Maya wanted for you," he said, his voice flooded with as much pain as hers. "And, I guess, at some point, I decided what was right was for you to know the truth. And I was so convinced of that, I never stopped to think about what came after."

Lottie didn't respond. How ironic for him to be speaking of truth, after what he'd done.

"How'd you figure it out?" he finally asked when she was still quiet.

"Tyler sent me a link to an interview she gave this morning; she mentioned Oak Grove. Wasn't too hard to put two and two together."

He nodded slowly. "Well . . . fuck. Obviously not how I wanted you to find out."

She stared at him. "Would there have been a good way?"

"No," he said after a moment. "I guess not." He lowered his forehead onto his palms. "Are you okay? After seeing her?"

Aidan's sophomore yearbook was open to a spread on their

homecoming dance. There was a photo of him, rose in mouth, dipping Anna dramatically on the dance floor. "I don't know," she said. He tentatively reached an arm around her; she allowed it. "It was kinda scary to be in the same room, you know? But also kind of a relief, to not have to wonder anymore."

"You think you wanna see her again?"

Lottie wanted to sit locked in that tiny studio for a year, force Anna to tell her everything, like she was pouring water from a pitcher to a glass. But her presence also felt so dangerously hot Lottie wasn't sure she wouldn't combust if they were left in the same space together.

"I think I have to. Does that make sense?"

He nodded.

Lottie slid one of the yearbooks closer to her and started idly flipping through. "You guys were really close, weren't you?"

"Yeah," he said, his voice tight. "We were."

"What was she like?"

"Driven, smart, witty. Also incredibly stubborn and hated admitting when she was wrong." He smiled. "But really, really talented, even then. I think we all knew she was gonna make it. It's almost like she didn't have a choice."

"You think we're similar?"

"I mean, you certainly look like each other, which is a little crazy for me. Especially now that you're at an age when I knew her, too. But, personality wise? I don't know. Anna could be a tough nut to crack. You're a lot sweeter." He squeezed her shoulder.

"But, like, the perfect pitch stuff, that must be from her?"

Aidan was preoccupied when he answered, thumbing through yearbook pages and lost in some moment from decades earlier. "Actually, no."

It was an odd answer. "What do you mean, 'no'?"

He snapped back to attention. "Nothing. I just mean, you

know, you're your own person, too. Not everything comes from her." He shifted uncomfortably in his seat.

Cold realization dripped down from the top of her head. "Do you know who my dad is?"

Aidan looked down at the counter. His right leg was wiggling nervously underneath.

"Aidan?"

He closed the yearbook in front of him, as if doing so would prevent any further slips of the tongue. But he wouldn't make eye contact with her.

"You know," she whispered, leaning away from him. It felt like the entire room had suddenly tilted on its axis. "Oh my god, you know. Did Mom?"

"No," he said quickly. "I promise, she didn't. She wouldn't have lied to you."

"Clearly not your problem."

Aidan rubbed at his temples. "Fuck," he muttered. "I'm sorry, that caught me off guard. I shouldn't've said anything."

"Too late. Who is he?"

"Lottie, I can't—"

"Who is he?" Louder.

"It's not my place—"

"It's my *dad*, Aidan! Is he in jail or something? Is he dead? Why wouldn't she want Mom to know?"

"Because he doesn't know, okay?" He practically yelled it, then took a moment to recover. "He doesn't know. He's alive. He's definitely not in jail. But Anna never told him about you. And I swore to her I wouldn't say anything. You've gotta talk to her."

Lottie stood up so suddenly from her stool it tumbled over. "You know what? Fine. I'm fucking sick of everyone knowing more about me than I do."

"Where are you going?" Aidan jumped up, alarmed.

"To go talk to her."

"Right now?" he asked, surprised.

"Yes, right now." She put a hand on his shoulder. "Alone."

Lottie called Anna as soon as she walked out the door, and before she had a chance to get in her own way. She was betting on her not picking up, anyway.

"Hello?"

Well, wrong on that front. "It's . . . Lottie."

"Oh! . . . Hey."

"I know this is kinda last minute, but are you around? Like, now?"

"Um . . . yeah. Yeah, I'm around. Are you okay?"

"I'm fine. I just—I think I need some answers. I think I'm tired of waiting."

It took her a few seconds to respond. "That's fair. You wanna come over?"

Anna was in a faded gray Brookfield sweatshirt and no makeup when she opened the door, hair piled on top of her head. It was hard to square this real-life version with the super-stylized shots Lottie had seen on album covers and in magazine spreads. They might as well have been two different people entirely.

"Hi," Anna said softly, and moved aside to let her in.

Lottie hadn't given much thought to who Anna was away from her music. Nearly everything she'd learned so far was about her songs or career. Her knowledge of anything else was limited to basically what Aidan had just shared. She wasn't sure what she'd find when she stepped into her apartment. It was gorgeous—loft, big windows, fancy open kitchen—but didn't seem particularly lived-in, minus the piano in the living room. No photos of friends or family, no tchotchkes perched on shelves.

"I'd offer you something to eat, but I'm not home a lot; I've got, like, old miso paste and mayo in the fridge? Vodka, too, but I'm guessing that's probably not how this is supposed to go," she said by way of greeting as she led her into the living room. "We can order something if you're hungry?"

"You sound like Aidan," Lottie murmured.

Anna stiffened slightly at his name as she sat down on her huge, low-slung couch and curled her legs underneath her. It was exactly how Lottie sat, too. She took a chair opposite; this was her first chance to get a good look at her; she'd been too panicked to do so at the studio. They did resemble each other, physically, no doubt. But Anna had that veneer of confidence that comes with money and adoration; Lottie recognized it from some of her own classmates. Underneath though, she could discern the chips, the scratches. And this, this she could recognize in herself: it was a stupefying mix of confusion and anger and relief.

"So where do you want to start?" Anna shifted nervously on her cushion. "I'm sorry, I'm not . . . great at this kind of thing." She motioned with her hand to the empty space between them.

"I wanna start with my dad."

Anna exhaled deeply, fully before answering, as if readying for a jump from a plane. "Okay. Understandable."

"I always thought you didn't know who it was. And then, you know, he's not on the birth certificate."

Anna's eyes widened. "Oh, god. I never thought about it like that. You must have thought I was . . . different."

"I didn't know what to think of you," Lottie retorted. "You made that kind of impossible."

She acknowledged this with a tip of her head. "Yeah. Guess I did."

"Anyway, Aidan let slip that he knows who it is. I got mad. And then I called you. And now"—she looked around, baffled—"I'm here . . . in your apartment."

Anna sat up a little straighter. "What'd he say?"

"He didn't tell me who it was. He wouldn't. But he said he—whoever he is—doesn't know about me."

"Yeah." She exhaled softly. "That is true."

"Why?" Lottie was surprised she could be this direct with her. Maybe the conversation with Aidan had knocked loose some of her normal inhibitions. Or maybe she was still too angry to care how she came across.

Anna seemed a little taken aback herself. "We're diving right in, aren't we? Well . . ." She took a minute to compose herself, pulling her hands protectively inside the sleeves of her sweatshirt. "At the time, when I was twenty-two, it seemed . . . easier. That he wouldn't have to wonder, too, the way that I would—the way that I have." She paused, pulling her knees up to her chest. "I wasn't really thinking of the long-term. I wasn't really thinking about . . . this happening one day." She gestured toward Lottie. "I was too young to get all the consequences."

"Was he a bad guy or something?"

She laughed lightly. "No. Not at all."

"I don't get it, then. Why would you wanna do all of that alone?" *And what if he'd wanted me?* Lottie was desperate to add. *What then?*

"I wasn't alone. I was living as a boarder with someone: Maeve. It was probably—definitely—more than she bargained for, but she took good care of me. You too, in a way."

"It's not the same."

Anna hugged herself a little tighter. "No. It's not."

"So who is he?"

Anna closed her eyes for a moment before she answered. "His name's Will. Pendleton. We went to college together." The admission seemed physically painful; Lottie could see how hard she was gripping her knees, almost willing herself smaller.

"He's a musician?"

She nodded. "A composer—a brilliant one. But he plays, too." She inclined her head toward the piano. "So you get it from both sides."

"He's the one with perfect pitch."

Anna stared at her, surprised. "Yeah, he does. Do you?"

Lottie nodded.

"Huh. Genetics." She shook her head with disbelief. "Wild."

"Okay, so what else?" Lottie couldn't let the momentum fade or she'd lose her nerve.

"So, what else . . . Well, we slept together before I left for Ireland and you were a nice little surprise souvenir." She smiled wryly. "Sorry, that's probably not what you were asking."

"I mean, I put that part together already. So you weren't, like, dating?"

"No. It was never really—I don't know, the right time or the right place for us. We loved each other, a lot, in our own way, though." She grabbed a pillow from the couch and wrapped her arms around it almost like armor. "He was my best friend."

"But you guys don't talk now?"

Anna shook her head. "It was too hard, at first. And then, it kind of felt like it was too late. Was just easier to keep the distance."

"So did you just like . . . ghost him?"

Anna nodded slowly.

"That's kinda fucked up. If he was a good guy and all."

"I know," she said quietly. "Trust me, I've had a long time to think about how fucked up it is."

"A long time to reach out, too."

Anna looked up, surprised, but didn't speak. It was hard to deny that Lottie was wrong. "It's complicated," she finally said, as if that were a satisfactory answer.

"Where does he live?"

"Boston. He teaches at Brookfield now." Anna pulled at her sweatshirt with the emblem.

"I'd like to meet him."

"I figured."

"I can't just, like, show up, though."

"I know." She seemed so small, hugging that pillow and sitting on that big couch in that big apartment. It was hard to imagine her commanding a stage. She was reserved: in her movements, with her emotions. It was a far cry from the jubilant, open-book nature of Aidan. Or the warmth of Maya, for that matter. "I need—I need some time."

"I think you've had enough."

The naked shock on Anna's face made it clear she was not a person used to being challenged much.

"You're gonna need to get to Boston."

"Yeah," she eventually said. "Guess I am."

# FIFTEEN

## Anna

*Boston*

May 22, 2024

**From: anna.buckley@gmail.com**
**To: w_pendleton@brookfield.edu**
**May 20, 2:56 AM**

Hey,

Hope you don't mind me blowing up your inbox on your work account, just figured you might check this one more. I'm gonna be up in Boston on Wednesday: you have time to meet for a drink? Would be good to catch up.

A

**From: w_pendleton@brookfield.edu**
**To: anna.buckley@gmail.com**
**May 20, 10:46 PM**

Hi,

Damn. Been a minute. I can make that work, though. Five Horses at 5?

Will

* * *

He was already there when she arrived. Anna could see him poking at his phone through the large front window; he was too engrossed to see her staring.

Will had changed remarkably little since she'd last seen him. Of course she'd tried to snoop ahead of their meeting, but he barely had a presence on social media (she probably wouldn't either, if it weren't mandated by her label). There was the same dusting of scruff on his chin, that same unruly hair. With a beanie pulled down over his forehead, he nearly passed for just another college kid. And he was handsome: the intervening years had carved away his last bit of baby fat, given him a hint of crinkle around the eyes.

Will looked up then and spotted her. Anna's breath stuck in her throat like a gumball. He gave her a half smile and an awkward wave. She managed both back and forced herself to pull open the door.

It was obvious the young bartender recognized her as she walked in, but she busied herself in her ice shaker, for which Anna was grateful. Delivering this news in such a public setting was less than ideal, but at least it meant the blast radius was contained. His reaction would have to be tempered by the presence of others.

And she did want to see him. Regardless of how long it had been, the hole—the absence of him—had never closed. She'd tried to grow bigger around it, to force it to disappear, but just succeeded in compacting it, making it impossible to dissolve.

She tried to steady her breathing as she approached him. He tracked her, with a touch of obvious trepidation, as she picked her way between the tables. And then, there she was in front of him. There was nowhere else to go.

"Hey, Annie," he said softly. He was the only person to ever call her that. No one would dare try now, anyway.

"Hey." She couldn't contain her smile.

Will maneuvered from behind the small wooden table and held his arms out tentatively for a hug. She didn't so much hug back as let herself be enveloped. It was an exquisite sort of pain, she thought, to have gone so long without a specific touch and still have it be so familiar. But the body remembers. He smelled the same, like pine soap and cotton.

"It's good to see you," he murmured half into her hair, before releasing her and looking her up and down. "You're still you."

"For better or worse." She sat down and stuck her hands under her thighs to keep them from shaking.

"So what're you in town for? You didn't say."

"Oh, you know, work stuff." She gestured vaguely and hoped he didn't ask any follow-ups. "How are you?"

"Good. Busy with wrapping up the school year. Working on a few pieces. You?"

"Gearing up for tour. I'll be back here later this summer." She hesitated, then added, "You can come, if you want? I'm happy to leave you a ticket. Or two . . . if you need two?" He wasn't wearing a ring, but her cursory-level Googling hadn't revealed either the presence or absence of a partner.

"I'm not—I don't have . . . I'm not married, if that's what you're asking. No kids, either. You?"

"No, not married."

"Well, good for us." He flashed a quick deprecating smile.

Anna forced a laugh. Her palm was itchy for a rocks glass. Will, evidently, felt the same; she could see the nervous energy in his eyes as they darted around the bar. "You, uh, still drink whiskey neat? I'll go grab us something?" He was already popping up from the table.

He returned promptly with two glasses and placed one in front of her. She took a slow, grateful swig, relishing the golden burn radiating through her chest.

"So it's been a while." His face was still so open. She hated herself for what she was about to do to him. She hated herself for what she'd done.

"Yeah—Oh! Congrats on the Oscar." A deflection, obviously.

He made a face, but he was blushing. "You didn't come all the way to Boston to tell me that."

"It's a huge deal, Will! And well-earned. That score was gorgeous."

"You saw it?" He looked dubious. "You hate war movies." She couldn't believe he remembered that.

"Well, I listened to it, if we're being completely honest."

"Knew it." He smiled. "But, thanks. I really liked your latest, too. That brass work was stunning."

"You listened?" She wasn't sure she would have, in his position.

"If we're really being completely honest? To them all," he said with an embarrassed shrug.

Her turn to blush. Did he have any idea how many songs were about him? "Yeah, me too," she added quietly. She loved playing some of his softer pieces on long bus rides between tour stops. They felt like old friends even if she was hearing them for the first time.

But this was not the direction they needed to be headed in. She downed another large sip. Her pulse was thumping uncomfortably into her eyes.

"You okay?" He tilted his head with concern.

She nodded quickly. "Sorry, just nervous to see you, I guess. Which is . . . not how it was." She put both hands around her glass to steady them. "I, uh . . . I need to tell you something."

He furrowed his brow. "Are you sick?"

"No! God, no. I'm fine." Another chug. She was nearly done already. "Fuck," she murmured.

He looked at her, then looked at her glass. "You sure you're—"

"We have a daughter." Four words. It was done.

Will stared at her, then chuckled lightly. "Oh yeah?" He leaned back in his chair, now a little more at ease after what he perceived as an ill-attempted ice breaker. "No really, what's up?"

Anna looked down at the table, tried once again to calm her ragged exhalations. She drummed her fingers slowly on the surface; it was impossible to make eye contact with him. "I . . . I couldn't go through with it," she whispered.

She felt him lean forward, but she couldn't look up.

"That was the plan. I didn't lie about that. But after I heard her heartbeat . . . I don't know, I . . . I couldn't do it." Around them, it felt like all noise ceased: the only sound she could hear was his own shallow breathing. "So I gave her up. To Aidan's older sister, Maya."

She waited for him to say something—anything—but he refused, so she went on. "It was a closed adoption; her records were supposed to be sealed until she turned eighteen. But Maya . . . Maya died, and she's legally emancipated now. Aidan gave her her birth certificate on her birthday and she tracked me down." She paused. "Her name's Charlotte. Lottie. She just turned sixteen."

His stunned silence felt like a wave about to crash. "Are you serious?" he finally said.

She couldn't answer and she couldn't look at him.

"Anna, are you fucking serious? Why didn't you tell me? Where is she?" A pause, then a demand: "Look at me."

She finally raised her eyes to his. The disbelief and confusion etched onto his face hurt more than any invective he could have thrown.

"Where is she?" he asked again, more insistently.

"New York. With Aidan."

Will pulled his beanie off and combed his fingers distractedly through his hair. "*Aidan* Aidan? Jesus fuck, Anna. When were you going to tell me if she hadn't found you?" He stopped to consider. "*Were* you going to tell me?"

"I don't know—I mean, yes, I would have, eventually. In a couple of years."

"In a couple of years. Well, lucky me, then." He looked around, as if wondering if this were some kind of terrible prank, and the gotcha moment was imminent. "Who else knows?"

"Basically no one. Just Maeve, for obvious reasons."

He nodded a few times, trying to process the onslaught of information, and took his own long swig of whiskey. "Okay. Okay . . . I need a minute." He propped his elbows onto the table and cradled his head in his hands. "I feel like I'm gonna pass out. Or throw up." He took a few deep breaths. She almost reached out to touch his arm, then thought better of it. "This is why you cut things off," he finally murmured, still looking at the table.

She closed her eyes. "Yeah. It is."

"Well, there's that mystery solved. Sixteen years later." He chuckled bitterly and slapped the table. She jumped. "What a fucking resolution."

She started to reply, then stopped. There was nothing to add that wouldn't make it worse.

He raised his head. "You have pictures?"

She nodded, then grabbed her phone and scrolled through until she found one of the school photos she'd asked Lottie to send.

"Here." She slid the phone across the table.

Will swallowed, then stared at the screen. Now, in such close proximity, it was easy to see which of his features Lottie had inherited. They had the same hair, of course, but also the same long neck. Even the same tapered, elegant fingers. He looked at the photo for minutes, not speaking.

"She's beautiful, Annie." He rubbed at the corners of his mouth. "Looks like you," he added softly.

"She wants to meet you."

He looked up from the phone. "You met her?"

She nodded.

"What's she like?"

How do you describe someone who grew inside you and then became a stranger? Lottie was both intimately familiar to her and completely alien, a favorite book in translation. "She's you. And she's me," Anna finally said. "I don't know how else to explain it."

Will nodded, shell-shocked, and put his head back down in his hands. "My mother is going to shit a brick," he mumbled to the table.

Christ, Betsy. She, somehow, hadn't factored in that telling Will eventually meant telling Will's family.

He exhaled deeply and sat up. "I need to go home before I say things that I . . . can't unsay." He finished off his drink in one long gulp. "And I need some time to sit with this. How long are you here?"

"Just tomorrow. I leave Friday morning."

"Think you can fit me in?" he said, deadpan.

"Of course," she said, chastened.

"I've got class at eleven—that'll be a fucking blast—but I can meet you after?"

She nodded.

He grabbed his hat, stood up, and started to walk away before turning around. "Will you, uh, text me that photo?"

She nodded again.

"Okay. Thanks." He raked his hands through his hair once more and turned his head up to the light. She thought his eyes looked wet. "Night, Anna," he said, and walked quickly out of the bar without looking back.

It wasn't surprising that Will was teaching. When Anna thought back to freshman year and how effortlessly he could draw classmates out of their shells, it made perfect sense that he'd want to help shape the next generation of musicians.

They'd arranged to meet at his office at Brookfield after his class let out. But faced with a rare empty morning in her schedule and loath to be alone with her thoughts, Anna wandered over to campus early. It was her first time back since graduation.

After the success of her first album, Brookfield had invited her on multiple occasions, each time sweetening the deal: deliver the commencement address, receive an honorary master's. But even contemplating setting foot on those grounds could induce vertigo. Shadows of Will would be everywhere, from the grassy central quad where they'd listened to Ives on Saturday mornings, to the cavernous recital halls where she'd watched him conduct his pieces dozens of times. So, via her publicist, she always politely declined, then made sure someone on her team donated to the scholarship fund as a mea culpa.

Finally stepping through those front gates made time feel very elastic. She'd first arrived here over twenty years ago, but could still walk the paths from the dining hall to the practice rooms to the dorms practically with her eyes closed. When she poked her head inside the library, the familiar smell of dust and ancient paper catapulted her instantly to being eighteen again: cramming for midterms while gulping someone's purloined Adderall, surreptitiously kissing her freshman-year boyfriend Marcus in the stacks, quizzing Will on the major composers of the Romantic period in one of the study rooms.

Almost without realizing it, she made her way to Jones Hall, where nearly all the music comp classes were taught. She looked at the time on her phone: Will's class had started about five minutes prior. Anna tried to get the attention of the student working the front desk, but she was deeply engrossed in something on TikTok. She didn't look up when Anna approached.

"Excuse me, could you tell me where Professor Pendleton's class is?" Professor. How could they be so adult already?

"Second floor recital hall, on the right." The girl pointed toward the stairs without taking her eyes off her phone.

Anna tapped the desk. "Thanks."

The girl finally looked up; her eyes grew big as she registered who was in front of her. "Wait. Aren't you—"

Anna smiled enigmatically. "Get that all the time," she called back, already walking up the stairs.

She figured she'd be inconspicuous enough that she could slip into the back of the class without being noticed. Maybe, with a baseball cap shoved low, she'd even pass for a student. Unfortunately for her, though, current Brookfield undergrads appeared to be far more punctual than back in 2003. When she opened the door, fifty faces swiveled around to look at her, except for Will, who was fiddling with his laptop to get the projector to work.

"Class starts at eleven, I may remind you," he said without looking up. He was in full professor mode: blazer with elbow patches included.

The students started giggling and whispering as they recognized her; a couple tried to snap a quick photo on their phones. Will finally got his slide deck working and stood up.

"What's with the noise, guys? I know it's close to lunchtime, but—" He finally spotted her standing alone at the top of the stairs. "Ah."

She hadn't meant to disrupt. But just for a few minutes, she wanted to see who he was now, who he was when he didn't know she was there. The window had closed, though. She couldn't tell how angry (or not) he was.

"Well, everyone, looks like we have a visitor. Meet Anna Buckley. We were at Brookfield at the same time." He smiled tightly. He was clearly furious but wasn't going to risk making a scene. Not when all the kids had iPhones and were trigger-happy with posting videos.

"Pretend I'm not here," Anna said with a little wave as she slid into a seat in the top row. "I just really wanted to learn about . . . scoring for a full orchestra."

More titters from the class.

"You heard her," Will said crisply. "Let's get to work."

After class wrapped, Anna got swarmed for selfies, which she happily obliged. These kids were her people: they lived for and breathed music like she did. Will was still down at the stage, gathering up papers and shutting down his laptop. He didn't acknowledge her until the last student had left.

"What are you doing here?" He was leaning over his desk with his arms splayed, looking down.

"I really am interested in scoring. And you're a fantastic teacher, by the way—"

"This is where I work, Anna. You can't just . . . waltz in and disrupt class."

"The kids didn't seem to mind."

"I mind," he said, a little loudly. "Let's please get out of here before the rest of them figure out you're on campus." He walked by her swiftly without making eye contact, but held the door open behind him.

Will's small office was exactly as she had pictured it: books stacked two deep, straining the shelves; sheet music piled precariously on the windowsill. A whiteboard had a few bars of scribbled notes, and a piano keyboard set up underneath it.

He collapsed into his desk chair and immediately put his head in his hands. "Close the door," he mumbled. Anna complied, then sat down in the seat across from him.

He inhaled heavily a few times and finally sat up. He looked awful: dark circles under his eyes, barely any color in the rest of his face. "I didn't sleep."

"Really."

"That bad?"

She nodded slowly.

"Great." He rubbed his eyes. "Great," he said again. "I don't . . . I don't know what to do here. I don't know what to feel. I don't know what to say to you." He looked out his office window. "And I always knew . . . what to say to you."

Outside, students were crisscrossing the quad, gesticulating to each other in excited conversation. Anna's longing to trade places was so sharp, she turned away from the view before it cut her further.

"I have a lot of questions, but I don't think I want to know the answer to any of them," he continued. "And you know what the worst part is?" He laughed bitterly. "I was really excited to see you. I feel like a fucking idiot."

Anna was at a loss for what to do herself. Anything she said would be putting a Band-Aid on wet skin: nothing would stick and he'd still be bleeding. All she could muster was: "You're not an idiot."

He acknowledged that with a snort before his attention turned to the piano. "Does she play?"

Anna smiled. "Yeah, actually. Beautifully. She got your ear for pitch."

Will's face relaxed into calm for the first time all morning. "No way. That's cool. That's . . . really cool."

"You want to meet her?"

He looked surprised she'd even asked. "Of course. That's probably the only thing I do know."

"I'm headed back tomorrow . . ." she began, carefully studying his face for signs of rejection, ". . . if you want to meet us there?"

He considered this, tapping a finger on his desk. "Yeah, I guess I can do that." He paused. "You know I'm gonna need to tell my parents, right?"

Anna winced, then nodded. Betsy's reaction terrified her almost more than Will's.

"You didn't tell yours?"

"No." She tugged at a loose thread on the hem of her T-shirt. "We haven't spoken in a long time," she added quietly.

He nodded, aware he was close to touching the perennial electric fence.

"Do you want me to go with you? When you tell them?" She said it without really thinking, but she meant it. All she'd done this week was tear through everyone like a virus. The least she could do now was try to lessen the symptoms.

Will exhaled and leaned back wearily onto his chair. "I don't know. This is gonna wreck them, Annie. You know how much they loved you. Pretty sure my mom's gone to a few of your shows without telling me." He smiled darkly.

Anna knew there were plenty of people who came to see her and never let her know. But the thought of Betsy there made her stomach hurt. "I should be there," she said definitively. "I owe them that."

He contemplated that while he gazed out the window again, then finally turned to look at her. "Yeah, I guess you do."

# SIXTEEN

**Lottie**
*New York*
May 23, 2024

Anna called just as Lottie was unlocking the door to the house.

"Did you do it?" Lottie said, cradling the phone on her ear.

"Yeah." She sounded defeated.

Lottie threw her backpack on the kitchen counter and put her on speaker. "How'd it go?" she asked tentatively.

"I mean, it's over with, at least. You can't really expect something like that to go . . . well."

"That bad?"

"We're still on speaking terms. Barely. So that's something."

"That is something."

"He wants to meet you." Anna's tone was a little more upbeat now. "A lot. I think he's gonna come down later this week."

"Oh. Okay. So, like, soon." Lottie found herself wandering to the piano bench; it remained her cocoon. "How did he—what'd he say? About . . . all of it."

"I think . . ." Anna paused for a long time. "I think, in some ways, this is what he's wanted for a long time."

"Meaning . . . me?" Lottie was incredulous.

"Meaning . . . the idea of you. Obviously, I'm sure he wishes the circumstances weren't"—she exhaled like a confession—"what they are."

"So he's not, like, angry? At me."

"No. God, no. He could never be that kind of person."

Lottie felt electric relief course through her hands and lightly ran her fingers over the piano keys. Maybe he was playing right now and wondering if she were, too.

"You'll like each other," Anna added. "There's a lot about you that's similar. In all the best ways."

Because of Maya's and then Aidan's (supposed) lack of knowledge about Lottie's father, he never figured as prominently in her daydreams. She'd been single-mindedly focused on tracking down her birth mom after Maya died, which from a psychological standpoint, wasn't hard to understand. Plus, as the daughter of a single mom, she didn't miss having a dad in the same way she missed Maya, because she'd never had one to begin with.

And until Aidan slipped up, she had assumed Anna didn't even know who her father was. So while it was a relief to find out he was alive and, thankfully, not serving a life sentence, her mental family tree was a sapling. She wasn't sure if adding a new branch so soon would snap it in half. And yet, he made sense. Another musician. One with perfect pitch, at that.

How much of her love of song came from him as opposed to her? Clearly, the two were more alike than different when it came to their careers, but at the most basic level, Lottie wondered whose innate rhythms she'd inherited. When she got so lost in Charlie Parker's fast-tempoed, golden harmonies that she missed her subway stop, was that Will? And when Joni Mitchell's *Blue* touched a place so deep inside her there was no recourse but to cry, was it Anna coming through?

She knew there was no right answer, nor, really, did it matter. But it felt good, at least, to finally be able to ask the question and have there be a plausible answer. For there to be someone, instead of just a blank spot on a piece of paper.

What was totally unexpected, of course, was Will's own considerable renown. In certain niche circles—modernist classical music, for one—he was a legitimate rock star (or whatever term might apply). His fans might not ask for selfies on the street, but, as she learned, when he premiered a new work for the Boston Symphony Orchestra or the NY Phil, it was always to sold-out crowds.

And surprisingly, although most classical music wasn't generally her speed, she loved what she'd heard of his. It was a lot more accessible than a stodgy Bach or Mozart: the tempos were often galloping, and he had a way of slowly incorporating every section of the orchestra that made his crescendos exhilarating. He had *fun* with it. And it turned out she'd heard a lot of his film scores, too: he was quickly becoming the in-demand composer for everything from war flicks to sci-fi epics.

He also, genuinely, seemed like a nice guy. She'd gotten a little more daring with her Googling of him than of Anna, figuring there probably wouldn't be anything too compromising on the internet for a contemporary classical musician. She was mostly right: there was a small but vocal Reddit community that did find him to be the "sexiest" of living composers, which she found hysterical, and a little gross. But it was also slim pickings, she'd have to imagine.

Her favorite article she'd found so far was an interview he'd done with *GQ* earlier in the year, when he was nominated for an Oscar for Best Original Score:

## *Maestro Will See You Now*

**Conducting, Composing, Scoring:**
**Is There Anything Will Pendleton Can't Do?**

*By Paul Einsiedler*

Will Pendleton might be the biggest name in music that you've never heard. The thirty-eight-year-old has a chance to be the youngest EGOT (that's Emmy, Grammy, Oscar, and Tony, naturally) winner ever if he snags his O at February's ceremony. And let's just say the house money is on him: he's nominated not once, but twice for two different film scores. Oh, did we forget to mention that he went to Brookfield and Juilliard and had a commission from the NY Phil before he graduated college?

Since then, he's written works for virtually every major symphony orchestra, from the Vienna Philharmonic to the Royal Concertgebouw, as well as penned some of the past decade's most memorable film and TV scores, for directors ranging from Scorsese to Gerwig. Maybe you've heard of them? . . .

And it went on like that for a few fawning paragraphs. But this exchange was Lottie's favorite bit:

***GQ***: What would you say your personal style is?

***Will Pendleton***: [*laughs*] Whatever's clean?

***GQ***: You must wear a tux when you're conducting?

***WP***: Sure, if it calls for it. If it were up to me, I'd do it in my sweatpants. It's a lot easier to move around.

***GQ***: So the pomp and circumstance of traditional classical music isn't your thing?

***WP***: Definitely not. I think it can be really alienating for a lot of younger would-be listeners. I'm trying to make sure we make new fans, not lose them.

***GQ***: What do you listen to other than classical?

***WP***: Oh, everything. I'm a pretty voracious listener. But lately, I've been really digging deep into stuff that came out when I was starting college. Something about that twenty-year mark, I guess.

***GQ***: Like what?

***WP***: A lot of Canadian bands, actually. Stars, Broken Social Scene, Metric. A good friend and I loved Feist at the time, so I've been rediscovering her.

***GQ***: It seems like you're on the go a lot, but what do you like to do in your downtime?

***WP***: I'm afraid this is going to be the most boring interview in the history of your magazine. I read. I'm trying to learn how to be a better cook. I have a place in upstate New York I try to escape to whenever possible.

***GQ***: What do you like to do there?

***WP***: I play a lot of piano by myself [*laughs*]. I like sitting outside on the porch and watching the sunset.

He seemed so . . . normal. And between Aidan—and now Anna's—more dramatic career antics, that was refreshing. It felt like her.

The next morning, Lottie had her last rehearsal with the Pembroke orchestra before their performance that weekend. She could readily admit that the talent within the group varied widely (to put it kindly), but at least everyone was on key by now. Perfect pitch was a gift, but it could also be excruciating when someone was horribly out of tune.

As they filed out at the end of the period, Lottie lagged behind, hoping to grab Mr. Shean's attention.

"You look like you have a question, Lottie," he said, gathering up his music sheets.

"Oh! Well. I've been listening to some new contemporary classical stuff, and I was curious if you knew who Will Pendleton was?" She could hear how high her voice climbed at the end of the sentence and hoped it wasn't too obvious.

"Yeah, of course. You see *Fire at Dawn*? He did the score for that. Gorgeous stuff. Pretty young guy, too. In his thirties, I think."

She didn't know exactly why, but for some reason, Mr. Shean's imprimatur mattered to her more than any award or accolade that Will could win. It moved him from the realm of national symphonies and Hollywood blockbusters to something much more accessible.

"So you think he's good?"

"I do. I like his work a lot, and not just his film stuff. He's done some pieces for the New York Phil that are incredible. But doesn't really matter what I think. Does his work make you feel something?"

She thought this over. "Yeah, actually, it does."

"Then his job is done." Mr. Shean gestured to the now-empty orchestra seats. "You know, I think one of the best things about music is how it can create a connection between two people: through time, through distance, through cultures. You can communicate without ever actually speaking. Will Pendleton composed something never knowing you'd hear it, but look what effect it's had." He shook his head in wonder. "Doesn't get much better than that."

# SEVENTEEN

**Anna**
*Boston*
May 24, 2024

She didn't sleep. Even with a Xanax and a whiskey chaser. This reentry—into the before—had her confronting people and places she never thought she'd see again: Brookfield, the Pendleton home. Him. Maybe, though, this was simply the reprise of the song. She'd have to wait to see if it played out in major or minor key.

They'd decided to meet Will's parents for breakfast at their house the next morning, before they decamped for New York. He picked her up at seven-thirty: unbearably early by her standards, but she wasn't about to make a fuss. If it were possible, he looked even more sleep-deprived than the day before, just now with more stubble and darker half-moons under his eyes. He didn't offer as much as a hello as she slid into the front seat.

"You sure you're okay to drive?"

"I'm fine," he said coolly.

In all four years of college, she'd never seen him angry at her. It was now the default. They drove in uncomfortable silence toward Brookline.

"What'd you tell your parents?" she finally ventured.

"That you were in town and we reconnected. That you wanted to say hi. Didn't want to freak them out over the phone."

"They've got grandkids already, right?" With four boys, there'd be a litter by now, she imagined.

"Funnily enough, no."

"You're kidding." Anna turned to stare at him.

"Nope. Charlie has yet to settle down, Ben and his wife are still trying, and Matt just broke up with his boyfriend."

"Matt's gay?"

Will chuckled. "That one took all of us by surprise."

"Huh." She leaned back in her seat. "So we're about to tell your parents they're grandparents for the first time. And we've kept their granddaughter from them for . . . sixteen years?"

"Should be a really fun breakfast."

Anna felt lightheaded. Will's parents, with their seemingly infinite hospitality and capacity for love, didn't deserve this. They should have a dozen grandkids, all tumbling down the stairs on Christmas morning, or making pillow forts in their living room. She leaned her head onto her forearms on the dashboard. "I'm gonna throw up."

"Welcome to the club."

They pulled up to the house about ten minutes later. It was just as beautiful as she remembered, now with springtime peonies in red and pink dotting the beds in the front yard. They sat in silence in the parked car, both loath to move first.

"What did you tell them happened after college?" she asked him quietly.

He flinched, briefly. "Not a lot. I think they could guess something went down." They were both giving a wide berth to discussing that phone call she made from Ireland. "And you know how they are; they didn't pry too much." He paused. "They asked about you for a long time, though."

The front door opened. Charles and Betsy appeared in the frame, waving down to them with wide grins.

"Let's get this over with," Will muttered, and hopped out of the car, throwing his sunglasses on.

"Anna! Welcome home, honey." Betsy squeezed her hard in an embrace. Then, in a whisper, "I *love* your new album."

Anna hugged her back just as tightly; she hadn't allowed herself to think about how much she'd missed them until now. "I'm sorry it's taken me this long to get back here."

"Well, we're glad to see you now." Betsy held her out at arm's length. "You're too skinny, though. Let's get you fed. Will, darling, why does your face look like that?"

"Great to see you, too, Mom." He brushed by them, giving his mother a perfunctory kiss on the cheek.

Betsy had already set up quite the spread in the dining room: smoked salmon, fruit salad, scrambled eggs, and a tall pitcher of (Anna would bet) fresh-squeezed orange juice. She'd missed these meals, too.

The bulk of breakfast passed by easily enough: there was so much to catch up on that it kept the conversation flowing, even if Will was far quieter than normal. Betsy and Charles updated her on the latest from the other kids, how they'd had to replace the siding on the Maine house earlier than planned because of a giant nor'easter. Anna filled them in on her tour plans for that summer, the new apartment she'd bought in Soho that she'd barely spent the night in.

At the end of the meal, she and Will gathered up the plates and walked them back to the kitchen. They had, so far, failed miserably at even attempting to bring it up. "How do we do this?" she hissed.

"I don't know. You have more practice than I do—what do you think?" He dropped the plates into the sink with a crash.

"Thanks for that."

"Sorry." He leaned over the counter, head low in defeat. "Christ, I feel like I'm sixteen and about to get grounded."

"We just have to rip off the Band-Aid."

"Like it's that easy? Fuck. I need a drink." He opened the fridge, peered inside, and grabbed a bottle of champagne, then popped it open over the sink. "Shockingly, for this household, this is all the booze that's in there."

They walked back to the table, Will holding the bottle, both of them eyeing the other to see if they'd start talking first.

"Oh, are we celebrating something?" Betsy asked hopefully, eyes darting between the two.

Will snorted. "Not exactly." He tipped himself a heavy pour and topped it with a teeny splash of juice.

"Everything okay?" Betsy asked slowly.

"No," Will finally said. Anna kicked him—hard—under the table.

Betsy looked from one to the other with alarm.

"Mom, no one's dying."

She put a shaky hand to her chest in relief.

"But we . . . uh. We . . ." He was floundering.

"We had a baby," Anna finished for him. "Sixteen years ago. I gave her up for adoption. Will never knew. Well, until a couple days ago." She grabbed the champagne and filled her own glass.

Betsy and Charles were staring at them, unblinking and silent. The only noise was the fraught ticking of the grandfather clock in the foyer.

Charles, uncharacteristically, spoke first. "You got her pregnant, Will? I didn't even know you two were dating."

Will cleared his throat. "We . . . weren't." This was excruciating.

"So you weren't together?"

"No."

"Did you use protection?"

Will rubbed his temples in deep irritation. "For fuck's sake, Dad! Does it matter now?"

Charles shrugged. "I was just curious."

Betsy drew a wobbly breath and eventually addressed them. "You had a *baby*? Where is she now?"

Anna couldn't bring herself to look up; she swirled her champagne in the glass instead. "New York."

Betsy nodded quickly, then pushed her chair back from the table with a loud screech. "Excuse me, one minute." Covering her mouth, she hurried out of the kitchen and up the stairs to her bedroom. She slammed the door so hard the glasses shook on the table.

"I'll go," Anna said quietly.

Will nodded.

Anna knocked softly, then opened the door halfway. Betsy was sitting on an upholstered bench at the foot of her bed, sobbing with her face in her hands.

"Hey," Anna said, unsure if she was invited to move any closer.

Betsy, still hiccupping, motioned for Anna to come sit next to her. "I'm sorry. I wasn't expecting that. You two. A baby." She paused. "I guess not really a baby, anymore."

"Please don't apologize," Anna said, taking a seat beside her. "That's not your job here."

Betsy reached out and interlaced her fingers with Anna's. "You must've been terrified. This was all happening while you were in Ireland?"

Anna nodded slowly. She was caught off guard by Betsy's grace in the moment. Her compassion made it hard not to wonder what she would have said sixteen years ago. *It all could have been so different*, she thought, Betsy's warm palm still in her own. It could've been so different.

"There will come a time when I will be furious with you," Betsy murmured, still grasping Anna's hand. "But right now, what I am is devastated that you felt you had to do that alone. We would've been there for you, honey. All of you." She wiped at the corner of her eye with her free hand. "What's her name?"

"Charlotte."

Betsy smiled softly. "You know that was Will's grandma's name?"

Anna shook her head.

"World works in mysterious ways . . . How is he?"

Anna shrugged after a moment. "I just blew his life up." She hadn't admitted that to herself until now. "But he's coming down to New York to meet her. And then, I'm sure she'd love to meet you, too."

Betsy's eyes filled up again. "I'd like that very much." They sat quietly for a few minutes; Anna leaned her head on her shoulder. "He was . . . not okay after you left. Not for a long time," Betsy finally said. "It broke my heart. But I didn't want to pester him, so I left it alone. In retrospect, that was probably not the best way to handle it." Betsy turned to face her. "What I'm trying to say is whatever happens now, you need to be careful with him. I'm not sure if he could go through that again. You understand?"

"But he's so angry, Bets."

"Can you blame him?" she said. "He'll forgive you. No one's ever understood him the way you do. He won't want to lose that again. I hope you don't, either." She patted Anna's knee. "We better get back down there."

Back in the car, still parked in the driveway, Will wearily leaned his head on the steering wheel and started laughing. Anna stared at him, bemused.

"Christ." He exhaled. "I'd find this all hysterical if it weren't happening to me."

"I'm surprised your dad didn't ask if I was ovulating."

"Well, to be fair, I guess we already know the answer to that." He smiled wryly, then shook his head in disbelief. "We slept together one time and this happened?"

"Twice."

"What?" He looked sideways at her.

"It was twice. If we're being accurate." Anna fought to suppress a smile.

He thought that over, then chuckled. "Guess so. Well, whatever. I should play the lottery more."

"Who knows? Maybe you've got lots of little Wills out there."

"That would be my fucking luck, wouldn't it?" He eased the car out of the driveway. Anna had always loved driving with him, for a reason she couldn't quite pinpoint. He was graceful in unexpected ways.

"So lots of ladies, then?"

He gave her a short snort. "Not exactly."

"Some?"

"You want my relationship history? That's rich, after everything you've neglected to share." He sighed. "You remember Jess?"

"Bassoon Jess?"

"Yep."

"She always had a thing for you."

"Yeah, well, we reconnected in New York. Dated for a while. That's been my only serious thing, really."

"Why'd it end?"

He shrugged. "Couldn't see myself with her long-term. Don't think she felt the same. It got a little . . . sticky at the end there. You?"

She shook her head. "Nothing serious. I'm on the road basically all the time. Doesn't leave a ton of room for dating. And it's harder now." She frowned. "You don't know if someone likes you, or the idea of you. Mostly seems to be the latter, which makes for pretty unrealistic expectations."

"They're surprised at your undying love for Teddy Grahams?" he said, throwing her a quick smile.

"They're delicious. Do not hate on the Teddys."

"They're gross. But what about, uh . . . Rory?" She could tell he was trying for casual. He'd failed.

She laughed. "You know about that?"

"I mean, your name shows up in headlines sometimes, Anna," he mumbled. "It's kind of hard not to click."

"Fair. Still can't believe that's a thing, but fair . . . So, Rory." She puffed out her cheeks. "Wouldn't say either of us really brings out the best in each other. Kind of an on-again, off-again thing."

"Then why do it?"

Anna's turn to shrug. Because the sex is good and he makes her forget what she's running from? "I think we keep hoping we're actually different people than we are."

"Who do you want him to be?"

*More like you?* It startled her how fast she thought it. "I don't know. A better listener? Less . . . wild? That's pretty much why we ended things last time."

He was quiet for a moment as he changed lanes. "I always thought—I thought he was the reason you . . . you know. 'Cause then, you guys were together—"

"Oh god, Will," she murmured. "No. No, that happened . . . after. He was never—"

The car in front of Will's stopped short. He slammed on the brakes and flung out his right arm protectively in front of her. "Sorry," he mumbled, whipping it back quickly as if touching her contaminated him. Maybe it did. They drove in silence for a minute or two. "So," he finally said. "You're in off-again mode?"

"Who's asking?" She turned to face him.

He kept his eyes on the road. "Loyal readers of internet gossip, of course."

"No one else?"

He shook his head. "No one else."

They pulled up to the Four Seasons; Will put the car in park. "I'm gonna go pack. I'll see you in the city."

* * *

Anna called Kendall as soon as she got back to her room. He needed to know, obviously, but she was already bracing for what would surely be a Kendall-sized reaction; he only had one speed. She resisted the urge to pour herself another drink: her head was already fuzzy from all the champagne.

"What up, Miss B.?"

"Hey. So, remember when you asked about Will? Pendleton?"

"Sure do."

"I . . . might not have told you everything."

"Yeah, no shit. Are you going to now?" Anna heard keyboard keys clacking in the background. "I'm Googling. Did something happen?"

"No. Well, not yet." She paused. "Are you in a calm place, Kendall? I need you to be in a calm place before I tell you what I'm about to tell you."

"I haven't been in a calm place since I took you on as a client. No offense."

"None taken."

"I'm sitting down. Talk to me."

"This stays between us, obviously. I'm just telling you in case it spirals. Which, I don't think it will." She collapsed onto the couch.

"Okay," he said slowly. "Obviously, you fucked. Is he married? Is he Trumpy?" More clacking. "Did you have a love child or something?" Kendall laughed at his own dumb joke.

Anna was silent.

"Hello?"

She blew out a big breath; she was getting pretty good at relating this story.

"I was joking," he said once she'd finished telling him. "Please tell me you're joking. Is it April? I haven't had time to look at a calendar in years."

"Funny, Will had the same reaction."

"This is for serious? You have a secret baby with Will fucking Pendleton?"

"I mean, she's sixteen now."

"Oh. Great." She heard him set the phone down, then muffled screaming. "Okay. What do you need me to do?"

"Nothing. I'm handling it. We're both going back to New York today. I just thought you should know."

"Yes, thank you for that not-at-all-last-minute heads-up. And what does *handling it* mean? Do I need to get NDAs out to anyone? Is this gonna pop up on *People* in like three hours? Who's Will's publicist? I should reach out for crisis control." Even more clacking.

She snorted. "There is negative chance Will has a publicist. But no one needs to sign anything. No one's giving any interviews. I've got this." She wasn't sure how convincing she sounded.

Kendall was quiet for a moment. "I'm sorry, let me rewind. Are you okay?"

"No, of course not." She closed her eyes and leaned back on the couch. Maybe she did need that drink. "It's a fucked-up situation of entirely my own making. But I'd gotten really good pretending this day would never happen."

"You want me to come over later?"

Anna sighed. "I think I've gotta be by myself for a minute."

"Understood. Get some rest, okay?"

"Highly unlikely, but I'll try."

"One more thing?"

"Yeah?"

"I'm proud of you, at least. For picking a hot baby daddy."

"Your emotional intelligence is staggering." Anna covered her eyes with her hand and let out a small laugh in spite of herself.

"That's why I'm great at my job. Later, kid."

# EIGHTEEN

**Lottie**
*New York*
May 25, 2024

"What're you gonna wear?" Sasha was lying on her back on Lottie's bed, playing with some new TikTok filter that gave her glittery, winged eye makeup.

Lottie stood in front of her closet, idly sliding hangers over. "I dunno. Does it matter?"

"*Does it matter* . . . Lottie!" Sasha sat up with a start. "Even I picked out something special for the occasion. I stole my mom's Celine." She smoothed down her tank top admiringly.

"Ew, Sash."

Sasha, after seeing Will's photos earlier, had no trouble pronouncing him hot "for a kind-of dad." Lottie felt this transgression was almost enough grounds to banish her from the house before he arrived, but she needed the moral support more.

"It's an objective fact. It's not like he's your *dad* dad, anyway." Sasha looked up from her phone. "Sorry, is that an okay thing to say?"

Lottie shrugged. "It's the truth."

"You realize you're, like, a *double* nepo baby now," she said, taking Lottie's picture with the filter. "Mr. Shean is gonna shit himself when he finds out."

Lottie spun around. "We're not telling Mr. Shean. We're not telling anyone else, remember? I barely know Anna and I haven't even met Will."

"Is she coming, too? I wanna meet her."

Lottie shook her head. While she was still unclear as to the exact level of animosity between them, even friendly seemed a reach. And, considering how convoluted the whole situation was already, it seemed infinitely easier to meet Will on her own; they'd made a plan to check out a new immersive music exhibit. If nothing else, it would be a good distraction if conversation stalled.

Lottie finally yanked a random red shirt off a hanger and pulled it over her head. That and jeans would have to do. She turned toward Sasha for approval. "Fine?" The doorbell rang before she had time to answer. "Shit."

Sasha grabbed her hands. "You ready?"

Lottie squeezed her back. "Probably not. We're about to find out."

From the top of the stairs and looking through the frosted glass, Lottie could just make out a blurry Will, standing in the vestibule between the two doors. Her knees suddenly buckled like rusty hinges. "Okay, I think I am nervous?" She paused halfway down and gripped the railing.

"Lottie, literally everyone likes you." Sasha was right behind her and put an encouraging pair of hands on her shoulders. "And he has to anyway, right? He is your dad."

"Kind of."

"Well, whatever. But he's related to you. That counts for a lot. Now, *go*." Sasha gently pushed her forward.

Lottie whipped her head around when she got to the landing, eyes large with panic. "What if I don't like him? What if he's, like, really awkward? Or mean?" She was aware she was stalling for time, but actually greeting him seemed unfathomable.

"Then, honestly?" Sasha looked at the door and then back to her. "You never see him again and you're right back where you started."

Lottie took a deep breath, nodded, then walked to open the door. Her biological father stood in front of her, his hands shoved nervously into the front pockets of his jeans. He was taller than she'd expected, but otherwise looked the same as he did in pictures: wavy brown hair like hers, a kind face. Horrifyingly, though, he was also in a red T-shirt. The two of them looked like they were about to take one of those dumb family photos on the beach where everyone is color coordinated.

"Hey," Will said simply, his face relaxing into a relieved smile.

"Hey."

They stood there awkwardly, staring at each other, neither knowing what should come next.

"Hi, Dr. Pendleton!" Sasha, bless her, called jauntily from the stairs. She walked right up to him and stuck out her hand. "I'm Sasha, Lottie's best friend. Come in."

Will, a little discombobulated, followed Sasha into the kitchen, looking around the foyer admiringly as he did so. "Oh, uh, great! Nice to meet you, Sasha. And you don't have to call me doctor," he added with a laugh. "I don't think anyone has since I defended my dissertation a million years ago."

"Trust me, she's been waiting to deploy that all morning," Lottie said dryly.

"Is Aidan here?" he asked haltingly as he scanned the kitchen. Little did he know this would be the last place to find him.

Lottie shook her head. "He's getting ready for Pitti Uomo."

Will looked at her blankly.

"It's a trade show, in Florence?"

"Oh. Is he gone a lot?"

"Um, depends on the season, I guess? He says hi, though. I know he'd like to see you."

"Same. We had some interesting nights when he'd visit," Will said, raising his eyebrows.

"Sounds like Aidan," Lottie replied with a grin.

Sasha looked from one to the other, taking the temperature of the room. "I think my mom is calling?" she said, already backing out of the kitchen. "I should probably head home. Nice to meet you Dr.—Will." She squeezed Lottie's shoulder on her way out.

"She seems . . . sweet," Will managed once she'd left.

Lottie laughed. "She is, I swear. Just a little overexcited."

Will looked at her, astounded. "You have the same laugh," he finally said. "Fuck." He chuckled softly. "I mean, sorry. I just didn't realize how much you'd . . ." He trailed off.

"Look like her?"

"Not just that. It's"—he gestured around her—"your mannerisms, the way you move." He shook his head, baffled. "I wasn't expecting that, I guess. Anyway." He exhaled a big breath, like a fresh start. "I'm Will. It's really nice to finally meet you, Lottie."

And then he smiled, and it was like finding your favorite glove that you thought you'd lost right next to you on the sidewalk. *Oh, there you are*, Lottie found herself thinking. *You've been here this whole time.*

Will had given her free range to plan their day, which, at first, had left Lottie stumped. What do you do with a sort-of dad that you've never met that's both low-stakes enough to be fun, but still gives you a chance to get to know each other? Thankfully, Mr. Shean had come to the rescue. Not that he knew it: he'd mentioned during rehearsal that week he'd visited a massive, spherical pop-up concert hall at the Shed. Perfect, Lottie thought: unique enough to be interesting, and it would give them a chance to chat music, which she would have wanted to do even if they weren't related.

And the hall, Sonic Sphere, was legitimately cool. It was

gigantic—sixty-five feet across—and seemed to be levitating in the middle of the cavernous, hangar-sized exhibit space.

"Damn," Will said, as the curtain parted and they approached the giant orb. "This beats Carnegie as far as entrances go."

Inside, instead of traditional theater seats, were netted areas made out of rope: the kind of thing typically found in a kids' play space, not a concert venue. Lottie and Will settled into one on their backs, the domed ceiling pulsating in a dozen different colors of light. She'd picked Steve Reich's *Music for 18 Musicians* for their show, figuring it was probably the one with which Will would be the most familiar.

"Do you know this piece at all?" he whispered to her before the show started.

Lottie shook her head.

"Ah." He grinned and put a hand over his heart. "One of my all-time favorites. Reich is a huge reason why I wanted to be a composer. A lot of minimalism can be so cold, but there's such . . . warmth in this. You can feel the breath and the heartbeats of every musician."

"All eighteen?" Lottie said with a cheeky smile.

"All eighteen."

The lights dimmed. They sat in silence for the next hour as the multiple pianos, marimbas, and human voices washed over them, the lights overhead dancing in time with the music. Chords flowed from major to minor and back again, or inverted in on themselves as each section pulsed rhythmically into the next. It was unlike anything Lottie had ever heard: she was transfixed from the first few bars. They were quiet for a few minutes after it ended, letting the music sink deeper into their skin.

"What'd you think?" he finally asked.

Lottie shook her head, clutching for the right words. "It's so many emotions at once. And there are parts that leave you hanging, like they're . . ."

"Unresolved?"

She nodded. "The musical resolution is not straightforward at all."

"It's kind of like life, right?" Will said, sitting up. "There's so much that gets thrown at you. And some of it gets resolved, and some of it"—he shrugged—"you just have to accept."

It was a sparkling New York spring day, the kind that makes you forget how ugly it'll be by August. They decided to walk the High Line after they left the Shed, weaving in and out of the many tourists taking selfies or posing with the statues.

"You just had a birthday, right?"

She nodded. "May third."

"2008?"

"Yup."

"Huh." Will looked as if he'd just solved a riddle.

"What?"

"That was the same night as my first performance with the Phil. Just a wild coincidence. Turned out to be a big day for all three of us, I guess." He exhaled. "Anyway. Anna tells me you play piano?"

"I do. But, you know, not like you two."

"Well, we have a few years on you. And it is our jobs. I'd love to hear you play, though—if you felt comfortable," he added quickly.

"Yeah, maybe? I actually have this kinda dumb recital tomorrow, for my school's orchestra."

"Really?" His face lit up like a little kid's.

"Oh, I didn't mean it like that." Lottie waved her hands no. "You, of all people, should definitely not come."

He put his hands up. "That's exciting, though. What're you guys playing?"

"'Rhapsody in Blue,' Copland's 'Rodeo'—it's a very patriotic program. 'Cause, you know, great time to be an American," she said with a dry smile.

Will chuckled. "But Gershwin! I love Gershwin. You know he published his first song when he was seventeen? . . . Hold on, one sec." He pulled his buzzing phone out of his pocket, glanced at it quickly, and shoved it back in with exasperation.

"You can answer, if you need to?" Lottie motioned to the phone.

"No, it's fine. Just my mom," he said sheepishly. "She's called, like, three times this afternoon."

"Your mom," she echoed. "So you have, like, a normal family, then?" She hadn't learned much about Anna's, but it didn't appear she really had one at all. And in the information overload of the past week, it hadn't yet occurred to her to look into Will's.

"Normal, maybe not so much?" He smiled. "But a mom, a dad, three older brothers. They're all pretty curious about you, as you can probably imagine. And by that, I mean my mother would literally run here from Boston right now, if I let her."

Lottie laughed. "Well, it would be great to meet all of them, at some point."

Would she call them grandparents? Uncles? She'd cross that bridge when she had to. But if they were anything like Will, she thought she'd like to know them, too.

# NINETEEN

**Anna**
*New York*
May 25, 2024

"I need to tell you something, but you have to promise you're not gonna act on it."

It was Will. He sounded more energized (and friendlier) than Anna had heard him all week. She narrowed her eyes at the phone, even though he couldn't see her. "Why?"

"Because I know you."

"You haven't seen me for over a decade," she said, somewhere between mock and actually incensed.

"Okay," he said, as if readying for a wager. "Lottie's school orchestra has a performance tomorrow, but she doesn't want us to go."

"Oh, we're definitely going."

"Anna!"

"You wouldn't have said anything if you didn't wanna go," she retorted. "You're only calling to get my blessing. I know how you operate, too. Tell me I'm wrong."

He hesitated. "They're doing Gershwin."

"You love Gershwin."

He sighed. "I *love* Gershwin."

"When is it?" She pulled up her calendar for the next day on her phone.

"Don't know. And I definitely can't ask without making her suspicious."

"Quinn—my assistant—can figure it out. She's freakishly good at this kind of thing."

"I don't know," he wavered. "Isn't this a big no-no for trust and stuff? We literally just met."

"Quinn can just find out when it is," Anna said reassuringly. "And then we can decide, okay?"

"Yeah, okay. Then we can decide." They both knew this was a lie.

"How'd it go today, anyway?" she asked carefully. Anna fully understood Lottie's reasons for wanting to meet him on her own, but she'd been jumpy all day waiting for a report from one of them.

"I mean, I need some time to process still, but good. Really good. She's awesome." He sounded relieved. And happy. "And maybe this is just me projecting, but I see a lot of me in her. Which is cool. Incomprehensible still, but cool."

"No, I get it," Anna said softly.

"It's hard to wrap my head around that she's mine . . . ours. Whatever you want to call it."

"I know. It's a mindfuck." It was also hard to wrap her head around having this conversation with him. So, she wouldn't. "I gotta go. I'll let you know what Quinn finds out."

As was no surprise to Anna, within the hour Quinn had not only found what time the performance was, but texted her a PDF of the flyer: 2:00 p.m. at Pembroke's main building. She sent it to Will as soon as she got it.

"Fuck," he texted back. "We're doing this, aren't we?"

"So are we texting her we're coming? Are we sneaking in and out? What's the plan here?" Will's nervous energy had always manifested in lots of frantic gesticulations. It was very conductorly of him. At the moment, as they were walking from his hotel to the school, he appeared to be in the middle of the finale of the *1812 Overture.*

"Well, we're not the most inconspicuous," Anna said. "You saw what happened at your class."

"Speak for yourself. No one knows—or cares—what I look like. *And* you came in late."

"Yes, sorry, Professor," she said, the words drawn out with sarcasm. "I say we just go, don't say anything. There will be tons of parents there: we can lose ourselves in the crowd."

He looked skeptical, but nodded. "I mean, I don't have a better idea?"

They arrived at the front doors a little earlier than expected: Will also walked fast when he was worried about something. They were debating getting a coffee when Anna heard Lottie behind her.

"What are you two doing here?" Lottie said slowly, approaching them like she was trying to scare off a bear at a campground.

"Shit," Anna said under her breath, and turned around. Lottie was wearing the sort of late-nineties spaghetti strap floral sundress Anna wore herself back then. She looked adorable, but also, quite pissed. "Okay, don't be mad," she said, trying for soothing. "But . . . we really wanted to come?"

Lottie glared at Will. "You told her?"

He lifted his hands up in atonement. "I'm sorry! It just kinda slipped out."

Anna opened her mouth wide in astonishment. "False!"

Lottie had turned beet red. "Oh my god, it doesn't matter. Just get inside." She ushered them both into the school's lobby, which Anna now realized, was actually the foyer of the mansion in which it was housed.

"This is so, so cringe," Lottie muttered as she hustled them down a long hallway toward the school's auditorium. She paused outside the double doors to address them. "To be clear, I'm not embarrassed by you. But I haven't really told anyone about you, either. And I've got too much on my plate to do it today. So if you're here, you are not here for me. You understand?"

They both nodded vigorously.

"Okay. I'm going inside. When you come in, you can sit somewhere in the back, stay quiet, and then you will leave when it's over." She looked sternly from one to the other. "We can meet up later, maybe. Got it?"

Anna gave her a thumbs-up.

She pointed a finger at them before pulling open the auditorium door. "Don't do anything weird."

Will stifled a laugh after she slipped inside. "Sound familiar?"

Anna frowned. "What?"

"That was literally you when you get bossy."

She rolled her eyes at him in response. He was, probably, not wrong, but she'd never give him the satisfaction.

Eventually, mothers dripping in Van Cleef Alhambra and fathers tapping distractedly on their phones started filing into the auditorium. Anna and Will dutifully grabbed seats in the back and kept to themselves, Will looking physically pained to have to abstain from chatting about Gershwin's impact on the American vernacular.

After a hush, the performance kicked off with Copland's "Rodeo," which had always been a little too jaunty for Anna's taste, though the girls handled it adeptly. Will, however, flinched whenever someone was off-key.

"You have got to stop that," she hissed, elbowing him.

"You know I can't!" he whispered back.

After some quick applause, the iconic clarinet glissando opened *Rhapsody in Blue*, a piece Anna had always admired for its seamless integration of jazz and classical into one swelling, joyous explosion of sound. It also contained a fairly difficult and athletic piano part. And while they hadn't discussed it, she guessed Will was equally curious as to how Lottie would handle it. But when her fingers tore across the keys during the cadenza with a bravura all her own, Anna realized she could untangle the knot of nerves deep in her own chest. Lottie was in her element. She communicated with the piano the same way Anna did: like two halves of the same circle.

"Jesus," Will whispered, astounded. "She's got it. She plays like you."

As Lottie pounded out the final fortissimo chords, Anna felt tears spring, fast and unwanted. How was it possible for her to be here, to be sixteen, to be playing Gershwin while they watched?

She glanced at Will, who had turned away from her as he rubbed his eyes. She nudged him gently as the applause started. "Are you crying?"

"No." But he was sniffling, just a little. "Are you?"

"No." She had to turn away herself. "I don't know. Fuck."

He shook his head slowly. "Fuck."

Anna looked toward the stage. Lottie was surreptitiously scanning the audience for them; she ventured a wave. In return, Lottie granted them an infinitesimally small nod of her head and an even smaller smile. Anna considered this a win.

They almost made it out of the school without getting spotted. And surprisingly, it was Will who sunk them, which later delighted Anna to no small degree. They were standing on the sidewalk when the school's music director approached them and tapped Will on the shoulder.

"Excuse me? I hate to bother, but you're Will Pendleton, right?"

Will, flummoxed, turned around. "Oh! Yep. One and the same."

Anna slipped her sunglasses on: her only line of defense. This was potentially going downhill fast, at least as far as Lottie was concerned.

The director's face broke out into a grin. "Oh man, what an honor!" He paused. "I was just talking about you with one of the girls this week. Can I ask who brings you here today?"

Will, Anna knew, was nearly incapable of lying convincingly. "Um," he stammered. "I'm . . . actually friends with Aidan Thomas? And he couldn't make it, so we came instead."

Anna would have stomped on his foot, but that probably fell under Lottie's injunction of nothing "weird."

"How wonderful." He turned to Anna and stuck out a hand. "Nice to meet you. I'm Nate Shean."

"Anna." She shook his hand.

He stared at her, unblinking. ". . . Buckley?"

She nodded slowly. "Also one and the same."

He laughed, a little stunned. "Well, this is more star power than we've ever had at one of these. Thank you both for coming, seriously." He shook his head in amazement. "Lottie didn't tell me about any of this."

"Yeah, I don't think she exactly wanted us to come. But it was a fantastic performance," she said. "And really special to see her up there."

"She's incredible. But I don't need to tell you that. I'm sure you've seen her over the years."

Anna nodded noncommittally. Lottie appeared in the front door just then and spotted the three of them talking before Anna could shuffle Will away.

"And there she is now," Nate said, beaming. "Excellent work today, Lottie. Not that I'm surprised."

Lottie shot them a death glare before composing herself for her director. "Thanks, Mr. Shean."

"I met, uh, Aidan's friends?" Nate said, gesturing to Anna

and Will. "What a nice surprise. You'll have to fill me in more later, yeah?"

"Yes, *such* a surprise," Lottie answered sweetly. Too sweetly. "Unfortunately, we have to get going. Now. Right, guys?"

"Right," Will said, picking up what she was throwing down. "Great to meet you, Nate."

"Likewise," he said, clearly still a little puzzled.

"This way," Lottie said, and started power walking down the street. "What did you say to him?" she demanded when they were a safe-enough distance away.

"That we were Aidan's friends?" Will said, wincing. Lottie made an exasperated face. "I'm sorry! I went blank in the moment."

"You had one job, you two." Lottie pointed a finger in the air. "One job."

"You sounded amazing, though," Anna said.

"Thanks." She brushed off the compliment with a wave of her hand. "But Chloe, on the clarinet—"

"Was a little flat?" Will finished for her.

Lottie smiled at him. "Yeah, exactly." She slowed her pace; she seemed to be calming down. "Well, now that you're here . . . do you want to come over?" she asked tentatively.

Anna looked at Will. He shrugged and nodded. "Yeah," she said. "Let's do it."

Anna knew Aidan had done well for himself, but even she was taken aback at the generous proportions of his town house. Lottie led them into the foyer, which was all creamy textures; sleek, modern furniture; and warm wood paneling. It was exquisite, and very Aidan.

"We can sit outside? It's nice out." Lottie was already headed through the sprawling kitchen to the house's backyard.

"Outside!" Will mouthed to Anna, eyes wide.

Lottie plopped into a chair on the flagstone patio; the two of them followed suit. "Sorry if I was a little . . . abrupt earlier. I'm not used to people coming to these things. Aidan's almost always busy. And, I *did* tell you not to come," she added pointedly to Will.

"We should've called," he said, shrugging his shoulders in apology. "I think we both just got a little excited to see you play. Once a music nerd, always a music nerd, right?"

"I don't think anyone would doubt you're still a nerd," Anna murmured. He gave her the middle finger in reply.

Lottie looked from one to the other, eyes hopping nervously between them. "Okay, but what'd you think? For real?"

"Anna cried." Will pointed a thumb in her direction.

Anna felt herself blush. "Whatever, so did he."

Lottie laughed lightly. "I'll take it. Guess I need to see you guys live now, too. Only fair."

"You have an open invite to any performance of mine," he said. "I've got a few in the fall."

"Same here. Tour's kicking off pretty soon, actually," Anna said. "What are you up to after school gets out?"

Lottie shrugged. "Probably working for Aidan. Normally, it's Paris or London. Sort of general intern stuff."

"That sounds just . . . horrible," Will said drolly.

"I mean, it doesn't suck. Less glamorous than it seems, though. It's a lot of trips to the post office."

Anna nodded in Will's direction. "What about you?"

He sighed. "Let's see. Not Paris? Rehearsing a couple new pieces with the BSO, prepping for the fall semester. It'll be fairly low-key."

"Would you guys ever wanna come on tour?" Her id blurted it out before she could override it.

Will chuckled, then stopped abruptly when he saw Anna's expression. "Oh, you're serious?"

Was she? Being in the same space with both of them for the

first time left her feeling centered in a way she couldn't really articulate. She wanted more.

"I mean, just for a little bit—it's an American leg, so not nearly as annoying as a European. Worse food, but fewer flights. You could be . . . my intern?" she said to Lottie. "And you." She turned to Will. "I could actually really use some help on the arrangements for the new stuff I'm working on. So I'd, you know, *hire* you guys. It wouldn't be indentured servitude or something." She had no idea where any of this was coming from. Her tour manager would be furious if he heard her.

They were both silent and staring at the ground. She'd taken it too far. Anna wondered how hard it would be to melt into the flagstones and evaporate.

"I don't know," Lottie finally said. "I'd need to talk to Aidan."

"No, I get it. It was dumb. Forget I said anything." Anna curled her knees up to her chest.

"I'm not saying no," Lottie said, looking up. "It could be fun. Could be good for all of us to, you know, *bond*, or whatever." The word *bond* dripped with teenage disdain.

Anna looked at Will. He was tapping out a nervous four-on-the-floor with his pointer finger. "I'd need . . . I'd need to think on that."

"Yeah, of course," Anna said quickly. "No need to make any decisions today."

# TWENTY

**Lottie**
*New York*
May 29, 2024

The end of the school year was always a blur in the Thomas household (if that was even an appropriate moniker for the two of them). Lottie in crunch time for finals, and Aidan basically a ghost, prepping for the twin gauntlets of Paris menswear and couture weeks back to back.

It had been three days since Lottie's performance: Will was home in Boston, and Anna was starting her intensive tour prep. Aidan was back from Florence briefly, before he left for Paris, but she hadn't had a chance to bring up Anna's invitation.

The offer gave her pause for multiple reasons. Did she actually want to spend her whole summer going through the armpit of America? Plus, she still barely knew either Anna or Will; it seemed risky to throw all of them together on a tour bus. But mostly, she felt like she'd be betraying Aidan on an almost cellular level if she went.

On the flipside: an unbelievable, and perhaps singular, chance to get to know her birth parents. Both of them. And while the three hadn't spent much time together, Lottie did already feel a sort of quasi-kinship toward them. Familial might be too far, but there was an ease to their interactions that was hard to explain away. Almost as appealing? Anna was offering her a way to immerse herself fully in music, a prospect so tantalizing, it made her fingers tingle just to think about it.

All this was to say Lottie was no closer to a decision now than she had been over the weekend, when Anna first floated the idea. But when she woke up that Wednesday morning to the chatter of both Aidan and Bee downstairs, she knew this might be her only shot for a long while to ask him in person.

"Third-to-last day of school!" Aidan said as she walked into the kitchen, giving her some quick jazz hands. "You have finals today?"

She nodded as she bit into an apple. "Physics and English," she said, mouth full. "How's prep going for you?"

He sighed dramatically. "I can't decide if the double-breasted blazers are a bad idea. Like, is it good retro or bad retro?"

"You'll figure it out."

"Appreciate that stellar vote of confidence," he said dryly. "But, speaking of figuring out: what office did you decide on? I should probably have someone start on your paperwork."

Lottie slid onto a bar stool across from where he was standing. "About that. What if I did something else this summer?"

Aidan stood up straighter. "Go on."

"Anna asked if I might want to hop on tour with her. Just for a little." She watched for his reaction carefully.

He remained impassive, except for darting a quick glance to Bee. "Did she? What'd you say?"

"Nothing yet. I said I needed to think it over. And I wanted to talk to you."

Bee was watching the back-and-forth like a spectator at the Open. "No," she declared.

Lottie looked at her. "What do you mean, 'no'?"

"You think you're going away for the whole summer with

a rock star?" Bee had, obviously, been invited into the circle of trust regarding Anna.

"It wouldn't be the whole summer, and she's not a rock star," she protested. "She's like, I don't know, an indie rock performer."

"*¡Es lo mismo!* And I know he gave you those papers"—she shot Aidan a look—"but you're sixteen. A tour? That's no place for you."

Lottie looked to Aidan imploringly. He exhaled. "I can't exactly stop you anymore. But I have to agree with Bee. Anna must be stretched so thin when she's doing one of these; who's gonna look out for you?"

"I'm not a child!" Lottie exclaimed.

"I didn't say you were," Aidan said patiently. "But Lottie, trust me, these things can spin out of control so fast. I don't want you ending up in a scary situation."

"I can take of myself."

"I know you can."

"I do it a lot."

Aidan was quiet while he took a sip of his coffee. It was the truth, obviously, but she hadn't meant for it to come out quite so accusatory. She tried a different tack. "What if Will comes?"

He raised an eyebrow. "Is Will coming?"

"Well, he's debating. I think."

Aidan thought this over. "I would feel better about it if he did."

Lottie cocked her head. "Do you not trust her?"

He hesitated. "I think she means well, with asking you to come. I'm just worried she doesn't really understand what it entails. And I don't want you to get hurt."

Bee shook her head. "*No me gusta.* Just go to Paris!"

Lottie put her hands up. "I'm not saying it's definitely happening."

"And I don't blame you for wanting to consider it," Aidan

said. "But I want to make sure you're going in with eyes wide open if you do."

The next three days felt Sisyphean and gave Lottie almost no time to consider either Anna's offer or Aidan's advice. The minute one final was complete, she had to start cramming for the next. It was a brutal cycle of poring over textbooks, regurgitating answers, rinsing and repeating. When the bell sounded on Friday afternoon, signifying the end of her US history exam and the school year, she was near tears from sleep deprivation and stress. All she wanted was to launch herself into bed and finally allow her brain some peace. But it was readily apparent that wasn't in the cards.

"So what are we thinking for tonight? Should we do a theme? White party?" Sasha had run up to her outside the classroom and linked arms.

Aidan had left for Paris already, and Lottie knew an empty house on the last day of school meant everyone would be descending like flies onto honey, whether she agreed to it or not.

Lottie groaned. "Can I take a nap first? I'm still having flashbacks to the Battle of Antietam."

"A *short* one. And then I'm coming over with Poppy so we can plan."

Lottie nodded listlessly. "Fine."

"I gotta clean out my locker. I'll see you in a bit." Sasha dashed off down the hallway, ponytail bouncing behind her.

"Lottie!" It was Mr. Shean. "I wanted to make sure I grabbed you before everybody scattered for the summer."

"What's up?" she said, adjusting her backpack over her shoulder.

"Not to be that super cheesy teacher, but thank you." He smiled kindly at her. "There are a lot of girls only in orchestra to pad their college résumés. And it's really awesome when I get a chance to teach someone who loves music for music, not just because Princeton likes it."

She smiled back. "Thanks. That means a lot, actually."

"What are you up to for the summer?"

Lottie shrugged. "Still deciding."

"Hopefully there's a way you can still be playing?"

She nodded. "Potentially. There's a chance I might tag along with Anna . . . Buckley. On tour," she said haltingly.

Mr. Shean's eyes widened. "Really? That could be quite the education. You should do it, if you can. Opportunities like that don't come around all the time." He hesitated. "So, Will and Anna, they're both friends with your uncle?" It was hard to miss the heavy skepticism in his tone.

"Yep," she said uneasily. "You know how fashion people are. Tons of friends all over the place."

He nodded, unconvinced. "Well, can't wait to hear what you decide."

"You and me both." She looked at the time on her phone. "I should go, but have a great summer, Mr. S."

"You too." He started to walk away and then pivoted on his heel. "Whatever you do this summer, Lottie? Just remember: it's okay to make your decisions from here"—he put a hand on his chest—"and not here." He tapped his head. "This?" He thumped his chest again. "This is where the music is."

Lottie arrived back at the town house just as a messenger approached, awkwardly pushing a large plywood crate on a trolley.

"Can I help you?" she asked as he steered the unwieldy package to the front of the garden floor door.

"I have a cake delivery for an Aidan Thomas."

Typical. "He's not here, but I can sign?"

He shrugged, unperturbed. "Whatever, I'm late already.

Where do you want it?" Lottie unlocked the door and pointed to the butler's pantry. Her phone buzzed simultaneously with a text.

"You get my present? Happy last day!" Aidan, of course.

"What is happening here?" Sasha gasped from the sidewalk, watching the delivery guy struggle to offload the elaborate, tiered confection onto the counter.

"Aidan trying to buy my love? I thought you were coming later."

She shrugged. "I got inspired for a theme for tonight; couldn't wait." She held up two large shopping bags. "Studio 54! That cake will be a perfect centerpiece, actually. Do you think Aidan has a smoke machine somewhere?"

So it was that by 9:00 p.m., Lottie's house had been transformed into that late seventies' bastion of iniquity, or, at least what a teenager assumed it might resemble. Sasha had bought a surfeit of disco balls in every possible size, which were now scattered on the floor, floating in bathtubs, and hanging from the railings all over the house. Sasha herself was in a silver sequined dress with a plunging V-neck, hair feathered like a Charlie's Angel.

Lottie eyed the whole scene curiously as she sipped on a Solo cup of champagne (there may have been some gaps in their themed supplies). "I don't even understand how you got all this stuff so quickly."

Sasha shrugged as she twirled, Sylvester's "You Make Me Feel (Mighty Real)" blasting on the house's sound system. "My mom has a lot of vintage YSL," she said, as if that answered the question satisfactorily.

The crowd started seeping in soon after: there were far too many boys in Warhol wigs, and more wide lapels and bell bottoms than Aidan would have been comfortable with. Lottie went for more of an understated look: black leotard under a pair of dark jeans.

"I feel your commitment to this theme, as the hostess, could be stronger," Tyler said, eyeing her outfit. He was in a truly atrocious maroon polyester suit.

"I'm Gilda Radner!" she said, offended.

"Who?"

"Only one of the greatest comedic minds of the last century. I Googled a picture of her outfit at the club," Lottie said, looking down at her top. "Also, Sasha planned everything, not me. I had, like, an hour to find something."

Tyler laughed. "Knew it." He raised his glass for a plastic clink. "You make any progress on you-know-what?"

She hadn't filled him in yet, and didn't really feel like doing so now. "Yeah, actually. Let's save that for another night."

"Right on."

"Yo, T! I need you on my team!" One of Tyler's friends was yelling from the kitchen, where a dozen or so of the boys were clumsily attempting to set up a game of flip cup on the kitchen island.

He shrugged and chugged the last of his beer. "Back in a bit."

Lottie watched him walk away. Maybe she should stay in the city this summer, for once. She could work at Aidan's New York office, spend some real time with Tyler, see where that led. Anna would be gone, Will in Boston. Things would be nearly back to normal. The thought was alluring in its simplicity.

She pondered all of this as she picked her way back toward the living room, where, much to her dismay, someone dressed as Michael Jackson was cutting lines on Aidan's small Noguchi table. Lottie stared down at him. "Really?"

The kid looked up, his fedora askew. "What? It's on theme, at least?" He bent down to snort one.

"Oh, for fuck's sake. Clean it up."

"Jeez. Chill." He brushed off the residue with his hand and rubbed an index finger into his gums. "You want, though?"

"No!"

The night felt like it was careening a little too fast and erratically to end well, the last car on a wooden coaster. There was a bristling, frantic energy to the crowd: the release of tension from the school year's end mingling with throbbing teenage hormones and too much—far too much—booze. Lottie was already feeling the tingling of a champagne headache in her sinuses.

Roars erupted from the kitchen as the boys finished the round. A slick of beer flowed down the counter and started to pour off the sides in sunny rivulets. Tyler cheered triumphantly, pumping his fist, as a girl—maybe dressed as Farrah Fawcett?—threw her wobbly arms around him. Lottie watched from across the room as he bent down to kiss her, both of them stumbling toward the back corner.

Oh, fuck this. Fuck all of it. The drugs and the sex and the same fucking people doing the same fucking thing every weekend. She was over it. And she needed things to stop happening to her and start making them happen, instead.

Lottie pulled her phone from her back pocket, quickly typed out a message, and hit send before she gave herself the chance to second-guess it.

"i wanna come with you."

# TWENTY-ONE

**Anna**
*New York*
June 2, 2024

She was still awake when Lottie's text pinged in at well past 1:00 a.m. The week leading up to tour was generally almost as busy as the tour itself. There were wardrobe fittings, daily rehearsals, and, always, at least one major disaster with a piece of equipment (this year, it was the skins for drummer Violet's kit). Somehow, wedged between it all, she was supposed to eat and shower. Sleep. All three were often more aspirational than reality.

Anna stared at the message for a good long while before responding, trying to parse her emotions. Ultimately, she surprised herself with how excited she was at the possibility of having Lottie along. But Will, keeping neither touring musician nor teenage hours, was certainly asleep. Anna was practically vibrating with anticipation, but she'd have to wait until the morning to call. It would be a tough sell, anyway: she could use this time to hone her pitch.

"She wants to come. On tour," she said by way of greeting when he picked up.

Will groaned a little. "Okay. I thought she might."

She paused. "She wants you there, too."

His reply was a deep, heavy exhale.

"Have you thought about it?"

"Have I thought about it? Yes, of course I've thought about it." His tone was wary, weary too.

"Could be a good fresh start?" she ventured. "With her."

"We didn't even get a start to begin with," he said, his consonants clipped. "Anna, do you understand what you're asking me to do, here? It's one thing to see you for an afternoon, but—"

"I can—I'd stay out of your way."

"Tell me, exactly, how one does that on a fucking tour bus."

"It's bigger than you'd think—"

"Jesus, that's not the point." Frustration laced every word. "The point is that you're asking me to come on *your* tour bus. On *your* tour. It's not exactly an even playing field."

"I'm trying, Will," she said quietly. "I can't cancel a whole tour. It's not just about me."

"That must be hard for you."

"That's not fair."

"I don't think you want to talk to me about fair," he said, voice rising. "And it's not like I don't have things planned for the summer."

"I know."

"We'd need to set some real boundaries."

"I know."

"I'd be doing this for her."

"I wouldn't ask you to do it for me," she said. "I wouldn't ask you to do anything for me."

He was quiet for a long time. "How many weeks are we talking?"

"So, I was thinking . . ." Anna stood in front of Will and Lottie; they were both looking up at her intently from the living room couch. All three were at a Midtown hotel, waiting for the tour bus to arrive outside. "It's probably better to keep this whole situation on the DL? I mean, Will, everyone will figure out we went to school together, but I think it's safer if no one knows who both of you are."

Will and Lottie exchanged quizzical looks. Anna started pacing the length of the room. "There's a . . . price to all of this, you know? There are people who want to know things about you who don't really have a right to. And look, I chose this, to a certain extent. But it's not really fair to put it on you guys."

"I mean, that's fine with me." Lottie shrugged. "I don't really want anyone else to know about you guys, anyway. No offense. You're cool or whatever. I just don't need the gossip, you know?"

Anna looked at Will. "I have neither rabid fans nor am I in high school." He put his hands up in surrender. "If this is what works for you two, fine. But, just so we're on the same page: you're both aware this is totally bizarre, right?"

"Trust me, tour is even weirder." Anna smiled, then picked up her buzzing phone. "Hey, Sal . . . Great, we'll be down in a sec . . . Oh, you made goulash for us?" She shot Will and Lottie a look. "Cool . . . Yeah, yep. Okay. See you soon."

"Goulash?" Will said.

"Told you it was weird." She hoisted her bag onto her shoulder. "You guys good? Ready?"

Anna had never brought anyone with her on tour—minus Rory for a handful of stops here and there, and he knew his way around a bus already. She was admittedly rusty when it came to accommodating others into her daily routine, and, obviously, the stakes were far higher with these two. She was desperate not to fuck it up. She wasn't even sure if she'd know if she did.

Lottie popped a piece of gum in her mouth and nodded.

Will sighed as he stood up; he looked resigned, if not exactly eager. "Yep. Let's get this literal show on the literal road."

Kendall was standing in the lobby when the three of them walked out of the elevator. "We're supposed to take pictures of you getting on the bus for socials," he said, engrossed in his phone. Anna had completely forgotten he was meeting her to see the band off.

"I'm in sweats, though?" She looked down at her outfit.

"It's whatever, people love the normcore." He finally glanced up and clocked Will and Lottie with a look of surprise. "Oh, hi. I'm Kendall, Anna's publicist." He walked up to Will and stuck out his hand.

"I'm Will—"

"Pendleton, I know. What are you doing here? . . . What were you doing up there?" he said slowly.

"Ken, manners, please," Anna warned.

"Anna, can I grab you real quick?" Kendall's eyes were saucer-big as he steered her into the corner of the lobby.

She nodded back at the two of them. "Guys, go hop on. I'll be there in a sec."

Will nodded, a little confused, and started guiding Lottie toward the hotel's doors.

"What is happening?" he hissed at her once they were out of earshot. "And is that who I think it is?"

"So they're coming with me?" Anna said, her voice pitched nervously high. Kendall started to protest and she put a finger up. "Just for a few weeks. And we all agreed to keep it under wraps, to make things easier. For them."

"For them, right. But, for real?" He looked pained. "What's your cover story?"

"Lottie's my intern. Will's . . . I don't know. He hasn't decided yet."

"Intern? Jesus. You're bringing a child over state lines?"

"She's emancipated!" Anna said indignantly.

"Great. Never mind, then . . . Anna, you're a very smart person.

You cannot think this is a good idea." He didn't wait for an answer. "But more important: Did you not think that bringing the baby daddy and long-lost baby on tour was maybe something I'd want to know? If this gets out before I have a chance to spin, I swear to god . . ."

"It's fine," she assured him, hand on his shoulder. "No one's gonna know who they are. They're just extra crew."

Kendall stared at her. "She looks like your literal fucking twin, Anna. You do know that, right?"

She thought this over. "Her hair is darker."

He closed his eyes. "I need a new job," he whispered.

Anna rolled hers. "You'd never leave."

"One of these days, I am gonna get there." He let out a deep sigh. "So how long is this cuddly little family reunion happening for?"

She shrugged. "Dunno. We'll see how it goes."

"I've actually never heard you say that. You plan the crew dinners months in advance."

"I don't know what you want me to say, here." She threw her hands up. "It's happening. Do I know how it's gonna go down? I do not. But I've gotta try, Ken. I'm not sure when I'm getting another chance," she added quietly.

She gestured to the bus and pulled her sunglasses down over her eyes. "Take whatever shots you need, and then we're out of here."

Anna adored her tour bus. Being inside was like its own little ecosystem: they had food, they had water, and, generally, enough whiskey to kill a Clydesdale. (She did ask her production coordinator to remove the booze for this leg though, with what she considered incredible foresight in regards to Lottie.)

She also led a rather solitary existence when not on tour: the opportunity to reunite with her band and crew family, even in tight quarters, was always a welcome change from being alone with her piano night after night.

The lineup of her bus and band had been the same for some years now: James on bass, Duncan on guitar, and Violet on drums. All three were session musicians by trade, but had performed on her last four or so albums and tours, making their mutual rapport both on- and offstage more akin to siblings than work colleagues. They had seen each other through breakups and marriages, deaths and births; they were probably as close to a support system as Anna had ever had.

The three slept in bunks on either side of a skinny hallway outside her bedroom; stacked three tall, there was plenty of extra space for Will and Lottie. *Plenty* and *space*, of course, both being relative terms on a tour bus. The label insisted on Anna taking the real bed at the back, which made her uncomfortable on the early tours, but as she was an inveterate insomniac, this morphed into a welcome perk.

"And this is the junk bunk." Anna pointed to a top berth on the right side. "It's where we store, well, all the junk we don't have another spot for? And breakfast stuff is here"—she gestured to a cabinet above the sink—"but you can tell Riley—she's the production coordinator—whatever you want to eat and she can send a runner to grab it." Anna realized she was rambling, but she couldn't contain her excitement on introducing them to what was such an integral part of her world. She'd clocked more hours on this bus than almost anywhere else, save for maybe her studio.

Will was taking it all in apprehensively. Lottie seemed to be always circumspect (Anna could see her genetics at work, there), but there was real delight dancing behind her eyes.

Anna opened the fridge, where a half dozen cans of root beer were neatly stacked on the top shelf. "This is for you," she said, looking back at Will. "I made sure we stocked your favorite."

He allowed himself a faint smile. "Thanks."

"So, questions? You can take any of the bunks here." She pointed to the right-hand stack. "And *always* feet toward the front when you're sleeping. Otherwise, you know . . ." She smacked her forehead with her hand. "No good."

"Morning, morning!" called a voice from the front of the bus. It was James, followed by Violet close behind.

Anna grinned and ran to envelop both in an embrace. "Shit, I missed you guys!" She pulled back to get a better look at them. "I love this pink, Vi," she said, fingering the fuchsia locks.

"New tour, new look, you know," Violet said with a smile and tossed her hair. James and Duncan may have been like the brothers Anna never had, but gloriously unfiltered Violet brought the fun.

James looked back to Will and Lottie and waved. Anna had texted all three to let them know about the new additions to the crew, but hadn't supplied a ton of detail. After this many years, they knew better than to ask.

"Will, Lottie, meet James and Violet. Duncan has never been on time for anything ever, but you'll meet him soon."

James smiled and pulled Will in for a quick bro hug, his full-sleeve-tattooed arm patting him brusquely on the back. "You probably don't remember me, but I was a freshman when you guys were seniors. I still remember your recital, dude. *Epic*. And never thought I'd end up stuck with this one." He elbowed Anna.

"Ha." She elbowed him back. "You never thought you'd be so lucky."

Anna's assistant, Quinn, stuck her head through the bus's door. "Are we all here?" She was holding the daysheet—the all-encompassing daily schedule for the tour crew—on a clipboard, yellow highlighter already unsheathed. Quinn was an excellent assistant—no one was more organized or dedicated—but she was also quite intense.

"One guess as to who's missing," Violet quipped as she walked to the bunks to stash her backpack.

Quinn made an exasperated face and highlighted something on the page. "Riley says we need to roll as soon as he gets here."

Anna's phone buzzed. It was Aidan. "Let me grab this real quick?" she said, walking back to her bedroom, then closing the door behind her. "Hey. We're on the bus."

"So this is really happening?" He sounded, at best, skeptical.

"Looks like it."

"Will is there?"

"Will is here. Not sure how excited he is to be here, but he's here."

"Well, glad he's there, at least. I really wanted to be there to see her off, but this is the absolute worst week to leave Paris." He sighed. "I don't love that this is happening, Anna."

"You've made that clear."

"I spoke to Will already, but you have to promise me that you're really, *really* gonna look after her."

"Aidan, she'll be fine. When I was sixteen—"

"She's not like you. Not in that way."

Anna bristled. "What's that supposed to mean?"

"I never worried about you standing up for yourself," he said. "I worried more about whoever got in your way. Lottie's different. She's not gonna tell you if she's hurting or if she's scared. 'Cause she's not gonna want to inconvenience anyone. So that means you need to make sure she never feels those things, okay?"

How strange, to be receiving parenting advice on your own child from your childhood best friend.

"And you're good?" he asked. "You feel like you'll be good with both of them there?"

"I will."

He paused. "You know what I'm asking."

"I do," she said quietly.

"I've gotta take you at your word. That's all I can do from here, I guess," he said. He didn't sound convinced. "Break a leg, Anna."

Aidan's phone call notwithstanding, between being reunited with her bandmates, the surreal nature of having Will and Lottie with her, and the sparkling promise of the Philly show just a few hours away, Anna was happier than she'd been in months. Years, maybe, if she really thought about it. The weather seemed to agree: while there had been thunderstorm warnings early in the day, threatening the cancellation of the whole production, the skies were now strikingly blue.

By the time they checked into the hotel and shuttled over to the venue, the load-in onstage was nearly complete. Anna was leading Will and Lottie around, introducing them one by one to the crew. All around them was the frantic hive of activity that was getting ready for line check: mic stands moving, cords unfurling, giant speakers rolling. Above, the lighting rigging was slowly being winched into final position.

Lottie craned her neck up. "You sure that's safe to walk under?"

"We'll find out, I guess," Anna said cheerfully. Lottie nervously sidestepped downstage, just in case. "We can get you up there with the riggers, if you want? You know your hard hat size?" she teased.

Will, meanwhile, had zeroed in on the Bösendorfer, sitting front and center onstage. "You finally got one," he said, tossing a glance back at her.

In college, she'd told him that when—not if—she made it big, her first major purchase would be one of the Austrian company's grand pianos. "If it's good enough for Tori Amos, it's good enough for me," she'd declared.

Anna grinned. "She's a cutie, isn't she? It's a 290." She gave it an affectionate little pat on its side. "You can try her out." She could tell he was doing his best to look disinterested, but even after such a long interim, she could still read his moods like a children's book.

Will walked a little closer to the piano and tentatively reached a finger out to test middle C. "Eight full octaves." He whistled. "I hope you write songs especially for it just so you can use those extra bass notes. Or at least play some Bartók." He skimmed the soundboard with his hand admiringly.

She gestured to the bench. "Sit down. I can tell you're dying to."

"Well, maybe just a little something," he mumbled, sliding onto it. He played a few bars of Philip Glass's "Etude No. 6," always one of his favorites. Out of the corner of her eye, Anna could see some of the crew stop what they were doing to watch with curiosity. He finally took his fingers off the keys and nodded appreciatively. "That's pretty good."

"Better be. Cost more than my first apartment."

She'd missed seeing him play. Will felt music with his whole body, whether he was conducting, or messing around at the piano for his own amusement. In college, she could almost tell what he was working on just from how he moved.

It struck her, then, that this was the first time the two of them had been on a stage together since his senior year recital. It felt like a lifetime ago. And it felt like yesterday. She was reminded of a phrase her French diction professor had loved to deploy: *plus ça change, plus c'est la même chose*.

The more things change, the more they stay the same.

# TWENTY-TWO

**Lottie**
*Philadelphia*
June 2, 2024

Lottie had nearly forgotten that there was a whole other world that Anna inhabited that wasn't just her studio. That she was, in some meaning of the word, an actual rock star. Arriving at the venue that afternoon—after nearly getting mowed over by a large, black rolling case emblazoned with ANNA BUCKLEY on the side—made her realize she'd underestimated the size of the mini-empire over which Anna presided.

She didn't seem like a despot, though, which was of great relief. Lottie had heard so many nightmare stories from Aidan about this pop star or that starlet, and how they might behave in public, but when it came to their staff, they were absolute horrors. Anna, however, took the time to introduce her and Will to everyone working onstage, from the sound engineers to the lead rigger. She knew all their names, but also their family members', where they'd been on vacation since the last tour, who'd had a baby. And the crew, in turn, seemed genuinely happy to see her: to be a part of this giant system of complicated gears, all rotating together to create a few hours where thousands could forget what came before or after.

Lottie was examining Duncan's impressive rack of guitars when Anna clapped her hands together at the front of the stage.

"Guys! Lemme grab you for a second?" She motioned for everyone to walk over; the crew slowly formed a semicircle around her. Lottie, unsure of where to stand, parked herself near the back.

"Well, we fuckin' made it." She grinned and the crew erupted into applause and hoots. "I'm so, *so* happy to be back. And before shit gets crazy, I wanted to take a second to say thank you. You guys put in insanely long hours every day to pull this off and I never, ever take it for granted. So bring it in, please." She stretched out her arms for a giant huddle; the crew moved toward her to form a tight circle.

"What are we saying on three?" Anna prompted.

"'Cheeseburger'!" someone yelled.

She laughed. "You hungry, Juan? Okay, you heard him. One, two, three . . ."

"Cheeseburger!" they all yelled in unison before breaking apart.

"Oh, one more thing before you go?" Anna called. "We've got a couple new crew members for a few weeks." She motioned to Lottie and Will. "Come over, come over." She waited until they both were standing, somewhat awkwardly, next to her. "I think most of you have met them, but this is Lottie, who'll be interning, and Will, who's . . . helping with arrangements." She lowered her voice dramatically, "Backline tech boys: they both have perfect pitch, so that could be helpful for tuning. *Not* that you need any help," she added with a laugh. "Okay, enough of me, go do your thing." She shooed them off and the crew began to scatter to their posts.

Riley, the production coordinator, and Quinn, trusty clipboard still in hand, approached the three of them. "Be ready for soundcheck in ten?" Riley asked.

"Yup, I'm good." Anna turned to Will and Lottie, tapping out a quick text. "Can I stick you guys in the seats for that? You've got fresh ears for all these songs."

Lottie looked to Will. "Yeah, sure," he replied. "Stage right, fourth row?"

Anna looked up, surprised. "Exactly, thanks. Quinn, can you show them the best way down?"

Quinn nodded. "Follow me," she said without looking back. She led them quickly from backstage to the orchestra section, pointed to the row without saying a word, and walked away.

Will watched her leave. "She's not exactly warm and fuzzy, is she?" he said, as he plopped into a seat.

Lottie snickered. "Not exactly."

"This your first time at a sound check?"

She nodded. "Quite the production."

"Yeah, right? Whenever you come to one of mine, be prepared for it to be . . . less loud. We don't have quite as many amps for orchestras." He grinned.

Onstage, Violet took her place at the drum kit, pulling her hair out of her face. Duncan, who did finally make the bus with minutes to spare, was twisting a tuning peg and quickly test-strumming his guitar.

"How'd you know? Where she wanted us to sit?" Lottie asked him, still watching the band warm up.

"Ah." He smiled. "In college, she always preferred for people to sit on this side, so you could see her hands when she played. And then she didn't have to make eye contact with you, either." He chuckled. "She's a creature of habit. Just figured her preferences hadn't changed much."

Anna finally walked onto the stage, holding a bottle of water, one in-ear dangling on her shoulder. She waved down to them with a smile and then turned back to the band. "Okay. Let's run through 'Breathless,' then I want to tackle 'Ivy' and 'Glitterati.' James, you were coming in late on that yesterday, so let's make sure you're really in the pocket. And D, you good with that?" She nodded to the guitar. "If not, let's get someone out here now; we've gotta get through a lot in the next thirty."

This was a fascinating transformation for Lottie to witness.

Anna, understandably, had been fairly deferential in the handful of interactions they'd had so far. But here, on her stage, she was all business. And the boss. It was kind of awesome.

Anna sat down at the piano and nodded to the band. Sticks already held aloft, Violet nodded back and counted them in: the song unfurled with a sticky, repeating bass riff. After a few bars, Anna leaned over the piano and began to play the first verse, pausing just for a second to gesture to the monitor engineer to turn up the sound in her in-ears. This was the first time Lottie had actually seen her play: her focus was impressive. It was just soundcheck, but you wouldn't know from watching her.

Will was taking it all in uneasily, arms folded across his chest. "She was this good even when she was eighteen," he said, shaking his head in disbelief. "It's almost not fair."

Onstage, Anna was belting out the last chorus, one hand held aloft.

"How's that sounding from there?" Anna called out when they were through, shielding her eyes with one hand, the other on her hip. The lighting crew was running through the various presets for different songs. She was splashed with red, then blue, then some sort of twinkly golden pattern.

"Piano needs to come up in the mix," Will called back. "Drums sound nice and crisp, though." Lottie nodded, too. Not that she had any clue, but it felt like sound professional advice to her.

Anna looked to her front-of-house engineer, hunkered over the soundboard a few rows behind them. "You heard him, Danny. He is, annoyingly, always right about this kind of thing." She made a face at Will.

"When are you checking 'Free Bird,' though? I was really looking forward to hearing that one," Will added, straight-faced.

Anna took a swig of water and stretched her arm out to him, middle finger raised. But she was smiling. "Will Pendleton, you can see yourself out for that one," she said directly into the mic. The sound reverberated loudly straight into the orchestra seats.

Will laughed: a real laugh. It was probably the first time Lottie had seen them joke with one another. She felt like she was getting a surreptitious peek at what they must have been like as teenagers, as friends. It was nice.

Anna turned back to the band, nodded, and rotated her pointer finger around in a circle. One more time through. She sat back down at the piano and they got to work.

Lottie had been backstage at Aidan's shows, but never at a concert. There were some similarities—far too many people, lots of headsets—but the mood at Anna's was a lot more jubilant. She likened it to Christmas Eve: there was a gleeful anticipation ribboning through every member of the crew.

After all, this is what they were working frantically toward every night. Lottie would soon become familiar with the achingly early walk-and-chalks, the relentless line checks, the chugging of the third coffee when there was no time to eat. Everything coalesced to bring them here, to whatever stage would act as church that night, where communion came in the form of drum fills and Anna's mezzo-soprano and the unbridled joy of the crowd.

She would also learn, as Will had correctly predicted, that Anna was very much a creature of habit. And unsurprisingly, she ran a tight ship when it came to the performance schedule: the run of show was calculated down to the minute and she rarely started late, unless there was a problem out of the crew's control.

After hair, makeup, and wardrobe were done, about an hour before the show, Anna retreated to her dressing room by herself. She'd sip ginger tea with a teaspoon of honey, steam her vocal cords, and run through her warm-ups, which, curiously, involved singing through a tiny metal tube ("It's called straw phonation," she'd said, when Will gave her the side-eye. "Look it up."). Riley would knock with ten minutes to lights down, and lead Anna and the band to the wings. Then came what would become Lottie's favorite part, although she almost felt like she shouldn't watch, it could be so intimate: all four gathered in a tight huddle, cheeks nearly touching, then each gave thanks to whatever higher power they believed in. It was one last chance for them to move as one before they splintered into distinct points of light onstage. Lottie found it to be very beautiful.

Riley would then direct James, Duncan, and Violet to their places, which would send up the first deep roar of the night from the audience. As they began to play, Anna would wait offstage, bouncing on the balls of her feet and as ready to explode as a racehorse jammed into her stall at the starting gate. When Riley finally gave her the cue to walk, the noise emanating from the crowd felt like a living, breathing creature. Lottie had never seen (or heard) anything like it. Anna would emerge into the spotlight waving, beaming, at home. She was the happiest Lottie would ever see her.

She was also almost unrecognizable. Anna favored a pretty dressed-down approach in her quotidian life: jeans and a T-shirt, barely any makeup. But for shows, the label insisted on a slightly more glam look, and, as Anna would tell her, it also had the benefit of keeping the two halves of herself—off- and onstage—in separate worlds.

For that first show in Philly, her team had given her a golden smoky eye and a flowing, silky dress to match the makeup, and curled her long hair in waves. She looked, Lottie thought, like a proper rock star. But it wasn't so much the style change that made her appear so markedly different, but her energy. Her posture, her bearing, how she moved through space was like comparing a housecat to a lion.

The Anna that Lottie had been getting to know was unequivocally human: she made mistakes; she had real fears and anxieties. But the Anna that took the stage that first night was a monarch addressing her subjects through wedge speakers, a preacher with a crowd wild for her sermon. They would have walked straight into the ocean if she'd asked them and never once looked back. Lottie found it hard not to wonder if that same bifurcation existed inside her. And what it must feel like to be so unencumbered, even for just a few hours. She wondered, too, what you had to sacrifice in order to get there.

The band kicked off the show with the lead single from Anna's newest album. She performed it standing at center stage, grooving and caressing the mic stand so sensually that, at one point, Lottie had to look away with secondhand embarrassment. The song "August Sands" was one of Lottie's favorite tracks, though: an upbeat ode to ephemeral summer love. Well, from what she could gather: Anna's lyrics were labyrinthine, at best. The crowd, of course, already knew every word and was dancing along with her. Anna's fans—Buckheads, to the devout—tracked her album releases and tour schedule with the fervor of the newly converted, even those that had been following her since the early days.

Once the applause finally died down after the opening number, Anna walked to the edge of the stage to grasp a few hands, and then situated herself at the piano. "Hey, everybody. Thanks for coming out tonight." She had to pause to let the cheers subside. "I've missed you," she purred. "It feels so good to be back out here." Somehow, she was able to flirt with all five thousand people simultaneously. It didn't compute that this was the same exhausted soul that was curled up on that big couch just a few weeks ago.

"I love you, Anna!" someone yelled out from the back rows. Anna shaded her eyes from the floodlights and blew a kiss.

"Marry me!" another shouted.

That one made her laugh. "Yeah, I don't think I'm exactly cut out for that. But"—she had a devilish glint in her eye—"can you cook? . . . Yeah? Steak? . . . Oh, you grill it? Okay, then maybe. Come find me after."

The crowd was clutching at her every word like she was

teaching them to breathe. She launched into an improv on the piano, still chatting. "You know, we've got a few new crew members this leg." She leaned over and caught Will's and Lottie's eyes offstage for a moment. "I'm not sure they know what they've gotten themselves into, with you guys," she said with a grin, in a mock whisper. "Be nice, okay? I won't make them come out to say hi, but, anyway, this one's for them."

The band set down their instruments as she played solo on the piano, her voice's upper register stretching nimbly into the highest reaches of the venue. It was a slow-tempoed number from her first album, *Cliffwalks*, one that Lottie could now see was probably about her, and Will, and everything that happened. The crowd, for the first time that night, was silent, transfixed.

Will and Lottie were watching it all unfold from the side of the stage, Will leaning against a column, incredulous and anxiously tugging on his backstage pass. He nodded at the stage. "This is what we always talked about. This is what she was always working toward. It's . . . unreal to finally see it in person." He shook his head in disbelief. "You can't take your eyes off her when she's up there."

It was at this moment Lottie realized that, while both would adamantly refuse to admit it, Anna and Will were still in love with each other. And while she was clearly no expert on relationships, even she could see this was probably dangerous territory for them to explore. There were so many rippled layers of hurt. And both were so desperate to make up for the time they'd lost, it was clear they might not reckon with why they'd lost it in the first place.

But it wasn't her place to get involved in their sticky mess, nor did she particularly want to. So she let herself join the congregation for the night, get subsumed into the bubbling frenzy of the crowd. She was ready to move however Anna said she should, breathe how she commanded, feel whatever she told her to.

# TWENTY-THREE

**Anna**
*Oklahoma*
June 13, 2024

The secret was that she was always terrified before the start of a tour.

She knew, objectively, it made little sense to worry: being on the road had been her default mode for over a decade now, and they routinely sold out the whole run before the first stop. But what we tell ourselves—and what we're told—when we're young is often the hardest skin to shed, it being so close to the bone.

"What if it's not enough?" she'd find herself repeating in the pit of the night, all the while urging sleep to come muffle the noise. It never did.

But once she was ensconced onstage for that first show, all of that pent-up excitement, and anticipation, and anxiety dissolved, pouring out of her like so much sweat. The endeavor would leave her totally, blissfully, drained; she'd sleep that first night—unusually for her—deeply and dreamlessly. Her body naturally found its happy, humming rhythm from that point: she allowed muscle memory to take over, allowed herself to get rocked from one stage on to the next.

Time on the road had a tricky way of unspooling, though. Overnight bus rides could sometimes feel like they lasted weeks, but onstage, two hours vanished in minutes. Before she knew it, they were nearly two weeks' deep: DC, Charlotte, Atlanta, Miami, New Orleans, Austin, and Dallas all behind them.

It was somewhere on that stretch that she'd finally convinced Will to help with arrangements for the new songs. Communication between them was tense, but no longer nonexistent, which was an immense relief. It also helped that she was mostly out of his hair: between press hits, sound checks, and the shows, there would be nearly whole days that passed without her seeing him. They probably both knew more about the other's daily schedule thanks to Lottie than their own conversations.

But one night, on a long slog west, everyone on the bus found themselves with a fat surplus of hours. Anna was in the bedroom, playing around with some new verses on her acoustic. Lottie was asleep already, and the other three were playing cards up front. Will appeared in her door, holding a mug of tea.

"Sounding good," he said, motioning to the guitar. "You've always liked that open tuning. C major seven?"

She nodded, not looking up. "Just messing around."

"You thought about what you might pair that with?"

She smiled, and finally met his eye. "Not yet. Something tells me you might have."

"Well, not really, but *if* you were gonna do something, could be really nice with like . . ." He hummed a few bars. "I could write it down, if you want?"

"Yeah, I'd love that, actually. Thanks." She patted the bed next to her. "Wanna sit?" He hesitated at his post. "It's still me, Will. I'm not gonna bite," she said quietly.

He grudgingly nodded, then took a perch on the farthest corner from her.

"You doing okay on the bus? You've never done one of these, right?"

He shook his head. "It's more dip in, dip out for me, one-offs."

"Must be nice."

"You'd hate it, I have a feeling. You like to be in motion."

She chuckled. "Someone once described touring to me as eternal adolescence, kinda kicking the adulthood can down the road. But even this goes by fast."

He took a sip of his tea. "Everything kind of goes by faster now though, doesn't it?"

She tilted her head to the side while she thought about it, still strumming. "Yeah."

"A year in college felt like a real *year*, you know?" He leaned back against the wall. "And now, I blink and the semester's over. And the kids keep getting younger—I mean, they're basically Lottie's age," he marveled. "It's just weird to be so far out of our twenties. I don't feel like almost forty. Not that we're old but, we're not . . . young anymore. I never imagined being here, I guess. It always seemed so far off."

"I wish I could be back there all the time," she said, setting down the guitar. "It did feel like the years went by slower, right? Like they were worth more." She paused. "At the time, all I wanted was to know what was gonna happen. I don't think I appreciated how fleeting it is, that moment where it's all out there waiting for you. And you haven't lost any of it, yet."

She shook her head, then leaned back in defeat on her pillow. "And then, all the sudden, it's like . . . I got swept up on this wave and popped out on another decade. And everybody here seems to know what to do: how to have a family, how not to . . . fuck up. I'm over here still treading water."

"It's not just you," he said quietly. "I have no idea what I'm supposed to be doing."

"Can I ask you something?"

He nodded, after a moment.

"Did you—do you want kids?" It was masochistic to even bring it up; she didn't know why she was.

He blew out a big breath before answering. "Yeah. I think I'd be pretty good at it." He hesitated, then shook his head. "Never mind."

"What?"

He shrugged, a little sheepishly. "I always thought if I had a girl, I'd name her Clara."

She smiled. "Like Schumann?"

He nodded, embarrassed. "Not really sure how to classify myself now, with Lottie. It's confusing. It's hard. What about you?"

She shrugged, herself. "I think I kept waiting for a time when I'd feel ready, or *be* with someone that made me feel ready. Haven't gotten there yet."

"You and Rory ever get that far? To talking about it?"

Anna hesitated. "Once. You can see where we landed on that. You?"

"Jess really wanted to." He was looking out at the dark highway from the bus's window. "I just couldn't see it, with her. That was really the beginning of the end, I guess."

"I'm sorry."

"Don't be. Would've been worse if I'd never said anything."

They were quiet for a few minutes, listening to the groans of the suspension and the scattered laughter emanating from up front.

"I know this isn't easy for you," she said. "I'm really glad you're here."

He acknowledged that with a stoic nod.

"It's never been the same," she said. "Making music without you."

He was still looking outside. A solitary car buzzed by. "I know."

Sometimes, she'd be listening to one of his pieces and a small phrase would jump out at her, like a grasshopper emerging from clover. She'd know it so intimately, it was hard not to wonder if he'd put it there for her. More than a few of her own songs held messages for him, too. Piano notes that tried to say what she could not.

"We could start off with something small?" She knew she was pushing her luck. "If it's too much, we can forget it."

He was nervously snapping and unsnapping the button on his shirtsleeve. "Okay," he eventually said. "We can give it a shot."

It was obvious that Lottie was not well as soon as they arrived in Oklahoma City. She was normally awake before any of them, but at nine, when the bus pulled up to the hotel, she was still fast asleep in her bunk. They let her rest while everyone else unloaded, but when she hadn't roused herself half an hour later, Anna and Will went to investigate.

"Hey," Anna whispered, pulling the curtain aside. "We're here." Will stood behind her, watching curiously. Lottie only groaned in response and rolled over to face the wall. Anna looked back at Will with alarm. "You think she's okay?"

He shrugged. "Feel her forehead?"

Anna gently placed a hand on Lottie's head. She was hot and a little clammy. "She's pretty warm. I think? You feel her." They awkwardly navigated around each other to switch places.

Will stuck his own hand into the bunk. "Yeah, she's hot." His brow creased with worry. "What do we do?"

She bit her lower lip, debating. "Call Aidan?"

"Tylenol works. She's not, like, six, you guys," Aidan said with a chuckle when they relayed the situation. "Give her a dose—the adult stuff—and some water. I'm sure she's fine."

"So this has, like, happened before?" Anna said, anxiously tugging on a corner of Lottie's sheet.

"A fever?" Aidan said, incredulous. "Yeah. Kids—even teenagers—get sick sometimes." He said it like he was addressing preschoolers. Perhaps that was warranted, as far as their caretaking abilities went. "I promise, you guys'll make it through. Just keep me posted."

"Do we move her? To the big bed? Or into the hotel?" Anna said after they hung up. She was peering with concern into the bunk. "I haven't gotten sick in, like, a decade. I think I caught every bug there was in my twenties from touring all the time and now I have super immunity. I didn't even get Covid."

"I'm not gonna ask what you were doing to get sick that much," Will murmured, still looking at Lottie's sleeping form. "I guess let's move her into the big bed? I can carry her."

Anna nodded and got out of his way. He reached in, easily scooped her up, and slowly maneuvered his way down the narrow hallway to the bedroom.

"I'm texting Riley to grab the venue doctor," she said, following behind them.

He laid Lottie down carefully on the bed, her eyes fluttering open for a second. "I don't feel so good," she mumbled, and closed them again.

"Just go back to sleep, okay?" Will whispered. He reached down and softly smoothed her hair back from her forehead. He did it as unthinkingly as if he'd done it for the last sixteen years. Anna felt like someone had plunged a hand straight into her chest and squeezed her lungs of every molecule of air.

"Anna? You guys still in here?" Quinn was at the bus's door. "You've got a radio hit soon."

"I can stay," Will said quietly, as he pulled the comforter up over Lottie. "I know you've got a ton of press this morning."

Anna hesitated. This felt like a test and she was pretty sure she was failing. "You sure?"

"Of course. Go do your thing."

"Text me?"

He nodded.

"Quinn! I'm here. I'm coming."

Aidan did turn out to be right: Lottie was fine. She'd caught some unspecified bug, according to the doctor, but she was only down for the count for about forty-eight hours. Will had kept her company while she slept during the day, and Anna had insisted on her taking the bed in the back when they did an overnight. By the time they arrived in Albuquerque, she was, thankfully, back to her normal self.

Will, however, was not. The two of them had actually made quite a bit of progress on arrangements during the Texas leg, but since Lottie's fever, he seemed to be irritated with her for reasons she couldn't quite discern.

Now it was that interstitial period between sound check and show. The two of them were camped out in the small artist's dressing room: a gray, windowless space with wan fluorescent lighting. Will was slowly pacing while he read a sheet of music, air-conducting with his free hand.

"Something about this section isn't working for me." He frowned and walked over to her. She was sitting on the saggy couch, marking up her set list with opening chords.

"Oh?" She peered at the sheet. "What's wrong with it?"

"I think this crescendo here is a bit much." He tapped it with his pen. "Maybe you should try to rein it in a little, more like, da, da, DA, da, da." He sang a few notes and looked to her for approval.

She considered it for a moment. "I don't know. I think it flows better how it's written. That's the real crux of the melody."

"Maybe try a quick diminuendo and *then* you ramp it up again?"

She sighed. "Can we leave it for now? I've gotta finalize the list for tonight . . . And I do like it the way I had it."

"'Course you do," he said under his breath.

Anna looked up at him quizzically.

"I just mean you generally like things the way you like them." There was a flick of bitterness in his words.

She decided to ignore it. "That's not true. I just disagree on this one."

"What about the viola I suggested for 'Blue Diamond'? Or the pared-down guitar for 'Kestrels'?"

"I'm considering those." She said it half-heartedly at best, and she was sure he knew it.

"Whatever." He walked away from her, eyes still on the paper in his hand.

She eyed him warily. "What's going on?"

Will clenched and unclenched his fist, then turned to face the wall. He was breathing heavily, slowly through his nose.

She started to uncurl herself off the couch. "I mean, look, if you really want to test it out, fine. I'll—"

He punched the corkboard with a shuddering thud. Startled, she quickly sat back down.

"She was my baby, too, Annie!" The words hung suspended between them for a moment, almost as if written in the air. "You had no right . . . You had no fucking right to leave me in the dark like that." He sunk down to the floor in a squat. "I'm trying so hard to move past this, to not think about everything I've missed. All the times I should've been there for her. But I've missed so much. It kills me to think about how much."

He looked up at her, eyes wet. "Objectively? You made a terrible fucking decision. The selfishness of it is just . . . inconceivable. I never would've thought you were capable of it. I never would have thought you could do something like that to me."

There it was. Somewhere, deep in her bones, she'd been bracing herself for this since the day Lottie was born. Anticipating it hadn't made it any less agonizing to witness.

"I would've been on a plane the minute you told me," he said quietly. "You know how much I loved—" He caught himself before he finished the thought. "Instead? I lost both of you." He sat down fully and leaned his back against the wall. "I would've given up anything you'd asked me to. You didn't know that?"

"Of course I did," she said calmly. "That's why I didn't tell you."

He raised his head, confused. "What?"

Anna leaned forward, forehead in her hands. "You would've destroyed your whole life for us, Will. I couldn't let you do that." She looked up. "You were at Juilliard. You had a commission from the New York Phil at twenty-two! You think you could've done any of that with a baby?" She almost spit the last word out.

"It wasn't your call to make!" He slammed his palm down on the floor. "You didn't even give me the fucking choice! None of that mattered as much. We could have figured it out."

"Yeah?" She sat up a little straighter. "What about me? You think I could've done this with an infant? You think I *wanted* to?"

He was silent.

Anna sat still for a moment, the words forming like marbles in her mouth. She had to spit them out or she'd choke. "I didn't," she finally said. "And if I'd had to give it all up, I think it would've killed me. She swallowed hard. "I'm not good at a lot of things, Will. But I'm good at this. I needed this."

He stared at her, astonished. "I would *never* have asked you to give any of it up."

"I know that. Of course I know that," she said softly. "But I couldn't have done this while doing that." She shook her head ruefully. "It almost doesn't matter: I would've fucked it up . . . us. Her." She inhaled deeply before continuing. "I, uh, had a pretty dysfunctional childhood. I think you've probably figured that out by now." She smiled darkly. "I wouldn't have known what to do, as a mom. And I couldn't risk doing that to her. I needed to break the cycle."

"Then—" He shifted uncomfortably on the wall. "Then, why didn't you . . ."

"Why'd I go through with it?"

He nodded slightly. With Lottie just on the other side of the wall, it was difficult for either of them to contemplate what had been the alternative.

"Because . . ." she started. "Because she was yours."

His breath caught. He slumped forward onto his knees like she'd ripped out his spine. "You could have told me all of this," he said quietly.

She hesitated before continuing. "I wouldn't have been able to say no if you'd asked me to keep her." Her voice barely registered above a whisper. "And you would've asked me to keep her."

This had all been inchoate inside her since she found out she was pregnant, but she'd never allowed it to take tangible form until now. Saying it out loud felt like a dam was breaking.

"Then it was never about me, was it?" He flicked the corner of the sheet music with his finger once, twice. "I don't know how to forgive you." His voice was level, but she could hear what was simmering beneath. "I'm trying, for her. I don't know if I can."

Anna nodded and closed her eyes.

Will wiped his cheek with the heel of his palm and stood up. "It's probably better if I head out after this stop. I think—"

"No, Will, please." There was more alarm in her voice than she intended. She recalibrated. "After the show, we can talk? And we've got an off day coming up."

He scoffed. "This always comes first, yeah?" He gestured around the room in disdain. "How's that worked out for you? Worth it?"

The question was a wasp sting; unexpected and searing. She was silent a moment. "It has to be."

He shook his head in disgust and turned to walk toward the door. "You know, sometimes I think all of this was the worst fucking thing that could've happened to you. You have built so many walls around yourself, Anna. You didn't need more reasons to keep people out."

He left, slamming the door behind him so forcefully she could feel it in her teeth.

# TWENTY-FOUR

**Lottie**

*Albuquerque*

June 15, 2024

While the temperature of Anna and Will's relationship seemed to fluctuate on metrics she couldn't begin to decipher, Lottie was very much enjoying getting to know each of them on their own.

Anna, surprisingly, considering her grueling schedule, meant it when she said Lottie could act as her intern. In the last two weeks, Lottie had accompanied her to local TV and radio spots, VIP fan meet and greets, and sat in on phone conferences with virtually her whole team, from her manager to the label. It was all eye-opening: there was far more to being a musician at this level than just the two-plus hours a night Anna was onstage.

But Lottie's favorite time to tag along was for hair and makeup before a show. It was the most relaxed she'd see Anna all day: no one generally bothered her during glam time, and her hairstylist, Jordi, and makeup artist, Elena, were hysterical together. It was here that Lottie was finally able to crack Anna's composed shell, just a little bit. And in turn, she allowed Anna to do the same with hers.

"Tyler sounds like a dick," Anna said as Jordi finished curling her hair. "I mean, I'm sorry you had to see him make out with someone, but sounds like it's for the better."

"He's not a total dick," Lottie countered. "He helped me find—" She stopped herself, realizing midway through the sentence. "He helped me with some . . . research."

Anna shrugged. "Fine. But high school boys all suck, anyway."

"Preach," Jordi said, brandishing the curler in her direction like a benediction.

"When do they start not sucking, though?" Lottie asked, sighing. "Does that happen?" Elena would often play around with looks on Lottie once she was done with Anna. Right now, she was dusting her eyelids with a bright green shadow.

Anna cocked her head to the side as she thought that over. "I'm not sure? I'll get back to you if I find out," she added dryly.

"Will doesn't suck?" Lottie offered.

"No, Will doesn't suck, that's true."

Elena raised an eyebrow at Anna in the mirror. "You ever gonna spill on that?"

Anna's eyes grew big. "Who said there's something to spill?" she said indignantly.

Elena sighed. "Please. Jords, back me up here."

"You are certainly backed." He was pinning pieces of Anna's hair for a half-up, half-down.

"We've known each other for a super long time, that's all," Anna said, trying for noncommittal. She caught Lottie's gaze, just for a second.

"In the biblical sense?" Elena grinned.

"Oh my god, you two are the worst!" Anna laughed, covering her face. "Enough! Let's please go back to Lottie's drama?"

Compared to the tilt-a-whirl madness of Anna's day, the time Lottie spent with Will was far more placid. They mostly did what she imagined you'd do with an actual dad: sneak out for lunch if they didn't like catering, go for early-morning runs at whatever park was closest to the hotel (Anna found this foray particularly egregious: "Why would you ever wake up early to do *that*?"), and, of course, trade copious music recommendations. He'd given her quite the education in contemporary composers—many of whom, like Philip Glass, she discovered she adored—and she introduced him, in turn, to the pop canon of the 2020s. He was particularly enraptured by the incisive lyrics of Olivia Rodrigo ("So young, but so wise," he'd said, shaking his head in amazement).

And while Lottie wasn't exactly the effusive sort, she was touched that he'd kept such a watchful eye over her while she was sick. He'd mostly quietly worked on music—either his own or Anna's—while sitting on the bed next to her. But every few hours, he'd quickly put a palm to her forehead, or coax her into drinking another glass of water. They were simple gestures, but ones she hadn't had in quite some time. They made her miss her mom.

But any thought of getting the three of them together for some sort of "family" time was dashed the night of the Albuquerque show. It was impossible not to hear Anna and Will yelling backstage in the dressing room. Obviously, Lottie could guess the contours of the argument, but the words themselves were, thankfully, muffled enough that everyone else was none the wiser. Even so, she watched the crew walk as slowly as possible by the door, in fairly transparent efforts to discern the reason for the fight. Adults, it turned out, were far more like high schoolers than Lottie had anticipated.

Eventually Will emerged, flushed and slamming the door behind him. Everyone quickly scattered out of his way without making eye contact; Lottie busied herself with ripping gaffer tape for spike marks onstage that were totally unneeded. He approached her; she pretended to be surprised.

"Hey, I'm gonna skip the show tonight, okay?" He looked shaken: red-eyed and distracted.

Lottie nodded, unsure of what to say.

"I might, uh, need to go *home* home."

"Oh." She didn't think it would be that bad. "Everything okay?"

He hesitated. "I'll catch you on the bus, all right?" He gave her a perfunctory pat on the shoulder and quickly walked toward the backstage door.

Anna didn't emerge from the dressing room and Lottie thought better of walking in. She didn't see her, in fact, until right before lights down.

"Let's fucking do this," Anna muttered from the wings, rubbing her nose as she strode onto the stage. There was a look of steely determination in her eyes that was a little frightening in its intensity. This was not an Anna that Lottie had seen before.

Riley, standing next to Lottie, watched Anna sweep by then chuckled knowingly and pressed the button on her walkie to address the crew: "Buckle up, bitches. We've got angry Anna on deck." A few responded back through the speaker with hoots and cheers.

As Lottie would learn, angry Anna was an occasional visitor during tours. And her shows were legendary: she wrung herself dry onstage those nights. There were certain performances that the crew would still reference with reverence: Cincinnati 2009, New York 2012.

"These are the best shows," Riley gushed to her as they watched her wail the chorus of "Glitterati." "I mean, for her? They're definitely the worst. But, they're the best. I mean, look at her."

Lottie hadn't been witness to a huge number of Anna's shows, but it was apparent from the minute she stepped onstage how differently that night would unfurl. Her aura was unapproachable and a little dangerous, as if you'd get shocked if you touched her. She played for almost three hours straight, stopping only to chug water (or, occasionally, whiskey) or sop up sweat with a towel. The crowd, which was always cranked to a fever pitch, was even wilder than normal, screaming as if they themselves were feeding off this newfound rage energy of hers. Lottie could see James, Duncan, and Violet exchanging worried glances during some of Anna's extended riffs and solos, as if wondering how long she could possibly keep this up.

Toward the end of the main set, Anna signaled to the band to take a break and then launched into a solo cover of Nine Inch Nails' "Hurt." Riley, puzzled, looked down at her set list and then clicked her walkie button. "Looks like we're going off-script, here, folks."

Drenched in sweat and bleeding from her elbow after banging into the drum kit, Anna was illuminated by a single spotlight while she sang. The audience, for the first—and only—time that night, was absolutely silent. She closed her eyes before she raspily whispered the pre-chorus, singing about what she'd become, about friends who leave in the end.

"Oh fuck me, this is brilliant," Riley said, laughing with astonishment.

As Anna sang the last line, she pulled off her guitar and threw it roughly toward the side of the stage. It landed with an audible crack and slid toward Lottie in the wings.

"We've got a smash, ladies and gentlemen. I repeat: we have a smash," Riley announced into the walkie. "Who had"—she looked at the date on her phone—"June fifteenth for the first breakage? Anyone?"

"Me!" someone squawked.

"That Tessa? Well done, my friend! I'll have your winnings for you after the show."

Lottie looked at her curiously.

"Ah," Riley said sheepishly. "You cannot tell Anna, okay? But we always have a running bet on when she'll break the first instrument. Earlier than normal this year. I'm surprised: didn't seem like it was gonna be that kind of tour."

"So this is a common thing?"

She shrugged. "Depends on the year, honestly." She paused. "Except for May. May is always bad. Thank god we started later this go-round."

"May is bad?" Lottie repeated.

"We've had a few with nothing broken at all," Riley continued. "We've had some where you absolutely don't want to see the bill I have to send to Phil." Phil was Anna's tour manager. "Those are generally Rory's fault," she added with an eye roll.

"Who's Rory?"

Riley looked as if she realized she'd probably said too much and turned back to the stage. "Doesn't matter, he hasn't been around in a while."

The chants were so loud after the second encore, the band went out for a third, running dangerously close to the venue's curfew time. When they finally took their bows, the entire front section surged toward the stage, tossing flowers and handwritten notes at her feet, their hands desperately reaching forward for a chance to touch her. More than one of them was sobbing.

"Anna, can we get a few shots?" The tour photographer had his camera aloft already as the band returned backstage.

"Jesus, not now," she snapped, pushing roughly by him. "Lottie, come with me." Anna motioned to her as she continued on to her dressing room, not even breaking her stride.

She was already peeling off her dress with irritation by the time Lottie walked in.

"Anna, you good? Want me to tell them to clear out at the meet and greet?" Quinn was behind them in the doorway, looking even more concerned than usual.

"No, I'm going. I'll bring Lottie." She looked at Quinn in the mirror while she started to take off her makeup. "Go get some sleep, okay?"

Anna was just in her bra; Lottie could count her ribs. And on her right-hand flank, she had a small tattoo that Lottie hadn't seen: a delicate circle and a half-circle attached to one another.

"You sure?" Quinn looked skeptical.

"I never cancel. See you in the morning."

Quinn hesitated, then closed the door behind her.

Anna rested her head in her cupped palms and inhaled deeply. "Did you hear? Earlier?" she finally asked.

"Kind of," Lottie replied. "Not specifics. Will looked pretty upset, though."

"Yeah." She exhaled and sat up, then grabbed an old Foo Fighters shirt from the back of her chair and pulled it over herself. "He is."

"Are you . . . okay?"

Anna glanced up at her, then noticed a pile of sheet music Will had left on the counter. "No," she said after a pause.

"Do you . . . want to talk about it?" Lottie ventured.

She smiled at her in the mirror, with a mix of pity and something Lottie couldn't quite put her finger on. Regret, maybe. "You're sweet. But, we've gotta figure that out on our own. If he'll let me." With her concealer now erased, it was starkly apparent how tired she was.

"How do you do it?" Lottie blurted out. "Go out there, if you're . . . not okay?"

Anna put down her makeup wipe while she contemplated that. "Because that space is sacred," she finally said. "Because even if it's all still waiting for you when it's over, at least out there, it's a few hours where you can forget."

She stood up and eased on a pair of jeans. "There are a bunch of fans who wait near the bus at the end of every show. I'm sure you've seen 'em." She looked down at her elbow, noticing the cut for the first time, and shrugged. "I have had some really fucking terrible nights before. But I've never missed this. Grab that bag?" She pointed to an empty tote in the corner. "Normally, Quinn does this with me, but I thought it would be good for you to see it." Anna glanced at the mirror one more time and swiped a streak of mascara away from her cheek. "Okay, let's go."

Lottie trailed her through the winding corridors to the backstage entrance where the bus was parked. The crew had already set up a rectangular barricade; there were about a hundred people gathered inside, holding variously shaped presents, pictures, and flowers.

"Just stick everything in there." Anna gestured to the tote. "I'll have you on photo duty, too."

The crowd spotted Anna at the door and started clamoring for her attention, yelling and snapping photos. A security guard with a badge reading TED appeared, seemingly out of nowhere, at Anna's side. "You ready, Miss Buckley?"

"Absolutely." She pulled a Sharpie from her back pocket. "Never leave home without one," she said with a smile, and prodded Lottie in the shoulder with it.

They followed Ted to the front of the barricade, where the crowd stood around ten people wide. Anna plastered on a big smile and started signing photos, records, even people's arms for tattoos. She posed for selfies, recorded voice notes, and caught up with fans whom she knew well. She was, at various points, doctor, and therapist, and friend. One pregnant woman even insisted on Anna touching her belly to bless the baby. This was probably the only point at which Lottie thought she looked uncomfortable, but she doubted anyone who didn't know Anna well could tell.

"How many weeks are you?" Anna asked politely.

"Thirty-seven," the woman said, beaming.

Anna looked surprised. "Well, I'm glad tonight didn't put you into labor. Gets a little rough at the end there, right?" she said, signing her album cover. "So I hear, at least," she added.

Lottie gathered all the handwritten cards, the paintings, and the baked goods (these, sadly, all got thrown out: couldn't be too careful). A few of the fans even asked what her own name was: Anna's diehards were almost as interested in everyone in her orbit as Anna herself.

And none of them, Lottie realized, had any inkling how staggeringly exhausted—physically, mentally, emotionally—Anna was. Nor, probably, did they care. She wasn't a real person to them any longer, but a vessel. Some cried with her about the death of their partner, others entrusted her with marriage proposal plans. She was impressively protean: shifting into some new version of herself depending on what every person needed. It was incredible to watch—Lottie was starting to understand why her fanbase was so fervent—but she couldn't comprehend how enervating it must be to do this nearly every night. The fans seemed so greedy, and it was hard to see what they gave her in return.

Finally, Riley came out and put an end to it. Tour bus drivers could only be on the clock for so long: they needed to roll out now. Everyone else was already asleep by the time they boarded; Anna and Lottie collapsed at the table up front. It was close to 1:00 a.m.

"Can I ask you something?" Lottie said, depositing the bag bloated with letters onto the counter. There must have been close to seventy.

Anna nodded in reply.

"Why'd you want me to see that?"

Anna leaned back on the banquette; there was no word to describe her but *depleted*. "None of this"—she swept her hand around the bus—"exists in a vacuum. None of this exists without *them*. It's one thing to see it from the stage, but that's not the whole picture, you know?" She pulled out a sticker-coated envelope and inspected it lightly. "It's symbiotic—the love, the care, whatever you want to call it: it goes both ways. I guess . . . I guess I wanted you to see that I know that—that I'm capable of understanding that." She stuck the letter back in and clasped her hands in her lap, looking down.

Lottie eyed the prodigious pile of mail. "Isn't this a lot to take on? Everyone laying their problems on you all the time?"

"I get asked that a lot. What I normally say is 'No, it's a privilege to have people trust you that deeply, love you like that.' And it is. It's an enormous privilege. But you want my honest, *honest* answer?" Anna leaned forward and put her chin in her palm. "I think it keeps me from getting too deep into my own shit." She gave a tired shrug. "Pass me the bag? I'll read these on the drive."

"It's late?"

"Yeah, well. I can tell there's not a lot of sleep in my future tonight." She slid out from the bench and stood up. "I wish you could've known me, before," she added quietly. "I know that doesn't make any sense. But it wasn't always this hard for me to . . ." Her voice faltered and she motioned to the space between them, instead. "Night, Lottie. Thanks for helping."

Lottie watched her walk toward the bedroom, shouldering the stuffed bag. Maybe, if both of them had been made of softer stuff, she would have rushed over to give her a hug. But their composition was all sharp angles; it was hard to see how they'd fit together.

The gash on Anna's arm was slowly purpling into a bruise that would take over her whole elbow by morning. You can only cover up so much, sometimes.

# TWENTY-FIVE

**Anna**

*Albuquerque to Phoenix*

June 15, 2024

It was a betrayal, Anna felt, to do that to another musician right before she took the stage. But as she'd done many times—too many times—before, she channeled all of that hurt, and anger, and disappointment straight into the show. And it worked, to an extent: by the time the band took their bows, much of her rage had dissipated, flying from fingers into piano keys and guitar strings.

Regardless of her mood, it always took hours to wind down after a show, and when emotions ran as high as they did today, she often found herself awake the whole night. The swaying of the bus was a familiar comfort, at least. She was attempting to read some of the fan letters when she heard a muffled thump from outside her bedroom.

"Ow! Fuck." It was Will.

Anna crawled out of bed and opened her door a crack. He was lying on the floor of the hallway, rubbing the back of his neck. She suddenly remembered how much he tossed and turned while he slept. At Brookfield, he was just as likely to be passed out on his dorm room rag rug as in his twin bed when she'd come grab him for breakfast. It was one of his quirks she'd liked best; she'd always imagined he was conducting in his dreams.

She stared down at him. They hadn't seen each other since he stormed out of her dressing room, and she had to admit she hadn't even checked to make sure he was on the bus when they pulled out.

"Some things never change, I see." She nudged him lightly with her toe.

"I'm fine," he grumbled. "And this hasn't happened since college, for the record."

"Need a hand?"

"No. Just landed on my neck funny." He rubbed it again. "Go back to sleep."

"I wasn't sleeping. You sure you're okay?"

"I said I'm fine," he snapped.

"Jeez, got it. Let me help you up, then." She extended a hand. After a pause, he grudgingly accepted. But as she attempted to pull him up, he let out a yelp and fell back down. Anna put a hand on her hip. "You are, in fact, not fine. Come lie down." She nodded toward the door. "I promise, I'll stay on my side of the bed."

"Give me a sec," he said, grimacing. "I'll be okay in the bunk."

"No, you won't. Look, I can sleep out here if you don't want me in there. You need a real bed."

"I'll get up in a minute," he said to the floor.

"William. Get back there. My bus, my rules."

He sighed heavily and finally nodded. Anna opened the door wider and gestured to the bed. Still massaging his neck, he carefully stood up and then crawled onto the mattress. In gray sweatpants and a navy T-shirt, he resembled teenage Will more than ever.

"You want the lights off?"

"No, it's fine. You can keep reading."

She stuffed the letters back in the tote and flicked off her bedside lamp anyway. "Couldn't really concentrate."

They lay there uneasily next to each other in the dark, listening to the gentle squeaks of the bus, the soft snores drifting from the bunks beyond the door.

He broke the silence first. "I asked Quinn to look into getting me a ticket out of Phoenix. I just wanted time to talk to Lottie first."

"Okay," she said quietly.

"I'm sorry this didn't work out." He was staring at the ceiling. "I know we both wanted it to, for her. But it'll probably be better for all three of us if I go home."

"I get it. I don't know what I was thinking, putting all of us on a bus." She chuckled softly. "Maybe we can try something a little lower stakes, when the tour's over."

"Yeah, maybe. I'm kinda in and out with gigs for the fall."

"Anywhere exciting?"

"Royal Phil at Royal Albert."

"Oh, I love that theater." She smiled. "My favorite to play in London."

"Yeah, mine too."

They were quiet again for a few miles. Outside, the white streetlights from the highway flashed rhythmically over them, almost like a heartbeat.

"When I was pregnant . . ." Anna started, then stopped. "I used to have this daydream of sitting in the audience with the baby while you were conducting. I'd point to the stage and say, 'That's your daddy up there, making all that beautiful music.'" She shook her head. "It was dumb. I don't know why I did it. I guess I liked imagining how proud you'd be to show her what you love, how proud I'd be of you." She paused again, the memory surging uncomfortably forward. "I liked imagining what we'd be like as a family."

She rolled over onto her side to face him. "I need you to know that I know you would have been a really wonderful father. It was never you I was worried about."

He was silent for a long time. "Will you tell me what it was like when she was born?" he finally said.

Anna closed her eyes. It had been a long time since she'd allowed herself to go back to that day. It felt like jumping into an icy lake: painful, then numb.

"I was at the keyboard trying to finish a bridge when I went into labor. That probably won't surprise you," she said wryly. "I really thought I could hold it all off until I was done."

"That . . . tracks," he said, throwing her a quick smile.

"That didn't end up happening, obviously. It got pretty intense really fast: we almost didn't make it to the hospital."

Will turned to look at her. "For real?"

She nodded. "She was ready when she was ready, I guess. Whether I was or not. Once she was out though, she only cried for a few seconds. Then she looked around, taking everything in with those big eyes." Anna smiled. "It's kind of the same expression she still has, now that I think about it. I remember wanting to know so bad what she was thinking. What your first thoughts might be when you're brand-new in the world."

She paused, wondering if she dared wade further than where her feet could touch. "Then they cleaned her off and laid her on my chest"—Anna touched hers—"and I couldn't believe how much hair she had, and how tiny she was, how beautiful . . . I couldn't believe you weren't there," she whispered.

He was quiet, the only sound the whiz of cars speeding by on the highway. The grief on his face was a visceral force. It knocked the breath out of her.

"You didn't deserve this," she said, staring up. "I'm sorry. I'm sorry. I am so fucking sorry I did this to you . . . To us." She tried to stifle a sob under her hand, but holding it in only made it worse. Soon, it felt like they were erupting from her every joint. She turned away from him, curling inward into herself.

Will gently touched her shoulder. "Hey, come here," he whispered. He turned onto his side and pulled her to him, wrapping his arm around her waist. He held her tightly as she wept, forehead pressed into the nape of her neck, shushing her softly the way you would an infant. They lay like that for a long time.

"Please don't leave," she eventually choked out. "Please. I can't do this without you." She rolled over, their faces now inches apart. His breath was warm on her eyelashes.

He reached up and smoothed her hair off her forehead, wiped her cheek with his thumb. "Okay," he finally said. "Okay."

Her own breath was still hitching. She took her palm and lay it on his sternum, in an effort to calm herself down, to let his syncopation take over hers. But his own heart was beating fast. This catalytic energy between them had never disappeared, she now realized, just had been dormant. Touching him again felt both dangerous and inevitable, plunging a hand into hot wax. The longer they lay there, the quicker her own pulse accelerated, matching his.

Wordlessly, she moved her hand to his cheek, grazing the side of his face with her fingers until her thumb came to rest softly on his lower lip. He inhaled with surprise, but didn't pull away. Cautiously, slowly, she leaned forward and kissed him.

"Is this okay?" she whispered, her forehead, warm, touching his.

He nodded a slow assent and pulled her in for a deeper kiss, slowly rolling on top of her. Grabbing one of her wrists from behind his neck, the other from his waist, he pinned both above her head. He needed to claw back some of the control he'd lost, she realized. And for once, she was willing to give it.

Anna let her back arch upward; Will pressed down onto her before releasing her hands to pull her shirt off. He bit her earlobe gently, trailed his mouth down the side of her neck, her breasts.

"Fuck, I've missed you," he murmured, kissing her hungrily—desperately, almost—as his hand found its way inside her. A small moan from her, then his palm hovering over her mouth to keep her quiet. There was a feral look to him, all of a sudden, one she'd seen just once before. Will reached down with one hand to ease off his sweatpants. This time, he didn't ask. And this time, she didn't want him to.

"Don't stop," she whispered. "Do whatever you want to me, just don't fucking stop."

# TWENTY-SIX

## Lottie
*Phoenix*
June 16, 2024

It was nearing ten before the door to Anna's bedroom squeaked open. Lottie was at the table, having a late breakfast of granola and yogurt while Quinn sat across from her, laptop out to organize Anna's schedule for the day.

Will emerged first, running his fingers through a mop of messy hair. He froze like a toddler with a hand in the cookie jar when he saw them staring at him intently.

"This isn't what it—I fell out of the bunk and tweaked my neck. Anna made me sleep in there."

Quinn went back to typing. "I didn't ask . . . And your shirt's on inside out," she said without looking up. Lottie stifled a snort.

He looked down to confirm, then tugged at his T-shirt. "Oh, so it is." He laughed nervously. "Hard to get dressed in the dark on the bus, right?"

Quinn took a sip of her coffee. "Not really."

"Oh. Well, I guess I need more practice to—"

"Will?" she said.

"Mm?"

"I really don't care." Quinn nodded toward the door. "But is she up? Glam will be at the hotel in about an hour."

Anna poked her head out. “I’m up, I’m up.” She finished tying a printed silk robe around herself and walked to the coffee station. “I didn’t realize how late it was,” she said brightly. “Haven’t slept that well in a while.” She turned toward the pot to hide her smile.

Will was still standing near the table, staring at Anna dumbly. “Yeah, me too. Slept really well.”

Lottie looked from one to the other, widened her eyes, and went back to her yogurt. This was an unexpected turn of events. But best not to let herself think too hard about what may have happened in that bedroom.

“You have a radio interview at one, but they’re streaming it, so you’ve gotta be camera-ready. Then sound check at five, and a quick M&G with fans who won a contest at seven. Lights down for the show at nine-thirty. Cool?” Quinn looked up at Anna expectantly.

Anna took a sip of her coffee and tilted her head from side to side. “I mean, I don’t have much of a choice, right?”

“Corrcct.”

Will slid in next to Lottie and reached for the box of granola, but Anna swooped in behind him and grabbed it just as he was about to stick his hand in.

“Hey!” he exclaimed.

“Hold on,” she said, reading the ingredients. “Yeah, no.” She looked at Quinn and Lottie and pointed a finger at them. “Sesame gives him hives. And he’s terrible at reading, apparently.” She smacked him gently on the back of the head.

“Ow!”

“Oh stop, that did not hurt.”

Anna looked at Lottie and narrowed her eyes. “What about you?” Lottie shook her head and shoved another spoonful of granola into her mouth. Realizing what she may have just inadvertently given away, Anna turned toward Quinn. “Just being safe, you know?”

Quinn stared at her for a second then went back to typing. "Will, did you still need me to get a flight out for you today?" She looked up over her laptop. Lottie stopped mid-bite to wait for his reply.

"Oh. Um, the . . . work thing I had isn't a . . . thing, anymore," he managed to stammer out. "So, I'm good to stay, for now."

Anna sat down across from him with a small smile. "Glad that worked out."

"Yeah, yeah. Me too."

Was he blushing? Both of them were acting supremely weird. Lottie nudged Quinn under the table with her foot, but she just glared at her.

Will grabbed a banana from a basket on the table, eyeing the box of granola warily. "I've been thinking about 'Saturn' that we were working on last week," he said, taking a bite. "It still sounds so wistful, you know? I was playing around with ways we could brighten up the chorus, so it wasn't quite so . . . sad."

Anna ruminated on that while she took another sip. She did look far more rested than last night. "I can see that. What're you thinking?"

He shrugged, his mouth full. "Hum me the chorus again?"

She obliged. It was a pretty melody, but he was right that the ending was somber.

Lottie, scrolling through TikTok, was only half paying attention. "Picardy third," she said, without glancing up.

They both turned to look at her. "I'm vaguely, *vaguely* remembering this term from freshman year," Anna said, scrunching up her face.

Will, clearly rewriting the whole chorus in his head, grinned. "She's right. You can keep the chord structure, but it sounds so much happier." He hummed it back to them.

"Huh," Anna said, surprised. "Will you look at that? The student becomes the teacher."

"I mean, she comes by it honestly." He looked about ready to explode from pride.

Anna raised an eyebrow. "From both sides, I'm sure."

"Maybe. Perhaps one side more than the other." He smiled mischievously, grabbed the spoon from Anna's coffee cup and clanged the side of the mug. "Anna, could you tell me: What note is that?"

She laughed. "Oh, fuck off, you know I don't know."

"Lottie?"

She looked up from her phone for a nanosecond. "A."

"Absolutely correct," he said, beaming.

"Lottie, give me your phone." Anna stuck out her hand.

"Why?" she asked, suspicious.

"Just for a sec. I'm not gonna do anything embarrassing."

Lottie passed it over, still skeptical.

"Just opening Spotify here . . ." Anna tapped the phone. "Let's see what you have downloaded, shall we? Okay . . . Will Pendleton. I see one, two, three albums. Not bad. Now, let's look for Anna Buckley," she said slowly as she typed in her own name. "And we've got one, two, three, four, five, and *six* here. Would you look at that?" She opened her eyes wide in mock surprise and slid the phone back across to them.

He peered down at it. "Can't help it if your demographic isn't quite as highbrow as mine."

"Hey now!" Lottie said, feigning offense.

"I believe the word you're looking for is *popular*?" Anna said with a pleased smile.

Quinn closed her laptop. "Okay. When you two are done with your dick measuring? Anna, you should get dressed and we'll get you over to the hotel. And, for the record," she said, standing up and looking at all three, "she's a fifty-fifty split."

Anna glanced at Lottie, alarmed.

Quinn sighed. "Relax, I'm not gonna say anything. But, come

on." She gestured to Lottie. "I have eyes, you guys." She walked away toward the bus's door.

"Sixty-forty," Will muttered under his breath.

Anna snickered. "You wish."

Being surrounded by genetic relatives for the first time was certainly a blow to Lottie's perceived sense of self. Some quirks that she thought were hers alone turned out to be inherited traits: Will, for example, was also a sun-sneezer. They'd discovered that when all three were stepping off the bus in Austin: both dissolved into fits as soon as the hot Texas glow hit their faces.

Anna had stopped to stare incredulously at the two of them before shaking her head. "You have to be fucking kidding me."

"Told you it was a thing," Will said as he patted her on the shoulder.

Apart from the obvious, like her ear for music or hair color, it had also been fun to discover some of their more esoteric connections: ice cream also made Anna thirsty; Lottie and Will were both lefties; none of them liked the smell of roses.

Even if all the connections made her feel a little less unique, being able to actually see a throughline from herself to another human being left Lottie feeling complete in a way she'd hadn't known was missing. It was as if she'd always been asking questions about herself into the ether, never expecting a response. And then, all of the sudden, the answers began boomeranging straight into her palms.

So when Lottie realized that Sunday was Father's Day, she wanted to do something for Will, but without upsetting the precarity of their relationship. While in Austin, she'd found a pristine vinyl copy of Bernstein conducting the NY Phil in two Gershwin pieces and picked it up for him on a whim. She'd squirreled it away in her bunk, but that morning, after Anna and Quinn left for the hotel, she nervously presented it to him.

"I got you something," she said shyly, unable to meet his eye as she proffered the record. "It's . . . Father's Day, today. And, I know you're not, like, you know. But I wanted to say thanks for taking care of me the other week." She finally looked up at him.

"Oh, wow. Thanks." He was clearly touched, but also looked like he might cry, which was a state she was definitely not equipped to handle.

"You probably already have it, anyway," she mumbled. "It's not a big deal if you don't want it."

"I don't, and I do. And I can't wait to play it at some point when we're not living on a bus," he said with a laugh. "But only if you'll promise to come over for a listen sometime."

She smiled. "We can probably make that happen."

The truth was, though, none of them had broached the subject of what came after the end of the tour. They hadn't even formally discussed how long they were planning to stay.

"I'd love that. And it would be fun to show you around Boston." He hesitated. "Can I give you a hug?"

She nodded. He squeezed her hard; he gave good hugs. "I'm really happy you found us," he said quietly. "I didn't know how much I needed this."

By the time Anna was finished with her radio gig, Will and Lottie had made their way to the hotel. Riley generally arranged the block so that all three had adjoining rooms: during the day if they weren't at the venue, they normally kept the doors open and hung out in the living room of Anna's suite.

"Have you guys eaten? You maybe wanna blow this popsicle stand?" she asked when she returned. She was in full-glam Anna mode: Jordi had given her a handful of tiny braids and woven in some gold thread.

"Are you seventy? Who says *popsicle stand*?" Will said, flipping through a *New Yorker*. "But yeah, actually, I'm starving."

He finally looked up at her. "Where are we going for lunch looking like that, though? Narnia?"

Anna grabbed a pillow from a nearby chair and threw it at his face. "You're disinvited. Lottie?"

She put her phone down and stretched. "Yeah, I could eat."

Anna eventually settled on a place called Duke's, which was not exactly a restaurant, but more like a corner store with tables tucked in the back.

"How'd you find this place?" Lottie asked, looking around curiously as they walked through a long aisle of souvenir socks on the way to their table.

"I have a restaurant list for every stop," Anna said matter-of-factly, pausing to finger a wool scarf. "Bars too," she added with a wink.

"Yeah, that's on brand," Will said, stopping to shake a snow globe with a desert scene. "You shoulda seen her spreadsheets for choosing classes in college. She's so type A, it's a miracle she ever made a decision on anything."

Anna made a face at him. "Lottie, ask him if his mother still buys all his clothes for him?" She tugged on a corner of his polo shirt. "This has Betsy written all over it."

A magazine rack on their right had a surprisingly large assortment of titles: Anna's face, in an arty black-and-white shot, pouted at them from the cover of *Elle*. Will's eyes lit up when he saw it; he grabbed a copy and stuck it in front of his own face.

"I am going to murder you," she muttered, trying to pull it down from him. "Lunch was a bad idea."

"This will never not be *so* bizarre," he said, flipping through to find her article. He cleared his throat theatrically. "'My musical practice is sacrosanct,' says Buckley. 'It's important to keep to a routine in order to really connect with the muses.' Anna. *Anna*." Will looked pained. "For real?"

"Hypocrite. As if you didn't have a *GQ* spread earlier this year."

He closed the magazine with a flourish. "In which I did not use the words *sacrosanct* or *muses*. But . . . you read it?" He smiled impishly.

She sighed. "Yes. I will admit that I read it, Maestro." She granted him a quick smile.

The whiplash of their interactions, from good, to bad, to back to good, was exhausting to keep track of. But Lottie would rather watch this playground flirtation than the frosty interactions of the past few days.

They eventually made their way to a small table in the corner, Lottie across from the two of them. It was the first time, she realized, that the three had been out in the wild together.

Her phone buzzed with a text soon after they ordered.

It was Will: "Watch this."

She looked up at him, confused. He grinned conspiratorially at her and nodded toward Anna, who was distracted reading the local ads on the paper menu. He reached over and tickled the inside of her forearm; she leapt what seemed like a foot in the air.

"William! Oh my god." Anna smacked him hard on the shoulder. "Are you five?"

He was doubled over in laughter. "Sorry, had to see if it still worked. You are the only person I know who's ticklish there."

Lottie kept quiet, but Anna clocked her nervous expression. "Oh no," she said, shaking her head sadly. "Don't tell me you got that, too?"

"Only one way to find out," Will said grimly, and lunged across the table for Lottie's arm.

"No!" Lottie shrieked, but she couldn't quite move fast enough. All of them were in hysterics at this point, the other tables starting to throw sidelong glances their way and whisper.

"Will, you're gonna get us kicked out," Anna exclaimed, laughing and wiping her eyes with the back of her hand.

"Whatever," he said, still chuckling. "Worth it."

* * *

For a generous portion of the crew, Anna's performance was the only downtime they received all day. That meant Riley, as the production coordinator, didn't always stay to watch the shows, but when she did, Lottie liked tagging along with her best. More than anyone else, she had eyes and ears on every element of the production. She also, for what it was worth, knew all the gossip.

The opener, a band inexplicably called Babytoof, had just finished their set. Riley and Lottie were standing backstage watching the crew tape down set lists on the floor. She nudged Lottie and nodded toward Anna and Will, who were standing about fifteen feet away; Will had just made her laugh about something. He also had his hand on her lower back.

"Looks like mom and dad made up," Riley said, raising an eyebrow.

"What? Oh, you mean . . ." Lottie was flustered. "Yeah, guess they did."

"What do you think the deal is with those two?" she said, still staring in their direction. "Sounded like some heavy shit yesterday."

Lottie shrugged. She wasn't nearly a good enough liar to say anything convincing right now.

"I feel a little bad for him, you know?" Riley said, tilting her head. "He seems like a nice guy. And with her, they don't even realize she's sliced them open 'til they walk away and they're bleeding all over the place." She turned back toward the stage, shaking her head. "Just a matter of time."

# TWENTY-SEVEN

**Anna**
*Phoenix*
June 16, 2024

The past twenty-four hours had had the quality of a fever dream, resting somewhere in that liminal space between reality and fantasy. Everything—from their fight to sleeping together—was a scenario that Anna had manipulated in her mind hundreds of times before. For all of it to crash from the imagined to the physical in the span of a few hours was a deeply confusing blurring of the worlds.

But to have the old Will back, with all of his goofy charm, and earnestness, and effusiveness, was spectacular. And he, in turn, could transport her back to who she was before any of the rest of it happened; even a small taste of that was addictive. But, of course, that other Anna didn't exist without him. If he disappeared, then so would she.

She didn't have the luxury to ponder this uninterrupted, however. There was hardly a waking hour when she wasn't doing some sort of promo for the album and tour, or getting ready for a show. And so now she was in Phoenix, sitting in a radio station green room with Violet and waiting to regurgitate the same tired stories she'd been telling for weeks.

Kendall was in town for another client's performance and had invited himself to the radio hit to catch up. He walked in a few minutes after they did, hurriedly typing out an email.

"And how are *you* doing this morning?" he asked, without looking up.

"Fine?" Anna said, cocking her head suspiciously.

"My Google Alerts beg otherwise," he said, flipping around his screen to show her.

"So does her guitar from last night," Violet added.

Kendall finally put away his phone and eyed her curiously.

"What now?" Anna asked impatiently.

"Nothing. Just, you've got that . . . freshly fucked look?" He waved his hand around her.

Violet cackled.

His jaw dropped. "Shit, am I actually right?" He laughed gleefully. "Who melted the ice queen?"

Will, of course, chose that moment to call. Anna fumbled to silence it, but they spied the screen before she had a chance to shove her phone into her pocket.

"Speak of the devil . . ." Violet murmured.

Kendall guffawed. "Couldn't see that one coming."

"That's not—we're working together, you know that," Anna said, attempting to regain some composure.

He snickered. "That what you're calling it?"

Violet opened her mouth in shock. "And lies! Need I remind you we live on a fucking bus? You're not exactly . . . quiet." She poked Anna on the arm with a wicked grin.

Anna felt her cheeks go hot. "He's already done a ton of work on the arrangements," she said, trying—poorly—to deflect.

Kendall rolled his eyes. "Anna, come on. I saw you guys in the city. The two of you were eyeing each other like fifteen-year-olds at Bible camp."

She groaned, relenting. "Probably not my best idea."

"Yeah, you think? What could possibly go wrong? But"—Kendall raised his eyebrows devilishly—"how was it?"

"How was *what*?"

"Give me something." He put his hands up like a supplicant. "I'm stuck in fucking Phoenix. Grindr here is horrific . . . And, actually? Now that I think about it, Will strikes me as the type who's kinda sneakily hung like a horse?"

Anna stifled a snort. "I am not answering that—"

"So that's a yes."

She threw a pen at him. "But it was good."

"Just good?" Violet said, unconvinced.

Anna covered her face with her hands and peeked at them between split fingers. "Fine. Very, very good."

Violet hooted and drummed her palms on the table. "That's my girl!"

A bright-eyed PA knocked just then and stuck her head into the conference room. "Hi! They'll be ready for you guys in five?"

By the time Anna wrapped the meet and greet after the Phoenix show that night, she assumed everyone else was already tucked into their bunks. But Will was still up, intently typing something into Sibelius on his laptop and munching on some pita.

"Those new?" Anna pointed to his glasses. "They're cute."

"My back hurts when I wake up, too," he said with a half smile, and pushed them up on his forehead. He nodded toward the bus's door. "How was it?"

"Fine. Everyone kept asking if I was okay . . . after last night's show." She raised her eyebrows and slid into the bench across from him.

"Are you?"

She shrugged. "I wouldn't even know how to begin to answer that," she said with a tired smile. "Are you?"

"Getting there." He pushed his laptop away and leaned back. "We should talk?"

"Probably. You really want to right now?"

He shook his head.

"Good. Me either." Anna craned her neck to look at the score on his screen. "What're you working on?"

"Nothing much. Lottie had a fun suggestion for this quartet piece I'm doing, just seeing how it sounds." He scratched his arm distractedly. "I think there might be a mosquito in here?" he said, looking around. "I'm getting bit by something." He rubbed at his neck.

Anna leaned in closer. "Roll up your sleeve?"

"Why?"

"Just do it."

Will pushed up the sleeve of his button-down; his whole arm was covered in small red welts. "Oh," he said, looking down.

Her attention turned to the pita in his hand. "Did you eat . . . hummus?"

"Yeah, why?"

"Oh my god," Anna muttered, tilting her head back for a moment and groaning. "You know there's tahini in that, right?"

He looked at her blankly.

"It's made from sesame, Will." She grabbed his other arm and pulled up the sleeve: more of the same. "Shit. Are you gonna go into anaphylaxis or something?"

"No, I'll just be very, very itchy."

Anna sighed and stood up. "Come with me." She walked over to a cabinet in the hallway and pulled out a small first-aid kit. "Let's see what we can fix you up with." She nodded toward the bedroom. "Go take your shirt off."

He smiled. "If you say so."

"Walked into that one, didn't I?"

"Sure did," he said, making his way by her.

The kit was, annoyingly, missing both calamine lotion and

Benadryl. Anna grabbed a washcloth and ran it under cold water instead. When she walked into the bedroom, he was already shirtless: hives sprinkled like confetti all over his chest.

"Jesus," Anna said, staring at him. "This isn't gonna help much, but it's all we've got. Where's it the worst?"

"My back, I guess."

She motioned for him to lie down on the bed. "My mom used to do this when I . . . got sunburned," she said softly, laying the cloth on his upper back and pressing down.

"That feels good," he said, the words muffled by the mattress. He let her do her ministrations in silence for a minute. "Are you ever gonna tell them?" he finally asked, turning his head to the side.

"My parents? I don't know." She moved the towel to his neck. "I'm not sure they deserve the chance."

He rolled over onto his side to face her. "If you ever want to talk about—"

"I don't. Not about that."

He nodded and lay back down. Anna resumed with the washcloth.

"Can I ask you something?" he said.

"Maybe," she replied, wary.

"You got a tattoo."

"That's not a question."

"Did you get it for her?"

She hadn't realized he'd spied that in the dark last night. "On her birthday one year; it's her sign." She sat up, gripping the washcloth tightly in her fist. He was circling territory she wasn't about to cede. "All right, I think that's about as good as it's gonna get for you 'til we find a pharmacy."

Will sat up himself and nudged her leg with his foot. "You know, there's a lot we can talk about. There's a lot we should talk about."

"I know . . . I can't, Will."

He nodded, understanding. He'd understand it all, probably. Which made not telling him any of it purely an act of self-sabotage. But that, at least, she understood.

Anna's booking agent's main directive was to cram as many shows into as small a window of time as possible. But there were always a few pockets during a tour where the crew was lucky enough to be presented with two—or sometimes even three—days in a row without a gig. When this happened in a mid-sized, Rust Belt city, no one was too enthused. But this year, they found themselves gifted with more than two full days in LA.

"Can we *do* something tonight?" Anna said giddily, as they pulled into the Beverly Wilshire parking lot.

"What're you thinking?" James asked as he scarfed down a bucket-sized bowl of Lucky Charms.

"Ooh, can we see a movie? I feel like I still haven't been in a theater since Covid," Violet said, already pulling up listings on her phone.

"Watching a movie with him is extremely annoying, no," Anna said, nodding toward Will. "Unless you want to hear how the score doesn't *quite* correlate to the intensity of the scene." He made a face at her. "Also, come on: we're in LA! We can do better."

"I wanna go bowling," James said, slurping up the last of his milk.

Anna wrinkled her nose and wiggled her fingers. "Can't. These babies are insured."

Will looked at her incredulously. "For real?"

"'Fraid so."

He shook his head. "Your life is strange."

"How about sleep in a real bed? Is that better?" Duncan called from the bathroom, where he was brushing his teeth.

"Ignoring that," Anna said. Her face lit up. "Oh! Karaoke? Remember that place from a few years ago?"

"Oh, okay. I could be down for that," Violet said, nodding. "I think I fucked one of the guys from MGMT the last time we were there?" she said, crinkling her nose in remembrance. "Anna, didn't you—"

Anna clamped her hands over Lottie's ears. "Moving on!" she trilled. "But yes to karaoke? We're in? Quinnie, my love, can you book us a table? And do you wanna come?"

"I'd probably rather get a Pap smear than sing karaoke with all of you," Quinn said, already looking it up on her phone. "But yes, I will get you a res."

"Also ignoring that," Anna said brightly, and clapped her hands like a little kid. "This'll be fun."

Quinn reserved them a large private room at Max, a no-frills downtown spot with neon lights swirling on the walls, cheap pitchers of beer, and karaoke in over a dozen languages. Anna immediately grabbed the large black binder of song choices. "Lottie, what's your go-to?" she asked, flipping to a new page.

"I'm not actually sure I've ever done karaoke . . ." Lottie said, curiously eyeing the space.

Anna looked up, mouth open. "Lottie. No! That's unacceptable." She slid the binder over to her. "But choose wisely. This is a tough crowd." She turned toward James. "Can we duet it, Jamie? It's been a minute."

James poured himself a glass of beer, held up a finger for her to wait, then downed half of it. "Ready."

A waitress swooped in with a tray of tequila shots and limes and placed it on the table in front of them. Anna quickly gulped one and made a face as she sucked on the wedge. "Ditto."

"So that's one down, how many more until we get Southern Anna?" Duncan drawled out the last words while grabbing a shot himself.

"That is not a thing," Anna scoffed.

"Oh, it's a *thing*, y'all." Violet, of course.

"Will? I know you've heard it," Duncan said, passing him a shot.

He knocked it back before speaking. "Will, I don't wanna go hooome yet!" he said in his best approximation of a twang. The rest of them roared with approval, minus Anna.

"I knew he was a real one," Duncan said, thumping him on the back.

"I pay all your salaries, you know that, right?" she said, pointing an accusing finger at them.

"Which is why we came out with you tonight," James said, grinning. "Okay, are we doing this, Buckley? I'm teeing it up." He stood and offered her his hand. "Shallow" lyrics flashed across the screen.

"Oh, you're choosing violence, I see." Anna gulped another shot before grabbing his hand. "Challenge accepted."

James had a deep, sonorous voice and, unsurprisingly, killed Bradley Cooper's part; Anna couldn't quite make it through Gaga's without laughing, but it didn't really matter. All of them—except for Lottie—were fairly buzzed already. The two finished to wild applause and took their bows.

Anna tossed the mic to Will. "I will bet you one million dollars I know what you're gonna sing."

"I am a man of mystery, Anna," he said, pretending to be appalled while he plugged in the numbers on the remote.

"Fine." She turned her back toward the screen. "'Dancing in the Dark' in three . . . two . . . one." She spun around just as the lyrics popped up and raised her arms triumphantly. "You're so fucking predictable," she said, and grinned. "God, I love it."

After Will muddled his way through the Boss, Duncan butchered "My Heart Will Go On," and Violet sang her heart out to No Doubt's "Don't Speak," Anna ceremoniously handed the mic to Lottie, who begrudgingly grabbed it.

"I don't even want to know how many Grammys you guys have between all of you," she grumbled, standing up. "I'm taking one of these," she added, choking back a shot.

Violet nodded approvingly. "All right, girl."

"Whoa, wait a minute!" Will said, leaning forward.

Anna, laughing, pushed him back gently. "She's fine, old man."

Lottie keyed in her song and stood nervously in front of them, shifting her weight from foot to foot. The twinkly electronic intro to Robyn's "Dancing on My Own" filled the speakers. She began, barely audible.

"Sing out, Louise!" Anna yelled, and started clapping to the beat. The others soon joined in.

Lottie covered her face with her hand, but kept going. And by the time she hit the chorus, she'd found her stride, belting it out with a gusto that Anna recognized as clearly as her own reflection.

"Damn, little miss has pipes?" Violet said, in awe.

Will was staring at her, slack-jawed. "Did you know she could do that?"

Anna shook her head, chuckling. "No." She leaned her head on his shoulder. "Comes by it honestly?"

"I'll give you that one," he said, taking a sip of his beer and resting his head on hers.

When Lottie finished, Duncan and James both scrambled to kneel on the floor, kowtowing exaggeratedly to her as she, red-faced, took her seat.

"Own it, Lottie!" Violet said, shaking her lightly by the shoulders and laughing.

Anna's phone had been buzzing nonstop since they'd arrived; she finally pulled it out of her pocket to look. A 423 area code had called multiple times; it flashed up again now.

"I'll be right back, guys," she murmured, trying to keep her voice level as she quickly walked out into the hallway. The bright overhead lights felt like a slap; she was already a little unsteady on her feet from the tequila. She squinted at the screen and finally answered the call.

"Hello?"

"Anna? It's Mom."

It felt like ice had shot through the phone and ricocheted down her arm. She almost dropped it. "Why are you calling?"

"It's your daddy, baby. He's dead."

# TWENTY-EIGHT

**Anna**
*Shelby County, Tennessee*
1989

It starts off small. You get your hand slapped when you stand on your tippy toes to reach for a chocolate chip cookie that's cooling on the rack. You pull it back quickly, rubbing it, unfamiliar with the fast, searing pain. *What's wrong with you?* he says, staring down at you from so, so high above. *Don't you know better than to take without asking?* You don't. You're three. He moves the cookies away to a higher perch, makes sure to tell your mama you're absolutely not allowed a single bite. Then, at dinner, he eats one in front of you, staring at you the whole time while he licks crumbs off his upper lip.

At five, during a July day so hot your eyes burn from the sweat seeping into them, you accidentally tip over a Big Gulp in the back seat of the car, the condensation on the cup making it slide out of your hands like a slippery striped bass. The Coke soaks fast into the fuzzy gray seat and spreads like blood from a wound; the ice piles up in your lap and makes your thighs go numb. You make the mistake of giggling, because it tickles. When he realizes what you've done, he pulls over on the side of the road, yanks you roughly by the arm out of the car, and lays you over the top of the scorching metal hood. You remember the cars whizzing by, swirling up eddies of dirt that scorch the inside of your nostrils. You remember seeing your friend Cassidy's mom drive by; she slows, but does not stop. You remember getting whooped so hard on your behind that you stand that night while you eat dinner. *Why don't you sit down, baby?* she asks you. You look at him, and you look at her, and you don't say anything.

At six, at your mawmaw's piano, you tease out your very first melody. It feels like rainbows coming straight out of your fingertips, like you've finally found the magic that's been crouching inside you all this time. You never want to stop touching these keys, and it feels like you couldn't, even if you wanted to. *Quit it*, he says. *I'm trying to watch the game. Quit it. Do you hear me?* But you don't, you can't hear anything other than this wondrous sound you're making from your very own mind. He slams his beer down, gets up from the couch, and then he slams the fallboard down on your knuckles. *That's what happens to little girls who don't obey their daddies*, he says. *Don't you forget that.* How could you? You couldn't move your hands properly for weeks. There's still a small dent on your left-hand middle finger that you rub when you're anxious.

At seven, you realize you can sing. And this gives you the voice you didn't have before. When he throws your library book into the bonfire because you were reading instead of playing tag with your cousins, you look him straight in the eye and tell him he's mean. *Mean?* He laughs, astounded. *I'll show you mean*, he says. He storms back into the house, the porch door screaming behind him. He emerges, eventually, with a black leather belt with a big, thick silver buckle and you don't have time to run into the woods before he grabs you. You scream yourself. It doesn't matter. Your mama—where was she before?—finally touches his shoulder lightly. *That's enough*, she says. But it's not, at least not for him. The belt leaves long, bright pink tiger stripes diagonally down your back. She doesn't say anything, just takes your hand, leads you up to their bedroom, and lays you down in her lap on your belly. She presses a cold washcloth down on the welts, tries to ease the sting, but it's too deep inside already.

At nine, school calls one afternoon when she's not home, but he is. Asks what those bruises are running down your legs like someone spilled grape juice on you and forgot to clean it up. Asks if you're getting enough to eat, because you seem too skinny and too hungry during lunch. Asks, *is everything okay at home?* But they don't really care; they're just checking a box. *Yes, ma'am. She's just clumsy. And built small. Thank you kindly for your concern*, he says. *What did you say to them?* he asks, when he hangs up. *What happens in this house is none of their goddamn business.* I didn't say anything, you tell him. Which is the truth. There's no one there to hear you. *You can wear pants until those are gone*, he says, staring at your legs. But he gets smarter after that: only leaves marks where no one can see them.

At twelve, you run away for the first time, trying to make your way to Nashville, where the music is. Where, maybe, someone will understand you, or at least the music that comes out of you. When he finds you walking down 12 South with your bag and your Discman, he pulls you by the ponytail into the back of his pickup truck. He kicks you in the ribs one, two, three, four times with those steel toes, and drives home without once looking back to see if you fall out when he takes a hard swerve. When you arrive at the house, she's waiting at the door and the look on her face is one you can't discern. It's not until later, much later, when you've lived more, that you recognize it for what it is. *Oh my god*, she's thinking. *What have I done?* She watches as he forces you up the stairs, pushes you into your room, and locks you in. He locks you in for two full days, even as you bang hard enough to put splinters in the door. She comes and sits outside it late into the night, when he's passed out in his stupid fucking chair and can't hear shit. *I don't have a key, baby*, she whispers anyway. *I'm sorry.* You pee in a water bottle and dream of making him drink it.

At thirteen, with the help of your middle school music teacher, you apply to boarding school and give her address as your own. When the big, fat envelope plops through her mail slot, she calls with glee to tell you they offered you a full ride, a full ride for all four years. A ride out of here, you think. *I'm leaving*, you announce to them, late into the summer. *They're gonna pay . . . for you?* he asks. *I think I hate you*, you say. And, still, to this day you're not totally sure what comes over you, but you spit in his face. He's almost impressed as he wipes it off his cheek, but then, he's just angry. He pummels you so fiercely that you change in the bathroom stall for the first month of school, terrified of your roommate finding out what's underneath. Terrified of anyone knowing where you've come from. When you're forced to go back home—once a year, for summer break—you do your best to avoid him. But one night, at a rare family dinner, he lunges for your neck when you insult him over something so ridiculous you can't even remember what it was. You grab a steak knife and slash him shallowly on his forearm. The blood springs out like tiny pomegranate seeds and you feel like Persephone, forced back to the underworld again and again and again. But this night: this is the last time he dares to touch you.

At eighteen, you leave again, this time for Brookfield, and this time for good. He watches you from your bedroom doorway as you finish cramming sweatshirts into your suitcase. *Who do you think you are?* he asks, almost amused. *I don't know*, you finally say, coming to stand right in front of him. His breath reeks of beer already and it's not even eleven. *But I'm not gonna find out if I stay here. I'm not gonna figure out what I need to say if I stay here*. He rolls his eyes. *No one gives a shit what you have to say, Anna. Don't be ridiculous. You'll end up back here knocked up and useless just like your mama*, he says with a smirk. You take a step closer. *You think I'd ever force this life on someone else? I'd rather die. I'm never coming back here*, you add, almost surprised it needs to be said out loud. *And I never, ever want to see you again.* And you don't.

At thirty-eight, you're alive but he's dead. *Fuck you*, you say. *Fuck you. Fuck you. Fuck you.*

# TWENTY-NINE

**Lottie**
*Los Angeles*
June 20, 2024

Anna was not okay.

They could all see it. No one knew what to do.

Lottie had pinpointed the start of the crumbling to three days earlier, when Anna had dipped out of karaoke to take that phone call. Her face was ashen when she returned, but she ignored the question when Will asked if everything was all right. She proceeded to knock back two, maybe three, more tequilas and insisted that everyone keep singing. Her bandmates—Lottie couldn't tell if they were oblivious or just inured—obliged, keeping pace with her shot for shot. By the time they left at last call, James had to fireman-carry her out to the waiting car, Anna bobbing in and out of consciousness over his shoulder. Lottie had never seen her anywhere close to that fucked up.

But the next morning, she was oddly energetic, scheduling a last-minute rehearsal for the band even though the show wasn't for two days. Lottie tagged along to the session, as much out of curiosity as a sense of duty. Everyone in the band was wrecked: none was expecting to be put to work just a few hours after the sloshing excess of the night before. Violet had to excuse herself twice to go puke; Duncan kept his sunglasses on the entire day.

Anna was pacing the length of the studio, lost somewhere deep inside herself. "Maybe we mix things up for the LA shows. I'm feeling like I want to rewrite the whole thing, you know?" she said, her fingers dancing animatedly around her.

Her manager, Toby, whom Lottie had heard during phone calls, but hadn't yet met, was sitting in on rehearsal. He was in his fifties, maybe, all business in dress and manner. "Anna, no. For a thousand reasons." His weary tone implied this was a battle of wills they'd fought before. "And you guys have been at it for three hours already; you should break for lunch."

Duncan nodded slowly. "I'm dying here. I need a burger."

Anna waved Toby off. "I'm not hungry. If they need to eat, fine, I guess. I'm gonna stay here, work on some solo stuff." She walked to the piano.

Toby raised an eyebrow. "You're not superhuman, you know. Food and sleep is good for you, too."

"No interest, thanks," she said, already engrossed in the keys.

Anna eventually, begrudgingly, allowed the band to return to the hotel a couple hours after lunch, but she herself stayed for the rest of the day. Lottie didn't have much of a desire to hang at the studios when she could be exploring LA, but something about this manic hyperfocus made her feel like Anna would unravel herself completely if left alone. Will texted around seven to ask if they were still there, and when Lottie answered in the affirmative, he said he was coming over himself to bring her back.

Anna was messing around, again, with the intro to one of the songs off *Constellation Story* when Will walked into the studio, brow furrowed.

"Hey," he said as he came up behind her at the piano, gently putting a hand on her shoulder. "You've been here all day. You guys should come back, yeah? Did you eat?"

She shook her head, still playing.

"Have you eaten at all today?"

Another shake.

"Jesus. Okay, come on, it's time."

She finally looked up at him, as if surfacing from a trance. "I don't need a babysitter, Will. I'm fine."

"You've barely slept and you haven't eaten. You've gotta come back," he said firmly.

"There's so much I need to sort out, still," she said, tapping her finger impatiently on the soundboard.

"The piano will still be here in the morning. You can't stay all night." He had both hands on her shoulders now and was leaning in close. "Please, Annie," he whispered. Lottie could hear the flash of desperation in his voice. "You're scaring me."

She eventually nodded, relenting.

The next day brought more of the same: the band's morale was visibly low from being drilled so acutely on what they thought would be actual days off. The simmering tension was enough to keep Lottie from rehearsal: she and Will went to the Broad Museum instead. They needed a distraction; Anna's erratic behavior had set all of them on edge.

"Are you worried?" Lottie finally asked as they wandered around one of the Kusama infinity rooms, their bodies multiplied in the mirrored, lambent space. The reflections made it feel like they were floating, untethered.

"Yeah," he said quietly. It was a little too dark to discern his expression.

"Do you know what's going on?"

He shook his head. Behind him, dozens of mirror Wills did the same. "I keep trying to ask, but she won't give me anything."

"Has she done this before?"

He turned to her, surprised at the question. It took him a moment before he finally nodded reluctantly.

"What happened?"

He looked down at the mirrored floor; it felt like an infinite drop from where they were standing. "She got lost. That's all I should probably say."

"Lottie! There you are. Can I ask you a huge favor?" Riley was visibly frazzled as she approached their table.

It was the morning of the first LA show. Lottie and Will were having a desultory breakfast in the lobby: neither had seen Anna yet. She nodded, her mouth full of cereal.

"Stacey, the merch manager? Is super sick with a stomach thing. Could you work it tonight?"

Lottie nodded again.

Riley put her hands up in prayer. "Oh my god, thank you. It feels like the wheels are off for this one, right?" She shook her head in confusion. "Okay, gotta run. See you later."

It being LA, Anna had a flurry of press appearances before sound check. And Lottie working the table meant she had to bypass Anna's hair and makeup session and the show itself: there was no way to see if she was still running on these adrenaline fumes.

Selling merch was at least a good distraction: the line tumbled seemingly endlessly outside the Greek. She didn't have time to contemplate much other than shirt sizes and poster tubes.

"Did you see on Deux Moi she was out at Chateau Marmont last night? We should have gone," a twenty-something brunette fan moaned to her friend as they approached the table.

"No way. Who with? The band? That new guy Will?" the friend—shaved head, glasses—asked.

Lottie stiffened. How the hell did they know about Will? And was Anna out last night?

"Is he the one who was in those karaoke pics?" the brunette said. "No, not him. I think maybe she was just out by herself?"

"That's very vintage Anna of her . . . Oh my god, what if she's back with Rory?" the friend squealed.

There was that name again. Lottie really needed to Google him.

"I hope not. That fucker's bad news," the brunette said, flipping through the sample concert program.

"I mean, maybe. I kind of love them together, though. And, didn't *Eleusinian Mysteries* come out after they broke up that one time? That album is *god-level* good." The friend finally looked at Lottie, who was glaring straight at them. "Oh. Hi. Can I get a keychain?"

She basically threw it at him. "That'll be twenty-five."

By the time the post-show crowds cleared out at the table, Lottie was nearly asleep on her feet. She'd just collapsed on top of her bed, melting into the duvet, when Anna knocked from the shared door and stuck her head in.

"Oh no, you're not going to sleep yet." She opened the door all the way and launched herself onto the bed next to her. "We get real after-parties for the LA shows! The label rents out a lounge somewhere, it's a whole thing. And not that you really care, but there's always a bunch of other musicians and actors. It's a scene." She widened her eyes, then popped up off the bed and walked to the door connecting Will's room. "He better not be asleep, either."

She knocked, then let herself in. The lights were off; he was definitely asleep. Lottie heard him groan as Anna presumably shook him awake. A few minutes later, both of them emerged back into Lottie's room, Will pulling a T-shirt on and rubbing his eyes, Anna beaming. "He's up now."

"Hold on, you want Lottie to come, too?"

Anna put a reassuring hand on his chest. "It's a private party; it's totally fine. No one's gonna post pictures or anything."

"I'm not worried about fucking photos, Anna." Will was suddenly wide awake. "I'm worried about bringing a sixteen-year-old to whatever the hell you're dragging us to."

"She can handle herself." Anna looked to Lottie. "Right? You can handle yourself." Lottie nodded, not knowing how else to answer. "It'll be a good time, promise," she wheedled, walking two fingers up his arm. "And I want you guys there."

Will looked to Lottie. She shrugged. "Fine," he said, exasperated. "I'd rather go than you go alone."

She narrowed her eyes at him. "What's that mean?"

"Nothing. Forget it," he said quietly.

"Everything is fine. I'm fine! But I'll be more fine once we get there, so, let's make moves, okay?" She clapped her hands. "Chop chop."

Anna's label had rented out a club called Mr. Franky's in West Hollywood. There was a handful of paparazzi stationed outside: the first time Lottie had seen them at anything Anna-related.

"They're definitely not here just for me," Anna said, laughing, as they walked by the bouncer. "Label PR probably called them for whoever else they're sticking on the list."

"But isn't this your party?"

She shrugged. "Nothing in this industry is really yours, if you're just the artist." She smiled wryly and pushed the door open.

As Anna had predicted, it was a scene. There was a DJ blasting something that was definitely not Anna's music, waitresses strutting by with specialty cocktails balanced precariously on trays, and at least a dozen actresses and singers who had worn Aidan's dresses on carpets. Anna got pulled away by Toby to chat with some C-suite brass as soon as they walked in, leaving Lottie and Will on their own.

He looked supremely uncomfortable, surveying everything with his arms folded gruffly across his chest. "This is . . . too much. This whole week has been too much."

Lottie pointed to the martinis whizzing by them. "Have a drink at least? We might be here a while."

He sighed and grabbed one off a tray. "I think you're right on that." He nodded toward Anna, who was now sitting on top of a banquette with Violet, toasting with shots. "Well, cheers," he said dryly, and took a sip.

Within the hour, the lights turned down as the music turned up. The handful of A-listers were attracting their own orbits: crowds hovered around them as if the proximity alone could siphon off some of their glow. Anna, meanwhile, was working the room, taking photos with VIP-level fans, or being escorted around by Toby to glad-hand. Every once in a while, she'd pull Lottie over to introduce her to someone—an old backup singer, an actor—and then flit away. Will was sitting moodily at the band's table nursing a beer but was clearly tracking all of Anna's movements.

At some point, an actor named Cooper something or other, whom Lottie recognized from a popular HBO show about college kids (the name escaped her: she'd snuck a martini or two herself), sidled up to her.

"You having a good time?" he asked, gesturing with his cocktail toward the melee around them.

She shrugged. "I guess. You?"

He smiled. "Better now that I found someone to talk to."

The two chatted lackadaisically for a while; Cooper was cute, but not a particularly riveting conversationalist. At some point, however, he must have read her disinterest as playing hard to get. He inched closer and closer until he had her pretty much cornered, then started kissing her neck; Lottie tried to push him off.

"Hey, bro. No thanks," she said, attempting to squirm out from under him.

"Don't be like that," he murmured, squeezing her breast before she had a chance to stop him.

"No, seriously, fuck off." Lottie tried to elbow him, but he grabbed her hand and pinned it against the wall behind her head.

"What the hell are you doing?" Will suddenly yelled from behind him. He grabbed Cooper by the shoulders, spun him around, and to Lottie's utter amazement, socked him right in the jaw. "She's sixteen, asshole! Get the fuck out of here." He pushed him away from her and put a hand on her arm. "Jesus, are you okay?"

Lottie nodded, wide-eyed, as she watched Cooper slink away toward the exit. "But thanks. Did you just . . . punch him?"

"Sure did. Only benefit of having three older brothers." Will rubbed his knuckles. "We're leaving, now, yeah? I knew this was a terrible fucking idea," he muttered as he took her by the hand and walked toward Anna's table. She and Duncan were in hysterics over something he'd just said. "We're going home," he announced to Anna.

"Oh, don't be like that," she said, still giggling. "Why so serious?"

"Because you're acting like a fucking child!" he shouted, loud enough to be heard over the bass. "I have no idea what the hell is going on with you. And you have no idea what just happened to Lottie because you're over here doing . . . fuck-all."

Anna stopped laughing; her eyes flashed hot with anger. "You wanna know what's going on with me, Will?" she said, sitting up straighter. "My dad's dead. That's what's going on. So, fucking cheers to that." She took a swig of her drink.

"What?" Will said, astonished. He walked closer to the table. "Are you serious? When?"

She waved him off. "Doesn't matter. He was an asshole."

"It does matter. Come home," he said, extending a hand. "Please."

Anna swatted it away. "Like hell I am." She was starting to slur her words.

"Anna, come on. This is not what you need right now."

She laughed, bitterly, and took another sip. "Like you know what I need. You don't know who I am anymore."

Will looked as if she'd slapped him. "Yeah. I guess you're making that pretty clear." He took a step back and shook his head. "Let's get out of here," he murmured to Lottie, then grabbed her hand and pulled her swiftly behind him through the heaving crowd.

# THIRTY

**Anna**
*Los Angeles*
June 21, 2024

Anna stumbled into her hotel room somewhere north of 4:00 a.m.; it took her five tries with the keycard. The past few hours were already a little too blurry to recall, like a watercolor painted with too-wet brushes.

To her surprise, Will was still up and sitting in an armchair in the corner of her room. Snapshots of their earlier argument began to coalesce into snippets of memory, but she still couldn't discern more than the outlines. What she did recall didn't seem terribly promising.

"What are you doing here?" she asked, but didn't wait for a reply as she made her way to the bathroom. "Just grabbing something real quick, then I'll go to bed," she added, trying for breezy. It was late—too late, really—but it was only one quick bump. That would be enough to push any lingering thoughts of home—of him—straight off the cliff. Tomorrow, she'd be fine without it. She would.

"It's not there," Will said from the chair. He sounded exhausted.

She froze, her back toward him. "What do you mean?"

"Just . . . cut the bullshit. It's late. I'm tired," he mumbled.

"Your nose was bleeding. At the club. You've barely slept for the last three days. I haven't seen you eat. Doesn't take a genius to put it together."

She flinched and tried to quell her rising panic before she spoke. "Let me explain—" She spun back around.

"No, let me finish." He was staring at the floor. "I can't risk you having that around, not with Lottie here. I chucked it, obviously. Unless you've got more stashed somewhere."

She hesitated, then shook her head.

He nodded and sat up. "Lottie's on a plane tomorrow. So am I." He paused. "I wouldn't be able to live with myself if something happened to her. Not after waiting this long. And it's not safe for her to be here anymore, not with you like this. And I . . ." He swallowed. "I can't do this to myself again, Anna. It's too fucking hard. You have no idea what it was like the last time."

She closed her eyes and sunk to her knees on the carpet.

Will looked more defeated than she'd ever seen him, hunched over with his elbows on his knees, his head in his hands. "You know," he began, "I left a ticket for you that night. That first New York Phil show, after we graduated. Now I know why you never could've been there." He chuckled lightly. "But at the time, there was still some dumb part of me that really thought you might show up." He was quiet, buried in the memory for a moment.

"I have left a center orchestra seat, fifth row, for you at will call every time I play New York," he finally said, looking up. "It's pretty masochistic because there's always an empty seat right in my sight line." He smiled grimly. "I think it got to be almost . . . talismanic at some point. I mean, I knew you weren't ever actually coming. But I liked writing your name on the envelope. Like you were there watching in some alternate way our lives could have gone." He exhaled what felt like a whole year's worth of breaths.

"Anyway." He stood up and looked at her directly for the

first time, hands shoved deep into his pockets, shoulders low. "It breaks my heart to see what's happened to you, Annie. But you cannot keep running from all of it forever. It's gonna kill you. So, as someone who loves you"—here, his voice cracked, almost imperceptibly—"I really hope you can find the help you need."

He walked to the door and turned around with his hand on the handle. "What a fucking waste if you don't."

It wasn't always like this.

For a long time, she'd had it under control. For a long time, it had been an occasional thing: when she was really tired, or really angry, or really sad, or maybe, all three.

There was a time, though, before it was under control. When it was an everyday thing. When she came very, very close to losing the thing that she'd given everything else up for.

Like nearly all her bad decisions, this one was also Rory's fault.

It was May 2009. Both of them were booked to play Primavera Sound in Barcelona: Rory's band as a headliner and Anna toward the very bottom of the poster. Not that she cared: it was her first major festival appearance and she was dizzy with the honor of even being asked.

They hadn't seen each other since the end of the Vagabonds tour, maybe six months before. And yes, they'd messed around some during that, but nothing serious and they weren't in close contact after it wrapped. Anna wasn't even sure she'd run into him there: the three-day festival took over the Parc del Fòrum, and backstage was almost as frenetic as the crowds themselves.

That cast of characters was interesting enough to keep her occupied even if she didn't find him. So many were heady with new fame and new money and new access to sex and drugs and people who would tell them yes even when the answer should most definitely be no. Consequences seemed like a state that existed for people out there, not here. Not here where everyone was beautiful, and talented, and so, so very young. Out of the lineup that year, at least a dozen would enter rehab before twenty-five. Three would be dead by thirty.

But Anna didn't know any of that then. She was actually having a pretty fun week: her set had been on the first day, but her performer's pass granted her access to any stage for the whole run of the festival. She dashed from Aphex Twin to Phoenix to Yo La Tengo, and nearly fainted when she bumped into Neil Young. The composer Michael Nyman, one of Will's heroes, was there, too; she kept an eye out for him all week, but never saw him. There was so much gallivanting, in fact, that she lost track of the date.

Then Maya called.

Anna saw the number and felt her face go numb. They hadn't spoken since Maya had left Ireland; Anna had said only to call in the event of a real emergency. She thought about not picking up at all, but knew that was only a short-term solution. Finally, she wove her way toward a quiet corner backstage and answered.

"Hey, Anna. Everything is fine." Maya's voice was always so calming. "I really struggled with whether to call. But, well, I want to do something special for Lottie's first birthday in a couple days. And I thought you might be able to help."

Anna's knees gave out before Maya even finished speaking. How could it have been so long and so short all at once? How did her body not remember even if her mind forgot? She took a few deep breaths before she responded and tried to sound casual. "What were you thinking?"

"I was wondering if you might record the lullaby you wrote? I can't play any instrument to save my life. And, obviously, I wouldn't tell her who it was from. You can say no, of course." She paused. "Are you at a show?"

"Oh, yeah. Kind of."

"I'm sorry. I didn't realize—"

"No, it's fine. Um, I'll think on that, okay?"

"Of course."

Anna hesitated. "But, she's good?"

"Yeah," Maya said softly. "She's wonderful."

"She's healthy?"

"Very much so. Just started walking, she's babbling a ton. Loves music. I can send pictures—"

"No. No, that's all right." Her hand was balled into a fist so tight she was worried she might be bleeding. "I'm sorry, Maya, I've gotta go."

"Oh, okay, sure. Well, you know how to find me . . . And you're okay?"

"Yeah. I'm fine. I'll be in touch?"

Rory found her maybe fifteen minutes later, sitting against a wall with her head in her hands. Outside on the stage, Deerhunter was absolutely shredding a guitar solo. The crowd was losing its mind.

"Oi! Buckley, that you?"

There was no mistaking that voice for anyone else's. She lifted up her hand in a meager wave.

"You look like rubbish."

"Lovely to see you, too." She stood up slowly. "Don't feel so hot, either. I think I'm gonna go back to the hotel."

"Hey." He put a hand on her shoulder, tried to meet her eye. "You all right, for real?"

"No." She gave him a tight smile. "Not really."

"Aw, but look where you are!" He gestured around him. "I just ran into Kim Gordon. Kim fuckin' Gordon! I nearly shit myself."

"That's . . . awesome. But, seriously, I gotta go." She started walking toward the exit.

Rory grabbed her hand and pulled her back closer to him.

"Hold on. I do have something that'll make you feel better. Truly."

She yanked her hand out of his grasp. "Yeah, I don't think so."

"Well, something that'll take your mind off it, at least. Whatever it is. Come on." He started striding toward the bathrooms.

Later, Anna would wonder what would have happened if she'd turned the other way. If she'd left. But the truth was if it hadn't been that day, it would have been the next, or the one after that. Rory carved four neat, white lines onto the dented metal ledge under the dirty bathroom mirror. "Ladies first," he said, brandishing a spooled euro.

"I shouldn't." She hadn't ever, either.

"You need a good bit of cheer. I can't stand to see your face like that." He reached up to tuck a piece of hair behind her ear and proffered the bill again.

She grabbed it from him and exhaled wearily, then bent down to snort a line. It burned; she coughed and rubbed her nose.

"There you go. Just give it a minute," he murmured soothingly behind her, then plucked the bill from her and did one himself. "It's Spanish shit," he said, tapping at the coke with the rolled-up euro. "Grand, really. One more?"

"I shouldn't—"

"Nah, I think you should." His dimples flashed. "We've got a long night ahead of us."

"Fine," she whispered.

He grabbed her ass while she did it and Anna found she cared not even a little. Once she finished, he spun her around roughly and kissed her full on the mouth, one of his hands already fumbling to unbutton her jeans. She didn't stop him this time. They fucked in one of the open stalls in the bathroom. Again, that night in his hotel room.

Anna did record the lullaby—only managing it thanks to Rory's steady supply. She sent the file to Maya on Lottie's birthday, and included a terse note not to call again unless it was an actual emergency.

It made everything easier, though; she wondered why she'd waited so long to try it. Back in New York, it was almost too simple to find her own dealer. Anna was amazed at the doors just a little bit of fame opened, even if most of them should have stayed shut. But she was already at work on songs for her next album and marveled at how little sleep she needed now, how much happier she could feel when she floored the gas pedal on her brain. What else might be out there, she wondered, that also made her feel this good? So she tried nearly all of it, mixing and matching the same way she stacked notes in a melody.

One night, maybe a year later at the Beatrice Inn, she lost track of the time, of the drugs, of the booze. Someone, she was never sure of who, called the ambulance. Kendall lost years off his life trying to keep it all out of Page Six. She probably never thanked him.

But that didn't mean that no one knew. When Anna had signed her record contract and finally gained a modicum of financial stability, she'd set up a will, leaving everything to Lottie. She'd also had Maya listed as an emergency contact, figuring if something happened to her, there'd be no one else to let her know.

Maya wrote her an email when she got out of the hospital, offering to pay for rehab, or therapy, or anything else she might need. Anna never responded. She was too ashamed to admit she needed help, and even more so that Maya (and Aidan, she was sure) knew what had happened.

Her record label, sensing her prospect as a cash cow, never raised the issue of treatment. She was too valuable an asset to be taken out of commission right then. Better just to keep a closer eye on her, milk her while they could. When she was bone dry, she could be someone else's problem.

They did, however, force her to sign a more stringent contract, one with provisions for cancellation of future tour dates or promotional appearances if they found out about excessive alcohol use or drug abuse. While she didn't have much of a choice but to acquiesce, it seemed so absurd that it had come to this, already: that she was just another dumb, rock cliché well before her twenty-fifth birthday.

But all of it—Maya finding out; the quick but terrifying hospital stay; the threat of losing the music—scared her enough to nearly stop entirely. Nearly. And that was how it remained, until everything began unraveling so fast she could only grasp at strings.

# THIRTY-ONE

**Lottie**
*Los Angeles*
June 21, 2024

As a rule, Will was an even-keeled, go-with-the-flow type. He was agreeable, without being a pushover. But by the time they maneuvered their way out of Mr. Franky's that night, he was practically vibrating from anger.

They were on the sidewalk, waiting for an Uber. Anna had not followed them outside. "You need to go home," he said, pacing briskly in front of the entrance.

Lottie looked at him curiously. "We are going home?"

He stopped walking. "No, I mean *actual* home."

"Will, it's fine. We're not gonna see that guy again."

He looked back at the door. "I'm not worried about him."

"Anna?" she asked, incredulous. "She's just drunk. You heard her, she's messed up about her dad."

He shook his head, still staring inside. The frantic chorus of Icona Pop's "I Love It" was drifting out from the open door. "I don't think that's it." He turned to her. "You shouldn't be here anymore. Neither should I. We can look into flights when we get back to the hotel."

She took a step backward from him. "Speak for yourself. I don't need to go anywhere."

"Lottie, you are too young for all of this." His face was stern. "And there's a lot you don't know, okay? It's gonna be better for everyone if we leave."

"Better for everyone? Or for you? And I can make my own decisions," she said, raising her chin defiantly. "You're not my dad."

He let out a hollow laugh. "Yeah," he said. "She made goddamn sure of that, didn't she?"

"That's not . . . That's not what I meant."

"But it's the truth, isn't it?" He walked away from her, hands on top of his head. "I would have stepped up, if I'd known. You know that, right?" he said, turning back around. "I wouldn't have done what she—" He shook his head to keep from finishing the sentence. "I think we would have been okay, you and me," he added quietly. "We would have been okay." His phone buzzed. "Car's here," he mumbled.

They rode home in stony silence, the LA traffic thankfully light at this hour. Will stared out the window until a brightly lit billboard of Anna, languidly supine on a chaise lounge and dripping in Cartier, reared up in front of them. Then, he looked down at his lap. The empty seat between them might as well have been a concrete wall.

"You know what? I'm calling Aidan," he said when they arrived back at the hotel. They were walking down the hallway toward their rooms.

"Stop, it's the middle of the night there!" Lottie tried to wrest his phone from him.

"He needs to know what's going on," Will said, moving the phone away from her. "And I promised I'd keep him updated."

Aidan picked up before she had a chance to intercept. "Will? Everything okay?" he said sleepily through the speaker.

"Hey, sorry for calling so late. And yeah, not so much—Lottie's fine," he added quickly. "I don't think Anna is . . . Lottie needs to come home—" Will opened the door to his room and the two of them walked inside.

"I don't need to do anything," she interrupted. "Aidan, it's fine. Her dad died; she's upset. She got a little drunk tonight."

Will let out a short laugh. "Yeah, it's more than a little. It's more than just drunk. And it's more than just tonight."

"Ah, fuck," Aidan groaned. "I should've known this was gonna be too much for her. But I can't believe she's pulling this shit again. I shouldn't have let you go, Lottie."

"What do you mean, 'again'? What are you guys talking about?" Her eyes darted from Will to the phone.

They both were waiting reluctantly for the other to address it. Aidan finally spoke. "Anna . . . struggled after you were born. I think it was a lot harder on her than she thought it would be. And she dealt with it in ways that weren't exactly . . . healthy. She told me she was clean. I believed her. But it's sounding like that's not the case, anymore. So, Lottie? I need you to come home. I know I don't have the authority anymore. But I'm asking you to trust me. Please."

Tears had been welling in her eyes for the last few minutes, but they started toppling down her cheeks now. She sat down heavily onto the couch. "We can't just leave her . . ."

"Yes, you can," Aidan said. "I'm not trying to be an asshole here, but it doesn't sound like she's looking out for you. So why would you stay?"

Lottie looked at the phone in astonishment. "Because she's my family? Because it took me this fucking long to find her? And now you want me to go?"

"*She's* your family?" Aidan exclaimed. "You just met her! And is this really how you think family should treat you? Strung out and dragging you to god-knows-where in the middle of the night?"

"At least she's fucking here! You never are!"

"Okay—okay! Guys?" Will put a hand on her shoulder and sat down next to her. "Let's table that for a second. Lottie, he's right: it is not good for you to be around her right now. This isn't healthy."

She wiped her eyes with the back of her hand. "What about what's healthy for her? If we go, then what? Who's looking out for her?"

"That's not your weight to carry," Aidan said softly. "It's hers. Please come home."

She looked at Will, who slowly nodded his agreement. "It's not forever, just for right now."

Will booked her a flight to JFK leaving the next afternoon, and one for him back to Logan. Before they went to sleep, he insisted on locking Lottie's interior door from her side, so Anna wouldn't be able to get in. She told him he was being ridiculous; he said he wasn't taking any chances.

She watched him fiddle with the bolt while she was perched on the edge of her bed. "You know, I didn't put it together until right now—something about you calling Aidan made it click—But I was there, when he told Anna my mom died."

Will turned around quickly, opened his mouth to say something, then changed his mind. Instead, he came to sit next to her on the bed.

"I don't remember a lot from those first few days after, but I remember when he flew out. I think that's when I knew things weren't gonna—that she wasn't coming back." Will reached out to hold her hand in his. "I'd had a nightmare—I was having a lot of nightmares. So I went to go find him and he was on the phone with someone . . ." Lottie felt like she was unearthing a set of bones: the deeper she dug, the more pieces she uncovered connected to one another. "And he said, 'She's gone. Can you come?' And it was quiet for a while. But then, he said—" Here, she had to stop. This was the point of no return; this was pulling out the skeleton. "He said, 'Then can you ask him to come?'"

She felt, more than heard, Will stop breathing. They both knew what Anna's answer had been. He was still for what felt like minutes, then finally he nodded, stood up, and walked out of her room.

Lottie knocked on Anna's door at 8:00 a.m. When she didn't answer, Lottie pounded.

Finally, she heard her stir and eventually approach the door. Anna opened it a crack, then all the way. Last night's mascara had drifted into dark half-moons under her eyes; she hadn't changed out of her clothes from the club, either.

"Hi," she said quietly, and moved aside so Lottie could step in. Anna walked over to the couch and lowered herself slowly, like someone much older. "I'm sorry. About last night. Things got kind of out of control . . . Are you leaving?"

"Yeah." Lottie was still standing in the center of the room, hands in the pockets of her sweats.

"I guess I would, too." Anna patted the couch. "You wanna sit for a sec?"

Lottie shook her head no. "Did you—Did you ever think about keeping me?" It tumbled out before she even realized she was thinking it.

Anna looked up in surprise. "No," she said finally. She said it simply. Definitively.

Lottie nodded quickly, felt tears prickling and tried to force them back.

Anna's expression softened. "I couldn't do that to you. I mean, look at me." She picked self-deprecatingly at her shirt. "You deserved so much better. You deserved someone like Maya. And, Jesus, Lottie, I'm so sorry she's gone. And I'm so sorry I can't be what she was."

"You didn't reach out, though," Lottie said, staring at her. "When she died. I know you knew."

Anna looked as defeated as Will had last night. "Yeah," she said quietly. "I did. Getting that phone call was one of the worst moments of my life. And I know it doesn't compare in the least to what you went through."

"No," Lottie said, her voice thick. "It doesn't."

"I wish I could have been the person that came," Anna said, looking down at her feet. "I wish I had a good reason for why I didn't, but the truth is"—she exhaled deeply—"the truth is that I was scared. I was scared to see what you'd been through. And I was scared of what I might do to you." She leaned back on the couch, staring at the ceiling. "I ran really far in the other direction, after you were born. Like I had to prove I made the right decision, that I was too fucked up to take care of you. Sometimes, I'm not sure I've stopped running."

"That's not true, though," Lottie said. Anna looked at her curiously. "I see how you are with your fans. You just save all of that for them. 'Cause you choose what they get to see of you, and they'll take whatever crumbs you throw at them. It's love, I guess, but it's love on *your* terms. That's not the real thing. And then"—she shrugged—"you don't have anything left to give to the people who actually know you, who actually care about the real you." She paused, realization dawning. "I don't even think you're worried about protecting me and Will from them. I think you're worried about them finding out you have us."

Lottie hugged her arms across her chest. "You know, I didn't care who you were. That you had this whole crazy life. But if this is what fame or music or whatever does to you? I don't want it. You can't even see what you're missing anymore."

Anna couldn't meet her eyes; she looked down at the carpet instead.

"I wanted to get to know you, 'cause I thought maybe that

would help me figure out . . . me. So, it sucks that you couldn't let me in. It sucks that I wasn't enough. But I guess it was dumb to think that just 'cause we're related, there would be . . . something there." Lottie wiped at her eyes impatiently. "Aidan was right; I never should've come. It was better not knowing," she said quietly. "I'm gonna go."

"Lottie, wait." Anna stood up from the couch and walked toward her, her own grief a mirror.

Lottie put her hand out to stop her. "Save it for them. I don't wanna hear it."

# THIRTY-TWO

**Anna**
*Los Angeles*
June 24, 2024

They were gone. And the absence was physical, a cold, heavy stone on her chest that made it nearly impossible to breathe.

To avoid thinking about it, Anna was grinding herself to dust, which wasn't particularly hard between press hits and the three shows at the Greek. The unrelenting pace reminded her of those splatter art paintings she'd made in elementary school: they could be beautiful when they were spinning, but to stop them revealed the mess behind.

She saw vestiges of the two of them everywhere, regardless: the empty hotel rooms, none of Will's sheet music detritus scattered on her couch, no Lottie to make her laugh during hair and makeup. She was right back where she'd always been during tours—alone—but it didn't feel familiar any longer.

Tonight was an off night, at least. After back-to-back-to-back shows (and after-parties), everyone in the crew was cranky, exhausted, and nursing multiday hangovers that had only been interrupted by the application of more alcohol. Anna, however, had clung to the overstimulation of the past three days with a death grip: anything to keep the dead quiet of her room (and the pounding roar in her mind) from swallowing her whole.

This didn't mean she'd necessarily been well-behaved on stage. During this week alone she'd cracked the neck of a guitar, snapped two tambourines, and slashed open her heel when she stepped on the whiskey glass she'd thrown.

"We're switching to fucking plastic," Riley had grumbled as she'd walked offstage that night, limping. "And you're wearing shoes."

But while the band had already begged off any more nighttime jaunts this week, Anna had no intention of slowing the cycle. And she was fine venturing out on her own: one of her favorite dive bars to hit during tours was here in LA, Frolic Room in Hollywood. Kendall called as she was getting ready to hop in the car; she picked up as she headed into the elevator.

"What's up?"

"Hey. Did Will punch—" The service petered out.

Anna looked at her phone, bemused. She called him back from the lobby. "Sorry, did you ask if Will *punched* someone?"

"Not someone. Cooper DeWitt."

"Am I supposed to know who that is?"

"He was at Franky's after the first show."

"Okay . . . so were a lot of people?"

Kendall was impatient. "He's on that big HBO show, *Undergrads*? And, apparently, got punched in the face by your boyfriend. His publicist called me screaming today; she just figured out who did it. They had to cancel his filming this week; network's pissed. I told her not my circus, not my monkeys. But you happen to know anything?"

"He's not my boyfriend," she said curtly. "And no, I don't. But doesn't sound like him."

"Well, let's hope there's no video. You enjoying your night off?"

"I'm headed out."

"Really," Kendall said flatly. "You sure that's a good idea? I feel like you could maybe use a break? I've seen you onstage this week. That cover of Joni's 'Little Green' was fantastic, though, I'll give you that."

"Thanks, I think? And gonna make the most of our last night here, that's all."

"Well, lord knows I can't stop you. Just don't punch anyone, okay?"

She chuckled. "I think I can manage that."

"I'll see you in the morning."

Anna loved Frolic Room precisely because there wasn't anything special about it. The drinks were cheap and strong. The crowd didn't give a shit who she was. It smelled like eighty years of accumulated cigarette smoke, spilled beers, and cheap perfume. It was perfect.

She grabbed a seat on a wiggly black pleather barstool and ordered a Guinness from the burly, taciturn bartender: this was dinner. On the jukebox was the Cranberries. She smiled; she'd had a soft spot for the Irish band ever since Doolin.

One Guinness turned into two whiskeys on the rocks. Her head felt pleasantly fuzzy, like someone had stuffed it with batting. And she'd managed to get the bartender to open up; incredibly and incongruously, he was a huge Kate Bush fan. She'd serenaded him with the chorus of "Cloudbusting" to his great delight.

He shook a finger at her. "You should sing, like, professional."

"Yeah, you should. Those are some pipes," lilted a voice behind her.

Anna swiveled around slowly. Rory was standing behind her, grinning, in a ripped Aerosmith shirt.

"Anna Buckley, as I live and breathe."

She stared at him for a second in disbelief, then chuckled softly and shook her head. "What are you doing here?" She couldn't tell if he had a preternatural ability to always find her when she was near a breaking point, or if she just existed in that state far more than she realized.

He motioned outside as he lit a cigarette. “Saw your posters. And you’re always here when you’re in town. Pretty sure we’ve been in that manky toilet together, too.” He raised his eyebrows conspiratorially. The bartender gruffly motioned for him to put it out; Rory waved him off and took a puff, instead. “Want?” He proffered the pack.

Anna looked aghast. “You know I don’t smoke.”

He chuckled, the cigarette bobbing on his lower lip. “Like you don’t have your vices.” He nodded to her glass. “What number are you on?”

She ignored the question. “You just happened to wander in?”

The dimples flashed. “Fine, I called Sal.”

Sal was her driver. He was the only person in her crew who genuinely liked Rory, at this point. But he was also a big fan of the Vagabonds, which probably clouded his judgment. Anna took a slow sip of her whiskey. “Guess I know who’s on the chopping block tomorrow.”

“Stop taking the piss, you wouldn’t.”

She smiled. “Nah, I wouldn’t. I’d miss the goulash too much.”

“You’d be the only one. Mind if I join?”

Anna hesitated, then gestured to the open stool next to hers. Rory leaned over to give her a kiss on the cheek. “You’re a sight for sore eyes,” he murmured, testing the waters by touching her thigh. “How long’s it been?”

She shrugged. “A year? Stockholm, maybe? It all kind of blurs together with you.” She gave him a sarcastic smile and tilted her head back to finish off her drink.

“Then it’s easy to pick up where we left off.” He took no notice of the dig, hand sliding between her legs now. “But looks like I’ve got some catching up to do.” He nodded to her empty glass. “Can I get you another?”

She could walk out. She could walk out right now. She exhaled. "Why not?"

She was wrenched out of sleep by the sound of frantic banging on her hotel room door. It felt like someone had driven nails deep into the center of each of her eyeballs. On her left, Rory was passed out, naked and spread-eagled. She looked down at herself. Her clothes were also missing.

"Motherfucker," she groaned softly.

"Anna!" It was Kendall.

She grabbed her phone off the nightstand: it was 9:00 a.m. and she had a dozen missed calls from him. Did she have somewhere to be? She honestly couldn't remember. The last time she'd had a bender like this was, well, probably the last time she and Rory were together. What was that pithy one-liner about insanity? Doing the same thing over and over and expecting different results?

Rory moaned as he woke up. "What is that shite?"

"Don't worry about it. Just stay quiet."

"Anna! I'm getting security!" Kendall yelled from outside, still pounding.

"Fucking hell," she mumbled to herself. "Ken, I'm coming! Gimme a minute!" She stumbled into a pair of jeans without underwear and threw a T-shirt on before realizing it was Rory's. Whatever. She closed the door to the bedroom before walking out to the living room, then opened the main door just a hair. She stuck her head out. "Hey."

Kendall was close to apoplectic. "Hey? Do you know what time it is? You have a photo shoot *in an hour* and glam has been waiting downstairs for two. Where the hell have you been?"

"Here, obviously." Standing up had, impossibly, made the throbbing behind her eyes even more excruciating. "I overslept. Sorry. Can we push it back a few hours?"

He laughed, a little maniacally. "It's for *Vogue*. You want me to call *Vogue* and tell them you got too fucked up last night?"

"I said I'm sorry." She opened the door wider so he could walk in.

Kendall scanned the room, clocking the empty vodka bottle, the couch cushions scattered on the floor. And her bra. "What the fuck were you doing last night?"

"Don't worry about it."

He snorted. "Easier said than done."

Rory sneezed loudly, just then, from the bedroom. Kendall froze. "Who is that?" he said slowly.

"Probably coming from another room," she mumbled.

He stared at the bedroom door. "Please tell me that's Will."

Anna ran her fingers through her hair. It felt sticky. She had no idea why. "Will went home a couple days ago," she said quietly.

"Anna, please tell me that's not who I think it is." Kendall started striding toward the bedroom. "That really, really better not be who I think it is."

"Ken, don't—" She tried to outrun him to the door.

"Rory?" he called out.

"Is that Kenny I hear?" Rory called back.

"That's not my name," Kendall whispered under his breath. "Yes, it is!" he cried with mock enthusiasm while flinging open the door. Rory was still ass-naked on the bed.

"Jesus Christ," Kendall muttered, and slammed it shut.

"Sorry, mate! Be dressed in a minute."

He turned toward Anna, eyes big. "Are you fucking kidding me with this? *That* is what you were doing last night?"

"I didn't plan on it, okay? We ended up at the same bar." She was aware how absurd it sounded as soon as the words left her mouth.

"Literally, only bad things happen when he's around." He

gesticulated wildly around the room. "This? This is bad." He pointed to her. "This is bad, too."

Anna rubbed her temples. "I had a rough week. And I don't even think we did anything."

"Oh, that's very reassuring, considering he's naked in your room." Kendall looked at her outfit. "And I'm pretty sure you're in his shirt. And your bra is in a different room . . . Rory?" he yelled at the door. "You need to be out of here in five fucking seconds or I'm posting pictures of your cock on Instagram."

"Wouldn't be the first time!" he shouted gaily as he opened the door, wearing jeans and no shirt. He looked to have added about five more tattoos since the last time she'd seen him. "But I'm gone, all right?" He turned toward Anna. "Always a delight, Miss Buckley. I'll grab that later?" He tugged at her shirt and then leaned over to give her a kiss on the cheek, which she tried unsuccessfully to avoid. "Cheers, then!" he said, slamming the door closed behind him.

They were both silent for a moment, then Kendall opened his mouth to speak; Anna put her hand up. "Just don't, okay? I know everything you're about to say. Let me take a shower and you can send hair and makeup up in twenty."

He sighed heavily and nodded, then started texting.

"I'm sorry about all this, really." Anna gestured to her dishabille. "Will leaving—Lottie, too, it wasn't . . . planned."

He put his phone away. "Shit," he said softly. "I'm sorry, kid. You gonna be okay?"

She shrugged. "Don't really have a choice. We've got a lot more tour left."

He hesitated. "Do I need to be worried?"

"Of course not." She found it hard to meet his eye. "I've been through worse."

Losing Will and Lottie and gaining Rory in the span of a few days had put Anna dangerously close to the mindset she'd had the last time she'd lost total control. Postponing a handful of tour dates would be the prudent call; she wasn't so oblivious as to not realize that. But it would never be a viable option: she was too proud to do that to herself, and too indebted to do it to the fans. She could see that any safety net she'd had was in tatters; she was still grabbing that trapeze and jumping off the platform, hoping her grasp was strong enough.

She did, however, take the extraordinary—for her—step of reaching out to someone, rather than a bottle of Bushmills. There was only one person who had been a compassionate witness to all of her hairpin swerves (and drives to the cliff) over the past decade and a half. Anna FaceTimed her after she finished the shoot and showered off the pounds of makeup and hair spray they'd had to shellac on to make her look presentable.

"Hi, love! . . . Oh, you look exhausted." Maeve squinted into the phone, concern etched across her forehead. "Are you sleeping?"

"What do you think?" Anna asked her with a small smile.

Maeve sighed. "I guess I know the answer. You all right? I don't think I've caught you since you left for tour. I was hoping that meant everything was going well."

Anna shook her head, then burst into very unexpected tears. "I'm sorry," she said, surprised at the force with which they were pouring out. "I don't know what's happening. I'm really overtired, I think?"

"Oh, sweetheart. I know this schedule is tough. I wish you weren't so far away." She hesitated. "You sure that's all?"

Anna knew she looked a mess, but she could never hide anything from Maeve, anyway. She shook her head again. "Will and Lottie left. And . . . I think I slept with Rory last night."

Her eyes went wide. "You *think*?"

Anna nodded slowly.

Maeve clucked her tongue. "You've got to put an end to that

one. The two of you have been making each other mostly miserable for, what, fifteen years, now? I think that's long enough."

She exhaled. "You're not wrong."

"Of course I'm not." Maeve smiled. "Both of you have more talent in your pinkies than I have in my whole bloody body, but that doesn't mean you're good for each other. You've got to stop falling back into him just because he's familiar. I promise he's not the only one who understands this life you've got . . . What happened with Will and Lottie?"

"I don't know. I . . . torpedoed everything."

"Is it fixable?"

"I don't know."

"Well, what do you want to happen?"

No one had asked her that in a long time. She thought it over. "I don't know that, either."

"Oh stop that, yes you do. I've never known you not to know your own mind."

"I didn't know it would feel like this. To have them go." Her voice was still quavering, despite her best efforts to stop it.

"She's your baby, Anna. And you made her with him," Maeve said softly. "It's okay to miss them. And it's okay to let yourself love them, too."

She was crying again; her body felt like a betrayal with this intensity of emotion. "I don't know what to do."

"You go get them! Fly back if you have to. You're a smart girl, figure it out."

Anna forced herself to nod.

"And for Christ's sake, tell that eejit to leave you alone. I'll tell him myself the next time he's home. But if I have to hear that name from your lips ever again, it'll be too soon." Maeve pointed at her through the screen. "Don't run from the hard bits, love. You'll never get to the good parts, otherwise. And I want you to get to the good parts." She paused. "I'm not sure you've seen them yet."

* * *

Anna didn't have to wait long before she had a chance to follow Maeve's directive: Rory appeared like an unwashed apparition as she was packing. They were finally headed out of LA; tour math made it feel like they'd been there for a month. She opened the door without letting him in.

"I'm gonna kill Sal," she said calmly.

"Just came to grab my shirt," he said, putting his hands up in defense. "Well, and maybe say goodbye?" He had an arm around her waist before he even finished the sentence.

Anna extricated herself with an eye roll and walked briskly to the couch, where his shirt was draped on an arm. "Here." She tossed it to him.

He caught it with a frown. "You mad?"

"I'm fine." Her delivery was far from convincing, she was sure.

He tilted his head, confused. "Did I do something?"

"It's got nothing to do with you."

"All right." There was a spiky, awkward pause. "Do you want to . . . talk?"

She snorted. "'Cause we're so great at that?"

"You are mad."

"I'm not. I'm just . . . done." She leaned back on the couch arm. "It's the same shit every time, Rory. We get together, we have fun, then we have too much fun, and I spend months picking up the pieces." She looked up at him. "I need . . . more than we're ever gonna give each other."

Rory tossed his shirt from palm to palm while he took that in. "We could have had more," he said finally. "You didn't want it."

Anna stared at him incredulously. "And you did?" She let out a sharp laugh. "Let's not rewrite history. I remember your face when I told you."

He shrugged. "I would've come around, if you'd wanted to. Just sayin', you could have had another go. Coulda kept one."

She was stunned into silence for a moment. "Get the fuck out," she whispered.

"It's probably for the better. I mean, look at you." He gestured to her, shaking his head in pity. "You would've been shit at it."

"Get the fuck out of here, Rory." The volume of her voice surprised her.

He nodded, acquiescing, then headed toward the door. "None of this would've happened without me," he said, suddenly turning around. "Before you go writing everything off."

"Jesus, you really think that highly of yourself?" She folded her arms across her chest in defiance. "And I don't know. Might've been better that way."

"Can't rewrite history, Anna. You said so yourself." He leaned against the doorway. "There's a reason we keep ending up like this, you know," he said, staring straight at her. "We're the same, you and me. You push everyone away, eventually."

Aidan called soon after Rory left. Well, to be more specific: he had been calling and Anna had avoided picking up. Her own tenacity, however, was probably matched only by his; it was only a matter of time before she'd have to relent.

"Hi," she said cautiously.

"Nice to see you're awake during daylight hours."

"We're headed out soon—not that I'm not normally awake now."

"Right, of course, you're the real mother of the year over there. Why don't you ask your daughter what she thinks? Oh . . ." He paused. "Wait . . ."

"Let me explain—"

"You know when everything started to happen for you, with the music and the awards and all that bullshit, Maya was so scared you were gonna ask for her back. Every time you popped up on TV or on the radio or whatever, the look on her face . . . I should've told her she had absolutely nothing to worry about. You are incapable of caring about anything other than yourself and that fucking piano."

"That's not true."

"I don't want you anywhere near her, you understand?"

"How is she?" She almost couldn't ask.

"Now you wanna know?"

"I've always wanted to know, Aidan," she said quietly.

"Fuck you, Anna. She's been through so much. She didn't need this." His voice was coming apart at the seams. "I trusted you. I trusted you with *her*. That last part's on me; I should've known better."

He hung up.

# THIRTY-THREE

**Lottie**
*New York*
June 25, 2024

Lottie was furious with Will for calling Aidan. She was furious with Aidan for convincing her to come home. And she was furious with both of them for being right.

But, in out-of-character moves for them both, Aidan told her he was coming back early from out east to be there when she landed, and she didn't try to stop him. Neither was exactly fluent when it came to discussing the hard stuff, but his willingness to drop everything to meet her spoke volumes.

Since getting back to New York two days earlier, Lottie hadn't left the house and didn't let her friends know she was there, either. Aidan had told his office he had Covid, and they'd spent a few glorious days ordering in dim sum, catching up on old seasons of *RuPaul's Drag Race*, and generally avoiding discussing anything that had happened earlier in the summer.

Lottie was fully aware this was a temporary fix (both Will and Anna were calling; she was ignoring), but trying to process everything from the last week alone was like trying to sight-read Beethoven's Hammerklavier; there was no way her mind could keep up. Plus, watching drag queens was a lot more fun.

Tuesday morning, Lottie awoke to the acrid smell of something burning and quickly galloped downstairs to make sure nothing was on fire. Instead, incredibly, she found Aidan at the stove, frantically trying to wave off smoke from a blackened pancake.

"You must really be worried if you're attempting to use a frying pan," she commented from across the kitchen.

"I had this whole plan," he said, sighing and still fanning away fumes. "I was gonna bring them to you in bed. With berries." Frowning, he took the pan off the stove and ceremoniously deposited it with a crash into the sink. "I'm not great at knowing my limits," he added with a chagrined smile. "I just wanted to take care of you, for once."

She joined him at the sink and gave him a hug. "Thanks. For all of it."

He kissed the top of her head. "It is the least I can do. But, favor?"

She nodded.

"Can you please call Will back? He's really worried about you. It's kind of sweet, actually."

She'd rather open that channel instead of returning Anna's calls, at least. She nodded again.

Will looked so unequivocally happy when she FaceTimed him that she immediately felt guilty for sending him to voicemail the past three days.

"Hey, you. Doing okay?"

She shrugged. "You?"

"Same boat. Not my best week. Whatcha been up to?"

"Not much, trying to avoid thinking about . . . anything, really."

"I know the feeling." He paused. "So, listen, this might be the last thing you wanna do. But I'm gonna ask, anyway: Any interest in coming up here for a few days? I can show you Brookfield, you could sit in on a rehearsal, we can listen to some Bernstein. I miss our chats. And I miss . . . you," he said, a little shyly. "I hope that's okay to say."

She smiled. He was open and kind in the same way her mom had been. They would have liked each other immensely. "You know? That might not be so bad."

"Love the enthusiasm."

Lottie laughed. "Yes, I'd love to come."

"And this is where I teach most of my classes." Will pointed out a handsome Georgian building as they walked by on a tightly manicured path. "And the biggest theater is that one over there; that's where we have the senior showcases."

"I watched yours," Lottie said, nudging him on the arm.

"Oh my god, why?" He shot her a look of horror.

"What? You were awesome. You both were."

"Senior apartments are over there." He was changing the subject.

Lottie peered over with interest. There were about four or five, white-painted brick with black shutters. "So which floor was it?"

"Which floor what?"

"Where you two, you know . . ." She raised her eyebrows.

Will blanched and stopped walking abruptly. Lottie burst out laughing. "I'm sorry. Too soon?"

He quick-footed his way by the rest of the dorms. "I am never talking about that with you, let's get that out of the way now."

"Fair. So, third floor?"

"Lottie!"

She'd caught a train up to Boston that same week. Aidan was all in favor and, obviously, she didn't have anywhere else to be. Will had picked her up at South Station and they'd dropped her stuff off at his place in Cambridge before heading over to wander Brookfield. The campus was quieter without the scrum of students populating the quads, but it was still fascinating to see the place that was so formative for both of them. Lottie almost felt if she squinted hard enough, she'd see the two materialize on a picnic blanket on the grass, or jostling over the keys in one of the studios.

After the Brookfield whistle stop tour, and a quick refuel for lobster rolls at Saltie Girl—Lottie's request—they headed to Symphony Hall. Will was creating a new piece for a chamber orchestra he worked with frequently and now that he was back in town earlier, he'd scheduled a few extra rehearsals.

"You don't have to go, by the way. I can drop you somewhere on Newbury," he said as they were getting in the car after lunch.

"Are you kidding? I'm dying to see you up there."

He grinned. "Excellent. I'm pumped for you to hear it."

The nine or so musicians who made up the group were already warming up in a practice room when Will and Lottie arrived. They started to stand when he walked in, but he hastily gestured for everyone to stay seated. It was fascinating to finally see him in Anna's position of power: he wore it more lightly.

"Good to see everybody," he said with a wave. "Thanks for indulging me on the rehearsal, too." He put an arm around Lottie. "I brought someone along today, hope that's okay?"

They turned to look at her with curiosity; she offered a small wave herself.

"This is Lottie. She's a pianist and"—he looked to her for approval; she nodded with a smile—"my daughter."

A few of them couldn't contain their astonishment and let out a surprised laugh; all nine pairs of eyes swiveled to stare at her, then him, then back again.

"Didn't see that one coming, did you?" he said, raising his eyebrows. "I like to keep you on your toes. But story for another time, ladies and gents."

Will gestured to a few empty seats in the corner for Lottie to sit down. "Holler if we're off-key?" He grinned at her before turning back and tapping his baton on the music stand. "And on that note, let's begin."

An orchestral rehearsal, unsurprisingly, was an entirely different beast than a production like Anna's. There was no crew buzzing around the wings, catching cases or hauling amps; there were no amps at all. Sometimes, they'd start in the middle of the piece, then double back; at others, he'd pull out just one violin or flute, and they'd mold the music together, like two artists on a single piece of clay.

Mostly, Lottie was amazed at how effortlessly Will was able to keep every instrument's sound distinct in his ear, while simultaneously crafting how they came together as one sonic entity. It felt like magic to watch him coax a melody out of wood and brass and air; she also couldn't help feeling a little proud. She sat through the entire ninety-minute session entranced, barely wanting to twitch a muscle for fear of breaking the spell.

"What'd you think?" he asked her once they'd wrapped and the musicians had streamed out, leaving just the two of them in the rehearsal space.

Like many of Will's pieces, it was contrapuntal: every instrument told a different but connected story. Thinking about the complexity of writing such a work made Lottie's eyes water, but listening to it was easy. It was transportive. And beautiful.

"It was fire."

He wrinkled his nose in confusion. "What?"

"I loved it," she clarified. "Really."

He beamed. "Maybe you can come back for the premiere of the real thing?" He looked at the time on his watch. "I've got something else I wanna show you while we're here, too. Come with me?" He motioned to her with an enigmatic smile and headed out the door.

"Where're we going?"

"You'll see. Close your eyes," he said, and grabbed her hand. "Promise I won't run you into a wall."

Lottie looked at him suspiciously, but clamped her eyes shut. He led her down a hallway; she heard a door squeak open, then he walked her about thirty feet forward.

"Okay. Open."

She was standing at center stage. In front of her stretched three levels of seating, with balconies banded in gold. Above, the ornate, coffered ceiling was glowing with a few well-placed chandeliers. And to her left, a grand piano, a glossy Steinway Model D.

He tilted his head toward it. "Wanna have a go?"

"Right now?" she asked, eyes wide.

He shrugged. "I don't get rock-star perks, but I can sneak you up here."

Lottie shook her head no vigorously.

"It's just us?"

"No, I know. I just get a little bit of stage fright when I'm up there alone and somebody's watching."

"Ah, fair." He paused. "Would you play if you were by yourself?"

Lottie nodded, after a moment. She could feel how beautiful the acoustics were in the hall even from the sound of their voices. To actually play would be exhilarating.

"Then pretend I'm not here at all." He smiled and jogged off to the wings.

Lottie watched him go, then cautiously made her way to the piano and took a seat. It was polished to a shine so slick she could see her reflection. The setting seemed to call for classical, so she launched quietly into Debussy's Deux arabesques. The sound that flowed from the keys and reverberated around the theater was crisp and bright; it was easy to understand why Will loved playing here so much.

"I'm not here, but if I were, I would barely be able to hear you. Play to me here," Will coached, beckoning to himself as he settled into a front-row seat. Lottie felt herself blush, but increased her volume to mezzo piano.

"Good," he said, nodding, satisfied. After a few bars, however, he stood up abruptly and ran to the very back row of the orchestra section. "Now here!" he called out to her.

She looked up at him briefly, a small smile escaping, and played mezzo forte.

"Well done." He hopped up again after a minute, this time vanishing through the doors back out to the lobby. He reappeared, eventually, all the way up on the second balcony. "For the cheap seats, Lottie!" he yelled out, hands cupped around his mouth. "Play it forte!"

She laughed quietly and obliged.

"Yes! That's it!" Out of the corner of her eye, she could just make out Will's jubilant fist pump.

When she finished, he applauded and hollered the way the crowd did at one of Anna's shows. "Damn, that was awesome," he said, leaning on his elbows over the balcony.

"Anyone ever tell you you're pretty good at this conducting thing?" she called up to him.

He shrugged. "Once or twice."

"Are you thinking about conservatory? For college?" Will asked as he took another bite of pizza.

They were back at his place: he lived just off Harvard Square in a sunny pre-war with bay windows and views of the Charles. Like Anna's, much of the living room was given over to a grand piano; unlike hers, it actually felt lived-in. Framed snapshots of his family littered the shelves, along with a handful of bobbleheads of Red Sox and Patriots players.

"Honestly? I haven't really thought about it. I guess that's coming up with junior year, though," Lottie said, spearing a piece of romaine onto her fork.

"I mean, you're really, really good. Brookfield, or Juilliard, or wherever, they'd be lucky to have you. And I'm not just saying that 'cause you have half my DNA." He paused. "I don't know, maybe I am. Feels like your birthright."

She mulled that over while she took a sip of root beer. "The last few weeks have kinda messed with my head, in terms of ever wanting to do this full-time."

Will nodded in understanding. "I can see why." They were still tiptoeing around what happened in LA. "But there's so much out there: there's what I do; there's what the band does, as session musicians, when they're not on tour. There are a million paths you can take in music that aren't . . . hers." He gestured to her with his slice of pepperoni. "I've seen enough kids come through Brookfield to spot the ones who can't live without playing. And I hate to break it to you, but you're sunk." He grinned.

She laughed. "Maybe. You guys are a hard act to follow, though. Might be tough if everyone knew how we were . . . connected, or whatever you wanna call it. Even if you do keep a Grammy in your bathroom." She pointed an accusing fork at him.

He swatted the comment away. "Forget me and forget her. If we'd never met, if this summer had never happened, how would you feel about playing?"

"It's like breathing," she replied quickly. "You can't live without it."

"That's what Anna used to say, too," he said quietly. "But there's your answer. You do it for you, not for anyone else. And you do it however you want to. But I don't want you to be afraid to take up space. I promise, Lottie, people will want to hear you. They'll want to know what you have to say."

* * *

"Okay, so they have these dates in the . . . pods, but they can't see each other?"

"Right, that's the whole point. That's why it's called *Love Is Blind*."

"But then when they get engaged, they can see each other?"

Lottie nodded.

"I think it would be more compelling if they didn't see each other 'til the wedding, right?"

"Oh my god, just watch, Will!"

His doorbell buzzed loudly, just then, startling them both. He turned to her, puzzled. "Did you order more food?"

She shook her head.

Frowning, he got up from the couch and went to check the front door peephole. "Christ," he muttered.

"Who is it?"

He turned around, combing his hair back with his hand anxiously. "My . . . mom."

"Your mom's here?"

"Will, honey, I can hear you," his mother said loudly from the other side.

He opened his eyes wide in apology to Lottie, held up a finger, then cracked the door just enough to poke his head through. "What are you doing here?" he hissed to her in a whisper that was, obviously, loud enough for Lottie to hear.

"I know you said you didn't want me to come—"

"I did—"

"But"—Lottie could hear her voice hitching—"that's my granddaughter in there."

"Mom, Jesus—hold on." Will closed the door and let out a deep exhale. "I can tell her to leave," he said, turning around to face her. "I have zero problem telling her to leave."

"It's okay," Lottie said softly. "I'd like to meet her, too."

"Yeah?" His face relaxed in relief. "You sure?"

She nodded with a smile.

He nodded back in confirmation, then opened the door. Standing in the frame was a prim blond woman in her sixties, who didn't resemble Will so much in features as in demeanor. Well, from what she could gather—his mother burst into tears as soon as she spotted Lottie on the couch. Caught off guard, Lottie quickly scrambled up and crossed the living room to her—to her grandmother—where she was immediately pulled into a deep, bosomy hug.

"Oh, sweet girl." She sniffled into Lottie's hair. "Oh my goodness." She paused for a moment to push her out to arm's length to inspect her. "You look just like your mama, don't you?" She touched the top of Lottie's head gently. "But that's Pendleton hair," she added with a grin. "I almost forgot my manners: I'm Betsy. And my lord, is it good to meet you." She clutched her again in a tight embrace.

Will was watching them with a mixture of befuddlement and pride, when he jumped slightly and put a hand on his vibrating pocket. "Sorry, Quinn keeps calling. I should probably see what she needs." He picked up and wandered over to the kitchen.

Betsy, now beaming, gathered both of Lottie's hands in hers. "Will you come sit with me? I just want to . . . look at you," she said, delighted. She wrapped an arm around her and led her back to the couch.

But something about Will's expression wasn't quite right. He caught her staring at him and turned away, hunching protectively around his phone and leaning deeply over the counter. In her ear, Betsy was peppering her with questions about New York and school and piano, but Lottie was only catching about every third word, instead focused on Will's form growing smaller and smaller.

In the kitchen, Will hung up. In the kitchen, Will's whole body seemed to come apart, and his head slowly came to rest on top of his hands.

And that's when she knew.

# THIRTY-FOUR

**Anna**
*Seattle*
June 30, 2024

She was swimming. It was warm and placid, currents gently moving like silk across her cheeks. She could breathe, too, somehow, the water flowing through her mouth as easily as song. Below her, orange and pink corals quilted the seafloor. Above, the sun refracted into bright beams, dappling her arms with bands of light.

But as she dove deeper, it grew cooler and darker. Pressure built up around her, squeezing her body smaller and constricting her lungs. The glow faded from her skin. She pushed ahead even so, understanding now she was on borrowed time.

The last fingers of light were swallowed up, then sound followed. She swam deeper into this vacuum: the water cold now, and her breaths shallower. There was no end and there was no beginning, just this endless black water churning her forward, or backward, or up, or down. Eventually, she couldn't keep it outside of her any longer. It filled her eyes. Her nostrils. Her lungs.

She couldn't breathe anymore. She couldn't breathe. Oh my god she couldn't—

* * *

"She's waking up."

"Okay, let's get ready to extubate, please."

At first, Anna heard it all as if from some great distance, like they were calling to her from the other shore of a wide lake. Then, the sound smacked her clear across the face; she felt her limbs start to shake, gagged from the tube down her throat. She couldn't speak and she couldn't take a breath; she tried to shake her head violently to dislodge it, and quickly felt a pair of hands on her shoulders to steady her.

"Anna? I'm Andrew, the respiratory therapist. We're gonna take this out right now, but you've gotta be still for just a couple more seconds, all right?"

She felt the bed rise up behind her, another pair of hands moving her into a seated position.

"I'm gonna pull it out on the count of three, okay?"

She was panicked, but nodded.

"Great. And then as soon as I do that, I'm gonna need you to cough as hard as you can. Ready? One . . . two . . . three."

The tube felt like razor blades as it traveled up her throat. She coughed deeply once it was out and then took a few heaving breaths, finally filling her lungs. In the moment, she wondered if that's what it felt like to be born.

"Good cough. Don't try to talk for a while, okay?" Andrew finally materialized in front of her. "You gave everybody quite the scare. You remember anything from the past couple of days?"

She shook her head no.

"That's all right. They'll catch you up on everything later. You're gonna want to rest, anyway." He gave her leg a quick pat. "Glad to have you back."

She was in the hospital.

Fuck. How many days had she lost?

As frantic as she was for details though, it soon felt like gravity had increased tenfold and was sinking her body deep into the thin hospital mattress. Despite her attempts to clutch at consciousness, she was soon swept into a heavy, dreamless sleep.

When she finally came to, Will was snoring softly next to her, sitting in a chair with his torso flopped onto her bed. He was also holding her hand. She smiled and stroked his hair lightly until he started to stir. He twitched, then sat up with a start, rubbing his face.

"Annie," he whispered, his voice catching. "You're awake." His eyes scanned over her, as if checking for cracks. There were a few days of stubble on his chin; his eyes were red and a little swollen. "Sorry. I just didn't know, at first, if you were gonna wake up. It was fucking terrifying."

Her throat was far too raw to speak; she squeezed his hand instead.

"Do you remember anything?"

She shook her head.

Will nodded weakly and exhaled. "So, you had quite the mix in you. Xanax, Klonopin . . . a lot of alcohol. Quinn couldn't wake you up, so she called 911 and they brought you here. You were in the ICU for a couple days; they had you on a vent, but, obviously, that's out. Now it's just supplemental." Will tapped his nose and Anna touched her own, not realizing until then she had a tube in for oxygen.

"You're gonna be okay. You're really, really lucky Quinn found you when she did." He gave her an exhausted smile. "You probably have a lot of questions."

"The tour?" she mouthed. Of all the things to be asking, she knew this was an absurd request. But everything else felt off-limits.

Will took it in stride, surprisingly. Or, she was just that predictably single-focused. "Right," he said, then swallowed hard. "I need to tell you something that's gonna be tough to hear." He took a deep breath. "Tour's canceled. Your vocal cords are gonna be shot for a while, anyway, because of the intubation, but you're in violation of your contract. The label pulled the plug."

She shook her head again, faster this time. Angry tears were already pooling in her eyes. Will climbed onto the bed and enveloped her without giving her a chance to protest. Her throat, her eyes, her limbs burned; everything was too exposed.

"I'm so sorry," he whispered. "But we've got to keep you safe."

It wasn't intentional. And the irony was that she'd already turned the corner: Rory was gone; she was planning to fly back to New York after the West Coast shows, force them to forgive her. It didn't matter what she might have to give them in return.

But she was so tired. And she also couldn't sleep. And so, she was taking something for the former, and something else for the latter. And some other things, too: things that made her forget why she had to take anything in the first place. She'd done all of this before, to be sure, but never this carelessly. It was hard to care when the only people she cared about had made it abundantly clear they didn't care about her.

It wasn't intentional. But, maybe, it was curiosity. What would happen if she drifted down and down into that black water until what had happened and what might happen disappeared?

But she was back on the surface, now, breathing real air. It had been about twenty-four hours since they'd pulled the tube. Her throat felt like someone had shoved a hot poker down it, but at least she was able to croak out a few words. She felt just as burned mentally, but was, at present moment, attempting to camouflage that as best one can while still in a hospital gown.

"Have you overdosed before?" One of the hospital's social workers, who'd brusquely introduced herself as Val, was in the process of reading a thorough (and thoroughly ignominious) questionnaire off her laptop.

"Just once," Anna said. "If that makes a difference."

Val clicked a button and continued. "In the past few weeks, have you felt that you or your family would be better off if you were dead?"

"I don't really have a family."

Val looked up. "Loved ones, then?"

Anna wasn't even sure she knew what that meant, anymore. "You can put no."

Val nodded. "In the past few weeks, have you wished you were dead?"

Anna anxiously twisted her hospital bracelet around her wrist, wondering how hard it would be to bolt from the room in her current state.

"Anna?"

"What? . . . Um, no."

"Were you trying to harm yourself or end your life when you took those drugs with alcohol?"

"Isn't that kind of the point?"

Val frowned. "Pardon?"

"Sorry." Anna cleared her throat. "Guess overdose humor doesn't really . . . land well here."

Val typed out a quick note, then closed her laptop. "Have you thought about what kind of treatment plan you might want to pursue?"

Anna looked up at her, puzzled. "They didn't say that I'd need anything once I left . . . My throat's already feeling better—"

"For your substance abuse."

"Oh. Well, that feels a bit dramatic," she scoffed. "*Abuse.*"

"Do you not feel it's a problem?"

Could she really say no while lying in a hospital bed after being unconscious for two days? She took a noisy sip of her apple juice through a straw instead of responding.

"I'll leave some info for you here, okay? There are a lot of options." Val placed a folder gently on her bed. "It's a long road.

And there isn't an end, not in the traditional sense. But there is a way forward, if you're willing." She nodded to her once. "I'll let you get some rest."

"I found a place for you," Will said the next day. "It's outpatient. Intensive four-week program near my house upstate. We can find you something longer-term in the city for after. But at least this way I have eyes on you for the first few weeks."

It was lunchtime. He was keeping her company while she refused to eat whatever gray, lukewarm porridge was on her tray. Since arriving in Seattle, he'd left only to shower.

"I didn't ask you to do that," she said carefully.

"Right, well, you'd never ask me to do that. You'd never ask anyone to do that. Doesn't mean you don't need it." He peeled a banana and handed it to her like she was a little kid. "You also need to eat."

"I know what this looks like," she said, gesturing in apology to the bed, the tubes, the everything. "I wasn't . . . careful. I can see that now. It won't happen again."

"You do know that's what everybody says."

"I'm not everybody."

"But why take the risk, Anna? Was all of this not scary enough for you?" It was hard to tell if his tone was harsh due to frustration or fear. Maybe equal doses of both. "It was for me," he added quietly.

"I can handle this on my own," she said evenly.

"I don't think you can." He was, it was clear, ready to go toe to toe with her.

"I don't need a program. It's a waste of time."

"Not if you want to reschedule the tour."

She froze in the middle of smoothing down her bedsheets. "What do you mean?"

"It's all in your contract—I spoke to Toby this morning—"

"You spoke to Toby?"

"They're not giving you the green light until you go."

Oddly, it was relief she was flooded with in that moment most of all. *Oh, it's here*, she thought. This is it. This is where you stop running. It was certainly not a finish line. But she could rest, all the same.

And so it was that on the night she was meant to be playing Vancouver, she was, instead, curled up on a wicker couch on Will's front porch in the Hudson Valley. His place was Will in house form, really: all big, cozy couches; picture windows with views of the Catskills; a huge stone fireplace that always smelled a little like woodsmoke.

It was nearing 10:00 p.m. now, the time when she'd normally be boiling over with anticipation to get onstage. Thinking about where she should be, instead of where she was, brought on a longing so intense it manifested as a sharp pain square in her chest. Adding insult to injury, she didn't even have any of her normal crutches to numb it. It was hard to recall when she'd felt this uncomfortable in her own skin. Well, that wasn't entirely true: she knew exactly when the last time was.

And, unsurprisingly, after the messy cocktail she'd ingested, she still felt like shit. She'd slept the entire flight to New York and again on the ride up to Rhinebeck earlier that day. Any conversations she'd had with Will hadn't gone further than discussing immediate logistics.

There was one bright spot, at least: above her, she could see stars for the first time in years, the Milky Way splashed across the summer sky like a piece of embroidered velvet. The view made her feel small, in a good way. Part of something.

She was wrapped in a woolly, red plaid blanket, balancing a mug of tea on her knees when Will poked his head out from the front door.

"Hey, you," he called softly. "Want some company?"

She patted a spot next to her on the couch. "It's beautiful here. I don't think I'd ever leave, if I were you."

"Yeah," he said, sitting down next to her with a sigh. "Most of the time I'd prefer not to."

They were silent for a spell, listening to the noisy orchestra of the frogs and owls in the woods.

"How's Lottie?" she finally ventured. It was the one question she'd avoided. The only one she wanted an answer for.

"Mm. Freaked out? But really relieved you're okay."

"She didn't want to come to the hospital, I'm guessing?"

He shook his head. "It was too much, I think . . . After Maya."

"I get it. I wouldn't have come for me, either," she said with a dry smile. "When we were learning French, in diction class, you know how they say I miss you?"

"How?"

"*Tu me manques*," she said. "You're missing *from* me. I didn't really understand that, at the time. I do now." All of her calls and texts to Lottie had remained unanswered. Every time her phone dinged, though, there was still that flash of hope, fast followed by a slap of rejection.

"She misses you, too. She just needs a little more time."

"But you didn't?" She rotated to face him. "Why'd you come? Why'd you do any of this?"

He was staring straight ahead, his expression inscrutable. "I thought you were gonna die," he said quietly, after a minute. "And as angry as I was, I wouldn't have been able to forgive myself if we'd left things like that." He turned to look at her. "You had my *baby*, Anna. And I know it's really complicated and confusing for all of us, but it also means we're gonna be in each other's lives whether we want it or not. So"—he exhaled—"I decided I'd rather work toward forgiveness. It's a hell of a lot easier than staying mad. And to be honest, no one else was gonna take your ass in." He nudged her shoulder with a smile.

She chuckled lightly and took a sip of her tea. "That is depressing and entirely true."

"What do you do, anyway, when you're not on tour? Like, do you see people?"

She shook her head slowly. "Not really. I'm either writing new stuff or working on the next album."

"Are you ever not working?"

She thought that over while pulling the blanket tighter around her. "No. It's my whole life. So, that's pretty fucking scary right now. I don't really know who I am without it."

He stood up abruptly and offered her a hand. "Then let's find out." She looked at him, confused, but let him pull her up. "I wanna show you something." He grabbed a lantern from the porch stairs and flicked it on. "This way," he said, already walking ahead.

"If this is your kill room, I'm gonna be really bummed out," she mumbled, picking her way down the cleared path behind him.

Will led her from the house to a small, red barn that she hadn't noticed on their drive in. He slid open the door and switched on the lights to illuminate a full studio, complete with a mixing board, sound absorbers on the walls, and a grand piano.

"This was my splurge after I did *Fire at Dawn*," he said, taking in the room himself. "And it's yours, anytime you want to come play. For fun."

"This is amazing," she said, craning her neck to look up at the exposed beams. "And thank you." She reached out to squeeze his hand.

He put an arm around her. "I know you've got a lot ahead of you, but I thought this might help. It does for me." He caught her eye for a moment and then pulled his arm back: they were both rationing their physical contact. It seemed safer that way. "Anyway, it's late, I'm gonna call it. See you in the morning."

It turned out the dense quiet of the forest had a better soporific effect than any sleeping pill. Anna woke up the next morning not exactly refreshed, but at least well rested. She even had the energy (and appetite) to whip up a batch of oatmeal pancakes, something she did on the regular when she was staying at Will's during school breaks, but hadn't attempted in years.

He padded downstairs about an hour after she did, eyes wide with wonder and hair sticking up every which way. "Am I smelling what I think I am?" he said, astonished.

She placed a plate in front of him as he sat down at the counter. "A small token of my gratitude."

"Oh my god, Annie. I haven't thought about these in years." He tucked in hungrily, stabbing a huge piece onto his fork and swiping it through maple syrup. "How'd you learn to make these, anyway?" he asked, mouth full.

She hesitated, but for once, didn't deflect. "My mom. Had to cook a lot for myself as a kid. Got really good at pancakes."

He swallowed his bite. "Have you guys spoken? Since . . ."

She shook her head. "Just when she told me. That night at karaoke."

Will nodded in understanding and put his fork down. "I know this isn't necessarily my place to say, but I think it would be good for you two to talk, yeah?"

"Maybe." She started rubbing down the kitchen counter with a dishcloth to give her hands something to do.

"And I know you're gonna have to do a lot of talking, once it all starts up," he continued carefully. "But if you need . . . more, I'm here, too. If you want."

She stopped cleaning and looked up. There was nothing left of her to hide from him: he'd already seen her scraping the ocean floor and was still willing to pull her up from the depths. If she couldn't trust him with the rest of her secrets at this point, she might as well bury herself with them.

So over the course of that sweltering July, she talked. She talked during hours of daily group meetings, where, it turned out, she wasn't quite as alone as she thought. She talked during grueling therapy sessions, which were as painful and as urgent as a surgeon slicing her open to remove an infected organ. She talked even though doing so felt like a naked betrayal to herself, one who had defended her privacy with a zeal bordering on religious.

And, as Val the social worker had said, none of it was the end of the road, and most days felt like all she'd done was walk in a fucking circle. She was used to exhaustion, no doubt, but exhaustion with a purpose. Her progress now couldn't be marked by ticket sales or the number of encores; it was, instead, virtually invisible. And this intangibility kindled a frustration in her so searing, she wondered nearly daily if it could ever be extinguished.

And yet. And yet, she was moving again. And moving, for once, at a pace that she'd set, which meant she wasn't running from something else.

All of this talking, paradoxically, made talking to Will even more necessary, finishing an unresolved melody, in a way. So, she told him. All of it. Stories of her mother, and her father. Of Ireland: of Maeve and Rory. Of what happened that first year after, and five, and ten. And he didn't pull away, and he didn't look at her differently. Anna had had these memories stacked high on her shoulders for so long that she'd forgotten what it was like to walk without them. But it turned out Will could lift them all so easily, could fling them out beyond the mountains. She could finally stand up straight.

And with him, she did discover who she was without the stage, without the crowds, without it all. They went swimming at dusk in the cool, lapping waters of the lake; they walked on dewy grass with bare feet while eating popsicles. And, of course, they played music. They played the way they did when they were barely out of childhood: for the pure joy of it, by intuition, in collaboration. They played not for an audience, or for a label head, but just for the pleasure of each other. It was like drinking cold, clear spring water, when all you've had for years was the empty fizz of soda. She hadn't felt so nourished in a long time.

Still, they remained painfully alert of their proximity. Almost as if there were a finite amount of times they were allowed to touch, whether hands brushing on piano keys, or shoulders leaning together on the couch. This new balance of theirs was so finely calibrated, it seemed a flinch in any direction might send it toppling. And Anna wasn't sure how many more times they could put it back together before it was too shattered to even attempt.

One night, toward the end of the month, when the sun had finally retreated and the air didn't feel so heavy, they wandered out to the deck after dinner with ice cream. Will had dipped inside for a minute and now opened the back door with a goofy grin, one hand behind his back.

"Guess what I found?" He presented it to her before she had a chance to answer.

Anna leaned forward, peering at it. "Is that . . . your old iPod?"

He nodded excitedly. "I already charged it, and—miracle of miracles—I found an adapter for the speaker." He plugged it in and started spinning the wheel to scroll through the songs. "I cannot believe this thing still turns on," he marveled. "Okay, ready? We're going back to 2003 with this one." The Postal Service's *Give Up* started playing quietly.

"Oh my god, I *loved* this album," Anna breathed. "Their lyrics break my heart. I still play this on the road a lot when I'm feeling lonely."

"Meaning, you're lonely a lot of the time?"

She wrinkled her nose. "That sounds so pitiful, doesn't it? But yeah, I guess so." She leaned back in her chair and looked out toward the sunset. "No one tells you it'll be like that, you know? They tell you about the money, the fans, the fame. They don't tell you how alone you'll be." She took a bite of ice cream and waved off her last comment. "I'm just feeling sorry for myself. I don't mean to throw all this on you."

Will chuckled.

She looked at him quizzically. "What?"

"But you *can* throw it on me. I want you to. You don't always have to brave the storm alone, Anna. There are no bonus points in life for that. And hot take?" He pointed his ice cream spoon at her. "Life's actually a lot more fun with friends."

Feist's "I Feel It All" started playing; Will's face lit up. "Remember this one?" He stood up from his chair and extended a hand. "Dance with me, Annie."

She raised a skeptical eyebrow. "You serious?"

"My house, my rules. Come on."

She sighed and allowed him to pull her up. They swayed gently on the deck, barely moving.

"You remember when we first met?"

She nodded.

"I lied, that night. The room wasn't double-booked. But I'd heard you play and I had to know who was making that music, who that voice belonged to. That was the best decision I've ever made." He paused. "The worst was not getting on a plane the minute you told me you were pregnant."

Anna felt her breath catch, but they kept swaying.

"I can't change that now. And who knows what would've happened if I had; we were so young. But having you back has meant"—he swallowed hard—"everything. I can't lose you again. So I'm here: whether you're at your worst or at your best. This is where I want to be. Where you are."

She could feel her eyes welling, did her best to blink it all away.

"I'm not asking you to make any decisions right now. And I know you might not end up where I am. I've made my peace with that." He tilted her chin up to look at her. "But I love you. I have never stopped loving you. I will always love you."

Anna lost her battle with the tears; they were careening down her cheeks now in hot rivulets. Will kissed her on the forehead and drew her in close. The iPod finally died and they kept on dancing, the only sound the gentle susurration of the crickets in the grass.

Kendall called while they were having breakfast the next morning. He'd had a hell of a month himself trying to stamp out all the rumors as to why her remaining tour dates had been canceled. The official statement claimed "exhaustion," but Anna doubted anyone actually believed that. To his credit, however, the real reason had stayed blessedly under wraps.

"Hey, Miss B. How's the wilderness?"

"We're in Upstate New York, not the Yukon. And you're on speaker."

"Same difference. Hi, Will. She behaving?"

"As much as she can be," Will replied, popping another piece of pancake into his mouth.

Anna made a face at him. "What's up, Ken?"

"So, listen. There's, apparently, something called the Tennessee Songwriters Hall of Fame. And they appear to be quite keen to induct a local gal like yourself next month. There'd be a ceremony, short performance. I checked with the label: they're okay with a one-off like this, it's good for image rehab. Especially since you're already in, you know, *rehab* rehab. But I need to know if *you* think you can handle it."

Anna puffed out her cheeks and exhaled. She was equal parts desperate and petrified to return to a stage. "Where is it?"

"The Ryman."

"The Ryman," she echoed softly. "Fuck. I've never played it."

"I know. And I know how much you've wanted to. So, Will? I'm gonna ask you: Can she do this?"

He looked to her. Anna bit her lip and drummed her fingers slowly on the counter. She finally nodded.

"She can do it," he said definitively. "She's ready."

# THIRTY-FIVE

## Lottie

*New York*

August 2, 2024

So, Lottie. Tell me what brings you here today."

"Mm. My uncle is forcing me?"

"All right. And why do you think he wanted you to come?"

"Do you want the adoption trauma? Dead-mom trauma? The meeting of the birth parents? Ooh, or maybe, the birth mom overdosing? I can keep you in business for a while."

Dr. Colman looked up from her notes. "Sounds like a lot on your plate for sixteen."

Lottie pulled and snapped the hair tie on her wrist with irritation. "It's been an interesting summer."

"So maybe we start there? You were with your birth parents for a few weeks, then came home last month when your birth mom overdosed, right?"

"You can just call them Will and Anna. And yeah, after I got back, then I went to London, interned for my uncle. I think he thought it would be good for me to get away. Now that I'm home though, he was pretty adamant I come see you."

"That is quite the summer. Have you spoken to Will or Anna since you left them?"

"Will, yeah. Not her. But they've been together for the last month while she goes to rehab upstate, so we're all keeping tabs on each other, I guess."

"How does that make you feel?"

"What part?" Lottie smiled dryly. "Not talking to her? I don't know. We just met a few months ago, so it's not like there's some deep relationship that's missing, you know? But we were all living on a bus together, so I think we got a lot closer, quicker."

"Would you like to talk to her?"

"I mean . . . yeah. I do miss her, surprisingly. I just—it was really scary when she went into the hospital. And I didn't go see her, because, well, I've been there before, with my mom. And I didn't think I could do it again." She paused. "After she died, it took me a really long time to not be afraid of everyone else around me dying. So, when everything happened with Anna . . ." She trailed off. "But, now I feel pretty bad that I didn't go. Like I kind of abandoned her, you know? And then the longer I wait to talk to her, the harder it is to pick up when she's calling."

"It sounds like you're concerned you did something wrong."

Lottie fiddled with her necklace while she thought that over. "When I moved in with Aidan, I think I wanted to be, I don't know, not a problem for anyone. I've always been everyone's second choice. So I try to be easy; I let other people call the shots, a lot. All the time." She leaned back on the couch. "I know I probably couldn't have stopped it from happening. I just wish I'd said something earlier . . . to her, to anyone."

"Are you still worried?"

"Less so. She's doing much better, according to Will."

"That's good to hear."

She nodded. "He said she's coming back to the city soon."

"How would it feel to tell her the things you just told me?"

Lottie pulled on her lip. "You know, it's funny. Obviously,

she didn't raise me. But there's certain ways we handle things, I guess, that's really similar."

"Why do you bring that up?"

"I think both of us have a really hard time being honest about what we're feeling, especially when it's the tough stuff." She paused. "And I think it's even harder for us to ask for help."

"Even recognizing that is a big first step, though." Dr. Colman put her pen down and looked at her directly. "And just because that's how it is right now, doesn't mean it's that way forever. Who you are is never set in stone."

"Wait, Will *punched* Cooper DeWitt?"

It was Saturday morning. Lottie and Sasha had attempted a run around the Central Park reservoir, but a late summer storm had sent them scurrying back to Lottie's instead.

"I still can't believe you saw all these people, though. I'm so jealous," Sasha moaned, rolling over onto her stomach on Lottie's bed. "But Anna and Will aren't together, right?"

"I mean, I have no idea what their deal is. But yeah, as far as I know, just friends."

"So did you see Rory O'Shea?"

"From the Vagabonds?" Lottie asked, confused.

"Well yeah, but he's Anna's boyfriend. Or was. I don't know, I can't really keep track." Sasha clocked Lottie's expression. "You didn't know."

Lottie shook her head. "I heard a few people in the crew mention a Rory, but I didn't put it together they meant him. He didn't seem like anyone's favorite, though." She flopped onto the bed next to Sasha. "For as much time as we spent together, I'm realizing there's still so much she didn't tell me."

"What'd you talk about, then?"

"Well, not Rory, clearly. But a lot, actually. Music, of course. What we liked to play, and how she writes her stuff, and everything that goes into touring and performing. And dealing with the fans, being recognized, all of it. Oh—and she made this great tea that she drinks right before going onstage; she said she'd never given anyone else the recipe." Lottie smiled at the memory.

"Have you guys talked yet?"

She shook her head again.

"I don't know," Sasha said, sitting up. "Maybe teaching you all of this stuff was her way of showing you how much she cares. And maybe some of the other stuff was just too hard to say."

Every once in a while, Sasha could hit the nail right on the head.

"Do you think I should start an OnlyFans for my feet?" she asked, wiggling her toes. "I mean, I kind of don't see a reason *not* to do it?"

The moment usually passed quickly.

After Aidan's pancake immolation, he'd vowed to finally learn how to cook properly. And, in typical Aidan fashion, he'd commandeered one of the chefs de cuisine from Daniel to give him private lessons. Tonight, they were working on coq au vin. Lottie, meanwhile, was in the living room, messing around with a piano melody that had popped into her head. The doorbell rang.

"Sweets, can you get that? I'm learning how to do a *brunoise*!"

"That sounds dangerous," she called from the living room. "But smells good in there."

They weren't expecting anyone for dinner and it was too late for a package delivery. Lottie opened the door to find Anna there with a Mets hat pulled down low on her face and hugging her arms nervously.

"Hi," she said quietly. "Will said you two were texting and you were home. Figured I'd try and catch you."

Lottie eyed her up and down, her hand still on the doorknob.

Anna did look far healthier than when she'd last seen her: alert now, and color in her cheeks. "You're a Mets fan?" she asked her dubiously.

Anna shrugged. "I relate to their struggle."

Lottie gave her a half smile and opened the door all the way. "Well, if you're here."

"Who was it?" Aidan called out.

"It's me, Aidan," Anna said, walking toward the kitchen. "Good to finally see you."

Aidan was not speechless often, but it seemed Anna could have that effect. He, thankfully, put his knife down before approaching her.

"Sorry I didn't call ahead," she said, stopping a respectful distance away. "I kind of hopped on the train without thinking."

"You've been doing a lot of that lately. Not thinking," he said coolly.

Anna acknowledged that with a nod. "I know. And I owe you an apology. A million apologies. That's part of the reason I'm here. Step nine," she said with a chagrined smile.

He glared at her, calculating her level of sincerity, then turned to Lottie. "Are you okay with her here? You can tell her to go, if you're not. *I* can tell her to go, for that matter."

"No, it's fine," Lottie said. "We should probably talk. We'll go outside?"

He nodded and then tracked Anna warily as they walked by him. "I'll be right here, if you need anything."

Lottie closed the patio door behind her and widened her eyes. "I don't think he's your biggest fan at the moment."

"Yeah, not so much," Anna said, settling into a chair.

Lottie took a seat next to her, arms folded across her chest. They sat in uneasy stillness, car horns and rumbling trucks punctuating the quiet.

"I'm not sure where to begin," Anna finally said, slowly tracing the iron pattern on the patio table with her finger. "It's funny, you know? When I'm up onstage, and there's thousands of people out there, I feel like I can say almost anything. But here . . ." She motioned to Lottie and shook her head. "I think you already know I'm shit at these conversations. I'm alone a lot; I don't get a ton of practice. I've had a lot of time this past month, though, to try to get better at it."

They lapsed into silence again; Lottie, for once, resisted the urge to fill it just to avoid the discomfort.

"The first time I felt you move, I was playing you one of Will's pieces," she eventually said, still looking at the table. "It was the strangest sensation, like you *knew*, somehow. I don't know, maybe you did. The longer I live, the more I realize there are so many connections we can't see." She paused. "It was hard for me to imagine what you'd be like, on the outside. I think, probably, 'cause I already knew you weren't gonna be mine," she said with a resigned smile. "I'd wanted you to have something from me, though. Something you'd have somewhere inside, wherever you ended up. So"—she chuckled lightly—"I spent a lot of time making these . . . in-utero playlists for you. Every night I'd—God, this sounds so ridiculous, but I had an old sweatshirt of Will's. And I'd put it on and then I'd take my guitar or I'd sit at the keyboard and I'd play you Bowie, or the Beatles, or Johnny Cash . . . or him. It kind of felt like the only thing I could give you, the music . . ." She trailed off. Even sharing that much seemed to leave her enervated to the point of silence.

"I don't know if I'll ever be able to say sorry in a way that makes up for everything I've done," she finally said, quietly. "No one means more to me than you and Will. But I've taken so much from you both. So that's tough to know. That's tough to live with." She nodded slowly to herself. "I'll understand if you don't want to see me after this, but I needed to say all of it in person."

Anna took a deep breath. "I couldn't see how big of a hole

I'd ripped in myself when I let both of you go. So many of the mistakes I've made since then were because I was just trying to fill it. And none of it ever worked. It probably only made it worse." She smiled darkly. "So, finally getting to be with you has been"—she exhaled shakily—"the scariest and the most wonderful thing that's ever happened to me." She paused for a moment to steady her breath. "Just because I couldn't keep you, doesn't mean I haven't thought about where you were or who you were with or how you were feeling every single day of my life." She finally looked at her directly. "And now that you're here, I can see that you're all the best parts of me, and Will . . . and Maya, and Aidan, too. But you're also you, and who you are is better than anything I could've dreamed up. I just feel lucky to have played a little part in having you here."

It was so strange to think that they'd shared a pulse at one point. How they were still almost strangers to one another, but that Anna had breathed for her. Lottie realized, then, that regardless of any physical distance, there would always be this incomprehensible, inexorable pull they'd exert on the other. Fighting it would be useless.

So she leaned over and gave her a hug, the one they both should have exchanged weeks ago. To be this vulnerable was a running leap off the high dive, was praying the water was deep enough. But she couldn't wait at the platform edge forever, and she didn't want to go back down. She'd come too far for that.

Anna squeezed her back tightly. And this time, they fit together: mold and form reunited. They held onto each other for a long time, not speaking; they didn't need to.

"I do like Bowie," Lottie eventually said, releasing her. "So, well done on that."

Anna laughed. "Glad it wasn't all in vain, then."

Aidan knocked on the patio door, then opened it, staring intently from one to the other. "We good out here?"

"We're good," Lottie said, smiling. "Can she stay for dinner?" She turned to Anna. "Can you stay?"

Anna looked at Aidan hesitantly. He sighed, then nodded his approval. "She can stay."

Anna leaned back in her chair and peered suspiciously into the kitchen. "But *you* cooked?"

"Hey, now," he said, offended. "A lot can change in sixteen years."

"You literally started lessons two weeks ago," Lottie said, looking up at him.

To everyone's surprise, though, the chicken was excellent. This probably had more to do with Aidan's professional teacher than Aidan himself, but Lottie was still impressed. After dessert, she scampered up to his office to retrieve the Oak Grove yearbooks. The three of them pored through all four; the shared memories in their pages potent enough to begin to repair some of the bond between two old high school friends. There were so many stories to tell, so many moments to relive that they didn't even realize when the sunlight slipped out, leaving them laughing in the dark.

# THIRTY-SIX

**Anna**
*Rhinebeck*
August 18, 2024

"Elton John?"

Anna scrunched up her nose in thought, then shook her head.

"David Byrne?"

She nodded and grinned. "Best night of my life."

"Okay, even I'm pretty jealous of that one," Will said from the couch, where he was bouncing a tennis ball off the wall of the barn studio.

Lottie was peppering her with questions on whom she'd performed live with while idly strumming one of her guitars. Much to Anna's delight, Lottie had finally relented and let her start teaching her how to play. Unsurprisingly, she was picking it up impossibly fast. And this filled Anna with such an unexpected, buoyant pride she was surprised she hadn't floated to the ceiling.

"So how many songs do they want you to do?" Will asked.

"Like seven, eight? It's not a huge set. But I lost a few weeks there with the, you know." Anna tapped her throat. "And playing Tennessee always makes me a little edgy."

"And no band?"

"No band. They want more of an acoustic, intimate type of thing. And that's making me weirdly nervous, too." She sighed.

"I feel like I'm gonna be under a microscope, 'cause everybody wants to know what happened with the tour." She dramatically played the first few notes of Beethoven's Fifth. "Always a ton of fun to get ripped apart on the internet, lemme tell ya."

"Yet another reason I'm glad I play classical," he muttered.

"Thank you, that's *so*, so helpful, Will." She gave him a wide smile and her middle finger.

The three of them were together for the first time since L.A. The tranquility of Will's spread, not to mention its seclusion, had felt like a much healthier place for her to prep for the Nashville gig. And he'd been more than happy to have her take advantage while he was getting sorted for the fall term in Boston. She'd been up here for over a week already, planning her set list, rehearsing on her own, and making sure her voice was fully recovered.

And recovery, of course, was not limited to her physical form, nor was it a state—she was beginning to understand—she would ever necessarily leave. But as relentless and exacting as she could be on herself while rehearsing, she now carved out time to attend meetings. It was a new normal that was not yet routine and still somewhat unbelievable. But then again, she'd think, as a text would ping in from Lottie while she was sitting on Will's front porch, nearly nothing was the same any longer. And it turned out even creatures of habit could survive without them or, shockingly, find better ones. When all of these adjustments chafed, however, which was often, she tried to remind herself what a gift it was to be able to move at all. And what a gift to hold someone's hand while she did so.

On a whim a few days prior, Anna had texted Will and Lottie, asking if they wanted to come keep her company for the weekend. They'd surprised her, instead, by showing up midweek on her birthday, rolling up to the house with balloons and a dozen cupcakes. At dinner, the two had loudly serenaded her with "Happy Birthday" on the upright, and all of them ended the night with fingers sticky from s'mores.

"Last year of your thirties, Annie," Will had said ominously while rotating a stick in the bonfire. "You where you thought you'd be?"

She took a bite of her s'more as she pondered that, looking amusedly from one to the other as they roasted their marshmallows. Both tilted their heads identically when they were concentrating. "Not in the least," she'd said, shaking her head in disbelief with a laugh.

Since then, they'd spent the last few days coexisting how Anna imagined they might have if they'd never splintered in the first place: arguing good-naturedly over who needed to change the laundry, piling onto the couch together to introduce Lottie to *Stop Making Sense*, taking turns playing DJ while they prepped for dinner. And for the first time in decades, she was sleeping: she'd even passed out on Will's shoulder one night on the porch while they were waiting to catch a meteor shower.

The power dynamic had shifted—how could it have not?—but it was to a place of better distribution. They were equilateral now, balanced. And that brought Anna a quiet, internal peace she hadn't known was missing. It was only when the two of them righted her bearing that she could see how off-kilter she'd been in the first place.

"The thing's next Sunday?" Lottie asked, curling her fingers around the unfamiliar strings and plucking.

"Yep. I've got a week to get it all figured out." They were keeping her company in the barn while she tested out a few stripped-down versions of songs.

"Can I come?" Lottie asked, putting the guitar down and leaning over the couch's arm. "This is your last show for a while, right?"

"You know . . ." Anna swiveled around on the bench to face her. "I would love that, actually."

Will lobbed Anna his tennis ball. "Well, I'm going if she's going." He paused. "Not on a bus, right? We can take a plane?"

Anna laughed. "We can take a plane."

"Can we get hot chicken?"

Anna threw him back the ball and an indulgent smile. "Yes, Will, we can get hot chicken."

Even after all these years, there was still something oneiric about stepping through the front doors of the Hermitage in Nashville. When Anna was growing up, a place like this was spoken of in such hushed, reverent tones, it might as well have been on the moon. And it seemed more plausible that someone like her would go to outer space than be the sort of person who could afford a night there. She'd probably been put up in a suite here half a dozen times now, but she never failed to whisper across time to her teenage self: "You'll get out. You'll get out. And you'll be here."

Kendall and Toby were both waiting for her in the hotel lobby; their anxiety so palpable she could almost smell it wafting off of them. They approached her cautiously, as if not sure she were fragile like a porcelain doll, or volatile like hot glass.

"I'm fine, guys," she said, preempting the questions. "But I did bring reinforcements." She nodded toward Will and Lottie behind her.

"I'm asking, anyway. You're sure you're good to do this?" Toby said, sizing her up.

"It's a little late for that, yeah? We're here. But yes."

"Excited?" Kendall asked.

Anna pursed her lips. "Maybe. Ask me tomorrow when it's all done?"

Kendall narrowed his eyes. "I don't love that answer. But we'll let you guys get settled. I'll see you at rehearsal."

Anna gave him a little salute before the two of them walked off. She turned toward Will and Lottie. "Hungry? My Nashville restaurant list is one of my best, if I do say so," she said with a pleased smile.

Will was about to answer when she heard her name called from across the lobby. In the split second it took to register whose voice it was, it was already too late to run. Her mother was quickly walking toward her, tears in her eyes.

"What are you doing here?" Anna said, alarmed, and took a few steps away from her. "How'd you know I was here?"

"It was in the paper you were coming in," her mother said, nervously wringing her hands. "Darlene cleans here now; she said they always put y'all up here. So, I drove over. Just wanted to see you, in person," she added quietly. Her dry blond hair was frizzing out of her ponytail; there were a few inches of dark roots, too.

"You could have told me," Anna murmured as she scanned the lobby for security guards.

"You don't pick up my calls, baby," her mother said, before registering Will's presence. "Is this . . . Will? From school? So nice to meet you finally. I'm Jennie." She extended a hand; he gave it a confused shake. "And who is this?" she asked in an awed whisper, taking in Lottie.

"Don't touch her," Anna said, struggling to keep her voice calm. "Will, can you take her upstairs?"

Will looked anxiously from Anna to her mother. "Um—"

"Now. Please."

"Of course," he said, putting a hand on Lottie's shoulder and steering her toward the elevators. Lottie craned her neck behind her as they walked away, concern splashed across her face.

"Is that . . . my grandbaby?" Jennie asked softly once they were out of earshot.

Anna's heart was drumming so fast she wasn't even sure she could take a breath. Her mother would be able to see through her lie as easily as a lace curtain. She finally gave her a curt nod.

Jennie's eyes filled up again. "Oh. She's beautiful. Spittin' image of you. I didn't know you had . . ." Her voice broke; she covered her mouth with her hand.

"That was intentional," Anna said tightly. "Why are you here? You need money?"

"No." Jennie looked hurt at the suggestion. "Just wanted to lay eyes on you. It's been a long time."

"Well." Anna gestured to herself. "Happy? I have to go—"

"Anna, please. I drove all the way here." She'd aged so much since the last time Anna had seen her; it was disconcerting to not be able to sync the voice to the body. "Give me a few minutes."

Even the thought of that was enough to make her hands shake. But Jennie looked so beaten down, so frail. It would be like kicking a stray dog to say no. "Fine," she finally said. "But upstairs, I can't do this with you in the lobby."

They rode up in the elevator in silence, her mother's familiar presence pressing on her like a bruise. Anna walked ahead of her down the hallway, opened the door, and allowed her to step in. "Let's make this quick."

Jennie took in the room with her mouth open. "So this is what it looks like up here . . ."

Anna gestured for her to take a seat. "Seriously, what do you want?" she asked, her fingers rat-a-tatting impatiently on the wall.

"To know how you are. Honest." She shrugged her narrow shoulders. "I saw you canceled your tour; I've been worried sick about you. Been praying for you, too."

"Thanks." Anna fought the urge to scream. "I'm sure that made a big difference."

"It's been a hard summer, with your daddy and all. Are you okay?"

"That he's gone?" She let out a bitter laugh. "I'll be fine."

"You know he loved you, baby. He just had his own way of showing it."

Anna scoffed at that and made her way to look out the window. "You don't need to defend him anymore, you know. He's dead."

"We did the best we could, honey. I did what I thought—"

"You didn't protect me!" Anna said, turning around abruptly.

"So whatever you wanna call the best? That was pretty fucking piss-poor." Looking at her mother was both impossible and unavoidable, like staring at your own bleeding, severed limb. "You knew what was happening and you did nothing."

Jennie looked down at the carpet. The silence between them ballooned by the second, pushed them further into opposite corners.

"I was afraid he'd take you from me," she said quietly. "And I didn't have anywhere else to go."

"So instead, you let him destroy us?" Anna shook her head in disbelief. "You have no idea how much of my life I've spent trying to get him out of my head. How many years I've lost trying to prove to myself that I'm not who he said I was."

"But you did, didn't you? Proved him wrong? Look at you. Look at where you are." Jennie swept her hand around the room. "Look at *who* you are."

"At what cost, though?" Anna said, coming to collapse in the chair opposite her. She felt so tired all of the sudden. "I gave so much of myself away. Things I can't get back."

It was quiet again, except for the occasional, insistent ding of the elevator outside.

"What's her name?" her mother finally asked.

Speaking it aloud felt like the breaking of some sort of oath. "Charlotte. Lottie."

"It's pretty."

"I didn't—I didn't name her."

Her mother nodded slowly, understanding. "I'm sorry," she said, looking down at her hands. "I know I should've done better by you."

"It's a little late for that, Mom."

"It's all I've got, Anna. I don't have anything else to give you. Nothing you'd want, anyway." She paused. "I was so relieved when you got out, you know. You'll never know how bad I wanted that for you. I just wish now I didn't have to love you from far away, that's all."

It had been so much easier to pretend she didn't exist. The few good memories Anna had from childhood were so precious, she hardly pulled them out at all, for fear of getting them dog-eared and too crumpled to decipher.

"Can I please meet her? Just this once? I won't bother you again, if that's what you want." She was crying now. Anna couldn't bring herself to comfort her.

She had lied to Will and Lottie about why she wanted to keep them a secret. But unlike what Lottie assumed, it was never because of some misplaced loyalty to her fans: it was always to ensure her own family never found them.

But what she couldn't see until today was that her mother's sacrifice was maybe not so dissimilar from her own. Regardless of whether their decisions were the right ones, they'd both made them, in part, to protect a child, even if they knew that meant a necessary cleaving of a shared future.

She wasn't ready for forgiveness. She might never be. But she was willing to give her this: a few minutes of pretending all those cords were never severed.

"That was some rehearsal," Will said, cautiously tracking her as she walked offstage.

"Damning with faint praise?" Anna asked, toweling the sweat off her face.

"No, not at all. Just . . . intense." He put his hands on her shoulders. "So, now I've gotta ask: Are you okay?"

She couldn't meet his eyes. "I don't know," she finally said. "I'm trying to be better here, with the honesty stuff." She raised her eyebrows at him. "So, that's the truth: I don't know. I wasn't expecting her to show up like that. Dredges up a lot of shit."

"I know. But, also in the interest of you being better, I need you not to pretend like it didn't happen."

Anna thought that over and eventually nodded, then pulled

away from him and walked to the edge of the stage. She sat down, dangling her legs off the side. "I've thought about when they'd meet for so long," she said, looking out into the rows of pews. "It's always terrified me."

"How are you now that they did?" he asked, coming to sit next to her.

"I never wanted her to know that world existed. I think I was hoping that she never would."

"Just because they've met now doesn't mean the past repeats itself," he said, staring out into the auditorium himself. "And it's okay if she knows where you come from; it's part of who she is, too. You know better than anyone that where you start out doesn't determine where you end up."

"You've gotten shockingly wise since we were in college." She leaned her head on his shoulder with a smile.

"Remember, I am a doctor now."

"Don't think you'll let me forget that one." Her attention turned to the balcony. "I wanna see it from up there. Come with?" She grabbed his hand and pulled him up, leading him to the stairs. They clambered up to the second floor and walked down to the front row, the stained-glass panels behind them casting colorful splashes onto the seats.

Anna leaned out over the balcony, peering down with a delighted smile at the stage. "I still can't believe I'm here," she said, shaking her head in awe. "The only time Tennessee ever felt like home was when I was singing in church. And now we're here . . . the Mother church. You can feel them, right? Everyone who's played here: Johnny and Hank and Dolly . . ."

"And Anna," Will said with a grin, nudging her with his shoulder.

"Guess so. I feel like an impostor, though. You still get that?"

He nodded. "All the time. That first show at Lincoln Center? I kept waiting for some security guard to come and tackle me. I'm still waiting," he said, chuckling.

They watched the crew perform their choreographed dance of stage prep for a few minutes in silence. "I have seen that piece live, you know," she finally said, still gazing down. "The one you did for the Phil after graduation."

Will turned to her, surprised. "When?"

"It was maybe 2014? We were in Denmark at the same time; I was playing Roskilde. The posters were all over the place for your show at Tivoli. I kept thinking that maybe I'd run into you on the street, or at a bar, or something. I scanned every table at every restaurant when we'd sit down, just to make sure you weren't there." She smiled sheepishly.

"Anyway, I ended up bumping my ticket back to New York, so I could stay to see it. I got a seat way in the back—that was all that was left." She paused, swallowed up in the memory. "It is such a beautiful piece, Will. My god. I was sobbing by the end. And I was so proud of you. All I wanted to do after was run backstage and tell you how much I loved it . . . I wish I had. Hearing it, seeing you up there, it made me miss you so goddamn much." She tried to force back the lump in her throat.

"I don't think anything has felt right for me since I left you. And I know it's taken me a long fucking time to realize that." She laughed softly. "I thought all of this was enough." She nodded toward the stage. "And it was, until it wasn't. I hate that we can't get those years back. And I hate that it's my fault. But I'm tired of holding onto shit. And I'm tired of feeling like I have to do everything alone." She turned to face him. "No one makes me feel more like me than you do. And most of the time, I know I don't deserve you. But I don't want to miss you anymore. I need you here." She put her palm on her chest. "So, there it is. I love you, too."

Will didn't say anything. He only smiled, grabbed her hand, and pulled her in for a kiss.

This place, that stage below, had been home. But now, he was too.

# THIRTY-SEVEN

**Lottie**
*Nashville*
August 25, 2024

Beginning her morning with a papercut wasn't exactly an auspicious start to Lottie's day. Luckily, Anna always traveled with an arsenal of vitamins, cold meds, and Band-Aids (even more so after Will's hives incident). The crew often joked she missed her calling as a Girl Scout.

But when Lottie knocked at her room, it was Will, bleary-eyed in a terry-cloth hotel robe, who swung open the door. When he registered who was standing in front of him, he looked as guilty as if she'd caught him in the middle of surfing porn.

"You're not room service," he finally managed to mumble, looking down at the carpet.

"You're not Anna," Lottie retorted. She narrowed her eyes and peered at his neck. "Is that . . . a hickey?"

He immediately smacked a hand onto it. "No."

"All right, then." They both stood there in awkward silence. "You know what? I don't think I need a Band-Aid that bad . . . I'm gonna go."

"Oh, okay." He brushed his hair out of his face. "You sure?"

"Yeah, I'll take a pass on going in that room right now."

"Will, was that the food or no?" Anna called from the bedroom.

"Morning, Anna!" Lottie yelled back gleefully.

Will, mortified, chuckled quietly.

There was a deliciously long pause. "Morning, Lottie."

She tilted her head at him. "I'm both grossed out and happy for you guys. It's probably a good thing I just got a new therapist." She nodded once. "Okay. Bye."

He nodded briskly back. "Bye." Lottie had never seen someone close a door so fast.

"So, there are two toothbrushes in your bathroom, Miss Buckley," Elena said with a grin as she dusted bronzer onto Anna's cheekbones. "And considering Jordi and I flew all the way out here, I think it's only fair if you tell us whose it is."

All of them were in Anna's suite while she got ready for the press line before the event. She blushed, and her eyes darted quickly over to Will and Lottie, who were sitting on the couch. Will shifted nervously; Lottie had to stifle a laugh. "Maybe I just keep an extra?" she answered.

Jordi snickered while combing out her hair. "Yeah, okay. You wear Speed Stick, too?"

The doorbell rang; Anna exhaled dramatically and grinned. "Saved by the literal bell? I'll get that." She sprang up from her chair and walked out to the living room.

"Oh my god, you're here!" Lottie heard her exclaim from the door. Anna walked back into the room a minute later, beaming, with her arm around an older woman with short salt-and-pepper hair. "There's someone here who you haven't seen in a very long time," Anna said to her, tipping her head toward Lottie.

The woman followed Anna's gaze, then covered her mouth in surprise. "I'd recognize that sweet face anywhere," she said, the words lilted with an Irish accent. "Oh my word, look how big you are! And gorgeous just like your ma." She reached out to touch Lottie's cheek, then drew her into a deep hug. "I was there the night you were born," she whispered to her. "And I've been thinking about you ever since." She looked back at Anna. "I said you two would make your way back to each other."

Anna smiled. "And I should never doubt you. Lottie, Will: this is Maeve, who I lived with in Doolin. And now, every once in a while, she'll allow me the pleasure of flying her out to shows."

"The good ones," Maeve interjected. "Paris is always nice," she added with a grin before turning her attention to Will. "Lord, I've heard so much about the both of you," she said, pulling him in for a hug as well. "Glad this one finally got her head out of her arse and figured out what was good for her."

Will laughed. "You and me both."

The doorbell rang again. Lottie went to answer this time: it was Kendall, distractedly typing something on his phone. He walked in without looking up or saying hello.

"Do you want the good news or the bad?" he said, once standing in front of Anna.

"Hello to you, too," she said, flummoxed. "And . . . neither?"

Kendall proceeded as if he hadn't heard her. "So, it's a sold-out crowd tonight. Well done on that." He sat down on the edge of the bed and exhaled. "But I just got a courtesy call from TMZ. Somebody at the hospital leaked your records. They're running with the story in a couple hours."

"What?" she said, alarmed. "They can't do that, can they?"

"Oh, they can. And they will. And unfortunately, there is no way you can skip the carpet tonight, so I need you to be prepared with a lot of 'no comments.'"

"Fuck," Anna whispered, and started to pace the room. "Fuck! . . . Ken, there's nothing you can do?" Her eyes were frantic, pleading.

He shook his head morosely. "I tried. They don't give a shit. I'm so sorry. You know I'd kill it if I could."

* * *

It hit while they were in the SUV on the way to the Ryman. Kendall's phone started pinging so furiously he finally turned it off. Will was lightly rubbing Anna's back as she stared out the window silently.

"I'm sorry, guys, for putting you through this," she said, nervously smoothing down her gown. "Again."

"The news cycle moves fast," Kendall said, turning around from the front seat. "Pray for a Taylor Swift headline?"

Anna smiled weakly and crossed her fingers.

When they emerged from the car, a flurry of photographers descended, all yelling variations on the same question. Anna, wincing, tried to cover her face as Kendall led the charge, plowing through them expertly on the way to the carpet.

"We'll see you guys inside?" he said to Will and Lottie, once they'd made it through the gauntlet. He paused. "I'll take care of her, promise," he added with uncharacteristic candor.

Will reached out to give Anna's hand one last squeeze before Kendall led her into the miasma of the crowd. They both watched her get swallowed up into the jabbering mass of people until they couldn't see her at all.

"That looked . . . rough out there," Lottie said to Will when they were finally in the green room.

He exhaled heavily, unbuttoning his suit jacket to sit down. "She's had a lot of shit thrown at her in the last twenty-four hours."

Neither could bring themselves to articulate the question they actually wanted to ask. So instead, they sat uneasily on the couch, trying to distract themselves with their phones while they waited for her to return.

Anna and Kendall made their way backstage about half an hour later. She was beleaguered, that much was obvious, but it was impossible to tell exactly how badly they'd damaged her defenses.

Kendall, meanwhile, was back on his phone, angrily typing. "Just making a list of all the outlets I am never fucking working with again. Might be a minute."

Will stood up immediately and walked to her side. "You okay?"

She started to nod, somewhat unconvincingly, then stopped abruptly. "Actually, can everybody get out? Will, Lottie, please stay, but can everyone else get the fuck out? Now?"

Kendall, Toby, and the handful of crew members in the room exchanged surreptitious, nervous glances with one another.

"You heard her," Toby said gruffly. "Move."

Anna waited for everyone to stream out and then walked to the door and turned the bolt. Will looked to Lottie with alarm, but stayed silent. Anna, meanwhile, sunk down to her knees, leaned her head onto the door, and started breathing slowly through her nose.

"Hey," Will said softly. "What do you need?"

"I need . . . I need to get out of this." She looked down at her navy silk dress and pulled at a strap in disgust. "Now." With a nod to herself, she started slipping it off. "Lottie, will you grab me some clothes from that bag?"

"Um . . . yeah, sure." Lottie hesitantly went to her duffel, dug out a shirt and jeans, and tossed them to her.

They watched in confusion as Anna quickly changed, then leaned limply over the vanity counter, staring at herself in the bright lights of the mirror. "I need to stop pretending that what happens out there stays out there. I need to stop pretending to be something that I'm not." She paused. "I'm not sure I know who I am out there, anymore." She caught their eyes in the reflection. "I know who I am here. I think that can be enough."

There was a rap on the door. "Miss Buckley? Five minutes to stage."

"Hey," Will said, crossing to her. He held her by the shoulders and leaned his forehead gently onto hers. "Fuck 'em up, Annie."

The stage was empty, except for the piano glowing under a warm spotlight. Anna walked out to an explosion of applause; Lottie swore she could feel the floor vibrate under her feet. Anna gave a quick wave to the audience, then settled herself at the bench.

"Thanks, everybody, for being here. This is really a lifelong dream come true, tonight." The audience roared loudly and Anna, blushing, waited for the noise to subside. "I wanted to start tonight off with one of my favorite covers, something I've been playing since I was a teenager." She raised her eyes offstage to Will with a smile, then launched into "Lilac Wine."

Her voice, thankfully, had recovered completely. She sang the first two verses as beautifully as Lottie had ever heard her do it, her vibrato strong and the notes achingly clear. But she started to waver as she began the third, the one with the lines about thinking and drinking too much. And then she trailed off completely, like candle smoke dissipating after you blow out the flame. She was frozen in front of the keys. The theater was suffocatingly, painfully silent.

"The fuck is this?" Kendall murmured, staring at the stage. "I've never seen this happen."

"Come on, Anna," Will whispered. "Come on, come on."

Lottie, heart pounding in her throat, cast her eyes around backstage. "Is there an extra set of in-ears?" When no one answered, she marched over to the monitor engineer. "I *said*, 'Do you have an extra set of in-ears?'"

Harried, he dug around his table, finally found a pair, and handed them to her.

"Lottie, what are you doing?" Will said, staring at the monitors in her hand.

"I'm taking up space." She clipped the pack onto the back of her pants and stuck the ears in. "Are you coming?"

“Out there?” he asked, eyes wide.

“Yes, out there. She’s drowning! What do you think we should do?”

He looked quickly from Anna onstage to Lottie, then nodded definitively.

Lottie took a deep breath and walked out, pulling Will behind her; the crowd started whispering in confusion. Anna turned around when she heard them approach, with tears in her eyes and a grateful smile.

Will sat down next to her and Lottie adjusted the mic up to herself at standing height. With a nod, he started the piece again and Lottie began to sing. Anna, now fully crying, leaned her head against his shoulder and reached out to grab Lottie’s hand.

The audience remained still as Lottie made her way through the song. She could feel thousands of eyes burning into her, but somehow, her stage fright had slipped off like an ill-fitting coat. She finished with a decrescendo, sustaining the last note barely above a whisper. There was a thick, shocked pause, then the crowd erupted into cheers.

Anna stood up and hugged her tightly, then kissed her on the cheek. “I love you,” she whispered. “Thank you.” She pulled Lottie down to sit next to her.

“Well, first time for everything, I guess?” Anna said into the mic as she wiped her face. She took a moment to compose herself. “Some of you probably know I’ve had a . . . tough summer. The only reason I am alive right now is because of the two people sitting on this bench next to me. And I am so fucking lucky they let me love them again.

“So, it’s about time I introduced them officially. On the piano, we have Will Pendleton.” She touched his shoulder. “And this one, with the big voice”—Anna clasped her hand—“this is our daughter, Lottie.”

# EPILOGUE

*New York*
Fall 2025

"Oh my god. Will! Emergency!"

Anna, in a full-length emerald-green gown, is holding a squirming, curly-haired baby out at arm's length when Will bounds into the room in a half-buttoned tux shirt, bow tie undone. Behind her, Aidan is chuckling with a pin held in his mouth, stitching the back of her dress.

"You made me sick for nine whole months and came out looking *just* like Daddy, so guess who gets to change this diaper?" She brings the gurgling baby closer, kisses her forehead, then holds her out to Will, nose wrinkled. "It's a bad one, babe."

"Will, if that baby gets poo on this silk, I swear to god . . ." Aidan mutters through gritted teeth.

Will, grinning at the baby, scoops her from Anna. "Say 'Uncle Aidan, *calm down*.' And there is no poop that is a match for my skills. I am a poop master." He swings the baby overhead, deposits her on the changing table, and unsnaps her onesie. "Oh Jesus, it's all the way up her back!" He stifles a gag.

"Told you," Anna says with a knowing smile.

Aidan finishes stitching and spins Anna around to examine her in the mirror. "I mean, literally had to sew you into it, but it is stunning, if I do say so."

"I've always loved your modesty, truly," she says to him in the mirror. "But it's beautiful. Thank you. Rivals your senior year collection."

"That was good, wasn't it?" Aidan loses himself in a day-dream for a second and then clamps his nose shut with thumb and forefinger. "Okay, I'll let you two finish with . . . whatever is happening in that diaper," he says, and makes a hasty retreat from the room.

Anna laughs and saunters up behind Will, wrapping her arms around his waist. The baby flashes her a toothless grin as she furiously kicks her legs. "Daddy said, 'Annie, let's make a baby.' And Mama must be crazy 'cause she said yes. She also didn't think you'd happen quite so fast," she adds in a mock whisper, eyes wide. "And now you're here and you're very cute, but I'm gonna remind him of this every time you have a blowout."

Will shakes his head, laughing. "I got my way, Clara. Don't listen to her."

Anna kisses him on the cheek. "You need to get dressed, too. But, you know, wash your hands first."

The front door opens with a clamor of voices. "Guys, we're here!" Lottie yells from the entryway.

"I'll leave you two to it," Anna says with a wink. Will salutes in reply and grabs another handful of wipes.

Lottie, Bee, and Will's parents are gathered in the apartment foyer with Aidan when Anna walks in. Aidan, naturally, is already making last-minute adjustments to Lottie's red gown.

"I both love and hate how grown-up you look in this," he says to her with a frown before kissing her on the forehead. "But I'll take all the credit for how gorgeous you are."

"Where's that delicious baby?" Betsy says by way of greeting, scanning the room for Clara.

"Outfit change. I think we're on the fourth of the day?" Anna says.

Will, now fully dressed in his tux with burp cloth flair, walks in a few minutes later with the baby over his shoulder. "Someone asking for this little lady?"

Betsy squeals and grabs her while Anna adjusts his bow tie. "You clean up nice. You ready?"

He nods, a little nervously. "Think so. No turning back now."

Betsy, rocking Clara, smiles over at them. "I don't think I'll ever get tired of looking at your mama and daddy together."

"Certainly took them long enough," Charles adds gruffly.

"Heard that, Dad."

Bee looks at her watch and points at all of them. "You're gonna be late. Give me that baby." She gently extricates Clara from Betsy and snatches the burp cloth from Will's shoulder. "*Dios mío*, it's like holding Lottie all over again." She smiles down at Clara and nods at Anna and Will. "You two make good ones, you know. Have more. Maybe just don't wait as long next time."

"Do *not* tempt him," Anna says aghast, swatting at her gently. She turns to address the group: "But we've got a world premiere to get to, yes?" She grins and claps her hands. "Let's go."

The main square at Lincoln Center is already awash with hundreds of people in their black-tie finest when their car pulls up. Kendall's waiting for them on the curb, looking—unsurprisingly—a little frantic.

"There you guys are. I've been holding off the events team for an hour. Step and repeat, *now*." He grabs Anna's hand; she looks back apologetically with a wave to Will's parents, but they usher them off with a smile.

The photographers' cameras start clicking rapidly as soon as Anna steps onto the carpet. She hooks arms with Will and takes ahold of Lottie's hand. The three of them pose together: a different sort of family photo.

"Can we get Anna alone, please? Anna alone!" The scrum of photographers yells from the pit.

She wags a finger at them. "Sorry, guys, not my night. It's his," she says, nodding toward Will.

"Anna? Will? Can we get a few words with you for *New York* mag?" One of the reporters on the press line is desperately waving her mic out like she needs to be rescued. Kendall leads them over.

"So great to see you guys out tonight. And congrats on the Grammy nom. Is this your first together?"

Will smiles broadly. "It is, and was very unexpected. I don't think either of us planned on recording and producing something together, but sometimes the music makes you and not the other way around."

"And I don't think that's the only thing you collaborated on this year?"

"There were a couple unexpected collaborations this year," Anna quips. "But we left the other one at home with a babysitter."

"How's new parenthood going?"

"Harder than a world tour. But I would say our lullaby game is strong." Anna laughs. "And Will is very much in his element. He brought the baby to rehearsal in a carrier last week."

"With ear defenders on," Will notes.

"It was annoyingly adorable," Anna adds.

"Can you tell if she's inherited those music genes?"

Will shrugs. "We'll see. She likes when her sister sings to her."

"Speaking of that," the reporter pivots her mic in Lottie's direction. "You planning on following in their footsteps? That video of you in Nashville went pretty viral."

Lottie shakes her head nervously. "I don't know. I love music. And it's cool we're all connected through that. But I'm still working on . . . charting my own path."

"Well, I can't argue with that," the reporter says. "Anna, what about you? When can we expect your next album drop?"

"You know, for once? I'm enjoying being in the here and now.

Even if we haven't slept since the baby was born," she says with a tired smile.

"Kudos to that. As for tonight's piece for the Phil: Will, what can you tell us about the inspiration?"

"When Anna was pregnant, and we got to hear the heartbeat for the first time"—his face lights up with the memory—"I think that was probably the most beautiful sound I've ever heard." He pauses. "I think it's also fair to say that the last couple years were the hardest of my life. So, there have been some high highs and low lows, recently. But we made it through." He gestures to Anna and Lottie. "Everything that happened—our heartbeats—are all over this piece. I couldn't have written it without them."

"Thanks so much, but we've got to get them inside," Kendall says to the reporter as he hurries them along. "Your tits are *enormous*, by the way," he whispers into Anna's ear as they leave the carpet.

She bursts out laughing. "You try breastfeeding an infant."

"Definitely won't. And never thought I'd hear those words out of Anna Buckley's mouth." He contemplates it for a second. "I don't hate it."

"Surprisingly? Neither do I."

"You look good, kid." He gives her a kiss on the cheek. "Really happy to see it."

A man with an earpiece motions to Will as soon as they walk into the Geffen Hall lobby. "Maestro? We've got to get you backstage."

Lottie raises an eyebrow. "Maestro, eh?"

"You're welcome to call me that, too," he says, grinning. "Oh, almost forgot." Will turns to Anna, reaches into his tux, and pulls out a small envelope with her name on it. "Your tickets."

"Thanks," she says with a wide smile, plucking them from him. "Been waiting a long time for these."

They find their seats next to Charles and Betsy in the center orchestra, fifth row. The lights dim soon after, and Will walks out to generous applause. Onstage, the musicians all stand at once, the strings section thwacking their bows with approval on their music stands. He steps onto the podium and swivels to face the audience, lifting a hand in greeting. Joy spreads across his face when he finally locks eyes with Anna in the crowd; he brings his hand to his heart—and she to hers—before pivoting back.

He waits until the concert hall is lush with silence before raising his baton. As he brings his right hand up to begin the piece at a forte, the music begins: a wave emanating from his body that splashes the whole orchestra with sound. True to his word, the music vacillates between exuberant and somber, minor and major key movements tumbling into one sonic river. It, somehow, encompasses their past and their present. Their future. On the podium, he is as balletic as he was as a teenager: graceful and purposeful. By the middle of the performance, there are tears streaming down Anna's face.

"You okay?" Lottie whispers, and leans her head on her shoulder, interlacing Anna's fingers with her own. Anna nods, smiles, and kisses the top of her head.

In the final few bars, the piece roars to a climax: strings, woodwinds, brass, and percussion forming a wall of sound that pulsates like a heartbeat throughout the hall. And then, Will leans forward toward the musicians, gently, beautifully, coaxing every instrument back to pianissimo. One by one, the percussion quiets to a stop, then the woodwinds, brass, and strings. Soon, just the piano is playing: slowly repeating an arpeggio. Each note of the broken chord hangs in the air like an exhaled breath, until finally, all three are sounded together.

A resolution; an ending.

# RESOURCES

While the characters in *The Encore* are fictional, many of the challenges they face are, unfortunately, very real. If you or someone you love is struggling with addiction, thoughts of self-harm, or is the victim of abuse, please reach out to the below organizations for help. If you are in immediate danger, call 911.

Substance Abuse and Mental Health Services Administration (SAMHSA): Call or text 988.

988 Suicide & Crisis Lifeline (formerly the National Suicide Prevention Hotline): The lifeline can also be reached by calling or texting 988.

National Domestic Violence Hotline: 1-800-799-SAFE

## NOTES AND ACKNOWLEDGMENTS

As a veteran journalist, it behooves me to flag a few instances where I took creative liberty with facts in service of the book's narrative. First, New York State does not have an official process for minor emancipation (though if anyone could sweet-talk a judge, I do think it would be Aidan). Second, there are a couple of timing fudgings: Sonic Sphere, while a real concert hall space, was mounted at the Shed in 2023, not 2024. Primavera Sound, similarly, takes place yearly in May, although not over the dates in the book. Eagle-eyed music fans, however, should note that those artists mentioned *are* who played the (epic) 2009 lineup.

Now, onto the thanks: First and deepest go to the two people without whom this book would not exist, Alison Fargis at Stonesong Press and Barbara Berger at Union Square & Co. Alison, thank you for loving and believing in these characters as much as I do. I've never been so excited to receive a 7:00 a.m. email as I was to get yours. Barbara, your keen eye chiseled this book into its best self. I am so grateful that my debut journey was a joy, and that is due to you and your team. Speaking of that team, thank you also to Union Square & Co. project editor Alison Skrabek, creative director Lisa Forde, art director and jacket designer Patrick Sullivan, interior designer Jeff Stiefel, production manager Sandy Noman, publicity manager Alex Serrano, and assistant editor Juliana Nador; as well as Addison Duffy at UTA.

My early readers, most of whom patiently read this book

chapter by chapter as it was being written, gave me the immense encouragement I needed to keep going. Special shout-outs to Christine Chitnis, Adrienne Gaffney, Sara Mercer, Ali Rosen, Katy Spratte Joyce, and Max Weisz: your tireless cheerleading, industry wisdom, and smart criticism were invaluable.

Diane Einsiedler, Hanna Kreiner, Meaghan Kilian, Stacey Olesh, and Allie Shean have shown me how beautifully and magically friendship can evolve over decades. I'm really sorry I couldn't work in "mounted like a picture frame." Next book?

To Devorah Lev-Tov, Lia Picard, Hannah Selinger, and Katy Spratte Joyce: thank you for being (kind of) kind.

I am indebted to the many experts who answered an untold number of my granular questions about their fields: Dr. Sarah Atkinson, Dr. J. P. Giliberto, and Dr. Ian Julie for medical terminology and protocol; Jennifer Bray on questions of Irish syntax; and Hanna Kreiner for helping me craft the therapeutic scenes. And a standing ovation for the music industry professionals who were so generous with their time: Timo Andres, Michele Hug, Ellis Ludwig-Leone and the members of San Fermin, John McRae, Dan Schlosberg, Claire Wellin, Naomi Woo, and Oussama Zahr. Any mistakes that remain in the text are solely my own (and probably not for lack of trying on their parts).

My endless gratitude also to all the composers and musicians whose sonic worlds helped to build this literary one: Tori Amos, Broken Social Scene, Jeff Buckley, Dan Deacon, Nils Frahm, Florence + the Machine, Future Islands, Philip Glass, the Postal Service, Michael Nyman, Overmono, Steve Reich, Maggie Rogers, Felix Rösch, Sampha, Stars, St. Vincent, and the Talking Heads.

I am fortunate to have had my love of words nourished and cultivated by spectacular teachers from the time I was a teenager: Kristen McElhiney at Sidwell Friends School, Sheila Fisher and Milla Riggio at Trinity College, and Arlene Hutton at The Barrow Group. Please don't tell me if you find a typo.

And finally, to my family, who have been unwavering champions of my work since I learned how to spell. Mom, thank you for teaching me how to read and love the written word, and for always being my biggest supporter. Laura, if only everyone could have a big sister as generous, loving, and hysterical as you. Mike, you are the other half of my circle. Thank you for urging me to make this dream a reality, and for giving me the space to do so. And Avvie, look! You're in print! I can't wait to read your novel one day, too.

Dad, while we're not fortunate enough to have you on this earthly plane any longer, I have no doubt that this book's existence was partially guided into being by your deft hand. We love you and miss you.

# PLAYLIST

If you're interested in learning more about the music mentioned in *The Encore*, see below for a selected, chronological (within the book) list of the artists featured, along with an album, piece, or set of compositions to start you on your journey.

**Maurice Ravel,** *Gaspard de la nuit*

**Sufjan Stevens,** *Michigan*

**Jeff Buckley,** *Grace*

**The Beatles,** *Let It Be*

**Chappell Roan,** *The Rise and Fall of a Midwest Princess*

**Frédéric Chopin,** Études

**OutKast,** *Speakerboxxx/The Love Below*

**Tori Amos,** *Little Earthquakes*

**Kings of Leon,** *Because of the Times*

**Feist,** *The Reminder*

**Kate Bush,** *Hounds of Love*

**Björk,** *Post*

**Maggie Rogers,** *Heard It in a Past Life*

**Janis Joplin,** *Pearl*

**Led Zeppelin,** *Led Zeppelin IV*

**St. Vincent,** *Masseduction*

San Fermin, *Jackrabbit*

The High Kings, *Grace & Glory*

Talking Heads, *Stop Making Sense*

Pearl Jam, *Ten*

Charlie Parker, *The Complete Savoy & Dial Master Takes*

Joni Mitchell, *Blue*

Stars, *Set Yourself on Fire*

Broken Social Scene, *You Forgot It in People*

Metric, *Old World Underground, Where Are You Now?*

Steve Reich, *Music for 18 Musicians*

George Gershwin, *Rhapsody in Blue*

Aaron Copland, *Rodeo*

Sylvester, *Step II*

Philip Glass, *The Complete Piano Etudes*

Olivia Rodrigo, *Sour*

Nine Inch Nails, *The Downward Spiral*

Bruce Springsteen, *Born in the U.S.A.*

No Doubt, *Tragic Kingdom*

Robyn, *Body Talk Pt. 1*

Phoenix, *United*

Michael Nyman, *Michael Nyman*

The Cranberries, *Everybody Else Is Doing It, So Why Can't We?*

Claude Debussy, *Deux arabesques*

The Postal Service, *Give Up*

David Bowie, *Let's Dance*

Johnny Cash, *Live at Folsom Prison*

Taylor Swift, *Evermore*

# TOPICS AND QUESTIONS FOR DISCUSSION

1. Lottie's legal emancipation sets the book's present-day chain of events in motion. Do you agree with Aidan's choice to go against Anna's (and Maya's) wishes? How much of his decision is predicated on Lottie's well-being versus his long history with and feelings toward Anna?

2. In the first chapter, Aidan says of Lottie's birth certificate, "whatever it says, [it] doesn't change who you are." Nature versus nurture is a central theme in the book: How much of who we are is fixed versus malleable? Is Lottie more a product of her upbringing, her genetics, or both? What about Anna?

3. Both Lottie and Anna describe feeling untethered or unmoored in the early chapters. How is their solitude alike? How is it not? What different choices do they make to find connection with others? How do you reconcile Anna's extroverted professional life with a personal one that is extremely solitary?

4. Anna choosing the pursuit of her art over raising a child forms the central crux of the story. Do you understand her motivations for doing so? Why was it such a binary choice for her? What would you have done in the same situation?

5. While Anna is adamant that telling Will about the baby would be disastrous for them both, what do you think would have happened if she had? How would it have affected each of their careers differently? Their relationship?

6. Anna says she's "happiest when she's busy." In what ways has being an extremely hard worker helped her? What ways has it been a detriment? Do you think her work ethic is due more to her love of music or because it's a way to avoid confronting her past?

7. Anna readily admits that what she endured while making her first album was, partially, what has made her so successful. There is also a long history of artists channeling their trauma back into their work. Why do you think translating deep emotions into song, painting, or other media can sometimes result in masterpieces?

8. We only learn a little about what Will's life has been like between college graduation and present day. However, both he and his mother, Betsy, make oblique references to him having navigated a difficult time. What do you think happened? There are also no chapters told from Will's point of view, which means we see him only through the lenses of Anna and then Lottie. How is he presented differently through each of their points of view?

9. Chapter 28—the flashback chapter to Anna's childhood—is told, unlike the rest of the book, in the second person. Why do you think this choice was made? How does it color your understanding of Anna's past?

10. Both the prologue and epilogue are told in present tense, while the rest of the book (except the flashback chapter)

is in past tense. Did you notice as you were reading? How does this change the reader's relationship to these beginning and ending scenes?

11. Anna's decision to hide Lottie's existence from Will could be seen as unforgivable. What about his life and personality allows him to ultimately move past what she's done? Would you be capable of doing so?

12. Lottie, while the youngest character in the book, is often the voice of reason. Why do you think she can assess the adults in her life so accurately? Discuss how her living situation might relate to this.

13. Part of Lottie's transformation over the course of the book is learning how to advocate for herself. What are examples in the early chapters where she's unable to, and how has she changed by the end? Who or what is responsible for this shift?

14. Anna is in a very different place by the end of the book: sober, in a relationship, mother to an infant, and taking a pause from music. How will these changes affect both her personal and professional life? What obstacles might be ahead for her? And in what ways is she now better equipped to handle difficulties?

15. Anna, Will, and Lottie all mention pulses and heartbeats at various points in the book. Discuss this motif's relation to music, as well as their connection to one another.